THE ROYAL NOTHINGS

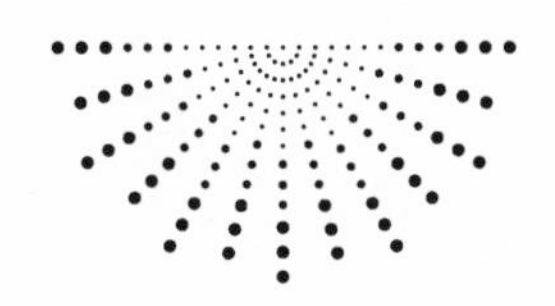

THE ROYAL NOTHINGS

VOLUME I OF THE GIFTBORN CHRONICLES

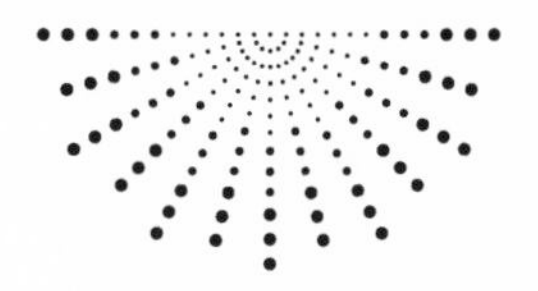

DREW BAILEY

Cover Design by S.H. Roddey

For every wallflower who has ever counted a song within that simply would not be denied. Follow the siren.

DRAMATIS PERSONAE

HOUSE LANIER

Princess Marsea Lanier, the eldest daughter, twenty cycles old

Prince Rembrandt Lanier, the eldest living son, and heir to the Throne of Lancastle, eighteen

Larissa Lanier, Queen of Lancastle

Prince Desmond Lanier, the eldest of the Lanier siblings, died during the coup of the Midnight Men at the age of nine

Whitman Lanier II, the last and former King of Lancastle, died during the coup of the Midnight Men at the age of fifty

Magwyn Lanier, Whitman's younger sister, Empress of Courowne

COURT OF LANCASTLE

Rhonyn Waldgrave, Ambassador of Lancastle, Queen Larissa's older brother

Merillion Casilvieri, a man of questionable character, and Marsea's mentor

Effie Cavendish, a cloth maiden, and friend to Princess Marsea

HOUSE HARVER

Raelan Harver, General and High Commander of the Lancastle

Royalguard Regiment, the eldest of the Harver brothers, Larissa Lanier's husband

Pion Harver, Raelan's son, twenty-two

Julia Harver, the daughter of Raelan and Queen Larissa, nine

Shelly Manson, Raelan's former lover, and Pion's mother (deceased)

Vaustian Harver, Viceroy of Lancastle, the middle Harver brother

Sylvie Harver, Vaustian's wife

Aeralie Harver, the daughter of Vaustian and Sylvie, fifteen

Ganedys Harver, the youngest of the Harver brothers

ROYALGUARD

Rhymona Curie, a battle-magus with a violent past, Captain of the Kingswatch company known as the Black Stags

Yurien Tenbrooks, a battle-magus of some repute

Bromas Aldridge, a Captain in the Royalguard, stationed in Lancastle

Wilhelm Marlowe, known as The Iron Black, a Colonel and Lord Commander of the Kingswatch

HOUSE VALENFORTH

Connor Valenforth, High Lord of Palatia

Lady Dree, Valenforth's wife

COURT OF PALATIA

Davrin Tarboril, High Commander of the Palatian Royalguard Regiment

Aramis Cedarholm, a Colonel and Lord Commander of the Crownswatch

Trydan Westerly, a magus and alchemist

SOUTHLANDS

Aiden Ashborough, an archivist at Perciya University, twenty-three

Stella Ashborough, Aiden's mother (deceased), a storied magus, and former archivist to Lancastle Library

Vincent Ashborough, Aiden's father, a winemaker

Autumn Ashborough, Aiden's younger sister, fifteen

Calem Reid, Aiden's close friend, and a fellow archivist at the university

Caitlyn Ellsbury, Aiden's girlfriend
Val, a mysterious sellsword that befriends Aiden
Xavien Ledgermaine, a barkeep at The Heart House in Port Tavernmast

FURTHER PLAYERS

Elsymir Beldroth, a y'deman huntsman
Broenwjar, Beldroth's wolf companion
Solomon Darrow, a magus and Oathsworn
Tetherow, a magus and author tangled in rumors
Wade's harlot, a barmaid with a dark secret

CHAPTER ONE

Rembrandt Lanier stared absently at the dancing flame emanating from the oil lamp at the hallway's edge, a billow of smoke rising from the pipe between his chapped lips, the scabbard of his watchman's blade resting idly against his shoulder.

The panting moans of Wade's harlot leaked out from behind the door he sat post, disturbing what would have otherwise been a most pleasant silence. Oh, but he could strangle his Kingswatch patrol mate, Liam Wade, to The Hood's Door for convincing him to assist in this lascivious dalliance, with a loose townie barmaid no less. Remy hoped she gave the daft bastard cock-rot. He certainly deserved as much if not worse.

In furtherance, he might likewise wring Van Wyck's neck for ushering him out to this gods' forsaken shithole with the Black Stags on the whim of some craven dullard's concocted delusion. He was a King after all, at the least a Crown Prince, a true blood royal, and the last surviving male of the Lanier ancestry. As such he deserved a modicum of respect. No, he damn well demanded it. The incorrigible Field Marshal should count well his ruddy luck stones Remy did not have him put to the stocks for such blatant insolence.

But these threats were merely idle fancy. For though Rembrandt Lanier was indeed the rightful heir to the Lancastle throne by birthright, the Midaran Commonwealth no longer recognized he or his bloodkin as rulers. In a single night, some fifteen cycles past, when he was but still a babe, the Midnight Men reduced his family, once lauded and beloved by near all amidst the Vaelsyn Empire, to mere gazing stock in a gilded cage. The namesake of Lanier thereafter became sullied by even the lowliest of servants and whoresons comprising Lancastle's hamlets. There had even been a series of wretched songs written about their plight. The surname had since become synonymous with the words weak-willed, pathetic, and foolhardy. It was for these very reasons that Rembrandt Lanier abandoned his dead father's kingdom last winter upon the dawn of his eighteenth birthfall. By his estimation, the court of Lancastle had devolved into a disease in the absence of a proper kingship and he'd had about as much as he could stomach of it. Besides, he had no mates to disappoint, no lover's hand to leave behind, and save for his half-sister Julia, he absolutely despised those that remained of his bloodkin. He also knew what they named him behind his back, and Rembrandt Lanier would serve as no man's puppet king. If Vaustian the Vile wanted the throne of a snake pit, he could very well have it. And, so it was, against his better judgments, that Remy enlisted with the dogs and drear of the Kingswatch, for better or worse, and to the nine hells with the lot of them.

Accordingly, here he now found himself, the Crown Prince of Lancastle, sitting sentry for one of the dodgiest degenerates in the Royalguard in a dimly lit hallway in a derelict inn in a scarcely cultured backwoods village in the middle of the evenfall during the darkest winter in a wolf's age. If ever there were a time for his kinfolk to wallow in the squalor of unjust karma, this was most assuredly it. He could practically hear Marsea's fake, annoying titter as though she sat in the hallway right next to him. The gods know, it would seem there was no distance far enough to evade his turncoat elder sister's bitchy haunt.

He took a long drag from his cob and listened wistfully to the tap, tap, tapping of a naked tree branch against the lone windowpane of the upstairs hallway before a creaking sound from the stairwell's bottom stole away his fancy. He took another pull from the cob and squinted into the lambent light to better focus his vision in preparation of his guest, then let his breath out. It was much too early to be one of his swordbrothers. Patrols would be out for at least another hour, some for another two. No, more than likely it belonged to some drunkard or one of the inn staff on their nightly rounds. Though mayhaps they were the dashing footsteps of

Gideon Ransford. Remy's heart began to hasten with excitement at the mere notion. Without a doubt, the innkeeper's assistant was the most beautiful creature he'd laid eyes upon since leaving the court of courts.

An innkeeper's assistant? Truly Remy? Your luck, you've more than like already met the man of your dreams and told him to piss off.

Truth's witness, as long as it wasn't Curie or Grim, he couldn't give two figs who rounded the corner. He had already been taken to task twice since Stag Company's arrival in Brymshire thanks to Wade's antics. A third time would be the final straw. He simply refused to endure another unjust scolding. If his cycles spent at court in Lancastle taught him anything at all, it was the difference between loyalty and exploitation, and his clemency only reached so far. He would not be made to look the fool, not for anyone, especially not a cur as witless as Liam Wade.

After a minute of waiting, Remy's curiosity reached its peak. Something about the spacing of the footfalls sat ill with him. Something vaguely familiar.

As he tamped the tobacco dry with his thumb, the revelation hit him. He imagined his cripple stepbrother Pion fighting each stairwell of Lancastle's citadel, left foot then right foot, one excruciating step at a time. Left then right again and again, a dozen times, and a dozen more, each one more grueling than the last, sweat beads forming a sheen about his brow followed by the continuous wiping of a cloth. It was quite unsettling to behold really.

By the time a deformed shadow emerged against the oil lamp's flickering tapestry, Remy practically felt the ache in his own ankles. He stowed his pipe in a jacket pocket and quietly pushed himself up from the floor, his eyes glued to the stairwell. Another ungainly footfall, and he inched the sword's cross-guard from the scabbard's mouth. Normally, he would have called out or perhaps feigned a cough to let the company know of his attendance, but something in his gut screamed to the contrary.

The tap, tap, tapping was all that could be heard save the footfalls, one foot, dragging, then the second foot, one after the other, two more stairs, one last stair, and the disheveled figure emerged on the landing before him.

"Miss Allison?" he whispered to the innkeeper's daughter, recognizing her by her willowy contour, though he did not dare approach. Something was horribly afoul about her. The Miss Allison he knew always had a bounce in her step and would have greeted him with a warm smile. By contrast, this version appeared unnaturally crooked and freshly hobbled.

Miss Allison's head snapped up at the sound of his inquiry, and she took a shambling step toward him, collapsing to the floor once her lame foot touched down upon its surface.

"Gods," Remy uttered as he backed away. A low clicking sound returned from the innkeeper's daughter as her silhouette contorted back up to her feet with a series of impossibly grotesque fractures.

"Emyria's tits, Toff," Wade barked as he slammed open the door of his bedchamber with no regard whatsoever for his nude state, "what in nine hells is all the bloody racket?"

The lamplight cast from the bedchamber unveiled to them both the most dreadful imagery either one had ever beheld.

"Curse the devil's wench," uttered Wade.

The right side of Miss Allison's once comely face had been ripped open from the edge of her mouth into the bone structure of her cheek exposing her gums and a row of snaggled teeth upward into a lump of malformed, half-masticated flesh that formerly housed an eye. The fold of skin that concealed the insides now hung down loosely against the side of her neck, which itself displayed upon its opposite side a chunk of missing flesh and a wellspring for the blackened blood discoloring the mantle of her cloak and the frontage of her dress.

Remy couldn't help but stare into the lone eye that had been left her. What once shown with a kindly chestnut shimmer had now become a sallow, lifeless milk shade.

Chasing a sickly groan, the innkeeper's daughter lunged at Remy, though he managed to dodge past her grasp with a sideswipe, sending her flailing body reeling forward, face first into the doorjamb behind him. She never stopped moving as she collapsed to the hardwood. She simply dragged herself hungrily forward in a violent serpentine crawl, screeching wildly as she shredded away the bruised skin about her ruined elbows with each clawing thrust at Wade's ankles. The light from the room revealed her right leg to be caked in blood and gruesomely mangled as though a rabid dog or a stray wolf had somehow gotten after her. Considering the severity of the maiming, it was truly amazing she had been able to move at all, much less ascend a flight of stairs.

Remy unsheathed his sword fully as Wade receded into the bedchamber, his whore atop the bed squealing madly at the clicking horror.

"What are you waiting for, Toff? Bloody kill it already," Wade howled, his voice breaking in the panic.

Without hesitation, Remy drove the point of his blade into Miss Allison's skull, halting the fiend's frenzied attack, and a pool of blackened blood formed beneath the ruin of her downturned face like spill from an overturned inkwell. He clutched fingers to his temples and closed his eyes. Remy had experienced an act like this before. The act of murder, of reaping a life, and though this act struck him just as profoundly as the first, it held its own rotten weight in misery.

When Remy shifted his attentions back upward to Wade and the barmaid, he found a lilac-skinned creature plunging a knife into his swordbrother's backside over and over and over again, her movements merciless, surgical, and quicker than an eyeblink; the movements of a trained killer, a devil meant for the darkness—an ashaeydir assassin.

Nothing of the gruesome scene made a mite of sense to him. Where was the bloody barmaid? What in the nine hells was happening?

The ashaeydir arrested Remy with a yellow-eyed gaze and a lopsided smile as Wade collapsed before her, spitting bright red blood by the pint-load. She then shifted the knife between her fingers from handle to blade, taking aim at Remy, and slung the bloodied instrument directly at his face. Remy spun outside of the bedchamber's doorway, narrowly avoiding the hissing blade before it stuck firm into the wall across from him, and without a second thought to the matter, he scurried down the hallway into the stairwell, abandoning Liam Wade as well as his watchman's blade still lodged inside the back of Miss Allison's skull.

Wade's cries of agony followed him down the stairwell to the ground floor and into the tavern, but Remy refused to turn back. Not with an ashaeydir killer about. It was only as he reached the doorway that he came to a halt, finding it slightly ajar. He nearly rushed out anyway, against all of his better judgments, but as his shaking hand reached to take the doorknob, the church bell sounded, followed by a baying of hounds, and the shouts of men and women scurrying to and fro about the cobble just inches away from him.

Where had all of this chaos come from? He inched the door shut and fell quietly against it. And perhaps even more troubling, how long had it been going on for?

A clicking noise from the back of the tavern drew Remy's attention, and he instinctually unsheathed the skinner knife at his waist. That five-inch blade was now the only means of defense presently left to him. From the shadows limped forth a figure in uniform wearing the corpse of Grayson Bedford, whose eyes in the wavering candlelight begot the same eerie spectacle that formerly possessed Miss Allison, and whose mouth and chin were caked in a beard of bright red. Remy glanced down at the cadet's waist where he found Bedford's sword untouched in its scabbard.

Gray, you craven fool, Remy thought, *wouldn't even pull the blade to save your own skin, would you?*

Remy doubted the blade had even once been married to whetstone since its issue. Nine hells, it more than like hadn't even left the scabbard. Though in Gray's defense, he had hardly begun his basic training before being thrown to the wolves. It was no secret the Royalguard had become desperate in recent months with rumors of a fresh ashaeydir campaign making the rounds. Subsequently, the Kingswatch began dispensing new recruits, some scarcely old enough to rightfully enlist, to the vanguard of battle. A favored few, like himself, received the skeleton's regimen of preparation at Nightsbridge before assignment to a company, but most were sorted with only the base combat knowledge they joined with. For Grayson Bedford, an unproven miller's boy from Elkmark, that misfortune had found him a most gruesome fate.

Though wretched circumstances notwithstanding, Remy decided he would have the cadet's blade before taking to the cobble. It would serve him a damn sight better than his skinner knife to be sure. Swiftly, he maneuvered behind a nearby table as Gray approached and began pushing it forward, using it as a buffer as he rammed it into his lost comrade, forcing the lumbering abomination to the hardwood beneath it. Unfortunately, Remy did not take proper account of his momentum during the act, and the miscalculation sent him sprawling atop the overturned table along with Gray, his face falling only inches away from the ghoul's gnashing maw. All that separated the pair was a thin layer of wood.

"For fuck's sake," Remy said as he shimmied to the top edge of the table and smashed the pommel of his knife into the crown of Gray's head.

However, the blow yielded no effect save to anger the abomination further. Remy smashed a second, third, and fourth time to equal results as the table teetered and tottered with the ghoul's violent shifts. Finally, Remy directed the blade downward so its biter protruded from the bottom of his fist. "I'm sorry, Gray," he said as he settled the steel into the center of Gray's forehead and began to push, driving it south with both hands until he felt the splintering of skull and the body cease thrashing and squirming underneath him.

More clicking from behind the bar shortened Remy's victory, and quickly thereafter, he stole away into the snowy darkness with the dead man's blade, leaving the horrors of the Krueger Street Innhouse to the devils of the past. He could only hope the ashaeydir from Wade's bedquarter hadn't decided to take to his tail.

Once outside, as anticipated, he found the cobble to be an utter madhouse. The clicking fiends were everywhere, like wildfire in a windstorm, as though their forms had somehow materialized from the decree of the encroaching mists. No doubt there was some sorcery to be found in it. As his Uncle Rho would say, *it was always something*. Brymshire's confined quarters would not long endure this manner of bedlam to be sure. Even a properly fortified citadel would struggle to defend against this count of savagery. Indeed, he wagered, the Kingswood would provide him his best chance of survival. As such, Remy decided to make for the southern gatehouse for no other reason than it was the nearest township exit.

He took a couple cautious steps forward and watched in awe as a pair of men tussled into the street before him from the black of an alley. The one with the odd-shaped club found his feet first and beat wildly at the other, smashing his opponent's head bloody before he was wrestled down by a third form from behind. Remy charged at the clicking attacker, cutting his sword down into its crown, but his reaction came too late. The throat of the man with the club had already been rent clean of his neck, and blood spurted profusely from the opening. Instinctually, Remy placed his hands over the wound to try to stop the bleeding, but there was nothing left to be done about it. He pulled away and flung the thick glaze of gore from his fingers.

Movement from inside the alleyway caught his attention, and he stared at the misshapen cluster in the starlight. It was an entire pack of the clicking bastards, feasting and tearing at an unrecognizable mass. The one nearest him turned its head and glared directly at him before contorting up from its repast. It took a moment, but Remy soon recognized the dreadful thing to be that of Lieutenant Grimbel.

A clicking sound below him wrested his attention away from Grimbel, and Remy recoiled as the man that had just bled out only moments before returned to the realm of the living, blank white orbs and all. Remy kicked away from the clicking ghoul and pushed himself up to his feet, scampering from the freshly made blighter and his approaching commanding officer.

A burst of white flame behind his flight ignited the mists, and within its brilliance, Remy circled about and beheld a most unlikely sight mounted high upon its necrotic destrier. A creature he thought to be of myth. His Uncle Rho had told him many hearthfire tales of the nasty bastards in his youth, of undead horrors named lich capable of resurrecting and commanding the grave-ridden, but Remy had always prided himself on his pragmatism and had thusly dismissed them as fairytale-folly. Yet gods' bones, sure enough, there it was, all ashen and emaciated, straight from the storybook's pages, cutting its icy sword down at a farmhand fool enough to charge at it with a meat cleaver of all things.

To be sure, Brymshire was fully at sixes and sevens now. This wasn't a battle. And this manner of butchery certainly wasn't for a cause. There would be no prisoners at the end of this carnage. There would be no surrender. This was slaughter through and through, wholly unbiased, outright slaughter. Kill or be killed. Every man for himself.

Remy wasted no time investigating further. From what he could recall of his uncle's stories, the lich were a horridly malevolent creation of the nether that required a highly skilled sorcerer to banish. He doubted Curie possessed such capabilities; mayhaps Tenbrooks might stand half a chance, though to be sure the watchman would have to see himself free of this fel madness first.

A block away, at the end of a far-too-narrow back alley, Remy peered around the corner toward the market that stood betwixt him and the southern gatehouse and found a young boy in the path's epicenter feeding over the corpse of a twitching woman. The boy could not have been older than six or seven cycles. From behind, an elderly man prodded at the boy with a pitchfork and waved a torch at it, but his threats did little to slow the young one's hunger. An instant later, a pair of ghoulish townsfolk ambushed the old man from the shroud of mist, dropping him helplessly to the stone, and the boy swiftly joined in on the fresher feast.

Without a word to betray his attendance, Remy turned away from the grisly scene and crept back down the alleyway whence he had come. It would seem the fates would have him work for his freedom this eve. As he came upon the end of the passage, a man carrying a young girl in his arms hobbled into his footpath, and instinctually Remy directed the tip of Gray's watchman blade at them, striding a few steps back into the shadows, halting the man in the starglow of the alleyway's mouth.

"On you go then," said Remy, his orbs beady and haunted.

The man stared at the watchman in disbelief, a subtle fever clear about his countenance. So too did the girl, all shivers and innocence. She quite reminded Remy of Jules.

I'm sorry. I'm sorry. I'm sorry. I can't help you. Go away. Just go away. "I said fuck off," Remy snarled, rearing the blade back for a strike. And the man shambled off in the opposite direction.

Bloody hell. Remy couldn't believe his state as he fell back in relief against the wall. Did he truly just frighten away a defenseless father and his little girl? The girl scarcely looked old enough to form words yet. *Every man for himself,* he reminded.

A clicking sound from the other end of the alleyway brought a swift end to Remy's deliberation, and he pushed away from the wall without a second glance, taking to a full sprint through the township, dodging and weaving around skirmish after skirmish, navigating the bloodbath by instinct's measure alone, not stopping for anyone or anything until he came within a block of the southern gatehouse, or at least what he believed was the southern gatehouse, for the settling fog had become so dense and the snowfall so thick that he could no longer properly determine his location. A pair of hunt dogs dashed across his ankles, nearly tripping him, and instinctually he followed in the wake of their wild tear. Perhaps the hounds of hell would lead him to some manner of salvation.

His world had become death and ash and the alien clicking sounds of the blight. What little that could be distinguished of the cobble had been recast in a thick smear of crimson and charcoal, erasing all memory of what once was. The fresh alteration displayed such a stark variation from its predecessor that it felt as though he had somehow been transported to a different town altogether and, moreover, with the arrival of a lich to a different world entirely. For what had become of Brymshire this nightfall was a hellish rendering that could only be likened to that of the nether realm.

Obscure forms bobbed and staggered and clicked about in every direction, the back and forth shouting of the remaining townsfolk singing out in consequence, with the sobs and screeches of the blight's victims serving as an endless chorus to the warring sides. But all the same, Remy clung to the shadows with his back ever pressed against a wall, removing the probability of a surprise attack from the equation. The only way he would be taken was if one of the blighters rushed in at him head on. Thusly he kept Gray's watchman blade up in defense of such a scenario. If another one of the bastards were bold enough to try him, he would make damn sure it regretted the decision.

"He wouldn't harm me." Remy heard a familiar voice call out as the southern gatehouse darkened into distinction. It was one of the Evers twins, no mistake about it. There wasn't another soul within all the highlands that sported such a crude accent as Jorem and Aldous Evers. "Not me. Not his brother. Never me. But she said he were an abomination, the fucking cunt, and that he had to die, and that she were gonna kill him if I didn't do it meself."

"So you murdered her?" Gordon Dennings spat harshly.

"What are you fools still doing here?" Remy said as he approached.

Dennings whirled around hotly, sword at the ready. "Toff. As I live and breathe. You made it."

"Something of the like."

"Where's Wade?"

Remy pursed his lips and shook his head.

"Shit fire."

"Grim and Gray too," he added.

"Chuffing hells, what in the nine fucks is going on? One second it's an ordinary nightfall, silent as the maiden's prayer, the next it's an utter shit-show."

"I should say our dear friend Carrington was true in his counsel, though the gods only knew what sort of hell he has cast us into. You should well prize yet, there's a bloody lich about the lot."

"A lich? Bugger all."

"It's the truth, hand to heart, back near Krueger Street. And an ashaeydir spy to boot. She was the one who stuck Wade. Stuck him but good too. And then she stuck him again and again for good measure. Made a right tatter of him, she did. And then she had a proper go at me just the same, but I managed to ward the bitch off by the skin of my teeth."

"Given this bedlam, you knew it had to be the fucking ashaeydir, the godless heathens. I had holiday in two weeks. The nasty cocksuckers just couldn't wait two more bloody weeks, could they?"

"The gods damn us all!" one of the Evers twins shouted to his lungs' extent.

"Steady on, mate," said Remy brusquely, shifting his weary gaze toward the twins.

"I wouldn't count my ruddy luck stones with that one, yeah," Dennings said. "You may want to have a better look at the spare."

Remy glanced past the standing Evers twin at the other who was slumped awkwardly over a dark mass. Upon closer inspection, Remy found the other gorging himself from a corpse's opened stomach, like a pig feeding over a trough.

"Jory killed the bloody baker to save his brother—or so he claims," Dennings said. "How's that for irony? Spend your whole life making folk food only to become food yourself in the end."

Remy glanced back and forth between the identical twins. With wobbly arms, Jory was shifting his sword back and forth at them, his eyes bulbous, bloodshot, and twitchy. Aldous, meanwhile, continued to make a rather messy meal of poor Miss Beam. As if the night had not already been surreal enough, watching the Evers twins in their current state was like gazing through some sort of mad before and after carnie mirror. "Emyria's lament."

"Aye, Emyria and the whole rotten lot of 'em," Dennings said. "Jory, mate, you understand of course Aldous cannot be allowed to endure in this manner."

"Piss off, ye fat shite," Jorem shouted. "I won't just leave him."

"Lower your tongue, fool, lest you join their lot, yeah," Remy hissed, the highborn coming out in him.

"I will afford you the choice of who ends it, Jorem, but this charade will not be allowed to persist," Dennings continued.

As if it could somehow sense its forthcoming doom, the creature that was Aldous Evers suddenly twisted its neck back toward the trio from the mound of ravaged flesh, a fistful of Jania Beam's entrails hanging low from its gnawing mouth, its orbs completely devoid of color.

"We don't have time for this," Remy said. "Kill him, stay, have a gods damned bloody tea party if you like, Jory, I could give a mummer's fuck less. But Brymshire is done. Tits up. And so is Al. There's nothing left to be saved here. I'm going to the mountain. It's our best chance to survive all this. I'll wager Tenbrooks and Curie are still there, and they will need to be warned of what's happened post haste. Now make your decision. Come with us or stay here and fuck along your merry."

Without another word, Remy sidestepped toward the gatehouse watching Aldous continue to partake of Miss Beam, extending Gray's watchman blade as a buffer between himself and the Evers twins, until he was passed. Once through the gatehouse, he took to a full dash into the starlit expanse of countryside beyond, riding the swell of his adrenaline. He didn't stop for anyone or anything in the open fields. The time for heroics had long since passed. He just kept moving through the cutting barley stalks toward the black wall of tree line that seemed a hopeless distance away. And for a short spell, nothing, save the ghoul's clicking, like crickets in a marsh, and his own ragged breath clouds registered, even as utter mayhem unraveled in the mists all around him. There were bodies everywhere, too many bodies. Some running like mad. Some crawling. Some crying over loved ones. Some fighting. And even more strewn about in bits and pieces. Remy dodged and shifted through the massacre as the gods permitted, though in this manner of murk, it was impossible to discern who remained amongst the living. Plainly put, Brymshire had become a potter's field, and it would be a total crapshoot as to who made it out of the stalks and into the forest alive.

Do not stop. Do not look back, he repeated as he neared the impossible dream of the Kingswood, vaulting an unmoving mass of flesh and passing into the obscurity of the forest pitch. He ran deep and long into the Kingswood before the frosty chill of winter eventually stole from him his ability to draw air, and he tumbled face first into a crude burrow, his adrenaline all but burned away. He sat up spitting dirt and watched in wearied silence as a cloth maiden struggled through the thorny twists of the wood with two ravenous ghouls trampling close behind her.

Dennings, who had somehow managed to stay close despite his size, ran one of the bastards through, freeing the woman from its scaly grasp as a third unseen blighter leapt atop the big man's back. It took a fourth and a fifth to finally wrestle him down, and even against such odds, he fought tooth and nail until the bloody end. Remy clenched his eyes shut as he listened helplessly to his swordbrother's howls and curses. There was nothing to be done for him, even if Remy had fancied himself the brave sort. He rather liked Dennings too. Damned shame to lose a decent soldier. They were quickly joined in a shrill chorus by the cloth maiden Dennings had only seconds before attempted to defend. The gods know she was a horrid screamer too, her cries resonating far beyond him, long into the country black.

CHAPTER TWO

Alone for what felt like hours in the aftermath of Dennings's mauling, Remy plodded, stumbled, and crawled through the dizzying wood to stay ahead of a pack of pursuing blighters, though he knew he was rapidly losing his battle with the demon of exhaustion. To have it true, at this juncture, he wasn't entirely sure he was even still being followed, but he believed that rest meant death and death could suck the piss from his limp cock after what he'd been through to get even this far. As such, he kept his eyes to the star map, his trek to the fore, and his mind on the prize: Palatia's iron gates.

Do not stop. Do not look back.

Oh, the treasures he would trade for a quaff of water, he thought as he mopped his forehead with the end of a shirtsleeve. Even a hand-cupped sip from a stream would be a blessed luxury. He had shed most of his armor since his escape from Brymshire to alleviate some of the extra weight bogging him down and hoped that the awry trail he left of it might also mislead anyone who had taken to his pursuit, especially a particular lichlord or ashaeydir assassin. Ghouls were one thing, but he was quite ill-equipped to duel beings endowed by the gift.

Reduced to jelly, his legs gave out on him about a league outside the village, and he collapsed to his knees and then fell motionless upon his side. He couldn't help but think about his family then. About Mother and Marsea and Jules. And if Jules missed him as much as he missed her.

His breath held as he suddenly realized just how quiet the forest had become. He rolled onto his backside and listened intently, but nothing moved. All was deathly calm, silent as the grave, just as it had been before the attack. He was mercifully free of the ghouls' insufferable clicking as though the assault on Brymshire had been nothing more than a soured dream. He tempered his breathing as he sat up and half-crawled, half-dragged himself through the mud to the nearest tree, leaning back into its shadow with a groan. Sleep had quite suddenly become his best mate, cooing most sweetly to him, though he refused to close his swollen eyes for fear of its consequences. He massaged his side instead, hoping his fall outside Brymshire was only bruising, not broken ribs. He couldn't afford such a detriment, not this nightfall, though he couldn't deny drawing breath grew progressively more difficult. *Damned body,* his throbbing mind complained as he scanned what little of the forest that could be fathomed through the vaporous snowfall.

Eventually, he fixated on a misshapen silhouette standing idle in the westerly distance, and he squinted and craned his neck forward to better define its profile. *It's just your imagination, Remy.* Its form appeared human in contour, but it did not move. It remained unnaturally still. *Your shit-rubbish overactive-imagination.* Perhaps it was just an oddly shaped tree, he decided after a full minute of gawking, unwilling to cater to his burgeoning state of delirium. Of course, that was it. It had to be. It was only his fear and fatigue playing tricks. Nothing was truly there. Nothing at all.

Old Ones, prophets, star maidens, Vael Mother, anyone, any bloody last one of you, I beseech you all, find me, protect me, love me, guide me free...

Crunch...crunch...crunch....

He halted in his prayer, and his orbs grew wide as dinner saucers. There could be no doubting it now. He held his breath and turned an ear eastward. Ensuing movement from the direction of Brymshire drew his attention thus, and he reflexively began to shimmy his aching body back up the tree until he reestablished his footing, using Gray's sword as a makeshift crutch. Once upright again, he stepped away from the tree with a rigid shuffle and shifted his watchman's blade to the ready as he awkwardly shambled away from his pursuer's footsteps. Quicker movement from the north had him spinning a feverish circle, but nothing could be identified or confirmed through the infernal fog.

Just ignore it, old boy. Rally on. Put one foot before the other. A thousand steps more. The gods favor you, remember. Do not stop. Do not look back.

Crunch...crunch...crunch....

"Bastard!" Remy screamed to his lungs' capacity, nearly at his wit's end with the games. "Come out and get yours, you foul piece of shit."

Crunch...crunch...crunch....

The movement was so close now he felt as though he could reach out and touch the vile culprit. *Damn this fog.* He aimed his blade in the movement's direction.

Crunch...crunch...crunch....

This time he had the fucker. He whirled around, quick as his battered body would allow, and finally unveiled the owners, though to his surprise, he did not find before him a pack of blighters. Instead, he found a most unexpected sight, a doe and its young fawn. How queer, Remy mused, for he would have thought such flighty beasts would have long since fled this place given the heightened state of tumult. With obsidian orbs, they both stood perfectly still watching their wearied guest with an equal measure of curiosity, the fawn cowering behind her mother's hind legs.

Remy lowered his sword in relief and couldn't help but chuckle to himself despite everything. It was perhaps the most beautiful occurrence he had ever beheld. As natural as was its participants, the scene itself seemed wholly unnatural, eerie and misplaced—haunting even, especially considering the otherworldly ambiance just beyond the wood, though the watchman could not in the least deny its wonderment. How could such beauty exist within such ghastly chaos? He took a gentle step forward, lost madly to the moment, and found himself reaching a hand out toward the doe as his emotions began to well.

"Hey," he said in a cold-clouded whisper, taking a second silent step toward the skittish creatures, then a third. He held his hand out flat, palm upward as he approached, the unequivocal vision of tranquility, and suddenly everything appeared to transpire in slowed motion.

The experience was surreal. The doe allowed Remy to graze the side of her neck without bucking off. Its fur was soft if not a mite bumpy from scratches and bites. Mayhaps it too had born witness to some of the horrid events of this nightfall. Mayhaps to it, Remy represented some manner of normalcy just as its own presence did for him. It was quite amazing how certain beings, even those that typically do not associate, could band together in times of peril. The fawn, however, remained timidly behind her mother, her frail legs frightfully awobble.

"Hey, sweetheart," Remy said to the little one as he traced the thin layer of fur atop the mother doe's side one last time. "It's all right, little one. It's all right." He reached down toward the fawn. "I'm safe. I won't hurt—"

"FOOL!"

The shout echoed across the dark expanse, dashing the delicate moment, and with the insult, all of the horrors of Brymshire returned to his psyche once more.

"Behind you," the voice bade.

Roused from his delirium, Remy hesitated but for a moment in his instruction before whirling about as a ghoul emerged from the mists. He lifted his arm just in time to fend it from biting down upon his shoulder. It caught his forearm instead, breaking its front teeth upon his iron vambrace, one of the few pieces of armor he had not yet discarded. All because he couldn't get the damned buckles unfastened earlier. Fortune sure had a funny way of showing her support.

The deer bounded away as he spun in their direction with the blighter's momentum, pressing forward with all the might his depleted frame would offer, jostling the creature through the pall of fog until a redwood appeared. He rushed the fiend into it as hard as he could and used its unbalanced footing to swing it back around him to the forest floor.

A second blighter made an attempt to ambush him from his blind spot, but an arrow took it clean through a milky-white eye, slowing its hobbled movements. Remy watched in horror as a bright sapphire scourge began to burn through the blighter's bloodstream from the arrow's entry point, boiling its withered veins from the inside out.

He recognized this man by his attire and build to be Aric Orinson. He was a logger, a family man, and a seemingly decent sort Remy had met a few days back whilst scouting the town perimeter with Wade. *Now is not the time for sentimentality,* he carped, as he watched the poor bastard struggle against the poison shredding through its insides. Remy kicked the sprawling creature in the chest as it clawed frantically at its melting aspect, causing it to stumble backward blind and defenseless, and as it faltered, Remy stalked mercilessly forward, spinning the hilt of his blade to gain impetus. With every ounce of adrenaline left to him, Remy slashed at the fresh abomination with a titan's fury severing Aric's smoldering head from its torso.

In confluence with the strike, Remy turned swift on his heel back toward the first ghoul, ready to be done with it all, but to his alarm found it being torn apart by the largest wolf he had ever beheld. Hrathgon's horror, it rivaled a grizzly in size, and in mere seconds, it gamely made of its victim an unrecognizable puddle of pulp and bones. Remy found himself frozen, caught somewhere between shock and sickness, as the great beast shifted its attentions upon him with fangs bared.

His guts nearly dropped from his ass.

"Broenwjar, thae quolo," the voice said from the mists, and the beast reluctantly concealed its fangs and came to heel, thereafter licking at its bloodied paws with indifference.

Remy collapsed to his knees at that and closed his eyes, wholly spent. If the beast deemed it so, he was a defenseless repast to be sure.

His thoughts pounded like a kettledrum, and his chest burned like a hearth. Dehydration had made of his tongue a doorstop, and the ache returned thus to his every joint and muscle. The parts of his body that were not numbed from the cold and overexertion had become stiff as the trees. Just an hour of rest and he would be fine, he told himself. He could at least maintain. Just one hour of repair and he might just make Palatia yet.

The sound of something hitting the ground and tumbling into his knee rescued him from the realm of his enveloping stupor, and his eyes cracked open to find a water-skin. *The gods are good indeed.* He hadn't a clue which one forged his favor this nightfall, but they would have the whole of his love from this moment onward. Remy fought through the fever to retrieve it, and his cold-gnarled fingers fumbled pathetically with the cap. Eventually, by the mercy of Myrenna, he coerced it off and shakily held the spout to his dried lips, sucking it down gulp by succulent gulp. Half of it poured down the front of his tunic, but he could not have cared less. Water had never tasted so wonderful. After all of this, he would never take her fount for granted ever again.

Footsteps approached from behind, and Remy glanced sidelong at the approaching figure. By the long, pointy ears, he discovered his savior to be y'deman. It was quite plain really despite his weariness, though Remy thought it more than a little odd that he sported the weaponry of the Ashaeydir Guard, the militia responsible for Y'dema's occupation and subsequent usurpation. Yet there they were. The fashion was unmistakable. Like no other upon the moon of Vaelsyntheria. The longer of the two curved, single-edged swords dangled inside a thin, black sheath upon his right hip. Remy knew its make to be named a mae'chii. And at the small of his back, no doubt nestled a second shorter blade of similar design named a sy'chii.

The y'deman appeared quite tall, gaunt, and uncharacteristically tanned for one of such a fair race. Remy rather thought the man appeared how he presently felt, which is to say well-worn and thoroughly beaten. Scars in varying widths and lengths crisscrossed painfully about his hardboiled countenance. There was a particularly nasty one that ate deep into the bridge of his nose, leaving a jagged blackened line across it and permanent bruises to fester about his darkly eyes. A long, braided ponytail of silver-gold fell against a thatched quiver and patchwork cloak. His tunic was faded and dirt-stained, his breeches frayed and hand-stitched, and his boots were threadbare and bandaged with ratty linens about the ankles. It was woodland attire to be sure, and far more rustic than any fashion Remy had ever beheld on a y'deman. Before this fell night, he had only ever observed their lot in bright, gaudy robes, shiny silken sashes, and unnecessarily lavish headpieces. Though he supposed most of the y'deman folk he had met before were royals and aristocrats, not huntsman as this fellow apparently was.

"Cheers," Remy managed with a rasp. The cold combined with his fatigue made his vocal cords quite uncooperative.

"We should be safe for a spell," the y'deman said in a strange accent of the common tongue. "You did well to survive the sortie," he continued as he scouted around the skirmish.

"Brymshire was no mere sortie," Remy said, perturbed. "Her sacking was an outright slaughter. Survivors be damned."

The y'deman turned back to him with a grim expression, his many facial scars stretching and enflaming with each twinge of movement.

Remy had never had such trouble at looking a man properly before. "They were commanded by a lichlord. I saw it with mine own eyes."

The y'deman's brow furrowed at that. "Baulrick Tamberyn, he's named. A real treat, that one."

"You mean to say you actually know this miscreation?"

The y'deman grunted something of a response as he removed his arrow from the mound of seared flesh and bone that was formerly Aric Orinson's head.

"I say, what was that arrow laced with? I've never seen anything quite like it before."

"Charonisk," the y'deman said. "Chandii magic. It boils blood tainted by the nether." The y'deman rested his bow against a tree and fumbled with something in his travel sack. "What's your name, lad?"

Remy squinted at the y'deman. True, the man may have saved his life, but something in his gut told him not to trust him outright. "Wade," he found himself saying, "Liam Wade." He doubted the poor dead bastard would mind. If anything, he should count it as a bloody honor. "And you are?"

"Elsymir Beldroth."

Remy seemed to remember something of the Beldroth name from summits past, but he couldn't define the memory past its whispers. He wanted to say it was typically given with disapproving connotations, but in all fairness, much of what the fae nobility discussed, ever drunk in their posh coffers, carried with it a puffed-up, condemning tone.

Beldroth retrieved a book from his travel sack and grimaced in disgust at its spectacle. "If I gathered properly, you are in route to Palatia, yes?"

"Seems so," Remy said, nursing his tender side as he labored back up to his feet.

"Hold," the y'deman whispered, leering in the direction of Brymshire, and instantly Remy's heart clawed up inside his throat again. "It would seem we are freshly short of time for pleasantries, Mister Wade."

"What is it?"

Beldroth was silent, listening intently before responding. "I cannot say for sure just now, but whatever it is, there are at least three or four. And they are moving much too quickly to be blighters." He turned to the beast.

"*Broenwjar thae vasjte.*" The wolf immediately reacted, padding a circle about the clearing, lifting its snout high into the air, before disappearing into the unseen mists. "Could be wolld. Could be worse."

"Wolld? You can't be serious." *Nothing was worse than the wildkin,* Remy groused, *bloody primitive savages.*

Beldroth offered him the strange black book from the travel sack. It was near as hideous as its owner, its rutted leather jacket bound heavily in twine and chains. "You must take this to Palatia," the y'deman ordered. "There you needst seek a woman named Tarboril."

"Pass," Remy said, shifting away from the archer. He wanted as little to do with this odd fellow as possible and even less to do with the wretched book. He may not be a giftborn, but he could certainly recognize a grimoire when he saw one. *And where there was a grimoire,* his Uncle Rho would say, *there was undoubtedly a bout of trouble.*

"Do you want to survive the night, boy?" Beldroth said sternly. "Don't be a bloody foolhard."

"Are you threatening me?" Remy's chin rose quite high just then, a lingering habit from his days amongst the nobility. "Do you have any idea who you are speaking to?"

"Threatening you? Trust it true, lad, if you have trusted anything in all of your days, if I wanted your life, I could have taken it with the greatest of ease. I could have had you clean from a league's passing or perhaps allowed the beast to dine on a fresher feast. Old Boy would have liked that. He rather prefers the living to the dead, if you must know. That is, if the blighters hadn't made a meal of you first. No, lad, what I am offering you is a deal. A deal that you would be most wise to accept if you could remove your head from beneath your pampered arse for long enough to hear it out."

Remy could not believe the gall of this vagrant. This ugly mongrel was indeed quite rude. One would think a man of such repugnance would strive to offer a decent personality, in the least a measure of proper social etiquette. But he was no longer inside the kingdom courts, now was he? And he was no longer atop the throne. A choice made of his own volition, he reminded himself. He could not speak to folk so harshly out here else he might find a red smile for the lecture. Out here social etiquette meant absolutely fuck all. Out here his name was just as rubbish as the next fellow's. He was no different than the lowliest of beggars and needed to remain mindful of such dealings. Out here, this y'deman dog was by all accounts his equal, unsightly or no. Thusly Remy bit his tongue to the man's affront.

"As far as I can tell, your right ankle is hobbled, you've more than likely broken some ribs, the gods only know what else, and that big, purple knot on your head screams of concussion. Without my help, you won't long outlast your pursuers this night, of that I can guarantee."

Remy glowered at the bastard from beneath his brow.

"However, I can hold them off. I can give you the time you need to reach Palatia if you can see to this one chore within her gates. It's really quite simple."

Nothing within the courtly kingdoms was ever quite simple. Truly this fellow must believe me the Vael's greatest simp. "If it's so bloody simple why not leave me here to the rot and do it yourself then?" A fair question, Remy thought, though he certainly could have approached it with less attitude, considering.

Beldroth beset him with a wolfish grin. It was a most off-putting guise and not at all the response the watchman expected. "I have my reasons, lad, just as you have yours for abandoning your duties to Brymshire."

"Abandoning my duties? How dare you. You know nothing of what I've been through."

"I know more than you think."

"Believe what you will, fae-fallen. You know nothing about me."

Beldroth smiled wider at that. It was without question the ugliest smile Remy had ever beheld. "Fae-fallen. Gods be good, it's been a spell since I've heard the tale. Brymshire was a winless battle, yes. I will grant you that, lad. Take solace in this. As far as I'm concerned, you made the right decision. Sometimes it is braver to run after all. I can appreciate that about you, Mister Wade. You have prudence."

Prudence? I have prudence? Truly this fellow's insolence knows no bounds.

"A lost art this day and age, I woefully declare. You would do well to hold on to that. There are far too many would-be heroes about puffing their chests out to this little quibble and that one, needlessly risking their lives, and for what? For Valor? Honor? Wealth?" He sucked his teeth at the notion. "A pox on all three I say. You are a survivor, Mister Wade. You have survived much tragedy in fact, terrible circumstances. I can sense this about you. As such you have become mistrustful yet quite clever all the same. Too clever by half some might name you. Certainly clever enough to recognize the cruel reality we are now trussed to. You are desperate, Mister Wade, yet take no offense, so am I—most desperate, I humbly confess. So why not help each other away from this desperation? Why not do yourself the favor, Mister Wade? Make the rest of this nightmare a bit more bearable? You say you are in route to Palatia anyway. What have you to lose from such a simple undertaking?"

"Farador's folly, fine. Give me the ruddy thing then," Remy grumbled, if only to stay the man's preaching.

"Ah, yes, I knew you to be the agreeable sort, Mister Wade. You have my gratitude. However, a bit of warning. In the interest of fairness. Should you stray from the task, should you break the deal in any way, trust I will know. I know a great many things, mind you. And knowing these great many things as I do, trust it true, I will find you. I will hunt you like a dog hunts the pheasant. And you will not like the consequences that follow."

"I said I would do it, didn't I?" Remy countered. "I'm good for my word, wretch. There is no more need for such intimidations."

"So you say." Beldroth studied the watchman with speculation. "Find Tarboril," he began where he had left off prior. "Tell her the Eld are risen."

"The Eld?"

"She will understand what this means. Though she may not understand why a lowly watchman knows of such affairs. If she or her brother give you any trouble say to them these words: *dweir ta ka'le du alé rinza.* Tell her this and you will have her ear. What you do with it in the after is your own stone to shoulder."

A howl of misery echoed forth from the not too distant darkness, and Beldroth pressed the book into Remy's chest.

"We are out of time. Tell no one else of the book," Beldroth said as he swiftly retrieved his bow and nocked an arrow to it. "And do not open it, Mister Wade. No matter what you may hear or what you might see. Never expose her pages to the woken world. Do you understand?"

"And what exactly might I see?" Remy asked curiously. *Not exactly the words one wants to hear after agreeing to such a dodgy task.*

"Let us hope you do not find out," Beldroth said, a mad fury seething behind his dark, sunken orbs. "Make sure it stays closed," he reiterated once more for good measure, and then he too was lost to the mists.

Remy Lanier did not once look back as he limped onward from tree to tree in the opposite direction, toward Palatia. Not even when he heard the din of battle break the silence whence he had come. Not even when he heard the shrieks of the dying return to the night. And certainly not when he began to hear the shuffling of footsteps yet again in the not too far away distance. *It was always something,* he thought, as he hobbled forward, right leg, dragging then left, *always something indeed.*

CHAPTER THREE

Aiden choked awake, his icy blues bursting open with all the uncontrollable fear of a night terror as a cramp rippled down the span of his right leg, twisting, burning, constricting, tearing, and finally settling thereabouts his calf. He jerked up quick, rubbing at it with a masseur's fury in the hopes of putting a swift end to the bastard's wrench, kneading deep and firm, back and forth, and gradually the pain subsided, as did the excitement from his dream's horror. Mercifully, neither one had been too terribly cruel this time.

Relieved of its ache, he fell back upon his pillow with a groan and violently yanked the blanket back over his head. "Fuuuuuuck." Hadn't even left the bed and it was already shaping up to be a bare minimum kind of day. At least, the mother of all hangovers had found him some bit of company this morning. His nose curled up in disgust a moment later as the stale reek of smoke and piss-rate booze fouled his nostrils. *Nothing quite like waking up to the stench of the night before.* He threw the blanket off him in disgust, eased his legs to the side of the study table serving as his makeshift bed, scratched at the ever-festering scar etched across the left side of his abdomen, and took a swig from a wine bottle that had been resting sideways upon the stones below. *The breakfast of champions.* After a quick stretch and pop of the knees, he grabbed a shirt from the top of his clothes pile, smelled it, and pulled it over his head. He had certainly done worse. "Come along, love," he said, swiping up the wine bottle by her neck as he made for the great hall of Withers.

"Someone's up with the birds," Calem commented indifferently from behind a tower of parchment and tomes stacked high atop the ever-cluttered registry desk.

"And they crow evermore for my wakeful lament, don't they?" Aiden mumbled as he plopped down in the chair next to his colleague.

"Fresh with the Tetherow bullshit already, hunh?"

"You can stow your animosity toward the man, dear brother. I'm well acquainted with your feelings on the matter." Aiden took another swallow from the wine bottle.

"Animosity?" Calem scoffed. "I wouldn't dare squander such a precious emotion on that two-bit pretentious tosspot, and quite frankly, I'm offended you thought I might."

"Capitol. Offend, offend. There's nothing quite like a good insult to start the day off proper."

"In other news, it would seem the bluecoats have found another body washed ashore." The mid-conversation shift in topics was not at all an uncommon occurrence with Calem. "It was another student. Evandrea Amersly, a third cycle. Apparently, she had gone missing last week around Manafell."

"Did you know her?"

"Not really. Evidently Penny shared a course with her last semester, but that's all she said about it. Some are already naming it the return of Baulrick Tamberyn."

Aiden shook his head as he downed another mouthful. He had grown quite weary of the cliff-side dropper stories over the past few weeks. It was such a sour nutrient for his already sour mood. If there was any one notion the archivist despised in the vast litany of concepts indulged by modern civilization, it was that of false empowerment, and if any one soul presently embodied such a despicable figure, it was most certainly that of the serial murderer known about the university as The Bayside Butcher.

"Folk are ever eager for a fresh bit of bullshite, aren't they?" Aiden quibbled.

"Aye, though say what you will of the publishing houses, scaremongering sells."

"Fucking halfwits, the lot. I daresay we are living in the age of the lotus-eater, aren't we?"

"Preaching to the chorus, mate."

"Baulrick the Bloodseeker was put to the pyre for his crimes. His body was doused with Eldn fire. The 'fuck you, you're dead, and there's no coming back from my ass' Eldn fire. There are yet still living witnesses that can attest to the burning for gods' sakes. Besides even if we completely tossed logic out the window and permitted the idea of some mad gravedancer's resurrection spell, these fresh murders are wholly incongruent with Tamberyn's pattern. His kills were premeditated... deliberate...ritualistic. He had a specific agenda in stow and specific victims. Whereas this latest killer's exploits seem to be entirely at random as far as I can tell. Furthermore, there were never any accounts of Tamberyn dismembering folk and dropping their body parts into the ocean that I can recall."

"Inspector Ashborough, ladies and gentleman."

The archivist unfurled a middle finger.

"Bit early for a nightcap then, wouldn't you say?" Calem commented. "Most folk would settle for a bit of coffee at this hour, yeah."

Aiden shrugged and took another sip. "And those folk can keep their nasty sludge water I say. Besides, I think her kiss rather suits me. Hair of the dog and all that."

"You mean to say it suits your ever-burgeoning state of apathy."

"Aww," Aiden brushed his long, straggly hair out of his face, smiled gormlessly, and batted his eyelashes, "you do still notice me."

"By your malodorous stench mostly. Mayhaps a bath is in order, yeah? You do recall what a bath is, right?"

Aiden sighed with a theatrical wind. "Fine brother, your cruel words have coerced it from mine lips. Drink or no, it was bound to escape one way or another I reckon. Besides knowing Caitie and Penny and Penny's unceasing gossip-tongue, I'm quite sure she has already blathered."

"Such is the true splendor of the opposite gender I'm afraid."

"Fuck all. What would you have me say, Cal? Part of me knows I should just bloody well end it. But I made a mistake. The biggest mistake of all, mind you. I allowed myself to become too familiar, too comfortable, too true. Plainly said, I've put in too much time to escape our past unscarred now. I know how she works. I know her intimately, every maddening detail, and she the same of me. I know her reactions. I know what pisses her off. What she loves. What she hides. And I think there is something to be said for that echelon of connection, nay, that echelon of dedication. It deserves more than a mere discarding and replacement. And yes, I know it has run its course thrice over now, and you've heard the tale a thousand times before..."

"Well, that's being generous," Calem mumbled.

"But sadly, pathetically, tragically, all the other bloody -lys, I love her still in my own little starry-eyed, mad-capped convolution. I know it's a fool's charade, but I don't wish her away from my life. I fear I'm not ready for that leap yet. Gods' breath, it hasn't even been a full three cycles and here I remember not long ago her seductive voice whispering to mine ear of tender tidings, childbearing, and a country cottage in Cedar Falls near her beloved cousin Emilie. Now that night seems a dozen lifetimes ago. And yet still I quiver to entertain the thought of losing her completely."

Calem notched his quill and pushed the wire-rimmed glasses back up the bridge of his nose, attending the daily emotional summit that had become his best mate.

"But, all the same, this nightmare cannot persist for the sake of my sanity's frail nature. Oi, it's all just confounding, confounding and pitiless, and I'm absolutely spent frittering my mind within its labyrinth of masochistic cruelties. I know all relationships take work, I know they're a learning process, but should they all be this impossibly complex and strenuous?"

What a demented digression, he thought. Had he truly become so morose? Still playing at love's young dream? Still woefully hopeful? Reduced to scant more than a pining, dithering tomfool? More often than not he scoffed at knobends of the like. *Fucking useless,* he carped. *How had it bloody come to this?*

Offering his own small form of comfort, Grandpa, a graying tom that had long ago seen fit to find residence within the archive, sprang upon the desk and nudged against Aiden's hand, forcing the archivist to rub his furry little head. Aiden scratched under his chin where he liked it most and then upon the scruff of his neck.

Calem eyed his friend speculatively for a moment, choosing his next words carefully, as he was well aware that Aiden could be quite sensitive about such fragile affairs. "And what would you have me say to such self-deprecating musings, dear brother? As the minstrels often sing, love is a most curious affair, rot, rot, rot." At that, in his perfected nonchalant manner, Calem retrieved his quill, dipped it twice in its inkwell, and went back to his writing.

"Is that all then?" said Aiden after a short silence.

Calem glanced up from beneath his brow. "What more were you expecting? A bit of ceremony? Shall I rouse the town crier then?"

Aiden took another swig of wine. "I call bollocks on that one. There's always something else with you, Cal. We've been mates for too long now. I know your expressions, and you had a 'but' expression there."

"A 'but' expression?"

Aiden scowled.

"I assure you you've heard the tale before," Calem said, "many, many, many times over in fact."

"Mayhaps I need hear it once more, yeah."

"Why must you cling so fervently to the past, brother? Why torture yourself so needlessly?"

"The gods know, I wish I held an answer to such a query. A bad mix of bloodlines would be my best guess."

"Well, let us not dredge up that bit, yeah?"

"Hand to heart, brother, I'd rather like to keep this day civil for as long as possible."

"And stand warned, of you and Caitie I've no more honeyed words left to spend."

"I wouldn't imagine you do."

"Very well. If I've said it once, I've said it a thousand times before: When has settling for something ever worked to your favor?"

Aiden stroked his bushy beard wistfully allowing Calem's question to resonate. It was a question he had heard a thousand times before, like clockwork, though for the thousand-and-first time nothing definitive came to mind.

"As banal as this is going to sound, I just don't want to see you get hurt again. Rhymona was enough for any one man to endure, but Caitlyn is a sprite of a different shade. I could see her breaking you even worse. She is an Ellsbury after all, and history has not proven their lot to be kind to the spirits of others."

"So, name it true, brother. Enough banter. Enough repetition. Do you believe we are unsalvageable?"

"Unsalvageable? Do you hear yourself? If you have to ask the question, then I'm afraid you already have your answer." Calem could feel the veiled expression of gloom come unmasked despite his desire to shelter Aiden from the awful truth. "Any tosser with a lick of common sense about them can see that you two are growing apart. And this is not just another rough patch, mate. This has plodded far past the days of rough patches. This is now the fractured remains of two very stubborn persons who simply refuse to accept the reality of their incompatibility."

A look of utter defeat plastered itself upon Aiden's guise as he raised the bottle once more to his lips.

"And there's the face," Calem said, running a hand through his sandy blond hair. "You're going to do something mad now, aren't you?"

"Mad?" Aiden took a long quaff, finishing the remains of the bottle before standing. "Mayhaps." He forced a smile. "You're a good friend, Cal, always have been."

"I do so try," Calem said in earnest.

"And trust it true, I appreciate you not saying something foolish. Mad seems about the proper name of it."

An hour hence, Aiden found himself standing passively at the island's edge, clutching the strap of his satchel as he peered down through the cloudworks at the humble township below. It was all he could do to conceal what little warmth he had stored from the archive. The unforgiving chill emulated his frostbitten ruminations, making the venom brewing inside that much more palpable, though the familiar scent of the salted surf briefly calmed his heartache as he watched the waves cascade pale and foamy across the shoreline. Staring out at the ocean always had a pacifying effect on his soured moods, the sun shimmering across her vast gray surface like that of an endless mirror. Somehow, despite his deep cadre of trusty friends, she was the only one that made him feel less alone. For it would seem she too was imprisoned by the throes of relapse, ever cursed to repeat her rise and recession. So loved yet so unloved. So necessary yet so neglected. It was by this manner that the archivist felt a kinship to the ocean. Truly, if circumstances permitted, he could idle here all afternoon and just simply watch her tide rise and recede with naught else to bother save the cold and the wind. *If only life were so ordinary.*

It was nearing midday when the archivist finally worked up the nerve to confront Caitlyn about their quarrel from the previous nightfall. Rheumy eyes and all, Aiden turned toward the soaring palisade spires in the distance and wandered through the rime-covered coppice that separated the university grounds from the cobblestone streets of the islet's bazaar. As usual for this hour, the market had become muddled with a diverse collection of wastrels, gossipmongers, and dandies. Folk Aiden generally despised and disregarded. Useless conversation was never particularly high on his agenda after all, especially not inside the tumult of his present temperament. Thusly he made quick work of the crowds, keeping his eyes lowered and his hands tucked deep within the recesses of his pockets. But for the breeze, good fortune found him in this endeavor, though it would seem the elements would have his guise quite feral this day, growing crosser and crosser with each passing avenue. He lumbered through all the same, muttering absently to himself until he reached the wrought iron gates announcing the Ellsbury's property, and it was with a prospering sense of approaching doom that he brushed down his windblown hair and passed through into a dense garden copse surrounding a quaint, stone walkway. A dozen stones in and he came upon a veranda where he discovered Caitlyn's mother having tea with another ostentatiously dressed woman he did not at all recognize.

"Milady, I hope the day finds you well." He lowered his chin, putting on airs. "Perchance, is Caitie about?"

"She is," the Lady Ellsbury responded in her typical haughty manner, her deep-set eyes burying him beneath a mountain of disapproval. "I believe you will find her upstairs in her bedchamber with her nose still wedged inside another one of those silly little fantasy gushes of hers."

"Heavens me, Adeline is the same way," the other woman disparaged as Aiden hurried past. "Truly I'll never understand it."

Aiden held no doubts that once out of earshot he would become the next topic of conversation. *Fucking uppity bitches.*

The entirety of the Ellsbury's manor was smothered in a painful mélange of luxurious gothic reds. Every time Aiden entered, he imagined himself being swallowed up by some dreadfully large beast that had somehow had its innards curated with an assortment of gold-trimmed mirrors, elaborate tapestries, and impossibly drab family portraits. Erected betwixt each hanging and work of art was a collection of large mahogany bookshelves and bureaus on which sat a seemingly endless number of tomes both fiction and non. If the Ellsbury's were nothing else, they were hoarders, spirited collectors, and voracious readers.

Aiden paused by the candelabrum tree in the downstairs hallway just below the stairwell and studied a recent burning glass of Caitlyn. It was one that he had taken of the Ellsbury brood at her graduation reception last summer. Magister and Lady Ellsbury loomed smugly behind their daughter, and to the right stood her Aunt Elena and cousins, Hannah and Emilie. He managed only a half-hearted smirk at the memory. Everything certainly seemed a lot cheerier back then.

The door to Caitlyn's room hung upon to a half, and he knocked so as not to startle her. Caitie's temper grew quite terrible when someone gave her a good spooking and that was the last thing he cared to contend with this day. As described, Caitlyn Ellsbury was still abed reading when the archivist entered. He dropped his satchel just inside the doorway and sat atop the end of the gossamer curtained featherbed watching her with his best attempt at doe eyes. Caitlyn wasn't giving an inch. It was quite clear she remained upset with him. So much so that she couldn't even be bothered to glance up from her pages.

"How are you?" Aiden asked as he poked at the bedspread concealing her lower half.

Caitlyn closed the book with an annoyed huff and turned the other way, sliding to the opposite side of the bed.

"Is this how it's going to be then?"

"Mercy of Myrenna, what would you have from me, Aiden?"

"It would be nice if you could look at me for starters."

Caitlyn sighed and offered a peeved glance over her shoulder. "I don't know what else you want me to say. You made your intentions quite clear last night, soused as you were."

"Come now. Surely you're not so deluded as to blame the entire thing on me now?"

"Oh, that's right, the great Aiden Ashborough can do no wrong. Sincerest apologies my worship, where ever are my manners? I must have forgotten to whom I speak." Caitlyn stood, lifted her robe from the rocking chair in the corner, and pulled it over her nightgown.

"Come off the vanity razz, Caitie. It's not fair and you know it."

Caitlyn whirled around hotly and scowled at him like a hunter stalking her prey. *Fuck me*. It might have been the most frightening vision he had ever beheld.

"Not fair? Don't you dare presume to educate me on what's not fair, Aiden Ashborough. You want to know what's not fair? You. You are not fair. Look at you. The state of you is utterly reprehensible. You look as a wildkin fresh off the binge. Your beard is atrocious, your hair a mess, you have little to no self-worth that I can readily discern, and thus far you have managed to do absolutely fuck all with your passion. It seems you are truly acquiesced to idle around with your lamentable friends frittering about the pathetic little pence you do actually manage to earn on drinking games and silly keepsakes, and this is every day and nightfall without end. Mayhaps even more tragic, you seem to possess no aspirations to do anything more, much less alter your disgraceful present course in the faintest. Gods' bones, Aiden, you've been alumni for going on two cycles now and you are living out of a bloody supply cupboard in Withers. You were crown of your order once. Most folk would kill to possess such a boast. By all accounts, you should have the whole of the moon in your palm by now."

Here we go again. Aiden said nothing. He understood that this one had been a long time coming for Caitlyn, and thusly he accepted her wrath with silent benevolence. If a character assassination was what she was after, then she could bloody well have it. It certainly wouldn't be the first time, and he had long ago tired of quibbling over the sour subject.

"Say something please. You know I hate when you disappear."

"And what would you have me say?"

"Anything. Gods, pretend like you care about one fucking thing, Aiden, just one real, meaningful thing."

"I'm here, aren't I?"

"I don't know. Are you?"

"Of course. What is that intended to imply?"

"I look at you now, and I know it to be you, truly I do, it's your same sad, beautiful eyes, and your same sad, funny smirk, and your same sad, over-serious demeanor, but I know these airs to be but fleeting reveries of a past version."

"A past version?"

"And I don't think you mean to be deceiving, I would never accuse you of such a horrid notion without proper reasoning, but ever since—you know—"

Say it, Caitie. Say her fucking name.

"It's as though you've become a different person entirely."

I thought not.

"You're cold and detached and you seem to have forgotten how to let folk in, even folk that genuinely care about you. And what's worse is the harder we try, the more you distance yourself. I have never felt so far away from you as I do at the present. Emyria's lament, we've courted for three cycles now and I feel as though I haven't a clue as to who you are anymore, as trite and clichéd as that is to confess. It's maddening really. Folk ask about you all the time and all I can truly tell them is that you are still working at Withers, occasionally subbing a lecture, writing a bit, and looking for a more stable position. I've even gone so far as to tell folk you're considering a transfer to Marrovard for a salary position. I lie for you. Do you know how embarrassing that is for me? What's worse is sometimes I catch myself starting to believe the lies—wanting to believe the lies, really."

"Gods," he hissed under his breath. "I'm sorry to be such an embarrassment for you, Caitie. But you should well prize, there are plenty of folk that believe what I do for a schill is an honest living. True, it's nothing dramatic and grand, but it's still decent pay, and believe it or not, I do occasionally enjoy what I do there."

"Rubbish. Gods, what a tale of rubbish. All I ever hear from you anymore is how much you hate what the archive has become and how much you hate all of Brumfield's changes to the curriculum and how the council has devolved into a nightmarish nepotistic corporation who couldn't give two figs about proper staffing much less the education of its students. Every day it's the same pessimistic rubbish on loop. It's always someone or something else holding you back, Aiden—the man who begot a thousand scapegoats you are. You know what's truly astounding is that through all of your ridiculous drunken rants, I've never once heard you hold your own self accountable. I've never once heard you even approach the possibility that *you* are the reason for all of your personal failures these past few cycles. I won't psychoanalyze you into the dirt like Rhymona did, gods forbid I ever approach the topic of Rhymona bloody Curie with you, but you damn well need to hear it. You, Aiden Ashborough, have not done a single thing to modify these changes you hate so much, which in my opinion nullifies your right to grouse incessantly about them. You're full of nothing but pitiful excuses now and they're all so ruddy tiresome. The gods' wept, I'll wager I've heard just about every last one of them under the sun at this point. You want to know what I think, Aiden? I think you are afraid. Mayhaps it is all subconscious, but I know you. You hate change more than anyone I have ever met. You would rather sacrifice your chances at success so long as it meant you didn't have to apply yourself. It took some time to arrive here, but I think you just might be the most selfish, irresponsible man in the entire Vael. You find niches so easily and all you do is settle into them, regardless of its effects on others, regardless of its effects on your own wellbeing. It's really quite cruel and doubly pathetic."

Aiden stared down at the floor as he cupped a hand over the lower half of his face, covering his mouth to prevent an ugly verbal backlash of his own. He could feel his body begin to tremble with sequestered rage as he considered Caitlyn's words. It was all he could do to contain the anger boiling inside of him. Caitlyn could condescend and harp with the most ruthless of the nobility, but he had never heard her take such an aggressive tone before, especially against him. Truly, it was such an oddity that he had the thought but fleetingly that it was spoken by a completely different girl altogether. "Well, if that's how you feel, I guess I don't actually understand what you want from me anymore." The words fell away from his tongue with a minimal degree of effort, as though he knew of naught other beyond their scope to combat their utterance.

"Honestly, I don't know either." Caitlyn pulled her hands off of her hips and let out a dismal breath. "Maybe I don't want anything from you anymore."

Aiden glanced up at her from underneath his brow as something sinister within grasped firm the vestiges of an ancient inferno. "Then name your desire, Caitie." *And murder me pretty already.*

"I'm fucking spent," she said as she sat next to him and slid in close. She smelled like a pastry shop filled with all the best kinds of pastries.

Somewhere between chocolate custard, apple strudel, and cinnamon roll. And the gods know it killed him every time. "I love you, Aiden. It is a nasty little condition I do believe to be permanent. Consult the gods and they will confirm this. But I'm just so bloody exhausted by the constant back and forth. And trust it true it's not just you. I would be loath to impress such a harsh title upon your head alone. It's this place, my mother, our friends, Kanton, university, all of it. Suffice it to say, my poor, addled mind needs a holiday."

"So you're leaving then?"

"Yes. I'm leaving."

"Just like that?"

"Just like that."

"To where? Cedar Falls?"

"Yes. Of course, Cedar Falls. I know this is difficult, Aiden, but I think this will ultimately be for the best…for the both of us. And I think that somewhere deep down inside you agree. What we had isn't working any longer. Our paths are diverging. Mayhaps they have already diverged. I daresay, just look at us. Aren't we the dashing pair?" She feigned a desolate smile. "You're day drunk again, and I've yet to leave my bedchamber."

Day drunk? This isn't even close to drunk, darling. I name this tolerant.

"Name me a prude, but this is no way to be. These are not healthy lives. We are poison to each other, Aiden. Surely you must see this. And what's worse is our fights are now rote and boring."

I can't argue there.

"Let us end this fool's charade before it gets to be unbearable, I say. Before we begin to resent each other. The last thing I want is for us to end up resenting each other. You must know this. I don't want you to despise me as you do Rhymona."

And there it is.

A state of disbelief settled upon him as he glanced at Caitlyn. It was all he could do to stem the panic welling up behind his icy blues. She had actually said the words. He had done his best to prime himself for this moment on the walk over, anticipating its actuality. By the nine, he had been anticipating its actuality for weeks now, but one can only muster so much preparation for the cast of heartbreak.

A million thoughts filtered through his head in that moment, not a one of them helpful in the least. And quite suddenly all of the care and sutures that Caitlyn had used to stitch shut his old wounds were fastly coming unraveled again. On the outside he was memorizing every inch of Caitlyn's countenance, from her warm honeyed orbs hidden beneath thick, well-tended eyebrows to the little beauty mark nestled upon her olive cheek just above her Cupid's bow, but inside he was drowning.

She's a siren, Aiden. A pixie. A false perfection. A pretty little holiday gush of a thing. A daydream of a life your society instructs you to want. This was never meant to be yours, she was never meant to be yours, try as you might to buck the system.

Every depressing thought he had ever conjured came to haunt, rushing in over him like a tidal wave, and suddenly his thirst for life had buckled to an unprecedented low. Her judgments from only moments before rang hollow in his ears as her fingers slipped in-between his. *And she has the gall to name me the cruel one? What fresh cup of hypocrisy was this one after?* He couldn't say with any measure of conviction, but he knew without a doubt that this was as close to the miseries of the nine that he dared allow himself.

Get away, his wits screamed through the settling vacancy. *Get far, far away.* Distance was the only remedy from such a callous perdition as this. Through the void, he somehow managed to find his legs again, pulling away from Caitlyn's disingenuous comforting. It was all an act, he knew. All conjured emotion. *Classic Caitie,* he mused. *She could turn it on with the best of them.* Calem had been right of course, as was ever his fair place to be. This was ten times worse than RC. At least Rhymona was an overtly cold-hearted bitch—a plunge the knife, twist the blade sort of lass. She had made it all too easy for him to loathe her. Caitlyn Ellsbury would offer no such satisfaction it would seem. Ironically, this very sentimentality was a significant reason for why he came to care for her in the first place.

"I have to go," he felt his lips say, but he refused to look her true again for fear of his findings.

"Aiden," Caitlyn whispered as he lifted his satchel upon his shoulder and drifted despondently out of her bedchamber and out of her life, the last soft caress of her fingertips shooting a pulsating shudder throughout the entirety of his being.

CHAPTER FOUR

The remainder of the afternoon was squandered on a languorous traipse back amidst the sprawls of Upper Kanton's bazaar. Sometime just before dusk, Aiden decided it best to disappear into Tyrenier Park, a labyrinthine patch of woodlands that swallowed up the entire southeast quarter of the island. It was the only place on the islet vast enough to seclude him from the rest of civilization until a time he deemed appropriate to return. He bought a cheap bottle of tilly-wine from Vintner's Parade and found an inconspicuous spot where one could bask in the dream-like sounds of the Aurabus Ocean crashing against the Midaran mainland in the not too far away distance. The scene was maudlin to be sure, though he found her an appropriate companion for his present mood, and mayhaps the best he could hope for considering the rather rotten circumstances.

He lazed back in the grass staring out at the sister moons inside the vast velvet horizon, doing everything within his control to sustain some semblance of a positive mindset. His vision trailed from the emerald behemoth Y'dema to her fiery sibling Ashira. Proud as princelings, the pair of them, especially during the winter months, when they always found display whether night or day (though a few months more and summer would have them, saving their spectacle solely for the deepest haunts of eventide).

Sadly, the sister moons' splendor offered but a brief respite from his growing pit of self-loathing. The gift that keeps on giving, that of self-loathing.

Oh, but if Mother could see him now. Some great figure he'd turned out to be. Barely scraping by, living off accomplishments long since faded, one shit bender away from beggarhood. Fortunately, astonishingly really, Brumfield hadn't yet gained wind of his head archivist bingeing and boarding at the library. Or mayhaps he had and simply did not care. That thought somehow pained Aiden even worse. Had he truly reached such a rank of insignificance?

"Cheers, Mother," he said raising the wine bottle skyward before taking a sloppy swill.

He thought of his sister at that, and the handful of letters she had penned him in the months that followed their mother's passing. It was obvious she had needed him as any younger sibling might need their elder after such a devastating occurrence. She was only fifteen, after all. Yet despite her pleas, he had done nothing. He knew not what to do in truth. The news had come without any warning at all. He remembered smiling when he ripped open her letter, wholly unsuspecting of the dagger lying in wait, his mind anywhere but tragedy. He knew Tam had applied to university for the harvest semester and assumed she was confirming her acceptance. He thought a joyous occasion awaited him. Hells, he'd been planning her acceptance party for months. But all of his merriment evaporated in the blink of an eye as he unfolded the parchment, and a chasm opened in his stomach.

He could remember the letter quite vividly. In fact, he could recite it line for line. Each word and sentence had been cauterized into his memory now. No doubt he had read it thousands of thousands of times to the present. It was simple and frank, as was ever Autumn's disposition. Her curtness and formality had always quite reminded him of their mother.

19 Jelnice 1828

Dear Brother,

My spirit has been dashed to bits and my heart benumbed of all proper function.

It tears my soul asunder to be the one to relate this most heartbreaking news, but it would seem I am the only one up to the task and you deserve to know.

Yestereve, mother took ill quite suddenly and repaired to the house to lie down whilst Father and I remained in the vineyard. An hour hence I returned to the house to begin supper and I found mother facedown upon the downstairs hallway floor. A large pool of blood had formed around her head from an apparent fall and collision with the entryway table. I will spare you the further details, but she did not survive the wound. I sent for Matthew immediately after finding her, but nothing could be done. She had lost too much blood. I am so sorry, brother. I know there are no proper words for tidings such as this. We will bury her on the morrow upon duskfall beside Nan and Dah. Dusk was always mother's hour, wouldn't you agree?

Please come home Aiden. I cannot do this alone.

Father needs you. I need you.

Deepest Love, Tam

Stella Ashborough was by and far the person Aiden cherished most in all the world, and quite suddenly this person was simply erased from his existence. He would never speak with her again. Never hear her voice again. Never feel her unconditional love again. At first, his mind refused to accept such a blow. His reaction in the weeks to follow was poor at best. Justly so, he went through every stage grief had to offer, some multiple times. He secluded himself from everything, his family, his mates, Caitie, everyone who cared a mite about him, and in his solitude, he drank himself into oblivion, one bottle at a time, one hour after another, one day into the next, until enough bullshit and alcohol buried the massive hole that had ruptured from his mother's passing.

Come home? How could he possibly go home?

He could barely cope with the loss himself. He would be no aid to Autumn or his father. More letters followed, and despite his fear of them, he kept every one and read through them often, far more often than he ought, especially whilst drunk, but to his chagrin, he could never quite bring himself to respond. His emotions always got the better of him in one way or another. At this juncture, after so much time in delay, even if his mind permitted such a whimsy as courage to find his fingers, he hadn't the faintest inkling what he might say or if it even mattered anymore. For as the days wore on into weeks and months and more letters piled atop his desk, the prospect of reply became increasingly more difficult. He had stabbed quill to parch a hundred times over, at varying times of day, sometimes sober, other times drunk, but each time his mind grew maddeningly blank. Mayhaps by this juncture Tam had written him off entirely. Given his negligent path, he certainly deserved as much. Months had passed since her last letter, and he had little reason to suspect there would be another. She must be so furious with him now, so disappointed in her older brother. The gods know, she had every right to be. She had once looked up to him so. But he knew he was right in this. He could not help her. He was saving her from another needless worriment. Their father would be burden enough.

He thought about the final letter, about the desperation and the ire that had been so meticulously phrased. It was obvious that Tam wanted him to feel the sting behind every word this time. She'd had enough. Apparently, their father had fallen into a terrible depression and could scarcely bring himself to leave his own bedchamber any longer, much less see to the vineyard duties. This of course left the tending and selling completely in Tam's hands—a task wholly ill-suited to a girl her age. The concluding line of the letter had struck him like a lance through the heart at first read. It was how he knew it would be her last attempt. Words most carefully placed and accurately aimed. They still haunted him horribly when, in a moment of guilt and regret, he would permit their ghastly presence.

He thinks you blame him for Mother's passing.

That was a most bitter pill to swallow—those sharp, simple words. Aiden questioned his own motives for days after initially reading the grim tidings. Did he truly blame his father? It was no high-held secret that he'd always been closer with his mother, he was her heart after all, but he never really took into account that others might view his negligent behavior in her wake as condemning toward her widower. Mayhaps if his father hadn't always seemed so gods damned resentful toward him.

The scar across his belly itched like a bad rash at the thought, but he ignored its call, downing a fresh swallow of wine in defiance as an image of Caitlyn filtered back through the rabble of his hometown, Gallea's Grace. He closed his eyes, allowing himself to fall deep within its bleak sanctum, deep within its welcoming embrace, like the sugary kiss of sweet, sweet medicine. The taste lingered on his lips, thick as lotus milk, and he began to feel the all too familiar tingling sensation in the flesh and bones beneath his eyes. The numbness wouldn't be far now.

When he made to stand again, he fell back over and had a laugh at his own careless hedonism. Three-quarters of a bottle in an hour on an empty stomach was not amongst his brightest decisions, but he was in another one of his moods, so he defiantly quaffed the remainder of the wine down, letting it streak sloppily into his beard, and hurled the bottle off the side of the island.

"The finest of Folkvale, my bleeding cock," he crowed into the unsuspecting breeze, struggling to his feet.

"I take it you did indeed find all of your hopes and dreams nestled low at the bottom of that poor wittle bottle?" a voice said from the blackened wood.

"Bloody hell," Aiden whirled around, his heart in his mouth. "Who goes there?"

After a moment of tarry, a short, sylphlike figure appeared from the shadow of an elm, a ghost in the nocturne. Aiden's eyes immediately befell the sheath at its side.

"If you have plans of thievery, I'll warn you forthwith, I've nothing of value to be had."

The figure snickered.

Aiden had not expected such a response. Did he know this person? Was this some manner of cruel-hearted lark? "You make mock of my vulnerability?"

"Trust it true, I mean you no ill will, young master."

Young master? Aiden decided her dialect was most assuredly of Southlands origin, but it also harbored within a sophisticated regality that he could not quite place. "No, of course not, you're only a hooded figure skulking about the forest after dusk. I daresay you might have set The Stranger aquiver."

"This is no forest I can assure you," the hood said as she took another step toward him. "Besides, could not the same be said of yourself?"

"I reckon that's fair." The archivist washed a hand over his face, collecting himself as much as the wine would allow. "And I'll readily admit I'm a bottle deep with no plans on halting."

The figure exposed a wineskin at her side, quick as a fox. "I suppose that makes the pair of us now, doesn't it?"

"Fancy that. A beggar's death for us both then," said he with a false cheer.

At that, the figure lifted the hood from its perch revealing a tempting pair of lilac haunters, a dusky complexion, and a long, wild mane of ash blond curls that she had attempted with middling success to wrangle into a ponytail.

"Fancy that," she echoed before she took a swig from her wineskin. "And prithee by the blood of the stars stow all of the trifling milady pleasantries. They vex me greatly."

"Do they now?"

"They do."

"And never before have I so desperately craved such a mannerly disposition," the archivist found himself saying, grasping at some semblance of composure. He imagined his younger self, freshly retched from his relationship with Rhymona, shaking his head in utter disappointment. He knew precisely what this breed of female could do to him after all, but evidently the wine coupled with the sudden throb of his cock was more than enough to introduce foolish scenarios once more into the shambles of his forethoughts.

"There he is." She was quick to the scratch. "Complete with all the subtle charm of your typical narcissistic giftborn sociopath, I see. And tell me scholar of magic most foul, does it delight your heart to wield such grand abilities?"

"It has before, if you must know, though, by the way you carry that iron at your hip, I wouldn't readily try your prowess with a blade."

"Keeping a careful watch on my hips then are we, young master?"

"There are certainly much worse trifles to mind in the twilit gloom, I most humbly confess."

"My, my, you are a cheeky lad aren't you," she said with a coy smile, "so much for all that ire and melancholy then, yeah. Some sad song about a lass named Caitie and a bleeding cock if I gathered proper."

"You heard all that, did you?"

"'Twas kind of hard not to. You were screaming it loud enough for every ear in Kanton to hearken."

"It would seem my heart has become slag with dwelling this eve. I'm quite rubbish with change, you see. Which is why I much prefer to keep to the present when I can help it. A present I must admit that has quite improved only just recently."

"Truly giftborn, your tongue is tainted by the silver."

"I've been warned of such before. Though if it pleases, I beg of you accept my most sincere apologies if I have been too ribald or presumptuous."

"Not at all. Your candor is actually...well, rather pleasant."

"Name's Aiden, by the way," the archivist said, extending his hand.

"Val," the woman said as she placed the wineskin within the creases of his palm. "Cheers to our lowly descent."

Aiden accepted her invitation, not wanting to appear rude, but was immediately taken off guard by the content's bite. "This is whiskey?"

"Daerynger to be more accurate," she corrected. "For to those that are so inclined should never be left to the wander without." She riddled off this last bit as though reading a slogan from a label.

"Gods." The archivist coughed and rasped through its aftereffects. "It's a rough bastard, isn't it?"

"I reckon it does demand a bit of an acquired taste," she said with a chuckle. "Those amongst the ports name her the Headsman's Kiss."

"I'll say. If death had a flavor, this would undoubtedly be it."

"Go on then, love, have another. It may be rough, but it'll get you proper right quick if that's your aim."

The archivist couldn't help but follow her order, drinking Val in as he slung back a second, far more generous nip of her offering. As exotically appealing as she was, she also carried about her an eerie ambiguity, though he blamed such vagueness on the phantasmagorical cast of starglow that swayed bright and dark betwixt the congested canopy of treetops. One moment she appeared as a woman in her in early twenties, perhaps no older than his own twenty-three cycles, the next she appeared nearer to her fifties, perhaps older.

"Gods' bones, how old is *that* bloody wretch?" Val commented on the tome that lay half-spat from the mouth of Aiden's satchel.

Aiden had become so distracted in his intoxicated state that he hadn't taken notice his pack had fallen open revealing his beloved Arcanum Volume IV. There was nothing overtly special about the tome at first glance. Were it to be judged by its cover alone, one might suspect it to be quite boring, filled tediously with archaic designs and garrulous pretensions. Its binding was once cast of a deep burgundy that had since faded tragically, the seam at the top had long since come apart despite numerous efforts by a novice needleworker to stitch it back to suitability, and the wealth of pages within were thin, foxed, and torn, many of the words worn from the aged parch altogether.

"Only the gods know the answer to that I fear," he said. "Old as the hills to be sure. The original print date has long since been blanched from perception."

"May I?"

"By all means. Careful though, many of the pages have come loose."

Val unbuckled the sheath at her side, resting it beside his satchel, retrieved the tome, and opened it as she plopped down in the grass. She skimmed half-heartedly through a few random pages, before stopping a quarter-length in to glance up at the archivist. "This is a grimoire, isn't it?"

"Indeed, it is."

"I thought this sort of material was not permitted beyond the archive's walls."

"It isn't. But this beauty belongs to me. It was given to me by my mother." He found a seat beside her, resting the wineskin between them. "And what of you?"

"What of me what?" she said, tucking the grimoire back inside the satchel.

He rapped his knuckles against her scabbard. "Well, it is quite curious now, isn't it, that a woman of your allure needst carry such a crude instrument at her side?"

"The better to protect myself, of course."

"I see."

"You're not one of those manly-men, women belong at the cookpot sorts, are you?"

"No. Gods. What? Don't be stupid." *Straight to the point was this one.* "I could give a fuck less what a woman wants for her life so long as she doesn't try to tell me how to manage mine."

"Steady on," said Val, "it was only a question."

"My mother was in the Royalguard, prize well," he continued, "a task largely considered man's work, as I'm sure you're well aware. She served as magus to some lord upstart in Lancastle some cycles back before retiring to the Southlands."

"Impressive."

"Aye."

"Well, I rather fancy myself more the courier type, if you must know. I protect those who have coin and happen to require such a service. Nothing more, nothing less. The kingsroad can be a rather dangerous place for travelers, as you can imagine. Bandits and bladehands and the like."

"And has it ever come to blades before?"

"Of course, it has. The tinker trade is as corrupt as they come. It puts foolish thoughts in the minds of hard, desperate folk. It can turn a good man rotten in the blink of an eye. Though, if it's all the same to you, I'd rather not delve too deep into such darkly coffers. It puts a rather grim damper on the drink, does it not?"

"No worries." Aiden decided he'd rather not push his luck with the Lady Swordsmith.

"Blades or no, it's not such a bad employ," she said gazing up dreamily into the field of stars overhead, "it suits me as well as any other job, I suppose."

"How is that then?"

"Well, I'm not much made for the company of others, if you hadn't discerned already. I'll readily admit I don't normally get on with folk as easy as I have with you to the present. Never have. Never will, I suspect."

"Woof." Aiden fanned himself. "Cage the charm school flirt over here."

"Don't misconstrue now. I like folk well enough. And most folk I don't mind being around, as in the vicinity of, but that's usually the extent of it. Truly, there is nothing more refreshing than a new face, but that's as far as I typically allow for. I like folk without permanent faces, you know? The type you meet without necessarily having to speak a word to them or remember them at all for that matter." She palmed the wineskin and turned it up. "I'm a loner at heart, I suppose, ever-cursed as the recluse. Fuck me, right?"

Aiden turned to his newfound drinking companion and his heartbeat suddenly began to hasten. She was a most intoxicating creature, this Val, her presence like a drug to his sorrowful soul, a drug he wished to explore with profound intimacy. In that moment, he wanted nothing more than to roll atop her and steal away a kiss, as juvenile as such an endeavor was to consider. He imagined the sweet, pillowy touch of her lips begging against his, the taste and texture of her tongue as he implored deeper and deeper, the overwhelming desire to undress her and explore her both inside and out from the very apex of her crown to the filed curves of her tiny pink toenails.

Val turned to her drinkmate, as though she'd somehow heard his inner urges within her own tangle of torments, and she brushed her unruly curls behind a perfectly shaped ear, presenting him with a breathtaking still frame of innocence. Her doll-like twilit orbs thence prompted an unfamiliar sensation from his racing heart down the sleeve of his left arm, radiating into the whorls of his fingertips.

"You may think on yourself poorly for such feelings," there was the hint of a smile pulling at Aiden's lips, "but trust I can relate in my own manner."

"I reckon we all have our fated paths to haunt," she said with unfettered ease. No doubt they were words she was quite familiar with.

"I reckon so."

"'And Death himself doth stalk within the twists and yawns of mine colorless shadow.'"

Bloody hell, did this sea drifter just quote Malthus Tetherow? RC was the only other person he knew that could quote from Tetherow's works with such casual aplomb. Most folk this day and age thought the old master's teachings little more than archaic hokum. Dead words from a dead age.

"Malthus Tetherow," he said, masking his surprise. "*Dysphoria Fields* if I'm not mistaken."

"Aye. Quite bookish of you, giftborn. You tend well your tomes it would seem."

"Quite literally, in fact. I've spent the better part of the past four cycles pretending at some manner of archivist to our fair university."

"Have you now?"

"Indeed."

"Well, even still, archivist is a right proper path, is it not?"

"It pays the rents, I suppose."

"By contrast, it would seem my path would have me portray the apparition," she said before shaking another sip from the wineskin, "a part that's come about me quite naturally I woefully aver. As such I've come to view myself as this sort of ghostly traveler evaporating from hollow to hollow never really making an impact anywhere. No worries though. It's the distance that defines me."

Why is it always the haunted ones that find me?

"Most folk don't want to see the true me anyhow." She stood. "They much prefer a pretty face—or an eager mouth—or better still, a wet cunny. They desire compliance, obedience, silent acquiescence." Val stared out into the sea of spectacular stars. "It's my great advantage," she continued wryly, "an honorable man can be taken off their guard by one so dispossessed of their own wellbeing, now can't they? It's unexpected by one in such a competitive trade as mine and in being so oddly, ironically, and perhaps unfairly, empowering." Val finished with a fresh smile, "and that is quite enough of all the doom and gloom, I say." She unclasped her cloak before kneeling down and began to unlace her boots.

"What are you doing?" Aiden couldn't help but ask.

"What does it look like I'm doing?"

"I don't know…stripping?"

Val glanced over at the archivist with a fox-faced smirk. "Don't you wish it so?"

It took but a moment more, and her boots were sent flying in whichever direction would have them, and just like that, she was off prancing about in circles and steps.

Try as he might, Aiden could not discern whether her sudden shift in moods was all an act to mask the freshly conjured pain within or if indeed the Daerynger had finally staked its claim. Either way, he was much too lit himself to properly mull such a worry and thusly began to unlace his own boots.

"May I have this dance?" Val curtsied as he approached, mimicking a belle at the ball.

"Do mine eyes deceive or has the Lady Swordsmith revealed herself a wild-eyed lush?"

Val held out her hand and gestured playfully for him to take it. "Hey, I got over myself, giftborn. Now bring your drunk ass over here."

Her hands were much smaller than he had imagined, though despite her rough trade, they had managed to retain some measure of their femininity, which of course only worked to enthrall him further. Like a sailor mesmerized by the beckoning call of a siren, he acquiesced, pulling her in close, positioning and repositioning his free hand awkwardly about her waist and hip before eventually finding a harmless spot at the small of her back. Her breasts were wrapped tight in linen bandages underneath her ashen blouse, making it impossible for him to discern their size or suppleness, but even still when she pressed in closer, his mind instantaneously began racing to all sorts of inappropriate retreats again. A moment later, she rested her head against the front of his shoulder and a most intoxicating scent washed over him. Her guise may have been lowborn, but she smelled clean, nobility clean, cleaner than nobility clean at that, like an ancient meadow after the first rain of springtide, like freshly blossomed cintas flowers.

Just as they found a gentle comfort in one another's embrace, the bends of their bodies meshing as one, Val suddenly twirled away from his cuddle, her hair screaming out like a blustering blizzard in the starlight's pour. The act briefly took him by surprise, but a moment later she whisked back into his chest with the delicate grace of a stage performer, her body taut and quite lissome. Though there was no music to be heard, every movement she made and led him on flowed to the rhythm of some exotic dance as though stolen from a royal house performance. He could almost visualize the scene unfolding around them, hundreds of posh revelers gazing at them in awe as each stride and turn Val made played for them a most compelling tale.

The pair danced and frolicked about the park for near to an hour, polishing off the Daerynger, before taking to the bazaar and then the university cobble. What ensued was a shiny, sodden blur—an unstoppable carousel of japery, drinking, and general waywardness.

First, there was the pubhouse and the mandolin player. This Aiden remembered with relative lucidity. The musician was quite talented, in fact, despite his melancholy, a rarity indeed within Kanton's confines. And his performance of *Lovers in Limbo* was something of the echelon beyond brilliance.

:How does one know where the devilkin goes when the devilkin knows you're awake?:

More pints, shots of whiskey, and a dash of shufa, and he and Val were off to the stars—mayhaps to Dalynisa herself. A planet made entirely of ocean, or so the starwatchers say. A mariner's wet dream more like. What a mad, mad, fucking mad realm this was.

Fuck Caitie.

Fuck Brumfield.

More pints and shots and forgotten words, and it was on to Billows with a group of seventh cycles, each one dressed like the whores and riffraff patrolling the harbor end haunts. What irony. Though he supposed even the educated and the wealthy were entitled to err from time to time. Since when had dressing like a tramp become an accepted manner of fashion anyway? If this development were allowed to persist, it wouldn't be long before one found a brothel for every street corner. Hah! That would be the day. Come one, come all. Send your kits to Kanton where they can have a lecture and a proper tug before the noonday bell tolls.

He couldn't be sure, but he thought he and Val might have snogged there in the candlelit dormitory hallway in front of anyone, everyone, and the council of the gods. What a spectacle the pair of them made. Though it was entirely possible it may have also been one of the whores or other riffraff.

Fuck Caitie.

Fuck Brumfield.

But mostly Caitie. Who was she to decide the design of their parting anyway? He might decide to despise her in spite of her wishes.

From Billows onward, it was just he and Val and the spinning streetlamps until they crashed through the portal of Withers. Once inside they danced like wildkin savages amidst her orchard of tomes, tossing the place something proper, and terrifying the piss out of poor napping Grandpa, who made himself scarce thereafter. They would have made a most brilliant pair of vandals, he and Val the Sellsword.

Fuck Caitie.

Fuck Brumfield.

And fuck Withers too.

Then he remembered he had a bottle of summer-wine stashed under his pile of clothes on the cupboard floor and somehow managed to slice open his hand trying to relieve the cork with a letter opener. He got blood all over his shirt and laughed at the sight of it, and Val stemmed the bleeding, wrapping it tight for him. Despite the spins, he remembered with unerring clarity her soft, tiny hands cupping and tending to his, his blood, vibrant and copious, discoloring the warmth of her nimble fingers. He studied her face in the lantern light as she tied a knot in the linen scrap around his wound, etching every tantalizing feature into the vaults of his memory bank, from the oblivion of her stormy orbs to her lightly freckled cheeks to her maddeningly taunting lips. Save her undeniable allure, she was nothing at all like Caitie.

Fuck Caitie, the fucking haunter. She could rattle her chains in someone else's ears.

Then came the night air like the kiss of a cellar banshee, bitter with brine, and the white sands, cold as the ice plains against his bare feet. It had been some time since he had beheld the shore at such a low tide.

Farador's folly, the shore? How was this possible? When did they leave the library? Moreover, when did they go down the lift? And mayhaps even more curious, where were his fucking boots? Had he forgotten them back in the archive? Or had it been in the park?

Fucking hells.

It was around this juncture that his consciousness began to betray him, and he settled down upon the beach, unable to keep his legs under him a moment longer. He thought Val was still there with him, but his body had had enough of the world and his eyes refused to stay open, so he bellowed her name aloud to make sure.

"Val," he crowed with a similar gusto to his tirade in the park earlier, cast from the deepest, darkest reaches of his soul.

"Hmmm," he thought he heard someone answer over the distant sound of waves dying against the shoreline.

:How does one know where the devilkin goes when the devilkin knows you're awake?:

It could have been anybody.

But then he thought he heard the sound of liquid shifting directions inside a glass container to the right of him. Or mayhaps the left? The whirling abyss behind his closed eyelids had long since deformed all sense of proper bearing. It was like navigating the blackest nadirs of the deepest ocean blindfolded.

However, a wind of cintas flowers washed over him as his head crashed violently upon the sand, and with its familiarity, he surrendered to the illusion of safety. It had to be Val. His escort. His lass. His warrior princess. He could never forget that most fetching scent.

She had opened up to him even though she hated new faces and companionship. Then she wrapped his hand and warded away all semblances of his prior sorrow. She was a real peach, Val the Sellsword. A real peach, indeed. Heaven-sent some might name her. And unlike Caitie, there was little doubt she would abandon him to such a witching wander as this.

By the gods, inside such a wander and afterglow, he could draw his final breath this night, under the freezing stars, in the sand with Val the Sellsword and all would be forever well. T'would be a most fitting end, he mused. One last victory for Old Aiden Ashborough. One last fuck you to this poxy world. This was the sort of last hurrah one only dared dream to go out upon, the very grail of expiry, that The Hood be kind enough to take us in our sleep.

"Cheers," he said at last, though it came out more like "cheese," before the tireless black drew nigh to claim the last of its circadian plunder.

CHAPTER FIVE

Frayed are the threads that cast shadows. Lush is the drear in their unforgiving wake.

Those were the only words scrawled upon the first page of the *Kingstome*. Marsea considered the unfinished volume her father's masterpiece. Of course, she had read through dozens of Whit Lanier's writings over the cycles, dozens of times, and had become intimately familiar with his prose, but the *Kingstome* proved itself something of a different beast from the rest. It was far less structured than his other works, painting a strange, chaotic picture of the last Lanier king's final cycles. Parts of it read like your run-of-the-mill memoir, but many of the scattered entries appeared more akin to a grimoire's passages or an alchemist's logbook.

Frayed are the threads that cast shadows. Lush is the drear in their unforgiving wake. Marsea trailed the words one last time before she closed the large, leather-bound tome, and sighed as the agreed upon hour of mischief and madness began to nibble at her toes.

She removed her glasses, placing them atop the book, and massaged at the bridge of her nose, spreading her thumb and index finger out across the soft patches beneath her eyelids.

"Father," she whispered, "I need you. I cannot—no, I refuse to rely on the maidens for such a task. They would be aghast to know my intentions this night, to know the thoughts that have riddled my mind these past few days. And so I am without prayer, without blessing, without protection. Save for you. If there is any connection left to us at all, please—"

Movement from somewhere outside The Cupboard halted her communion, causing the hairs on the back of her neck to prickle, and she held her breath. *Please watch over me, guide me, love me, and keep me safe.* The words echoed as she listened to the footsteps beyond. They were faint, barely a thing at all, and yet, in the hanging silence, they were all she could hear.

The Cupboard, in all of its mystery, was her secret. Her sanctuary. The one place she felt safe enough to step outside of herself and dare to hope. It was the one thing her bully of an elder brother had given her before his passing. Verily, it was all she had that she could name her own. And as such, she decided no other should know of its whereabouts. Not even Remy, her younger brother. Not even her own mother, the Queen. Neither one could be trusted with such a secret in her estimation. Not that either one would have cared a mite anyway had she actually been more forthcoming about it.

Mayhaps more surprising, she had not yet told Vaustian. He held her heart, after all. She loved no other more. But she did not trust him to leave it alone once he knew of it. No doubt he would have had the place scoured from top to bottom. And the tomes he found the most useful he would have had brought to his private solar, away from her access. He was a voracious collector with an insatiable hunger for more. More, more, more. More of everything. That was Vaustian Harver. The entirety of The Vael was scarce large enough for his countless fancies. She knew her secret would be a ruin once put to his care. She loved Vaustian, truly, madly, woefully, but she was no lackwit. If her twenty cycles in this world had taught her anything, it was that too much trust was poison, especially whilst kept by the ones adored most.

Marsea stood as the footsteps faded, and quietly placed the book four deep inside the nearest stack, lining its edges precisely to the pair surrounding it. They were her father's books, all, ancient and arcane, passed down from generation to generation, stacks upon stacks of them lining the walls of the small, hidden nook at the back of Lancastle Citadel's massive archives, most towering high from floor to ceiling, nearly enough to fill an entire study, and they were all she had left of him, all she had left of her entire family's once-storied legacy.

Marsea had read most all of them in the cycles since her father's passing. Some many times over. But this particular book was her favorite. To wit, it had no name, so the princess had secretly taken to naming it the *Kingstome*, as though it were a famous blade or some such rubbish. It comprised her father's personal writings, words that always seemed to calm her when she grew horridly anxious, which admittedly happened far more frequently than she should like. Often enough that she nearly had the thing memorized now. She placed the whorls of her fingers against the *Kingstome's* spine and closed her eyes, asking her father once more to grant her some measure of protection this night. Anything. Anything at all would do.

After a moment of repose, she retrieved her too-big glasses, "gran glasses" Vaustian named them, returning them to their perch upon the crest of her button nose, and pulled her long, honey-gold hair back into a bunch. She stared into the candle's flame one last time and inhaled, collecting the woodsy, bookish scent of the room as though it were a kiss of perfume, and she breathed it out slowly, banishing the flame's hungry flicker once more to the darkness.

Quiet as the tomb, Marsea inched the hideaway door forward and peeked out into the lantern-lit aisle. As far as she could tell, the coast was clear. She waited a beat and swiftly squeezed through the doorway's narrow opening, making sure its hidden latch secured properly afterward.

Stealing in and out of The Cupboard was one of the rare instances in which she counted her diminutive stature as an advantage. Moreover, every time she withdrew, she couldn't help but wonder how her father had managed it all those many cycles before.

On tiptoes, Marsea crept down the aisle toward the next one over, careful not to betray the eerie hush of the long, cavernous chamber. *And whose lovely footsteps were those?* she wondered as she stole toward the archive's heart, her curiosity gaining the better of her again. A fool's charade, mayhaps, but she simply had to know. She feigned a hauntling's presence, breath buried down, as she danced from shadow to shadow, wary to evade the lantern light's pale amber fury, stepping lighter as she came fast upon her company.

Another three rows in, midway down the aisle, she found Effie Cavendish in the fire glow silently leafing through a book.

"Effie," Marsea greeted as she casually strolled into the aisle.

"Eeep!" Effie jumped, near to the next moon over, emitting a strange sort of half-yell, half-crying sound as she fumbled her book to the stones and fell back against the bookshelf. "Your Highness," she replied, her face near red as her long, mossy mane, struggling to collect herself proper, "deepest apologies. I could have sworn I was alone."

"I should be the one to apologize," Marsea said, sliding her glasses back up her nose, fighting to conceal her amusement, "it was not my intent to frighten you so."

"Of course not, milady," Effie said, bending down to retrieve the fallen book. "I'm afraid I startle far too easily, always have."

"*Humping Your Nan*," Marsea said, inspecting the book's cover. Now this was a surprise indeed coming from a cloth maiden. *Effie, you tart.* "I daresay, are you sure the Lirae Mothers would approve of you reading such...cheeky material?"

"I...er...um..." Flustered, the cloth maiden gripped the beaded rosary around her neck.

Marsea had never beheld shame so barefaced in all her days. *Shit.* She could tell immediately her friend was taking it poorly. "No worries, Ef, your secret is safe with me," she added, hoping to ease the cloth maiden's embarrassment. *Now smile.* Her lips curled up against their nature. *Brilliant, Marsea. Not awkward at all.* "Love Fawkes. Fucking hilarious. Truly. *Humping Your Nan*, *Sensible Jest*, *Dead Soulmates Society*. I've read them all, end to end."

And they say all the classics are dead.

Effie tucked the book back into its cranny and smiled sheepishly.

"I know it's easy to just say," Marsea began candidly, "but you should be more confident in yourself, Ef. You are an amazing person. I hope you know this."

Effie's features brightened considerably at that.

'Tis a damned pitiful irony of the human psyche that one can offer such keen advice on certain delicate matters, but nary accept them when it involves their own affairs.

You don't have time for this, the riven thing inside reminded. "Right," the princess said. "Well, I must be off then. See you at devotions on the morrow?"

"Of course, milady." The cloth maiden bowed, still nervously clutching her rosary. "Have a blessed evening."

"And you the same," Marsea replied with another manufactured smile. "Also, I recommend skipping ahead to chapter six. That's where it actually starts to get good."

CHAPTER SIX

Marsea hugged close against a redwood, tightening the hood around her waxen cheeks before peering around the side at her prey. It would seem by his squat and the rather vulgar choice of language that her mark was having a keen go at a shit in the distance, the elements be damned. Her face wrinkled at the realization, and she leaned back against her looming safeguard. *Of course, he is, considering the vexation of the past few days, such would only be the proper way with this one.* Though all revolting circumstances considered, she certainly could not have purchased an easier stab at her mark. Mayhaps her father watched over her this eve, after all. And with the promise of such a precious favor, a fleeting wander of warmth swept over her.

Ganedys Harver had proven himself a rather difficult man to corner over the past few days, which Marsea conceded was more of an undersight on her behalf than anything of note the wretched tosspot did himself or was capable of. She slowly unsheathed her sword as she gazed across the snow-buried expanse to where her prey was finishing his business and took a deep breath to settle her racing heart.

His grunts and curses shifted into song as his belt began to jingle, and she hurried into action, a pale shadow against the frightful snowfall's sorceries, zigzagging from tree to tree behind her quarry, gaining ground with each decisive step. She could only hope the howling wind would be enough to obscure her crunching footfalls in the ever-thickening shroud of winter. She halved the distance with a trio of lunges, and drew a second blade from a tasseled sheath at the small of her back as a baleful expression twisted across her innocuous guise. Cat-like, Marsea maneuvered ahead of her mark, her dancer's feet halting flush behind another monstrous redwood as she prepared for the ambush.

"Unveil yourself, slitpurse!" Marsea heard Gan bellow as she melted against the tree. *Shit.* "You're about as stealthy as a buggered whore, to have it true. Gods' breath, the entire hollow could hear your approach from a league's passing." The words were followed by the cold, flat scrape of a sword being drawn free of its scabbard.

So much for surprise, she grumbled, nudging her glasses up with the back of her wrist. *Was anything ever easy anymore?* Marsea swallowed hard and clutched firm the handles of her blades. *No turning back now.* She stepped out from behind the tree, fear all but consuming, and brushed back the hood of her cloak, revealing her youthful aspect to the Royalguard colonel.

Gan's eyes grew wide at the visage of his assailant, and his lips curled into an impish grin. "Nine hells, isn't this rich? They finally let you loose from the cage, did they?"

Externally Marsea shrugged, cool as a cucumber, but internally her blood was practically punching holes through her veins.

"My brother sends his fucking whores to do his dirty work now, is that it?" Ganedys Harver prodded.

"You have become a liability, Ganedys," Marsea heard her voice drone on in repetition of Vaustian's words. The viceroy's words had always instilled a certain measure of confidence that she typically lacked. A measure of confidence she would no doubt require to see this nightfall through. "You have only yourself to blame in this."

"Hard words from a soft mouth," he scoffed. "But I can see you've got some kind of spirit in you now, don't you? Delighted to see Old Vaustian didn't fuck it *all* out of you just yet." Gan took a step to his left. "Though I suppose your death was always mine to take, wasn't it? And there were yet so many opportunities over the cycles. To think I could have spared myself all this bloody trifle. I only wish I could see the look on my asshole brother's face when I send your pretty little head back to court on that tiny bitch sword of yours."

I say, someone thinks mighty well of himself, doesn't he? "The scars that bind us and all that, right?" she taunted.

"Oh, you would do well to keep those words off your tongue, whore."

At that, everything slowed, and Marsea felt the pull of her right leg, followed by the push of her left, one step forward, then another, her strides quickly hastening into a calculated sprint. She had never much been one for trading useless barbs after all. Not when there was work to be done, and certainly not when she had the favor of her forborne in tow.

Ganedys Harver was a pillar of a man by comparison to her short stature, so her first order of business would be to bring him down to her level. He might own the size and strength, but she had speed and agility, and a mite bit more insight into his flaws. She had watched him in tourneys and lessons on numerous occasions before, and though he showed little in the way of weakness in the sparring yard, he had earned quite the reputation for wielding a rather nasty temper. Mayhaps a temper she could goad into aggression at the detriment of his defense. Marsea knew him to be especially explosive once deep in his cups, and he was well deep this night. He was like a wild beast in that way, primitive, impetuous, and predictable. Nevertheless, even if she were to rile the beast into carelessness, her strikes would need to be flawlessly executed to gain the upper hand.

She drove in low to start, and his first cut nearly put her in the grave. She managed to parry the strike, but it sent a burning tremor up the length of her arm from wrist to shoulder. She spun away and steadied her plight as best she could, recovering just in time to send his subsequent thrust wide of her belly. Suddenly her sword became heavy as a slab of stone. Not the most promising start, but she soldiered on through the sting. *Keep him moving. Keep him guessing. Find your opening.* Ganedys lunged after her again, no doubt hoping to have her done quick, but she was much the quicker, backpedaling like a fencer, keeping her blades between them, dodging and blocking his swipes and stabs, all the while gambling the correct position of each ensuing effort. They clashed and swayed inside a feral dance, back and forth, like a cat and mouse, between the towering redwoods, until finally her heel caught awkward against a root and she fell backward into a violent tumble. A great gust of wind circled about just overhead as she rolled frantically away, each turn dampening her clothes in snow and muck. *Stars save me*. The sodden bastard nearly had her. Just like that.

Tender and muddied, Marsea plowed forward and scrambled back to her feet, fastly repositioning herself in a defensive stance, but Gan denied her any chance at a full recovery, chasing after her again with a throaty growl, his officer's blade flashing about her in unforgiving waves, driving in at her with unnatural ferocity, closer and closer still. It was all she could do to keep his iron at bay, and with each joining blow, it became woefully evident that her spill had taken more than a little something from the mobility of her offhand shoulder.

Nothing from her sparring lessons with Vaustian and Cas had prepared her for such a vicious onslaught, for such outright savagery. To say she was outmatched and ill-prepared for such a tilt would have been a most egregious understatement. Nine hells, simply remaining upright challenged her at this juncture. Her knees had begun to wobble errantly under the pressure of Gan's hacking and slashing, and the fingers of her main hand were practically benumbed of all feeling. No doubt their grip would begin to betray her sooner rather than later. She desperately needed to shift the tide of the game and soon, for at their current pace she was not long to remain in this one.

Gan managed to rout her completely soused, and despite her best efforts, the fat, ugly lout showed little sign of fatigue. She couldn't hope to return his dogged tear even on her best day. She was simply too small, too thin, too weak, and too untried to withstand such a dreadful fever and intensity. So, she decided she would allow him a small victory, if only to sell the switch, to soften his approach. He held the control in a contest of blades, any fool with half his sight could see as much, but there were many more methods to fell a man than brute combat. In the case of Ganedys Harver, he'd become a slave to his ego eons ago, and as such, grew into a proud and pretentious bully who thought far too well of himself. That overconfidence would ultimately prove his undoing. In this, she had to believe.

Marsea parried and blocked and dipped and weaved, waiting for the perfect opportunity to prize him the win, and finally, mercifully, it came. His officer's blade curved out with a reverse swing from a rather nasty dig, and she let her sword tear away from her grasp, reeling back wildly with the move. She spun about and stumbled to the ground, struggling to maintain her footing before collapsing fully upon all fours. Afterward, she could feel Gan stalking toward her, just over the bend of her shoulder, his boots crunching with menace over frozen thistles behind her, though she did not dare look back at him. She had to maintain her concentration. The gambit left no room for error.

All eggs, one basket.

For you, my love.

Here we go.

She fought her mounting state of panic as she crawled forward, inch by tried inch, grasping tight the dagger in her left palm, keeping it close at the ready. She could only hope he wasn't clever enough to simply run her through right then and there—that his arrogance would worm forth to stake its claim. Marsea produced a desperate fit of coughing as Gan arrived upon her side, and he bellowed out a hearty chuckle at her suffering.

"Such pageantry, little lamb. Bravo. You put on a jolly good show, I'll grant you that. But tell it true, is this all you've got in you?" She heard him spear his officer's blade down into the mud just behind her ankle. She could feel its steel hum biting for a taste of her lifeblood.

There he is. She almost smiled.

"I suppose all in your bloodline are equally as pathetic, aren't they? Your father, the craven. Your brother, the deserter. And your mother, the shameful turncoat."

At that, Marsea halted in her crawl and pushed up from the muck into a kneeling position, abandoning her dagger before her in the snow. *Wait for it. Bait him in.* She flexed her aching hands to regain some measure of feeling in them. *Make him believe.* A moment later, she felt Gan brush his fingers up the top of her spine onto the nape of her neck before gripping tight a fistful of her hair.

"And then there is you, now isn't there?" He wrenched her head back so he could look at her straight. "You're a tough cookie, aren't you? A real puzzle-box sweetheart, yeah?" he spat, jerking her up to her feet, strands of gold tearing out from her scalp.

He's only a man, Marsea. No different than you or any other. **A slab of meat.**

"How dare you presume to bring me before The Hood's Door." He buried his big, heavy fist in the small of her back and let her drop back to the mud, her glasses falling from her face in the process. "Who are you to steal upon your lord with a blade in the dead of nightfall?"

The air caught fire, and Marsea wheezed and hacked as her back and side wailed in agony. She crumpled onto her side and stared through blurry eyes at her dagger not but a few feet away. *He's only a man.* It was all she could do not to go after it. Though she knew it was yet too soon. Gan would still be on his guard, and as dumb and drunk as the big ox was, he would still be expecting a fight from her. She had to maintain the ruse, if only for a bit longer. Woefully, she'd become well acquainted with this tired, old game. She had lived it all her life. Submission would prove her salvation yet again, as it had on so many occasions before. Of this, she had no doubts. It was her lone constant.

The Royalguard colonel dropped to a knee beside her, palmed the side of her head, and pressed her face down into the muck. "This is where you belong, whore," he whispered into her ear, his breath reeking of booze and the maidens only knew what else. "This is where your entire fucking miserable family belongs." Marsea moaned and spluttered, coughing and spitting once he let her back up.

Let him have it. Just a bit longer. Only a man.

"You know, I never understood what Vaustian saw in you. You seem about as ordinary as the next harlot to me." He straddled atop her, forcing her onto her backside as she flailed and beat at him, stoking his amusement further. "That honey pot of yours must be a damned sweet one to have my brother wrapped around your little finger like you do, lapping at your tits like you're his fucking wet nurse."

"Fuck you," Marsea hissed between her teeth, throttling him on the side of his head as hard as she could, ever careful to maintain her ruse.

Ganedys countered with a punch every measure as cruel that split her lip, followed by a second that rattled her cheekbones.

Her vision dimmed from the blow as yellow-white symbols flickered before her eyes.

Only a man.

In all her cycles she had never suffered such a jarring impact, by man or otherwise. Her body went limp, and a great swelling began to form upon the side of her face. In that moment everything stopped. Her thinking stopped, her breathing stopped, and her struggling stopped. All was perfect, silent, and serene, as though she were floating atop an endless ocean where the currents dared not tread.

Use it, she heard a voice call from within. **He's only a man, Marsea. A slab of meat. Now use it**.

NOW!

Calm and composed, as though it was all she knew, her pinky hooked inside a ring dangling loose from a string at the cuff of her sleeve and with its gentle tug triggered the revolution of a tiny metal fulcrum, which produced from the sleeve's depths a second slender dagger. Before Gan realized what was happening, Marsea shoved the blade deep inside his belly, and with all the screaming strength she could muster, she carved it upward across the whole of his fleshy front.

"Bitch," he howled in disbelief, clutching at her wrist and forcing the blade out of his gaping stomach, but the effort came much too late. The damage was done. His devious days had quite suddenly found their full count.

As he lifted away from her, his entrails began to spill out between them like water from a busted levee, and Marsea drove in at him again to finish the job, intending to penetrate the vile bastard all the way through, to make him feel every ounce of pain he had ever inflicted against her, and every ounce more he had beaten out of Remy, but this time he was ready for it and his hand caught hers, crushing her fingers around the blade.

It was an act of desperation, a fucking fluke, and it screamed within like the touch of a crone's cauldron. Such was her luck when greed beguiled her toward the star of madness. She cried out like a banshee as he mangled her fingers across the knife's twin edges.

"What…did you…do?" he rasped as she shrieked and dug the fingernails of her free hand into his face, running bright red lines down his cheek. "What…did…" his grip weakened as he labored for breath, "you…" he whispered one final time before his words became blood and he toppled away from her.

Caked in gore and chunks of viscera, Marsea kicked away from his convulsing body, nursing her injured hand against her chest until she put enough distance between them to feel safe again.

She watched him in silence, her breathing heavy. One eye a watery muddle, the other tiny and unwelcomed inside the misshapen lump that now resided upon the left side of her face.

Only a man. And now one less left to the world that could bring her harm.

A large pool of blood began to form before his face, and his eyes grew vacant and colorless.

Gingerly she lifted her throbbing arm away from her chest, unlacing the concealed blade's vambrace, and took a series of quick breaths before wriggling the infernal contraption over the bright red mass that remained of her hand. The agony burned so deep it was almost cold.

Marsea shook all over, and the beck of hysteria forced a miserable whimper from her swollen lips as she inspected her wounds. She found her pinky now missing above the top knuckle as well as her ring finger above the bottom. Their parts were simply gone, gone as a distant memory, leaving behind a pair of hideously misshapen nubs. Her middle and index fingers fared little better as both showed deep lacerations down to the bone that continued oozing profusely. Yet, somehow, she was still alive. In fact, despite the loss, she had never felt more alive in all her cycles.

The masters will be pleased, she told herself as she struggled to her feet, her body trembling violently. *You know what must be done now. Just keep your wits tight a little longer.*

Doing her damnedest to isolate her mind from the horror that was her left hand, she wedged it underneath her armpit to stem the bleeding, collected her glasses and dagger from the snow, and struggled to roll Gan's massive corpse over onto his backside. *Just as Cas said.* She rallied on. *Pry the eyes to blind them.* Before she could think twice about it, she jammed the point of her dagger down into Gan's dead orbs, right then left, relieving them from their hollows. *Break the jaw to muzzle them.* With the heel of her boot, she stomped down upon his jaw until she heard a cracking noise. Tears, fat and relentless, began to well and blur her vision and snot began to run uncontrollably from her nose into the cleft of her busted top lip. How had she found herself in such a ghastly business as all this? *Sever their hands and feet to keep them still.* Fitfully, Marsea rolled up the sleeve of Gan's right arm and struggled to cut through the flesh and bone at his wrist, her own health waning in the process. *Only a man. A slab of meat.* It was difficult enough to grip the hilt properly, much less apply pressure with it. She began to feel queasy by the third strike just as the hand became detached. The eyes and the jaw would have to do, she decided. She could stomach no more butchery, not in her current state. The man was dead, besides, and dead meant dead full limbs or no. *Then burn them screaming to sell the spirit.* She fished a book of matches from the inner pocket of her coat and groaned at the fresh predicament of having one good hand left to her. *This, girl, is how the wolld tether the dead.*

She fitted the matchbook between her front teeth and tore a match away with her good hand. *Good riddance to bad rubbish,* she thought as she struck it against the matchbook's binding, bringing about a tiny flame before a puff of wind took it out promptly. She moaned at the misfortune and tore free a second match. However, as she lifted it to strike the binding once more, a twig snapped inside the darkness just over her shoulder and she whirled around at the disturbance. Her one good hand fell upon her dagger, quick as a whip, and she held it out defensively, glaring down the darkness with her one good eye.

The wood was eerily still as she glowered and waited, tense and breathless. Slowly she rose to her feet, and as she came to full height, a bloodcurdling howl claimed the nocturne, shattering the bubble of silence. It was much too near for comfort, much too near indeed, and without a second thought to her duty, she bounded away from the freshly undone corpse with all the heave and haste her battered body would allow for.

Gan was dead, she told herself again and again during her reckless flight. *And dead was dead, whether it was burned to ash or passed through the belly of a beast.*

The masters would be pleased. And most importantly, so too would her heart's desire.

CHAPTER SEVEN

"Lovely bit of fiction you have here, Master Toff," a voice spoke from the space just over his shoulder, stirring him from his rest. There was certainly no mistaking that expressionless rasp, ever cast in utter disapproval of everyone and everything within sight of her footpath.

Remy glanced behind him to find Rhymona Curie seated upon the bunk next to his, leafing through a book. With a groan he rolled back over, thinking quite little of it, his mind nearly surrendering to the beck of slumber yet again, before the remnants of his last memory wormed its way to the fore of his consciousness accompanied by an overwhelming sense of dread. He popped up quick as a wink from underneath the bedsheets, his body screaming at him with each sudden shift and turn, and ripped the book from her hands, snapping it shut and winding the silver chains tight about it once more. "Are you mad?" he barked. "Do you know what this is?" The y'deman's final words came back for the haunt at that, and Remy couldn't help but imagine the wretch's beast having a fervent go at him, tearing him apart limb by bloody limb.

"Naturally," Rhymona said, sporting her very best go-fuck-yourself smile. As usual, her attitude emerged far too cavalier for comfort. "It is a grimoire, silly. If you've seen one, you've seen them all, I'm afraid. Though I must admit by the look of this one's bindings, it has seen many more sunsets than you or I. And the night writing is a fun new twist. Which begs the question, does it not, of how exactly such a relic has suddenly found itself within the possession of a nothing watchman?"

Her words conveyed the utmost level of condescension, as did most words that left the mouths of the giftborn, as if to imply he was somehow incapable of understanding such an entity as a grimoire. Amongst their lot, Remy had come to know Curie as an especially prickly sort, soil-tongued and defiant to the bone. By all accounts, she appeared little the part of a scholared magus, and he doubted she ever would. Not with the particular brand of devil she housed within. To further emphasize her unruliness, she favored dark leathers and a fur cloak in lieu of the more traditional robes worn by most of her magian peers, and she brandished about a hatchet she affectionately referred to as "Fucker." She once told him she named it such because it was that much and worse to wield it, but she much preferred the bastard's weight to the pig-pokers they issued to the guard. *If things were going to get bloody,* she went on with her words of stone, *they may as well get real damned bloody, yeah.* Even still, knowing all of these things about her, Remy stared at the snow-haired sorceress utterly dumbfounded.

"The Stranger take me, Toff, you look as though I just kicked your fucking puppy. Learn to take a bloody jape, mate."

"What was in it?" he asked, wild-eyed. "What did you see?"

Curie shrugged. "Little of note. Novice incantations mostly. Nothing one couldn't pick up in a semester at university. It was really quite disappointing."

"But nothing happened? You didn't see or hear anything?"

"I heard you whimpering in your sleep like a suckling babe after his fucking wet nurse."

Remy's face wrinkled in irritation. *The gods know Curie could be a mouthy bitch when she wanted,* though he knew the squabble would hardly be worth the bother. Rhymona Curie was the least of his worries besides, especially considering what he had seen unbound in Brymshire.

"Where are we?"

"The barracks," the magus said as she stood into a stretch, "just outside the citadel. A patrol found you wandering just east of the northern gate earlier this morning. They said you were mad with fever, cursing your lungs hoarse, swinging your sword about like a right proper nutter. They tossed you in a cell for your efforts, the fucking halfwits." She snorted. "You would think they might have recognized the bloody King of Lancastle, yeah. Needless to say, by the time we got to you, you were well gone to the black. Even the smelling salts had no effect."

"And what of Brymshire?"

"Boney and Shore reported in a few hours before the Palatian guard found you. They claimed Brymshire lost; rumors of the blight at hand, rot, rot, bloody rot."

"Rumors of the blight?" Remy scoffed. "Understatement of the cycle, that. Make no mistake about it. The hollow was a ruddy slaughterhouse."

"We wagered as much by the reports to follow. Tenbrooks wanted to take a patrol to gain a better lay, but Marlowe refused to send more to what he named a senseless death. Especially not his most seasoned."

"Colonel Marlowe is here?"

"Aye," she said, "arrived just yestereve."

"Well, I must say, Marlowe proved the wiser in that," Remy said. "And did their tidings include the presence of an ashaeydir spy or a lichlord?"

"A lichlord?" It was perhaps the first time Remy had ever seen Rhymona Curie appear even vaguely surprised. "No, as a matter of fact they did not." She brushed her boyish hair from out of her eyes. Her gaze had suddenly altered from puckish to inquisitive. Remy rather thought she might have been attractive once, but her many cycles of dark-dabbling had taken a most unfortunate toll.

"Baulrick Tamberyn, he's named." Or so Remy hoped. Though he had to wonder why the y'deman would bother to lie about such a small matter as the creature's identity.

"Baulrick Tamberyn?" An eyebrow arched. "And how came you about such an outlandish theory, I wonder?"

"I have my ways." Remy decided it best for the time being to keep mum about his y'deman friend.

Curie's razor-thin lips curled upward with amusement. "Is that right?"

"Tell me Curie, you've been in Palatia some time now, have you perchance heard the name of Tarboril floating about?"

"Tarboril, Tarboril, let us see. It seems vaguely familiar I must admit, but I'm afraid there is nothing yet for it. Should I know this name?"

"Not necessarily. Though, I have it on good repute they are the owner of this wretched eyesore." He retrieved the grimoire from the end of the bed.

"Gone for a few days and you return with all sorts of oddments and intrigues. I must say I quite approve of this new Toff."

"I don't know whether to be wounded or charmed."

"Take it as you like," she added nonchalantly. "You're welcome by the way."

It took him a moment to understand her meaning, though it was quite evident that someone had nursed him back to his middling present condition. Many of his cuts and bruises had disappeared altogether, including the welt on his temple; however, his ribs still clung mightily to their soreness. It was a damned sight better than what he last remembered though, to say the least. He knew a turn in health of such magnitude could only be swayed by one thing: the use of magic. Something he had heard former Lord Magus Xavien Ledgermaine once name The Spellbind. He noticed four empty blood candle wrappers crumbled atop the lower end of her bunk.

"You did this?"

"I couldn't very well leave our poor wittle Toffy-woff to suffer, now could I?"

"You pulled from The Spellbind?"

"I did. And what would you know of such affairs?"

"I know it can be deadly. Not that I'm not appreciative."

"Trust it true, you're not out of the woods yet. In fact, you would do well to take it slow for a spell," Rhymona said. "I was able to mend some of the lesser cuts and bruises, but your ribs are another story. They will have to heal on their own."

"And, how are you?" Remy had heard horror stories about the consequences of The Spellbind on its bearer. It was said that blood candles were more addictive than shufa and twice as unforgiving, causing fever, sweats, chills, hives, and horrid hallucinations, amongst a host of even more damning side effects.

"I will be fine. I didn't delve too deep. Just enough to bring you round."

"I'd say four binders is fairly deep. How long were you...?"

"Not long enough to matter, Toff. Fucking hells, are you growing sweet on me?"

"Don't flatter yourself. I'd simply rather not have your wellbeing on my conscience, is all."

"I should say you're well fucking safe there, lieutenant, though full fucking marks for pretending to give half a toss."

"Captain Curie," hailed a nasally voice from the corridor outside, interrupting their row. They both shifted toward the doorway, and a moment later, Goran Tavernys appeared inside its frame. He was dressed tidily in the gray and crimson uniform of the Royalguard, sporting blond, wavy hair and a well-minded mustache that he was known on occasion, though not this particular one, to curl about the ends. Remy rather disliked the man, to have it true. He thought Tavernys ostentatious and vainglorious to excess, a rather off-putting pretense from that of such lowborn stature, but to the man's favor, much of his keep he had earned the old-fashioned way, as the elders name it. Being born the son of a farmhand, Tavernys had already ascended far beyond most of his station. Such was the will of a practiced sycophant, Remy figured, and Tavernys portrayed the part consummately.

"Ah, excellent you're awake, Your Highness," Tavernys greeted with a certain measure of smarm, his arms tucked neatly behind the small of his back.

"Remy will do."

"Of course, milord."

The nerve of this hayseed, Remy thought. *Mask it with pleasantries all you like Tavernys, I can still hear your contempt.*

"The Lord Valenforth and Lady Dree were quite distraught over the tidings of your ill health."

Bloody doubtful.

"I apologize for the rather crude accommodations, but the Lord's Hand was worried you too might be diseased."

"'Tis no matter," Remy said. "I expect I would have done the same were our roles reversed. The blight is an unforgiving affair, is it not?"

Tavernys bowed his head. "Most unforgiving, Your Highness, Lord Remy, though the small council will be most pleased to find you hale and hearty again."

One could hardly call my state hale and hearty. "I am sure they will," said Remy bitterly. *The gall of this insufferable truckler.*

"It would seem Lieutenant Shore was not quite so fortunate."

"And what is that intended to imply?"

"Suffice it to say I have not yet beheld the man myself, but news arrived of his, shall we say, odd behavior some hours past. The Palatian guards that arrived upon the disturbance at The White Rose found him erratic and glass-eyed. They tried to speak some sense to him, but he was non-responsive and showing signs of disease, making some strange clicking sound with his tongue. They say he grew increasingly more violent the more they tried to calm him and eventually had to put him down for fear of harm to others. The tale is it took three of them to subdue the loon. Upon closer inspection of the body thereafter, there showed prominent bite marks and scratches that had blackened and festered upon his arms and shoulders confirming the blight's presence. I say, it was a right stroke of luck they caught it before the disease spread to anyone else."

"Most assuredly," Remy agreed. "By my account, it took mere minutes to ravage Brymshire's quarters."

"Presently, he is being kept in the castle cellars under observation."

"What?" Remy said. "I thought you said they put him down."

"Yes, they put him down. But they did not kill him. We can't very well have our own being murdered out in the streets for any and all to see, now can we? It would create a panic."

"As well it bloody should." Remy took a step toward Tavernys. "These folk deserve to know the truth. They deserve to know what's out there, what's coming for them…"

"Now is not yet the time, Your Highness, Lord Remy. Cedarholm's orders..."

To the nine with Cedarholm's orders. "Very well, but I should like to observe the fiend for myself," Remy said. He held no fondness for the man. In fact, Remy knew nothing at all about this Shore fellow, but he wanted, nay, needed to behold the disease up close again. He needed to look the rotten fucker that had come hungering after his lifeblood time and time again dead in its ghoulish face.

"I suppose it could be arranged in due course, Your High…Lord Remy, but for now we must remain vigilant, which brings me full to the point of my visit. The council is set to round upon the hour. Lieutenant Shore's turn will undoubtedly be discussed as well as Brymshire's fall. As such, we will need our best and brightest in attendance. Your presence has been requested, Captain. As will yours be Your High...Lord Remy. It would seem you have been granted a rather unique perspective in all of this."

You have no idea.

"This threat is the most formidable Palatia has seen in decades, and we cannot succumb to its whims. We cannot allow this fair kingdom to endure the same fate as Brymshire and Hearth and the other western wood hollows. There have already been sightings within the last few hours of the blight-ridden within a half-league of the northern gate, and they grow closer as the minutes pass. The kingdom is presently on high alert. We already have archers lining the parapets, patrols being sorted, and scouts in the wood. An attack is expected imminently. But we cannot allow its birth. Any uprising against Palatia must be quelled before it can even begin. These are Colonel Marlowe's words exact. He states Van Wyck is aware of the situation and has prepared a centuria of men to join in the city's defense, but it will take at least another day or two for their arrival, providing the snowfall lets up."

"And what are they proposing until then?" Remy asked, though he suspected little in the way of positive news.

"To be honest, milord, given that you and Boney are the only known survivors of Brymshire's fall to present, the council was rather hoping you might have some insight to impart of this fresh enemy."

Nightfall sang of winterdust and burning leaves as the trio left the barracks for the citadel. Beyond the rising mists, the heavens held little cheer in reserve. All the sky appeared as grim and gray as the sepulcher. Decidedly, it was a shade only the deepest depths of midwinter could conjure. Fat snowflakes cascaded down from the pit of clouds above, blustering about wildly in the warring winds. It had been near a decade since last Remy visited the mountain kingdom of Palatia, long enough that he had completely forgotten about the city's overabundance of jagged stairwells and steep inclines. There must have been a thousand such steps from the barracks to the great hall of the Palatian council alone, each one more trying than the last.

Remy paced Curie and Tavernys, a few steps behind. Despite the uneven terrain, the upper half of the city was truly quite enchanting to behold. Stone columns tall as redwoods and twice as thick surrounded each courtyard, well-tended shrubberies scattered hither and yon along the walks, and glistening golden statues of lords and generals past in each epicenter. Everything in Palatia seemed exaggerated and oversized, Remy thought, *including the egos he was soon to indulge.*

A pair of massive golden braziers burned brightly, crackling high into the heavens, just outside the large iron-pitted citadel doors where a throng of Royalguard soldiers found warmth from the cold. The majority of the lot were Palatian bloodcoats, but a few clusters of Kingswatchmen shifted along the outside of the bunch. It took little effort to pick the two divisions apart.

Those of the Kingswatch wore mismatched leathers, mostly coats of ash or faded black, and their faces carved into sullen and sour lines, their weary eyes downcast. A few puffed despondently at pipes, others drank from steaming flasks, more still were nervously whispering amongst their closest, and one rather ragged looking fellow was marrying a whetstone to his blade, though not a one of them paid the trio a bit of mind as they navigated past into the sea of gray and crimson city guards hovering in-between the great hall's breach. By comparison, the bloodcoats seemed in much higher spirits, cracking jokes and singing songs of glory and gods. Clearly, they hadn't the faintest inkling what awaited them outside the city gates.

Damned halfwits.

Bearskins and wolfskins alike adorned the stone floors of the great hall, hissing sconces lined the support columns, gold-rimmed tapestries on fields of gray and crimson hung high about the lifeless walls and timbers, and parch-cluttered tables of ancient oak rose to either side of the crimson-carpeted center walkway. Dozens of candlesticks and curiosities were placed about the tabletops to keep the many stacks of parchment in proper placement. A familiar figure arrayed in burgundy robes paced near the opposite end of the great hall next to a short, pear-shaped soldier named Blaney Chilton. Given the dour set of Tenbrooks's face, Remy doubted much good was being had from the discussion. All the same, the magus stroked at the salt and pepper tuft at the jut of his chin and let the soldier continue.

"Look what I found," Curie crowed as they approached, "fresh from the mouth of madness."

Tenbrooks eyed Remy warily, his silver irises screaming forth like glinting daggers against the dark-skinned plain of his weathered face. *Must all giftborn act as such pretentious shits?* "Milord, we are all relieved to see you back among us."

As indicated plainly by your scowl, Remy thought. "As am I."

"Dire news, as you might have guessed. Lieutenant Chilton here has just informed me of a rather large host of blighters half a league from the eastern gate."

"Though they appear to have thopped in their march," Chilton added through a fresh lisp bought from a drunken tourney yard brawl with Gordon Dennings some weeks back. "They've been like that for hourth, juth thanding there, idle and thilent."

"Confirming our suspicions of a lich," Tenbrooks said.

"A lich, an ashaeydir, wolld, nine hells, I think I saw a bloody wngar in the lot."

"An ashaeydir?" Tavernys bristled.

"Aye, a nasty one too. I witnessed it murder Wade right before mine eyes, and it nearly sent me to the hells along with him."

"Curious," Ten said, "though not all that surprising, considering. It would not be the first time the ashaeydir have employed the dead to their means. Gravedancing is practically a rite of passage to their lot."

"I'm fairly sure this one was in hiding," Remy said. "And it was the only one I crossed. I certainly couldn't say with any degree of promise the two parties were actually in cahoots."

"Though a bit fucking convenient not to be, wouldn't you say?" Curie questioned.

"Wrong place, wrong time?" Tavernys posited.

"Regardless, we must be prepared for either scenario," said Tenbrooks tersely. "The ashaeydir are reactionary creatures who pride themselves on chaos and unpredictability. They hunger for it, lust after it, and thrive on it. Such abstract tactics delivered them victory on Y'dema. No doubt the same could be had here."

Remy knew well the record of the ashaeydir's campaign on Y'dema. Uncle Rho was always keen to a good history lesson when the mood so struck, and he could be quite the storyteller once the wine took hold. He described the initial ashaeydir occupation of Y'dema as an act of desperation whose swift and decisive victory produced an appetite for further conquests, conquests that, unlike the fae, the children of The Vael had managed to stymie for the better part of a century. Remy couldn't help but think about the y'deman at that and how he spat in the face of pride and valor and honor and even death. What a curious creature was that one. A man seemingly bereft of fear. Or perhaps it was common sense, given his bizarre crusade. He wondered if Beldroth and his beast were still alive amidst the cold, the trees, the dead, and their sea of rot. For reasons he could not explain, despite the man's threats and impertinence, Remy rather hoped so. In fact, in these grave and harsh growing times the world might benefit a great deal from a man such as Elsymir Beldroth.

"I got a look at Lieutenant Shore while you were away," Tenbrooks was saying to Curie as Remy drifted back into the conversation, pushing away from the table he had slumped against. "Wes is with him now, though his condition appears grim at best. Be that as it may, Wes is determined to find a remedy with what scant time we still have left."

"A remedy?" Curie snorted. "You can't be serious." Tenbrooks's expression remained as grave as ever. "For what," Curie scoffed, "for death? The fucking foolhard. 'Tis a fruitless endeavor, that. Last I checked dead is dead is fucking dead, yeah?"

"Tell that to the bathtardth marching outthide our gateth then, yeah," Chilton said.

"Gods fucking wounds, scab, is that you then giving your Captain sass?" Curie returned, ever quick to the counter.

Chilton's face blanched. "I'm thorry thir…er m'am…I uh…"

"Lack of oxygen to the brain no doubt," she deduced. "The mountain air can be a right fucker on you lowcountry boys I'm told."

"Yeth, m'am…"

"Captain," she corrected smugly, placing a hand upon her hip and the other atop Fucker's eye.

"Captain," Chilton said woefully, lowering his eyes.

"You can stow the discord, Captain," Tenbrooks said. "Marlowe was in support of the decision, so best just to let it alone."

A loud clamor resonated out from behind the chamber door they stood before. The racket was chased by a booming voice and followed by what sounded like a squawking bird. Confusion spread across all of their faces, except Tenbrooks, who simply shook his head and blew out a heavy breath.

"Fucking hells, was that The Colonel?" Curie asked with a titillated smirk.

"More than like," Tenbrooks grumbled. "He and Cedarholm have been at each other's throats like a pair of rabid pit dogs for the better part of the past hour."

Remy remembered Cedarholm from summits past, always lurking about the Lord Valenforth's ever-widening shadow, whispering about his ear like a busy little gnat. He could picture the grating curmudgeon now: his gaunt, narrow face, his bird beak of a nose, and his dark, beady eyes, always scowling about as though someone shit in his stew. Though all said, given the Crownswatch commander's recurring disagreeable disposition, it would be of little surprise if someone actually had before.

"Marlowe is demanding we wait it out in the city until reinforcements arrive," Tenbrooks explained, "but Cedarholm wants to send his men on the offensive."

"And what sense does that make?" Remy had to ask.

"Cedarholm believes it will be the wiser to keep the enemy as far away from the city as possible for as long as possible. And I daresay as much as it vexes me to share the man's opinion on any matter, I quite agree with this one."

"But we have the high ground," Curie put in. "Why needlessly waste lives?"

"For now, we have the high ground, but given what I beheld of Shore and what I know of the lichlords, once the bastards begin to storm the gates, it's only a matter of time before they get through. The only real question is whether they can batter down the walls or if they mount the piles of their own to top it. The lich care not about their subjects, and they care even less about methodology. All they care about is the success of their venture. As such, the blighter assault will be vicious and unceasing. And what contingencies do we have once the inevitable occurs? We're atop a mountain range. There are only so many options left for retreat."

Remy had to admit, despite his initial opposition, Tenbrooks was making a rather compelling argument. But even still, it was much too soon. He couldn't imagine rushing back out into the same nightmare he had only hours ago struggled so hard to escape. Surely such an endeavor was suicide.

"This is an outrage." Cedarholm burst through the chamber doors fuming. Poor Chilton took the brunt of it as the right door swung out wide into his arm, and he jerked away from the impact with a series of curses, rubbing furiously at his elbow. Cedarholm halted but briefly in his ire and eyed Remy up and down with a sneer before continuing his march through the great hall toward his waiting men. Tavernys's face wrinkled with distress before he fell in line after the irate Crownswatch commander.

Through the council chamber's doorway, at the head of the Lord's round, Remy found the cause of Cedarholm's anger in the form of a heavyset man clad in black and fur. Wisps of white-gray hair receded into a thicker patch about the back half of his head, his squared jaw shown rough with stubble, and his lone eye set hard as Helanderan steel. Remy had never actually seen the man before, but he had heard the many tales, tales that would turn a man bedsheet pale to grant them credence, at least in the manner Uncle Rho told them. They all came flooding back to him inside the man's daunting presence as he trailed Tenbrooks and Curie inside the council chamber.

Colonel Wilhelm Marlowe. The Iron Black, he was titled amidst the commonwealth. The Undying, by many more. Nine-Lives, he was named amongst his closest, though most of their lot had long since gone to the grave. He'd lost his shield arm in the infamous ashaeydir Siege of Skagaten some cycles back and his right eye to a turncoat swordbrother that had a go at him whilst he slept some seasons later. But neither job brought him death. They only made him colder, harder, and angrier. Some said he was a god returned in human guise, though Remy scarce believed in such hogwash. To Marlowe's credit, however, he certainly portrayed every inch of the part. Remy had never beheld a man more weathered by the brutality of war than the misshapen figure that presently stood before him. All the same, he'd never beheld a man as august, either.

"Your Highness," Marlowe greeted, his craggy expression softening only slightly, "we feared for the worst and yet here you stand. It would seem you are Waldgrave's nephew through and through, aren't you? Your uncle was a tough bastard too, back in his day, and one of the finest swordsmen the guard has ever begotten, I daresay."

"I appreciate your kind words Colonel," Remy said as he approached.

Finally. A man with a proper head about his shoulders. "Uncle Rho always spoke quite highly of you as well, sir."

"As well he ought." The man had a deep chuckle. "The gods know I saved his sorry arse from The Hood's Door more times than I can count." He held up his lone hand. "But then again I've only five fingers to work with."

Remy forced an awkward smile. At least he hoped it was an awkward smile. It would seem even in the direst of times he was still absolutely dreadful at feigning some measure of good old boy comradery. At this point, he doubted it would ever come to him naturally.

Behind Marlowe, tucked deep inside the chamber's corner with a haunted, thousand-yard gaze was Waylon Boney, Remy's apparent lone co-survivor in the sacking of Brymshire. Tall and strapping, Boney found a similar age to Remy, though it was obvious by his body language he came from peasant stock, mayhaps from Illery or Elkmark. Verily, he was not at all the sort of figure one envisioned at the namesake of Boney, and even less the sort of figure one envisioned within the present cast of company, yet here he was nonetheless, a wayward sheep amongst a pack of wolves.

In the chair to Marlowe's right sat the bejeweled High Lord of Palatia, Connor Valenforth, who appeared drunk and utterly disinterested in the matter at hand despite its rising magnitude. To have it from Harver and the Lancastle cabinet, Connor Valenforth was an embarrassment and an utter mockery of one of Midara's once great families. He had once overheard Ledgermaine tell his uncle that the sod hadn't even the competence to lord over a pig farm, much less a kingdom. However, unlike Whit Lanier, Valenforth had remained staunchly compliant to the demands of the Midnight Men over the cycles and thusly had been allowed to maintain his life of comfort and opulence without trouble. Remy found it exceedingly difficult to hide his disgust at the sight of the gutless craven.

To Valenforth's right, sitting perfectly prim and proper, was an enchanting blond woman Remy had never seen before, though he presumed she would be the High Lord's latest wife, Lady Dree. Much had been made of her presence in the royal courts since their marriage last summer, much indeed, and little of it kindly. As with the High Lord Valenforth, there was most assuredly an air about the woman that sat ill upon Remy's scruples.

A dashing young mystery with an impossibly chiseled jaw leaned against the wall behind Her Ladyship, trim body clad in dark crimson armor. His cold, suspicious eyes met Remy's but briefly before the watchman's gaze shot to the left side of the round where sat an elderly man Remy knew to be named Sir Henry Thwaites. To name the councilman long in the tooth would have been a horrid understatement. These days the man appeared positively decrepit. No doubt one could still find willow wood trees with fewer seasons to their count. But to his repute, for all his many cycles, few could equal his wisdom and experience.

Between Thwaites and Marlowe hunched the final member of the lord's round, a frail wither of a man scarcely wider than the gnarled cane that provided him support. Remy knew him to be named Charles Northam, a former soldier who had been rendered a cripple during the Siege of Skagaten. It would appear the cycles since had proven quite unforgiving upon him.

A motley bunch Palatia has amassed to their small council, a motley bunch indeed, Remy mused, though he had to admit despite his mislike of the High Lord Valenforth, he already preferred their lot to the one he had abandoned in the court of Lancastle.

"King Rembrandt," the High Lord Valenforth slurred. "It's lovely to see you hale again. I feared we might have lost another Lanier."

Another Lanier. As though we are but leaves on the wind. Remy despised the bright and dainty way words fell away from the High Lord's tongue. "It was tough sledding there for a mite, I must admit, but as the wise old master's cant goes, sometimes 'tis better to be favored than skilled."

"And here I thought it was better to be favored than sober," Northam grumbled before turning up his goblet.

"Favored or no, one can only count their ruddy luck stones for so long before they're due a mite bit of strategy," Marlowe said.

"I take it, given Cedarholm's tantrum, that we're to take a defensive approach?" Tenbrooks asked.

"Indeed," Marlowe clarified. "Inside the gates, we have some two centuria Crownswatch soldiers and another thirty Kingswatchmen. Coupled with men and women fit to fight, we should have near five hundred capable defenders, with another pair score beyond the gates and more on their way from Nightsbridge."

"Forgive me, Colonel," Remy dared, "but these numbers are not near enough. Not against what I witnessed in Brymshire."

"It will have to be enough," Marlowe rumbled, his merriment from moments before all but a distant memory. The gods know, he had a voice that could silence a room.

"A report just in from the vanguard claims a large number of the blight amassing to the east," Tenbrooks echoed Chilton's message.

"Let them fucking amass, I say," Marlowe spat. "The longer they wait the better fortified we become."

If nothing else, the man certainly wasn't short on confidence.

"Additionally, Lanier has confirmed the presence of a lichlord," Tenbrooks continued, "and of an ashaeydir infiltrator within Brymshire's quarters."

Marlowe watched Remy's reaction, the knuckles of his lone hand pressing white and firm against the table before him.

"It's true on both accounts, Colonel," murmured Remy. "Though I may have some bit of good news in all of this." All eyes were on him, though none of them looked particularly hopeful. "During my escape, I happened upon a possible solution to slowing the blight. A substance named charonisk."

"Charonisk?" Tenbrooks questioned, "of the Chandiian custom?"

"I must confess, I know it by name only," Remy said, "though I can attest to its efficacy. It sets to flame blood wrought of the nether."

"Lovely. All of our hopes and futures lie in the revival of a dead man's alchemy," Thwaites croaked.

"Bah," Marlowe quieted the old coot. "And how came you upon such prized information, Lieutenant?"

"An archer," Remy blurted out before he could conjure a less daft explanation. "He arrived to my aid outside the township when I came under attack by a group of blighters. Shot one with an arrow that tore through its flesh like wildfire, burned it down to bone and ash in a matter of seconds. It was like nothing I had ever seen before. When I later questioned him about its properties, he explained that the arrow had been laced with charonisk." It was at this point that Remy noticed how intently everyone was staring at him, everyone save the High Lord, of course, who couldn't be less interested.

"And where is this archer now?" Marlowe asked.

"After the blighter attack, a troupe of wolld approached our respite, and we became separated in our flight. I fear he did not fare as well as I did."

Marlowe turned an inquisitive eye on his most trusted magus, apparently unconcerned with any further specifics. "Is this charonisk something we have access to here in the city?"

"Mayhaps," Tenbrooks responded, "but it could take some time to gather. I am familiar with its means, but I will have to learn its properties."

"And you believe this a worthy venture in the time we have left?"

Tenbrooks shifted his attentions toward Remy, seemingly gaging his response by the watchman's reaction before nodding his head. "I believe our Kingship believes his words to be for truth and therefore so do I."

"Then away with you," Marlowe ordered, "time is of the essence. May the gods be with you. Take Curie if—"

"No!" No one was more surprised than Remy by his sudden outburst.

Marlowe's hard expression returned. Even Valenforth stirred from his sodden reverie, staring at him with mouth agape.

"I need her," the watchman king said, his chin held high. Just over his shoulder he could feel Curie beaming brighter than a midsummer sunrise.

The gods know I may never live this down.

CHAPTER EIGHT

"Fucking brilliant. The looks on their faces," Curie delighted as she led them down a torch-lined corridor toward the castle cellars, her grin spread ear to ear and apparently unending. "The look on Valenforth's face." She made a dramatic expression of utter horror to compete with the High Lord's before she let out an amused titter. "What a fucking twat."

"It wasn't meant to be a jape. Lest you forget, I've seen what's out there," Remy quibbled. "Keeping a magus near seemed an obvious choice."

"Obviously," Curie beset the watchman with a devilish smirk. "The gods know. Must we always be so offended?"

"Who's offended?"

"Mmm, let's have a think, yeah?"

"I'm not in a mood for rubbish, Curie," he grumbled.

"Very well, straight to the point then. If I'm to be your minder, I reckon—"

"My minder? That is not what this is at all."

"Sure," she said offering a wink and an awful little fang.

"We are merely temporary partners," he explained, already beginning to regret the words.

"We sure as shit are, and as your partner, I think it only fair we operate on the same page, yeah?"

"Of course."

"Then I should like to know more of this archer from the wood."

"Well, I am afraid you've had about all I know."

"I find that rather hard to believe."

"Do you?"

"I daresay, for a highborn you are an exceptionally terrible liar, Remy."

"And I daresay I mislike the context of your insinuation."

"Do you now? And *I* daresay there is quite a simple remedy for such a simple mislike now isn't there?"

Remy remained silent as they turned a corner down another similarly dark, empty passageway. *You may as well tell her, old boy. You're not likely to find a trustworthy companion in this entire camp, and you're going to need her around a while, assuming you still have a while left to linger.* "Before we continue, I need to know I have assurances with you."

"Assurances?" This of all things stopped her dead in her tracks.

"I need to know if Palatia goes tits up, you are with me, Rhymona."

"Rhymona?" She twirled about and took a seductive step toward him chased by a second that forced him against the wall. Her eyes glistened wildly in the flicker of torch fire. "My, my, my, Rembrandt Lanier, you are a cheeky lad, now aren't you? All of this formality and talk of tits had from milord's lips. It's quite enough to confuse an old-fashioned girl from Synner's March now, isn't it?"

"Again, context," he said, his throat suddenly dry as the dustlands.

"Fuck context." She placed a palm flat against the wall beside his head. "This has gone on well past context, hasn't it? Last I checked, only the tramps call me by my ministry name." She pulled in close. "And the tramps are after one thing and one thing alone from a lowly southern belle such as I, now aren't they?" She held for a breath before turning away with a snort and a dodgy grin. "The nether take me, Toff." She was practically parading down the passageway now, "I'll tell you quite plainly, even if we weren't buggered to the nine atop Fuckwit Mountain and surrounded by a thousand ravenous corpses, the word assurances would mean exactly shit all to me."

He brushed down his ruffled coat. "Well, if nothing else, I appreciate your candor."

"Oh, my prince, my lord, my gracious worship, you have my blade and my gift both. You have my cunny too if you wish it yours," Curie cooed with a practiced courtesan's call, her words flush with sugary lilt and falsities. "Were those the words you were hoping to hear, Master Toff?"

"Something of the like," he said, unmoved.

"Prize them well, Crown Prince, they only go so far. And that's about as close to a fucking assurance as you're like to get from me. We can't all be as graceful as your ladies of court, I'm afraid. Now fair is fair, yeah. Your archer friend, spill."

"You should know you will be compensated handsomely for your services."

"I expect I will. No doubt the King's coffers run deep. Now stop stalling."

Remy cared little for Curie's attitude and even less for her demanding tone, but it would seem for the time being they shared a common path, like it or not. *Stiff upper lip*, Uncle Rho would say to such a scene. "He introduced himself as Elsymir Beldroth," the watchman began. "And he was y'deman. Though he scarce looked like any y'deman I had ever seen before. His face was covered in grotesque scars, and he was dressed the part of a vagrant. The gods know he reeked like one too. He also got on with a set of ka'rym chii."

"Sounds like a real character, this Beldroth," Curie said as they halted before a door bound and studded in pitted iron.

"Our meeting was brief," Remy confessed. "Quick as a dream really. He saved my life and relayed me the lichlord's name, but before I knew it, I was on the run again with the grimoire in search of a woman named Tarboril. Our entire encounter could not have lasted more than a few minutes' time."

"Mmm," Curie grunted with a thoughtful expression before pounding the bottom of her fist against the door. A moment hence it screeched open, revealing a gangling bloodcoat soldier with a thin, severe face. A familiar clicking sound echoed from further within the chamber, and Remy's hand immediately dropped to the hilt at his side.

"Gods wounds Tucket, you bloody imbecile, I told you there were to be no interruptions." A dark-haired man in brown robes rounded the corner removing a mask from the lower half of his pockmarked countenance. "Your Highness," he said, stopping abruptly, "my apologies. I was not told to expect such eminent company."

"It was a spur of the moment decision," Remy said. "The council was not apprised."

"Of course, milord." Westerly bowed his head. The mage appeared exactly like the odd sort of wretch one would imagine spends the majority of his hours skulking about the castle cellars. "And you invited It along with you," his expression swiftly changed to that of disgust, "how fantastic."

"Go open a vein, Wes," snapped Curie as she stepped past the magus to inspect the rest of the chamber.

"Always a pleasure, Captain."

"Tenbrooks tells us you fancy yourself some manner of gravedancer now. I suppose I shouldn't be too surprised nothing has actually been accomplished."

"To the contrary. Mayhaps there is no apparent improvement in the subject, but my experimentations are not wholly without merit. In fact, I have thus far confirmed a number of questions we previously held about our enemy."

"Is that so?"

Remy drew his sword as he approached the dreadful miscreation. The oil lamp's dance on the table next to it only intensified the fiend's apparent horror. It hardly looked a man at all anymore and reeked horridly of decay and decomposition. Its putrid odor fouled the chamber, setting the eyes awash with tears and twisting the stomach toward nausea. Remy cupped a hand over his nose and mouth to cut the stench. The creature that was Jon Shore had been stripped of its shirt and boots and was shackled at the wrists and ankles against the far wall. Its discolored skin shriveled tight against its bones, baring a pair of twig-like arms and a jagged ribcage that protruded unnaturally over a sunken belly.

"To begin, it is undoubtedly the same blight from centuries ago," Westerly said with an unsettled edge to his tone.

"You speak of the Black Dawn," Curie said.

"I've studied the manuscripts end to end. I've double-checked the illustrations. There can be no mistaking it. See for yourself." Westerly waved his hand in the direction of a table on which lay a three-pronged candelabrum and half a dozen opened tomes. "They are the same. In the case of Jon Shore, it would seem his change was brought about by a scratch across his upper right arm. By the length of the marks, it was undoubtedly made by a woman or a child. Either way, he hadn't the faintest inkling when it raked its nails through his linens and across his flesh. He couldn't have known. And he would have thought little of it in the after. Initially, it appeared no worse than any ordinary scratch might. Doubtful it hurt any different..."

Remy's study shifted to Shore's arm, where a blotch of deep black festered and branched out inside his veins beneath the skin. Shore's head tilted to the side as it returned Remy's glare, its clicking dying to a lowly murmur. For a split second, it almost seemed intelligent.

"Based on Boney's statement, they ran into a bout of trouble in the wood about a half-league outside of Brymshire. It was during that scuffle he believes the scratch occurred. That was roughly four hours before the change in behavior was reported at The White Rose, which was now roughly twelve hours past."

"You mean to say the nether did this to him in less than a day?" Curie asked.

"It is what happens to the infected if the nether parasite is unable to feed properly."

Remy held Shore's milky-white orbs and defiantly lifted his sword up to the creature's heart, the tip drawing a thin line of blackened blood. It was the same color as Miss Allison's and Gray's. Shore's clicking rose in volume at the threat.

"Milord," Westerly said. "Piercing the heart will not kill it."

"I am well aware," Remy said, his attentions never leaving that of Jon Shore's repulsive shell. "The brain must be destroyed to kill it."

"Indeed. From what I can deduce, it is the primary means of control for the parasite. Once it enters the body, it entrenches itself at the base of the skull and spreads from there. It would also seem that the parasite requires blood as sustenance to remain on this side of The Pale. It feeds on others so that it does not leech its vessel dry."

"And what do you suppose happens if they are left unfed?" Curie asked.

"I suppose we shall soon find out, shan't we?" Westerly responded coldly. "Though by Lieutenant Shore's withered appearance, it would seem they become fastly malnourished and emaciated, mayhaps leading to a more permanent form of death."

"Is this sort of behavior not unlike the wolld?" Remy said, turning away from Shore.

"I will grant you it is quite similar, milord, but the wolld consume their prey because they believe it gives them the strength and abilities of their kill. The blight consumes human flesh to maintain their existence upon this side of The Pale. They are parasites of the lowest form, most desperate to survive. In the greater criterion of the nether, I would actually more liken their lot to that of a tiny woodland tick."

"So then we fucking starve them out. Let them eat each other. Or wither away. Problem solved, yeah?" Curie said as though it were but a minor inconvenience.

"A plan sound in theory, yet potentially calamitous in practice. There is simply no telling how long we would have to hole ourselves in this place for such a strategy to work. It could be days, it could be weeks, it could be a cycle or longer. We might starve ourselves."

"What other choice do we have, if a mere scratch can cause this?"

"As of yet, I am unsure what a mere scratch might do to you or me," Westerly said with a most devious expression. "The nether is a form of magic after all, is it not, discarded and diseased as it is? True, it might kill us all the same. It may very well turn us into horridly dreadful abominations far beyond the like of this poor fellow. Then again there is the possibility it may have no effect at all..."

"The gods know, Wes, stop bumbling about," Curie carped. "What are you suggesting?"

"I was very nearly ready to extract a sample of Lieutenant Shore's blood to test with that of mine own before your intrusion, I will have you know." He quickly shifted to Remy and bowed slightly. "Forgive me, Your Highness."

"Not at all," Remy said, sheathing his blade. "As you were then."

"You heard His Royal Highness," Curie sneered. "Let's be on with it then. We haven't got all nightfall, have we?"

"Very well," Westerly said, raising the mask back over the lower half of his face, and retrieved a serrated instrument from the workbench behind him.

Instantly, Remy recognized it as a kindleblade. It was quite unmistakable really. No common forged blade could possess such an unnatural translucent shine no matter how well polished the owner kept it. This particular one was quite wide, almost resembling a butcher's cleaver, with odd symbols engraved across its flat side and jagged edges cut along its sharp end. It appeared a rather gruesome thing designed to inflict extreme levels of pain. On this account, however, it was used quite delicately as Westerly extracted a blood sample from the creature's ruined arm.

Atop the workbench was an opened glass jar containing what appeared to be human blood inside. Carefully, Westerly eased the kindleblade into the jar, and the trio watched as the nether-tainted blood trickled sluggishly down the edge of the knife, collecting and culminating briefly at the tip into a single fat teardrop, before dripping down quietly into the uncontaminated blood sample below. Quickly, Westerly screwed the lid shut, and Remy felt his breath catch at the union, though nothing of note happened at the outset.

"Well, that was disappointing," Curie said after some time had passed.

"What does it mean?" Remy couldn't help but ask aloud.

"I don't know, milord," Westerly answered.

"It means we are still in the same shitty boat we were a minute ago," Curie quibbled as she began leafing through one of the tomes atop the study table.

"Mayhaps a modicum of patience is in order?" Westerly contested.

"Fuck your patience," Curie scoffed. "This is a massive waste of time."

"No." Remy swiped the jar from the workbench and studied it only inches away from his face, swirling its contents about from side to side. That couldn't be all there was to it.

"Mayhaps such an endeavor may require a larger sample," Westerly said as he retrieved a second jar from a shelf above the workbench.

"Wait," Remy said as something began to move beneath the blood's surface. The trio watched in awe as the black spot absorbed the blood and grew into a small worm-like entity that appeared fully animate, circling about the bottom of the jar.

"Nasty looking bugger," said Wes as a series of tentacle-like appendages began to sprout from the creature's core giving it a spider-like appearance.

"I'll say," Remy agreed. He set the jar back down atop the workbench.

"Curious," Westerly said.

The creature rounded about the jar's bottom, quicker now, though seemingly unaware of its restricted surroundings, before its movements began to stagger and cease altogether. At that, its legs became detached from its body, one by one, and its black outer shell began to fade to a white shade, flaking away piece by tiny piece until it became nothing more than a small mound of ash.

"Bit odd, that," Curie said, breaking the momentary hush.

"It turned into a spider?" Remy said dumbfounded.

"Of course, it did," Westerly said with a mad chuckle. "Fantastic!"

"Fantastic?"

"I hate spiders," he divulged.

"And that is fantastic?"

"No, but we've another insight into our enemy, haven't we? The nether feeds off of hate and fear, does it not? It will do anything to get under your skin, so to speak, to gain the advantage. You understand. Thusly, once it fed of mine blood, it manifested itself into one of the things I hate and fear the most. Gods' bones, can you imagine the manner of psychological torture it must cause its host once it has taken control? Fear by fear, stripping the host of everything it once was, breaking the mind and flaying the spirit, until there is naught left within but a vast, unknowable darkness."

:You will...gain nothing...from this husk.: Lieutenant Shore's shell arrested the chamber with an eldritch tongue, gutting the group of all prior excitement. ***:There is...nothing...you can do...to stop...what's coming.:***

"Baulrick Tamberyn?" Remy said without thinking, imagining the ghastly lichlord towering high atop his necrotic steed, and Shore's milky-white stare settled on the watchman before letting out something like a laugh at the inquiry. "Do I have the right of it, then?" Remy dared further.

:The deserter...is it?: It inquired in return. ***:Pity...the wildkin...didn't finish the job. Your Highness would make...a most welcome addition...to our little rebellion.:***

Remy drew his watchman's blade, causing Shore to croak with laughter yet again.

:You...had better keep that iron close...boy.:

"How do you know me?"

:How...do I know you? You reek...of Lancastle privilege, boy. I could smell...one of your blood...from the other side of the Vael.:

"And what do you want?"

The sheen of darkness in Shore's clouded orbs suddenly vanished.

"What is the purpose of all of this?"

No response.

"Baulrick Tamberyn? Is that your name, fiend?" Remy bellowed, though nothing more arose from the creature. "I demand an answer!"

What life that remained in Jon Shore's body departed at the hollow threat, and he collapsed to his knees, his momentum ushering him forward into freefall, before the shackles caught him, suspending him upright in an awkward half-collapsed position. Ash began to spill forth from his open mouth, and the group watched in awe as the parasite within became expelled.

Silent as the grave, Curie hefted Fucker from its haunt at the edge of her hip and strode across the chamber, her footsteps light and controlled. Straight up to the suspended corpse she floated, like a child in a meadow, as though it were the easiest affair in all the world, and without slowing, she reared the hatchet back and hacked it down into the nape of Jon Shore's neck, once, twice, and a third time, sending the poor diseased bastard's head rolling across the stones and into the shadows.

Remy, Westerly, and Tucket all stared at the mad magus in the after, each one displaying a variant expression of shock.

"Well, I don't know about you lot," Curie said in her typical undaunted manner as she walked past the horrorstricken trio, "but I could use a drag, a dram, and a fucking pint right about now."

CHAPTER NINE

"Nine hells, The Butcher get another one?" Aiden heard a thick country voice say in the nearing distance, interrupting the echoing chorus of *Lovers in Limbo* dancing loose upon the fringes of his dreamscape.

"Naw, just a wayward tosspot," a second voice responded. Something tapped against his foot. "Wakey, wakey, begs 'n achy."

"Balls of Agault, this one reeks like the bloody gallows," said the first.

"Aye, he's certainly put me off breakfast another hour, he has. I'd say he went after the black pretty hard last night."

"I'll say. And it's a right stroke of luck he's not a corpse, considering."

"Ain't no luck in it. This one's kissed by the gift to be sure."

"Tosh, this one ain't no ruddy giftborn. No way."

"Aye, he is at that. Sure as the winter's a cunt and the sea is wet. They all got a way about 'em, you see—a certain presence, mind you."

"This one's presence favors more a privy's appeal than any manner of civilized sort I ever seen. I say, you reckon we ought to summon the guard?"

"Hah! And witness how wasted our taxes truly are? Shit on the bloody bluecoats, I say. They're about as useful as a fart in a tempest. I'd sooner join the lad in his sodden rot than entertain a single word from one of the king's fucking wasters."

The archivist struggled to open his eyes at the sound of conversation being held just above him. Only the right one cooperated. The other one remained defiantly shut. With the one good eye, he glanced up at the burly figure silhouetted against the rising sun behind him. The man was puffing at a pipe and carrying the full gamut of fishing gear, Hammershoden rod, deep sea net, and double den tackle box. The other fellow, off to his side, Aiden could see a bit clearer. He sported a curse of a rat-face with considerably less meat on his bones. They were an ugly-looking pair, to be sure. Both wore drab, colorless rough-spun clothing, the dress of the peasantry, and smelled every bit the part. Aiden did not recognize either man, but then again, he didn't much associate with those of Kanton's lower half. He rather thought the most of them grating simpletons.

Before Aiden could utter a sound of acknowledgment, the rum began to come up, spraying forth like a spigot twisted at full flood. Fortunately, he was sober enough to shift on his side so as not to wear it. *Splendid,* he thought. Next followed the ale. *Lovely*. Then the Daerynger. *Fantastic*. And lastly, the bottom-shelf wine in short order. 'Twas a damned good thing he had very little pride to begin with, damned good indeed, else he might have had to feign embarrassment as well, and he was rather rubbish at feigning much of anything at such an early hour as this.

"Oye, this one's hurting me just looking at him," the rat-faced angler said, shifting away from the pathetic display.

It took only a minute more for the archivist to expel himself near to proper again, slobber hanging thick from his bottom lip well into the wilds of his beard. No doubt he appeared a ghastly savage, though to have it true, Aiden was simply pleased it hadn't run free from both ends. The gods must be smiling on him indeed this lovely day. He wiped the spittle and vomit from his face with the mantle of his shirt. He had certainly done worse.

Afterward, he sat up and inhaled, allowing the smells of the Aurabus Ocean to envelop him. "Nope," he said as he turned to his side and retched again. He began to laugh midway through this bout and broke a long spell of morning wind that played in tune with his off-kilter laughing and bingeing. *There's the dignity killer*. What a piss-poor mess he had become. The gods were most certainly smiling at this sad, shitty spectacle and howling mad right along with him. Come one, come all, come see Aiden the Fool, once crown of his graduating order, now a retching, farting, floundering street dweller.

The rat-faced angler dropped a flask in the sand beside him. "For the sake of The Vael, have a drink, mate."

"Cheers," Aiden said as he fought to compose himself and sipped at the flask slowly. To his surprise, he found the contents within to be water, a bit brackish, but otherwise plain old ordinary water. He chugged the remainder of it down in a series of gulps and spit the last of it out to clear what remained of the evening's comeuppance.

"The only thing I ever seen do this to a man be a woman," said the burly one.

"Aye," Aiden managed as a memory of Caitie flickered through his thought stream. It was of the first morning they awoke in the same bed together, back when he still owned an actual bed. Her smile was the first thing he opened his eyes to that morn. Instinctually he brushed his thumb over her beauty mark as he had done a thousand times before. If only he could awaken to such an enchanting vision every morn, he remembered thinking as the tops of her bare feet began to rub against the bottoms of his. Her honeycomb eyes, yet still encumbered by the influence of slumber, belonged solely to him in that moment and instantly all of his pain over Rhymona evaporated like the mist in daylight.

This one would linger for a while, he knew. It was amongst his most cherished of memories.

"Everything all sorted then?" the burly one asked over his shoulder, plainly ready to be done with this little bother.

"Sorted," Aiden said. "Cheers." He offered the emptied flask back to the rat-faced angler.

"All you, mate," he said as they continued on toward the piers.

Irony of ironies, that. Even the lowest of the low have grown to pity you, Aiden. And thusly he found the only problem with waking on a beach. There was no pillow available to readily scream into.

Aiden watched after the anglers for a while before turning toward the sea, at which point he realized he had a bloodstained linen cloth wrapped around his hand. "Shit. Truly Aiden?" he grumbled as he gently slipped the makeshift bandage over his palm and fingers to assess the damage. "Ah, hells." It wasn't pretty. He arched his hand out as wide as he could and briefly studied the under flesh. It was dark and crimson, revealing a small trickle of dried blood at its lower edge. He sniffed at it, but no odor arose from it. At least it wasn't infected. He carefully eased the bandage back over the wound and worked himself up to his feet. Nothing so dire a binder and a bottle of red couldn't mend.

"Bugger all," he groaned as he glanced down past his hand at his bloodless toes. "Where in the nine fucks are my fucking boots?"

"Speak of the devil," he heard Penny groan the moment he shuffled into the great archive.

From behind a tall stack of tomes atop the registry desk she appeared, a short, plain-faced girl with long mouse-brown hair. It was obvious she wanted him to understand her irritation without delay. No doubt it had been left long to the boil. Thusly, Aiden grumbled something of a response, hoping it might be enough to appease her, though knowing good and well it wouldn't be even on his best day.

"So how's the crippling alcoholism going?" she kept on, her tiny hands wrapping around her tiny waist.

"Fantastic well, actually," Aiden said with his best attempt at a shit-eating grin, "I appreciate the ask. And I see your sarcasm has made some improvements."

"Can we not, you two?" Calem groaned as he straightened the stack before him.

"I daresay Ginny Rivenbark certainly had a thing or two to say about how fantastic well it was," Penny bit back.

"Who?" Aiden swiped up a tome as he approached and tossed it to Calem.

"The fifth cycle strumpet you were snogging in Billows last night. I must say it was a sad spectacle even for you, Aiden."

The archivist had a snort, and the taste of bile returned to his mouth.

"You think this funny?" Penny hissed.

"I daresay it's not not funny."

"Ugh." Penny covered a hand over her nose. "I can still smell her stench on you from over here."

"That would be the retching and farting more than like."

"Gods save me. Must everything be as a joke with you?"

I don't know. Must everything be as a lecture with you?

"Penny, lay off," Calem said, adding the tome Aiden had tossed him to one of the towering stacks. Aiden had no doubts Cal had a meticulous system in place for the mess he had made. Say one thing about Calem Reid, say he is a man of order and consistency. For every measure into disarray as was Aiden, Calem seemed twice as organized.

"Lay off? Are you seriously just going to brush this one under the rug as well? Look at this place. It's an absolute wreck. No doubt Brumfield would have him exiled if he found out, and that's if he was feeling generous." *No doubting that.* "There are dozens of priceless, centuries-old tomes just carelessly strewn about the floors, of which there is no telling how many are now ruined beyond repair. Not to mention the broken ladder. And then there's the blood and sick in the cupboard. Are you going to mop that up? Because I'm certainly not. And we both know His Majesty won't get to it for at least another week, if it's seen to at all."

"Pen..." Calem started again.

"It's fine Cal," Aiden said. "I probably deserve it."

"Probably deserve it? You deserve it unquestionably," Penny continued. "And you wonder why you and Caitie are having problems?" She spread an arm out wide. "This. All of this is precisely—"

"Were having problems you mean," Aiden was quick to correct. "Though I'm quite sure you are already well aware, so let us curtail the dance of aspersions—for both of our sakes, yeah?"

At that, there was an awkward moment of silence between the trio, complete with knife-cutting tension, long-faced scowling, and folded arms. Aiden thought he heard a pin drop somewhere near the back wall of the great archive. *Mayhaps in that dank, dingy place some bored tosser gave half a mummer's fart about Penny's useless bloody opinions.*

"Why do I even bother?" Penny rolled her eyes, grabbed an armful of books from a stack on the floor, and stomped off down an aisle.

"Of course, you know this is a good thing, brother," Calem reassured in a low voice once Penny was out of earshot. "You may not see it quite yet, but trust it true, this is for the better."

"Yeah," Aiden said, scooping up another book from the floor and placing it atop the nearest stack. "But sometimes better is bullshit."

"Utter bullshit, mate," Calem agreed, moving the book to a different stack. "But you've managed worse."

"Sorry to put you in a spot with Penny."

"If it wasn't you, it would be something else. Her trials are up next week, and it's put her in a rather foul temper, to say the least."

"If that's the case, then she can bloody well sod off. My morning has been foul enough already without her pitching in."

"It's not like that. She cares about you."

Aiden scoffed.

"She does. Do you think she would be here if she didn't?"

"She is here for you, Cal," Aiden said. He was no fool to the politics of the highborn. "She can't have your sterling reputation dashed to bits by some fuck up, lowborn, back-hollow bumpkin, now can she?"

Peeved, Calem lifted a stack from the registry desk and drifted off toward the War and History section. Aiden knew immediately he had overstepped his bounds. He knew Cal detested when he demeaned himself to such a degree, especially when he used their disparities in societal hierarchy as the crutch.

"Such is the true splendor of the opposite gender, yeah," Aiden quipped as he followed after his friend.

"I know you probably don't want to sort this right now," Calem said, an intense edge to his tone, "but what is the purpose of this sad beggar skin you now seem so obnoxiously keen to parade about the township?"

"The gods only know. Tell me how you truly feel, mate."

"That wasn't a dig. I'm quite serious, yeah. I mean it's bad enough you're off your face ninety percent of the time, but now you're consorting about with the riffraff, slatternly riffraff at that, for all the world to see. Not to mention…"

"Oh, *come* off it, Cal, truly, what did you expect? How long have we known each other? Don't act as though this is some fashion of newfangled behavior for me. I was working Caitie out of my system all right."

"Acting a belligerent prat is working Caitie out of your system?"

"You have your way, I have mine."

Calem frowned. "I won't play the smug card with you Aiden, as much as you would love to have it. And I'm not your old man, so I won't bother with a lecture. However, I will be forthright. You deserve as much I suppose."

"You suppose I deserve as much, do you? Well fucking dandy, that. Reckon I'll have to agree as well then, won't I?"

"And I am glad you agree," Calem said, a rare air of aggravation clear in his tone. "Though I am quite curious when exactly it was that you decided giving up and becoming a sad, sulky degenerate was your best course of action."

And bandage right off. Aiden smirked. It was not the reaction he expected of himself, but somehow it felt quite natural. It was almost as though a tiny devil lord was tugging upward at the crook of his mouth.

"I mean look at this place, Aiden. I hate to beat a dead horse, but it's practically in tatters."

Aiden glanced around, humoring his friend. Without question, he had put in a consummate effort wrecking the place.

"And what's worse is you're nowhere to be found in the after. Naught hide nor hair to be found of you save a puddle of blood in the supply cupboard. Another hour and I might have had the coats on watch for you, especially with the Bayside Butcher about. You can imagine the kinds of dark scenarios that ran through my head."

Aiden stood silent and took the verbal thrashing. Cal had never come at him so hard before.

"Why are you just allowing yourself to waste away in this middling poshed up prison anyway? It's quite beneath you, now isn't it? And it's quite clear you're absolutely miserable stewing in it. So for Veradon's sake, why are you still here?"

They were questions he had asked himself a thousand times over, but to wit, he had never once had them from Calem. They sounded quite queer coming from Cal to have it true, as queer as his anger, but quite sobering all told, and he hadn't the faintest inkling how to respond. The devil lord smirk had rather suddenly become a distant revelation.

"Gods, you must know I hate to come at you so hard, brother, but I've let it go on long enough. You're not right. All told, I don't know what to properly call how you are now." *Troubled, spineless, grasping come to mind.* "It's like I am watching you from outside this invisible bubble that is very rapidly taking on water and very near to filling, and try as I might to pull you from its capture, my efforts only seem to hasten your dreadful fate." *How very Galloway of you Cal, though I must admit it's positively adorable you still think I am salvageable.* "For a while I thought you would simply work it out yourself, I hoped and prayed you would, but as the days pass, it seems more and more to have gone down the other way, hasn't it?"

"Trust, I am slogging through it, slowly but surely," Aiden said with feigned confidence, fumbling about for one of his many masks. In the least, Cal deserved a few words of explanation, though they were only just that. "You know how I am. I'm like a phoenix, yeah. True, I get low at times, nine hells, I go six feet under on the worst of days, but I'm not much made to be down with the worms now I am?" He offered a contrived grin. "Besides, I've come to think it's well past time for a holiday back home, isn't it?"

Calem's expression brightened marginally at that. "No doubt Tam would be overjoyed to see you again."

"I wouldn't be so sure."

"What's not to be sure about? She is your sister, isn't she? Your blood-kin. Of course, she will understand. She knows how close you and your mother were. She knows how hard it must have been for you to lose her. Tam may be young, but she is remarkably intuitive and doubly empathetic. I could sense that from the very moment I took her company." Calem smiled cleverly. "The gods know she's a damn sight more intuitive than her older brother."

"And the gods know I'm not yet soused enough to carry on a conversation of this magnitude."

"You brought it up, mate," Calem said as he forced a rather thick volume on The First War of Kings into a nook much too thin for its many pages, pounding at it with the bottom of his fist to finally settle it in place. "And it's been a while in the well to be sure. I know you harbor a lot of guilt over Tam. I see it on your face every day. But for once you've managed to scrounge up a halfway decent idea, haven't you? Now it's only a matter of seeing it through."

"Well, aren't we just the very beacon of positivity this morning."

"I think Gallea's Grace will do you wonders, in all earnestness. It may be difficult at first, but I think once you see your family again, it will all begin to sort itself out. Besides, all affairs considered, I would say you are due a mite bit of favor, wouldn't you agree?"

"I say, Reid, do I detect a bit of pander in your loathsome lilt of optimism?"

Calem's smile faded. "Mayhaps, though I must admit there is an underlying motive behind this kindred connivance."

"Mmm, fancy words, those."

"Fancy words that beget harsh words I'm afraid," Calem appended. "Words I have struggled with over the past few days. Words I have grown to detest. But I suppose their time has come at last, if ever there were a proper moment for their permission."

"And so I wait with bated breath."

Calem set the stack of tomes down at his feet, marking the gravity of the coming conversation. "I recently received a flyer from Brumfield."

Aiden's icy blues hardened at the mention of the Headmaster's name. Brumfield had had it in for him ever since he and Rhymona began courting in his second semester. Say one thing for Harper Brumfield, say the man could carry a grudge. Brumfield despised Rhymona for her rude and rebellious behavior and therefore by association despised Aiden as well. Try as he might to make amends in the cycles to follow RC's expulsion, Brumfield would have none of it. No doubt had his mother not stepped in, Aiden would have been expelled all those many cycles ago right along with her. As affairs stood, he has since been on thin ice with the Headmaster and never more so than most recently.

"There is no easy way to say this, so here it is cold as the bladehand's kiss. The council of magisters has decided to suspend your services for the remainder of the present and harvest terms." Truly Aiden wished he could be more surprised. "Effective immediately, they have named Nigel Head Archivist until they find a more permanent candidate."

"Boone?" Now, this was a surprise. "Over you?"

"Naturally they offered me the post first, but of course, I turned them down."

"Is that so?"

"I start my internship at the Ministry in Marsoon. What sense would it make to govern the ship for two months and vacate?"

"I suppose they could have done worse than Boone."

"Much worse, I'll say. Could you imagine Gethan or Mosby running this place?"

"Oi. I'd rather not."

"So you are not cross then?"

"Cross? What's there to be cross about? I've been a shite archivist for quite some time now, haven't I? To be honest I'm amazed I've lasted this long. Brumfield must be getting soft in his twilight." They shared a laugh at that. "Besides, it's been you and Boone and Penny keeping this place afloat for some months now. The mantle is rightfully passed. No doubt it will serve Boone a damn sight better than it ever did me."

"I must say you are taking this rather well."

Aiden shrugged. "What would you have me say, Cal? Now and then there comes a point when you know it's time to move on. I'm making my peace with Kanton the best way I know how, but you know how I am. I'm a real difficult fucker when it comes to being told what to do." He had his mother to thank for that. "But the fates are forcing my hand this time, it would seem, and who am I to defy the almighty fates? What great figure am I to delay the inevitable? Besides, bucking up to Brumfield would only be another senseless headache. And just now I'm quite over my stable of minor inconveniences." It was at this juncture that Aiden noticed Calem's utterly bewildered expression. "Come now, what is that look for?"

"The gods only know. Who is this imposter before me and what has he done with the real Aiden Ashborough?"

"Oh, that old tosser?" he started with a sinister tone. "I've locked him away where naught dare tread and fed the key to the furnace. May he live long and rot."

"Poor sod."

"Ah, he was a whiny twat, wasn't he? To the nine with his lot, I say."

"The gods help us all if you become warden one day."

"You have no idea, mate."

"In all seriousness though, you know I'm here for you, right?"

"I know."

"No matter where you go or what you do. Mum will see to your affairs if need be. You are like a second son to her, I hope you know."

"I know." *Tabbie Reid has always done right by me, Cal, trust I am well aware. But love only suffers so much.* "And I thank you. But I don't think I'll be around these walks much longer. I have my own mum to see about."

"I know the words are unnecessary, but I thought I would say them anyway. We're family you and I, until the bitter end."

"Until the bitter end, brother." Aiden turned back toward the registry desk, hands on hips. He could only stomach so much sap in one morning. "I say quite the task some asshole put us up to today, isn't it?"

"Indeed, a real wanker that one, but we've certainly managed worse."

A smile found Aiden's lips in spite of it all. "That we have, old friend. That we have."

CHAPTER TEN

Princess Marsea sat abed staring miserably at the bandages wrapped firmly about her disfigured left hand.

She awoke from a series of fever dreams to find her body a mass of bruises and the left half of her face swollen like a grapefruit. But none of that mattered. Those wounds would eventually mend. She considered herself a rather fast healer, besides. Instead, she had become fixated on those that never would, turning her veiled hand from knuckle to palm, gently caressing the nubs of her freshly shortened fingers. Cas had done his best, considering, but she'd taken a severe mangling from the hidden blade, a mangling that likely couldn't be salvaged by even the best of the commonwealth's surgeons. To the touch, their absence offered a strange tingling sensation. It almost felt as though they were still with her, curling inward with the remaining others.

Almost.

Are we all simply destined to live these miserable half-lives? Wishing at fairy tales and feeling like different people than the world perceives us to be?

She frowned and with her good hand removed the pin from the end of the bindings fastened just above her wrist. She had to see them again, her hideous, misshapen nubs. She had to know the extent of the damage whilst sober.

And what will they say about you now? There goes Marsea, she seems a nice enough lass, good spirit and all, but one must wonder how such a lovely girl could collect such an assortment of ghastly scars.

In the least, much of her aches had subsided thanks to the lotus milk. A most wondrous concoction, milk of the lotus. She had forgotten how lovely it could be, really. For it had been many cycles since she had last required its effects. At the thought, she could faintly recall the cramping and aching in the bones of her ankles, feet, and toes from her time taking ballet. Her frown deepened. Yet another disastrous venture her mother had forced upon her. She loathed even the thought of her dance instructor Mistress Veranski. What an absolute horror was the Mistress from Maidstone, in particular with her unrelenting demand of proper pointe work. As such, there were many nights Marsea could barely stand after her lessons. And though it had been a decade since she had last stepped inside her ballet slippers, she held no doubts the rigors of Mistress Veranski's class would ever remain with her. Marsea shook the vile memories from her mind as she slowly began to unwind the bandages, layer by layer, each layer a slightly darker shade than the previous.

"Milady," Yuna uttered from the window seat, though Marsea paid the handmaiden no mind. She simply kept unwinding the strip of linen end over end.

That she had some feeling in her index and middle fingers gave her hope. Though she certainly wished she'd had more time to sift through the snow for the missing halves of her pinky and ring finger. Mayhaps Cas could have reattached them, made her hand appear halfway normal again. Such was not her luck, however. Was it not enough that the gods had stripped her of her pride and independence? That they had robbed her of a family and a proper childhood? What great cruelty had she wrought that should have them now thieving for her beauty as well?

Marsea could vaguely recall stumbling through the Kingswood into the back alleys of Lancastle Proper toward the keep, her ruined hand tucked well beneath her armpit, her body slowly failing her. Fortunately, the princess of Lancastle was quite adept at navigating her kingdom's quarters. It was, after all, within Lancastle's confines that she had spent the entirety of her existence prior to this past new cycle's eve. Nigh twenty cycles worth of exploration and she had mastered near every nook and cranny inside the kingdom walls, every bend and twist, every hidden passage, every forgotten side street, every hall of every wing within her citadel, even the pits and the lower quarters, though she rarely bothered down so far. If she wished to have her eardrums defiled by hags and creeps, she would sooner consort with those of the dungeon ilk than traipse a quarter mile through the hustle and bustle of Lancastle's malodorous cobble.

As for how she arrived in her bedchamber some hours later, she hadn't the foggiest. She remembered turning down Jawns Street to avoid a band of carousers, leaning heavily against the building stonework, her breath forming cold clouds before her face, concentrating on the sway of the streetlamps above her, before they dimmed, and a great dark chasm swallowed up the remains of her light. Thereafter, her eyes next opened inside a lotus-induced stupor. She found a cloth draped over her forehead, a bandage swathed about her hand, and Vaustian Harver reading from a tome at her bedside. Her love appeared quite smart in the fuzzy flicker of candlelight. She tried to speak to him then, but her words passed scarce better than a mumble, scarcely words at all really, though enough to lure his attention, and he placed a hand, warm and masculine, over her one good one before she was yet again whisked away from the land of the conscious.

"Milady," Yuna said again, this time a bit firmer.

"What?" Marsea topped Yuna's sternness, her frustration woefully evident.

"Lord Casilvieri said you must let your bandages settle a while. He instructed me to..."

"I couldn't give a pair of figs what Cas has instructed you; it's my hand and I will do with it whatever I please."

"Lord Casilvieri told me to come find him if you disobeyed, milady."

"Then go find him," Marsea hissed as she went back to unwrapping.

Yuna set her knitting needles aside and knelt at Marsea's bedside. "I beg of you, milady. Lord Casilvieri can be rather…"

Marsea paused for a moment and scowled at her peculiar handmaiden, daring her to complete her sentence. It was mayhaps the one physical feature she derived from her father. She had her mother's distinctive button nose, Waldgrave silvery orbs, and curly blond hair, but even all of that could not diminish her king father's fiery Lanier glower when it reared its ugly fangs.

A rapping at the door interrupted their tense silence, and both of them shifted their attentions toward the chamber's entrance. Marsea recognized the knock and immediately beset her handmaiden with a desperate, wide-eyed gaze. Instantly, she began shaking her head.

Yuna waved a hand down, instructing her ladyship to lie back low beneath the covers as she slowly edged toward the door. Marsea dropped back upon her pillow and slipped deep within her blankets before closing her eyes. Blind beneath the covers, she listened as Yuna took a breath, gripped the doorknob, and opened it to their visitor.

"Marsea?" a familiar voice wormed inside her bedchamber, its cast full of deceit and court-bred sophistication.

"Milord, the lady is still asleep," Yuna whispered.

"Do not lie to me, Yuna. I heard her scolding you only moments ago."

Marsea heard the light click of a cane atop stone and a shuffled step inward followed by a second and a third before her mattress shifted with additional weight.

"Sister, I know you are awake," the voice said. Marsea kept perfectly still. "I heard you were attacked yestereve in the courtyards. Name me a bleeding heart if you must, but I've grown ever so anxious in the hours since."

Is that what Vaustian is telling folk? Marsea shifted slightly underneath the blankets, gently folding the quilt from over her head, her champagne locks spilling out wildly around her.

"Oh dear, oh dear, oh dear, what did that monster do to you, my sweet Seasea?" The oil lamp introduced Pion Silvertongue in a ghastly light, though there was scarce a flame in all The Vael that had done him much favor. What bit of handsomeness his Harver blood had earned him had been stolen away by his pallid orbs and a malformed leg, though he had long since learned how to manipulate those shortcomings to his advantage. Spidery hair hung low in long, black tendrils around his gaunt features, and his thin lips pursed into an unsightly smile.

"I'm fine, thank you," she said.

"Your eye says otherwise," he said tenderly, reaching a pale, skeletal hand toward her, but Marsea turned her cheek away.

"Why must you wound me so, dear Seasea? I only mean to offer you comfort."

"I'm fine, Pion. Your comfort is unnecessary."

"And how is the paw?"

"It's fine."

"Is it now?" He frowned. "Seasea, why must we play at these silly games? Do you not tire of them?"

"I'm not playing at anything," she said with tamed innocence. *Because you're a fiend and a schemer and a devious lech.*

"You must know I only want the best for you, Seasea. Larissa had me come for you. She was quite distraught when father gave her the news." *So, she couldn't come herself?* "She worries about you, you know." *Like the moons worry about the sun?* "Jules too."

"I know," she offered for civility's sake.

"Uncle says they've put the guard on high alert for this mugger of yours. Some Vardain fellow, I'm told. Utterly reprehensible what he has done. No doubt he will take a long turn in the stocks for his foolishness, and he should count his ruddy luck stones that's all he bloody well gets. Mayhaps they will take a hand in recompense for good measure."

Vardain? What in the nine hells? Marsea had never even heard the name before. No doubt it was some lackwit that had rubbed Ravenholme the wrong way. "Yes," she mumbled weakly. "Capitol news."

"Capitol news?" Pion beset her with a curious gaze. "You seem unsure."

"Unsure? Not at all. The gods know I hope he gets the noose."

"Is that so?"

"What is this truly, Pion? What are you after? Did Mother have you come to interrogate me as well?"

Pion frowned at that. "My apologies, love, of course not. You needn't paint me the snake in all this. It was only an observation. I meant not to make you cross." Pion slithered his dainty hand atop the quilt over the hill of her knee. "Though you should well prize that scowl of mistrust is quite unbecoming of her ladyship."

Spoken like a true Harver. She moved her leg away from his reach. "I will take that under advisement."

"Ah and yet there are still more ill tidings to impart, dear sister." *If only they belonged to their bearer.* "It would seem you were not the only one to come under attack yestereve."

She feigned ignorance as best she could.

"Yes, yes, yes, and I am afraid mine Uncle Ganedys was not near as fortunate as you were." *Fortunate? You name losing half a hand fortunate?*

"In fact, he was found butchered to bits in the middle of the Kingswood."

"Truly?"

Pion nodded, indifferently.

"I daresay considering your kinship you do not seem too terribly broken up about it."

"I admit fully I bore little love for mine Uncle Gan. Even from a young age. I thought him an abusive brute and an obnoxious drunkard, a foul embarrassment to the name of Harver, and a witless lout through and through." *Odd words coming from the family whelp.* "But nevertheless, his murder cannot go unheeded. Father and Uncle Vaustian have already opened an investigation, though it would appear his attack came at the hands of a wolld scouting party."

Marsea found relief to hear that Casilvieri's plan hadn't completely failed. One less worry to fret over. "What business have the wolld poaching this far south?" she played along.

"Surely you have heard the rumors of the wildkin uprisings in the north?"

Vaustian had mentioned something of it during their last tryst, but he spoke of it as little more than a fleeting nuisance so indeed she thought scant little of it. Cas, on the other hand, had been the one to order Gan's murder in such a fashion. She knew he was a northerner, born of the Hetland somewhere abouts the wolld kingdom called Colbengrad. No doubt his experience with the wildkin savages gave him a distinct advantage in all of this. *Clever Casilvieri,* Vaustian would say, *clever as all ever was that one. Too clever by half,* Marsea granted. And she couldn't help but wonder if Vaustian had been in on the decision to brand the wolld as Gan's attackers. Likewise, she couldn't help but wonder what else he and Cas were hiding from her. "Mmm," she managed.

"Evidently the savages are no longer content with their patch near The Scar. I can't half blame them, all affairs considered." He stood and hobbled to her window, looking out over the vast kingdom below. "This city," he began after a brief silence, "these people..." He let the words linger before turning back to Marsea, a darkly lament about his countenance. "Something foul this way wanders, sister. I can feel it in my bones. I can smell its rotten stench on the winter winds. And these wildkin attacks, your mugging, Uncle Gan's murder, they are but a prologue for something much worse." Pion sat down atop the window seat shaking his head. "The bluecoats have been in a pother for weeks now, centuries being sent to the north without return, draft boards being placed all about the kingdom hollows, and yet no one is talking about it. I daresay, when did we all become so bloody complacent? When did we decide we were all content enough to simply ignore the obvious? Only the gods know, I fear. We are all too busy nattering on about whose Lord's birthfall it is next week and which belle Prince Halfwit from Beggarshire is sending dowry for. The weak, pretentious foolhards."

Marsea watched Pion as he continued his ranting. There had always been a certain degree of edginess to him, but this fresh version teetered on the cusp of madness. She had never seen him so worked up about anything in all the days she had known him. Meanwhile, Yuna stood still as a statue with her hands bundled up over her mouth, fear prevalent in her nervous eyes.

"And now there is an attack in our citadel courtyards, against the princess of Lancastle of all folk, right at our bloody doorstep, and yet do you know what filled the content of my last conversation? Lady Marisol of Valasta, too deep in her bitters again, bedding some nameless bard just in from Debynshire."

"That is quite enough, Pion," a gruff voice added from the doorway, startling the princess. "Lady Marsea requires her bedrest."

"Smiler," Pion sneered, "ever the beacon of merriment." The distaste between the two men was nearly palpable.

"Is there not another chamber nearby you can readily defile with the latest gossip rag?" Casilvieri said.

"The gods know," Pion returned. "Is this what now passes for suitable bedside manner?"

"You would be wise to keep that tongue in check, wretch, lest you find yourself without."

"And you've proven my point yet again, charlatan," Pion answered with a certain measure of disgust before shifting back to the princess. "Apologies for any affront, milady. I will relay your mother and Jules your love. Rest well," he added with affection as he passed through, each hobbled step followed synchronously by the click of his malformed cane.

With Pion departed, Marsea shifted her full attention on the impeccably dressed figure at the chamber's entrance. For all intents and purposes, Merillion Casilvieri looked the part of any long-standing noble house member, save for the rather off-putting scar that ran the length of his left cheek. Vaustian introduced him to the court as a renowned high seas admiral that had spent many cycles away at trade in the far east, but the princess knew better. It was but a clever ruse to conceal the true identity kept within, an identity that unquestionably carried with it a dark and violent past. She doubted the hetlander had ever even been aboard a ship, much less commanded one.

He cleared his throat and turned with a dour guise to Yuna, who had all the while remained as inconspicuous as a fly on the wall. Realizing her gaffe, the handmaiden bowed, removed herself from the chamber, and quietly closed the door behind her. Casilvieri waited a moment, listening to her footfalls fade down the corridor, before shifting his attention back upon the princess.

"I brought you some soup," he said as he set the steaming bowl atop her night table. "I would imagine by now you are quite famished."

"I'm sorry," Marsea said nervously, ignoring the offering.

Cas smiled as he grabbed the chair from underneath Marsea's vanity desk, dragging it loudly across the stone-tiled floor, before swinging it around backward against the end of her bed. "There is no need for apologies," he said as he settled down upon the seat. "All told, I would say you performed quite well. Ganedys may have been one of the Vael's greatest foolhards when it comes to social etiquette, but you put a blade in his hand and he could be as ruthless as the inquisition."

Marsea couldn't agree more.

"The damsel card was a bold strategy, bold indeed. It nearly sent you to ruin. But your execution with the hidden blade was absolute perfection. No hesitation. Nearly felt the blade myself you drove it in so deep. I daresay up north, in The Pits, you'd have been named a gods damned bloody legend for such an unexpected upset." He had a laugh. "And you'd have had a fat purse for the King's Road to boot."

"You were there?"

"Of course, I was there," he said, removing his glasses and taking a cloth to the lenses. "You think Vaustian would allow his Marsea dearest out so far from home on her own? Trust only suffers so much these days I'm afraid."

"And you did nothing? I could have been killed by that savage!"

"Oi, before you go about placing blame, I was instructed to watch, not participate. Times are tough on the exiled these days. You understand. Made of me a right proper yes man, it has. In any case, this was your lesson to learn."

"My lesson to learn?" she said, foxed.

"You were a housecat amongst strays. It could not be avoided if you were to survive."

"*If* I were to survive?" She couldn't believe what she was hearing.

"Now you have a clear understanding of just how near to death our company keeps every hour of every day. Tell me, Marsea, in all of our sparring sessions, did you never think to question what they were for?"

"I..." she started before her words disappeared. She misliked his tone, as though there were some underlying meaning outside of the obvious.

"The gods know, girl, are you uncertain then? Were my training sessions of such piss-poor quality as to apparently shun response?"

"To learn how to properly wield a blade," she blurted, if only to slake his badgering, though she knew good and well it wouldn't.

"Tut. No Marsea, they were not to instruct you how to wield a fucking blade. I know damned well you know how to wield a blade. Even the thickest of dullards can wield a blade when driven to it. They were to instruct you how to not die. And despite your apparent ignorance, it would seem something of their practice hit the mark, didn't it? Besides, as I recall, you asked for this." He placed his glasses back upon their perch. "Do you remember, Marsea? You told me you were ready. You told the Viceroy you were ready. Looked us both proper. And neither one of us held a blade to your throat to do so. Am I to understand those words were now false?"

"They were not false," she answered plainly.

"Did you then deceive us, Marsea?"

Marsea glowered out the window into the storm clouds beyond, considering her next words carefully. Though she knew there would be no way to win this conversation. There never was where Ravenholme was concerned.

"Well, girl?" he goaded further. "Out with it then."

"I didn't lie or deceive you," Marsea answered tersely, her silver orbs flickering with untamed ire, her good hand continuing to unfurl her bandages.

"Ah, and there she is." A smirk returned to Casilvieri's disfigured guise. "And the gods know it's a most exquisite affair, isn't it? That was what I was hunting for. That face right there. Do you hear it now, Marsea? Do you sense it calling to you? Do you feel its teeth breaking the skin? What you feel right now, Marsea—the hate, the anger, the lament over what was stolen from you. Use it." He stood rigidly and casually strolled over to the window. "The experience is yours and yours alone. You made it yours. You fought for it. You earned it. Now embrace it. Accept it. Keep it close to heart. For that is the balance. That is the reward. This fury you feel presently, this hatred you feel for me and my betrayal, it can be conjured until you kill it, until you relinquish its power. It is yours and yours alone. And prize well, as ugly a thing as it is, it can provide you with great strength when you need it most." He turned back toward her, leaning against the wall, arms folded across his chest. "Folk are so eager to dally along naming things good and bad, or black and white, as though the world were ever such a simple matter, but there is no good or bad, no black or white, at least not anymore, not in this poxy version of a civilization, now is there? There is only useful and expendable. And as shitty as things appear in this moment for you, Marsea, you've managed to create something quite useful for yourself, now haven't you?"

Tears in her eyes and poison in her soul, Marsea lifted up her bare ruined hand between them. "Does this look useful to you now?"

Near to the entire hand, down past her wrist, shown a bloated violet bruise, jagged lines of yellow and red bearded the outsides of the lesser injured areas, and sutures rose up and down the great swell of her palm and remaining fingers like the seams of a dollmaker's haphazard rescue. The nubs of her ring finger and pinky were an unsightly mass, stitched shut at their knuckles, and wrapped tight with a string at the base to keep them together and immobile.

"A small price to pay for ascension," said Cas as though it were the most obvious affair in all the world.

"I can barely move it."

"It will mend in time, girl. And you will be the stronger for it. Trust I've seen far worse."

"How dare you belittle my pain, Cas." She knew immediately that she had overstepped her bounds, but the words would not be denied.

"You think you know pain, girl?" Cas pushed away from the wall with an uncharacteristically theatrical flair. "You think losing a few lengths is the worst of it?" He fitted a pair of fingers inside his mouth pulling something loose, and she realized a moment later he had removed his teeth. "Think again."

Marsea had never seen anything like it in all her days. Casilvieri stepped close into the light of the oil lamp and smiled wide showing his darkened, toothless gums. His entire face drooped with the omission, as though it were a mask and not a face at all, before he fitted the false teeth back in place.

"The bottom row is even worse," he promised.

Marsea shuddered to think how he would have even come about such a strange curiosity as false teeth.

"Wildkin attack when I was still but a boy," he answered her silent question. "Many wolld tribes collect the teeth of their prey and fashion them into necklaces and bracelets and what have you. Some tribes even use them as currency. Though typically their taking is done after the victim is dead and tethered. However, it would seem this particular wildkin was a right proper nutter." He presented her the palm of his right hand, revealing a bubble of scar tissue near its epicenter. "She pinned me to the ground with a dagger, right here. Hurt like a devil's wench too. I wailed like a bloody banshee, I did. Then she stuck me twice in the belly with the other before she fitted the blade against the corner of my mouth and sliced outward. I screamed and screamed as she began to carve away at the flesh beneath, but it purchased little sway. Reckon it was around the fourth pulled tooth I lost consciousness. I suppose I should count my fucking hag stones the bitch didn't take my tongue as well."

"No more," Marsea pleaded. "I understand."

"You understand, do you?" A bushy eyebrow arched.

"Yes."

"You understand that self-pity is utterly useless?"

"Yes."

"Do you, Marsea? Or is this you telling me what I wish to hear?"

"I want to understand," she said anxiously.

"Then let us be done with this senseless song and dance. Say the words and fucking swallow them."

She held his hard, unforgiving glare, and her entire body began to tremble uncontrollably. *What is happening to me*?

"Enough sulking, Marsea. Enough hiding. Enough dithering. Fuck the stars. Fuck your fears. Fuck the past. Fuck all that ever was before this moment. Assume the present is all that is and all that ever will be. Live every breath as though it were your last. It's the only way to savor even an ounce of freedom in this poxy world, of that I can promise you. Now take control and say the ruddy words, girl. Say them and swallow them down."

She hesitated.

"Chuffing hells, you knew what this was when you got involved," he barked, his hand collapsing against the hilt at his side. "I didn't see to your task out in the wood just to see you cower in the after. Now say the damned words, Marsea. You owe me this. You owe yourself this."

She was no stranger to Cas's scolding, but there was something quite different about his tone this time. Something grave, almost sinister. Something deadly.

Say the words, a voice from deep within the folds of her consciousness bade her. *They're only words.*

"I will not let my past define me," she sputtered, as if the words were being ripped from her throat against her will. True, she had thought them a thousand, thousand times before, they even haunted her dreams most nights, but to wit, she had never once spoken them aloud.

"Again," Cas commanded with all the wrath of a seasoned Royalguard colonel.

Marsea's glare hardened, her fierce Lanier spirit taking root once more. "I will not let my past define me."

"Again," he said, driving a fist into palm.

"I will not let my past define me." She nearly matched her mentor's bellow and bluster, staring daggers through him, all of her pent-up emotions beginning to spill forth. "I will not let my past define me."

"Again, Marsea, and gods dammit, make me believe it this time."

And for the first time in many quintweeks, Marsea smiled true. It was a smile of defiance, and it felt crooked against the fresh swell of her fat lip and busted cheek. *Damn you, Cas.* "I will not let my past define me. I will not let my past define me! I will not let my fucking past define me!" By the last chant, the back of her throat burned as though she'd just slammed back a dram of whiskey.

"Gods damn bloody right you won't," he avowed. "First thing you say in the morn, last thing you say in the eve, every day until there are no more. Is that clear?"

Marsea nodded obediently, her chest heaving from the sudden rush of adrenaline, and with her good hand, she brushed her hair back from out of her face.

With a satisfied gait, Casilvieri strolled to the chamber door and turned back toward her. "You should well prize, girl, despite your injuries, you performed impressively. You certainly surpassed my expectations. But rest assured, Ganedys was only the beginning. He was but the first chip to fall, and there will be more to follow. Many more."

The princess lowered her gaze to her ruined hand.

"The winds of change are stirring for a long overdue hunt, Marsea. Best to mind your bedrest while you still can. And do have a bit of the soup, yeah. You will most definitely want to be fresh and fit for what comes next."

CHAPTER ELEVEN

It took the better part of the afternoon to piece Withers back to suitability, and by the end of it, Aiden was utterly knackered. He burned through a pair of binders to mend the cut on his hand, and some hours later, after a fitful nap atop his rickety, old table-bed, found himself on a most familiar footpath. A footpath, on this nightfall, born more of routine than any true whim of desire.

So much for all that alone time, he groused. *Damned bad habits.*

Quiet as a country mouse, the archivist found an inconspicuous table in the dimly lit back corner of the Brass Lantern Pubhouse. As good fortune faired, the tavern was a tick on the slow side this eventide, occupied mostly with the circadian suspects.

Small comfort to know some things never change.

Sid and Monty were already half-lit, hovering at the end of the bar in their usual haunts, heads hung low, their cigars arresting the air in stags and drags. Trixie's man, Jim Ellis, cluttered the first booth nearest the entrance with a jotter, an inkwell, and a stack of tomes, no doubt fast at work on his next editorial. And Captain Cork and his latest band of unruly primitives were making a raucous game of it at one of the tables across the way, though Aiden only recognized a few of the faces. A bluecoat is a bluecoat is a bluecoat, he reckoned. More than like, the most were transfers from The Bulwark and fresh cadets, bright-eyed underlings Cork hadn't yet forged an opportunity to properly swindle. In any case, their green-faced lot certainly had the swamp donkeys swarming about early, some real dodgy barkers too by the looks of it. May they ever evade the candlelight's smolder.

"What'll it be, sugar plum?" Madi asked as she sidled up to the end of his booth all tits and smiles.

"Evenin' Mads," he greeted, all southern boy charm, "the usual. Cheers."

"You should well prize, love, we've a stand-in cook this week. Wicket's on holiday with his lass 'til the fifteenth."

"No worries. I haven't eaten a proper sup in days at this point, so he won't catch much fuss."

Madi's darling grin widened. "No he about it, hun."

"No?"

"I'll be making sure it gets the proper seeing to. But you'll have to bug Trixie for yer pints I'm afraid. Can't very well be in two places at once, now can I?"

"I reckon not."

And with a wink, she was off to the kitchen. Aiden couldn't help but follow her hips until she disappeared around the corner. Afterward, he drifted absently to the bar and waited for Trixie to finish serving a fresh round for Cork's table. He wasn't in any hurry after all, and quite suddenly he had more than enough to occupy his thoughts. His morning conversation with Calem in particular. Had he truly told his brother he was leaving? Was he truly sacked? Was this finally the end of university for him? It seemed quite abrupt, considering all of the pain and frustration and build up involved, that one day he should be in the middle of a horrid mental maelstrom and the next utterly unshackled and tossed gently to the unsuspecting breeze. Though truly, by his standards, he reckoned such a dramatic turn seemed about the proper way of it—the only way of it really.

"The king's lads are giving you a hell of a run tonight, aren't they?" he commented to Trixie once she returned to the counter.

"Aye, they are," she said blowing loose strands of auburn hair out of her face, "but they're paying honest if you can believe it. Far be it from me to let 'em dry out."

"I only hope they've left some for the rest of us."

"Reckon that'll depend on what yer after, love," Trixie said as she began to dry a freshly rinsed mug with a damp hand towel.

"Medgar by chance?"

"Alas, sorry, hun, been out for a few days now. Hope to have some in by the week's end, but supplies through Sutheryn have become quite scarce since the troubles in the west began."

"Bandits again?"

"Not sure to be honest, could be the bloody Butcher for all I've heard, though it certainly seems a mite bit worse than bandits and bootleggers by the delay of things." Aiden was not at all sure how to take her uneasy expression, so he remained silent. "Anyway, 'tis a bother for a distant day, that. You've come for a drink not a debate, haven't you?"

"Sure, of course," he said, though all told, he still hadn't the faintest inkling why he had come. *Damned bad habits indeed.*

"If it's ales yer after, we've Soldiers, Rumsie, Castlewood, and Stone's Cast. Think we've still a bit of ciderwine as well, though Cork's boys are making remarkably quick work of it."

"Make it a Castle then," he said as a raspy mumble joined the soft pluck of lute strings from the tavern's corner, "and a double dram of your hardest whiskey."

He turned toward the balladeer as Trixie sorted his order. The man appeared haggard and legless and every measure as old as the tune he set to strumming, some strange meld of "Bella Susannah" that took on a mid-ballad shift to "Autumn Orchard Stroll." Aiden decided he quite liked the revision. The two songs blended exceptionally well into one another. Who would have thought? In spite of the rowdy Royalguard soldiers, it presented the room with a fitting sort of melancholic serenity.

As always, Trixie was exceedingly generous with the double dram, and Aiden quaffed it down in a trio of gulps as though it bore within some aspect from the meaning of life. Though to prospect, it only left him with a bitter expression and a temporary sore throat. As he turned the glass on its head, she arrived with his pint of Castlewood, its dark brown cast flowing neatly to the brim. *Damned fine barkeep that Trixie Foxworth, damned fine indeed.* One of the few folk he might actually miss of Kanton's crowd.

Aiden took a sip and closed his eyes to drown out the raucous, nodding along with the balladeer's next song. Some woeful requiem about a lowly lord's lost lady dearest. What more could he say? The trollied sod spoke to his heart's lament with this one, and for a trice, Caitlyn wormed her way back into his weary and wounded mindscape. This time he didn't want to dismiss her, however. He wanted her memory to linger a bit. He wanted to feel her freshly made scar. He needed the hurt. It cast a most appropriate ache in light of all the change that had found him this desolate dayfall. Besides, as queer as it yet felt, Kanton was already in his past whether he chose to accept it or not. He was but a ghost to her cobble now, a guest that had long overstayed his welcome. And Caitie had made her decision unquestionably clear. Though, he reckoned, in truth, it had been made some time ago between them, and like everything else, became lost to the void of habit somewhere along the way.

You deserve this pain, he thought as his eyes cracked open.

He watched the balladeer as the man poured every ounce of his lifeblood into his craft. He supposed affairs could be worse, considering. In the least, he hadn't yet found himself on the level of this tormented creature. And with even the slightest turn of fortune, mayhaps he never would. *Oi, may the luck stones prosper,* he put up a poor man's prayer for it and took a swig from his mug. Then he dug a poor man's tip from his trouser pocket and ambled back toward his table.

When he arrived, he found a most unexpected surprise awaiting him. She was short enough to stretch out the entire length of the booth and keep hidden, though she kept her cowl up anyway. And the gods know she had a phantom way about her.

"Fancy your kickers," Val said playfully, in reference to the raggedy-looking socks sheathing his unshod feet. "Is this the new winter fashion then? Beggar posh."

Jaw slightly hung, Aiden slid into the booth across from her, and a familiar scent of cintas flowers swept over him. Its catch was every measure as intoxicating sober as it had been during his bender. "So, you are real, then."

"Am I real, he inquires? I say, is this how you get on greeting all the little lasses then?"

"The gods know I was pissed to the nine last night. Indeed, I thought there was a strong possibility I might have dreamt you up."

"Dreamt me up? Blushing maidens moon, there goes that silver tongue again, quick as ever. You've a real problem there, you have." Val sat up straight and leaned forward. "Little bit of advice, yeah. You might care to buy a girl a pint first before you go ahead flooring her knickers."

Aiden couldn't suppress a smirk at the cheek of this woman, and he cleared his throat. "Val, was it?"

"It was." She leaned back. "I suppose it's a victory you've managed to retain even that, given the turn of our little jaunt last night. You were proper fucked the last I saw of you, spouting off about the Ministry and the council of magisters. You would do well to mind the company you keep with such venomous words by the way."

"I will keep that in stow."

"Though how could I fault you? Truly, I was scarce better to wit. Woke up with a world-class banger myself. That Daerynger's a real fucking knobend, yeah?"

Something of the evening's end came back to him at that. "You left me."

"I left you?" she said astonished. "As I recall, it was you who left me. I wrapped your hand there, all nice and neat, told you I was going to grab some ointment from my bag, and when I came back to the library, you and the wine were gone as the ghost. Not a drop left in the house. Way to leave your lady in the lurch, Sir Gallant."

Aiden had no account of any of this. *Me and my old mate, lost time, having another therapy session, no doubt.*

"How is the hand, by the way?" Val asked.

Aiden laid it out palm up on the table between them. There shown only the ghost of scar tissue in its place. "Put a couple candles to it. Good as new." *Good enough, in the least.* It wasn't as clean as RC's work, but it would do.

"Would you look at that. He's some talent beyond the drink, after all."

"Something an old friend taught me."

"And where was it you got off to with all the wine, I wonder?"

"The beach, evidently," he said, a few of the puzzle pieces beginning to spin into place. "And I only know that bit because I woke there…"

"I say, this Caitie lass did a real number on you, didn't she?"

"She's certainly played her part, make no mistake. But I didn't exactly do myself any favors either."

"Hot plate coming through," a voice said from behind him, and Madi appeared a moment later with a steaming plate of chicken, peas, and rice, seasoned with gravy and rosemary.

"Ah, this looks amazing, Mads," Aiden said, "smells great. A feast fit for a king, it is. Cheers."

"You're most welcome, sugar plum." She turned to Val. "And for the lady?" Val silently tugged the front of the cowl down further over her face. "All right then," Madi took the hint, "enjoy, love."

His eyes practically salivating, Aiden scooped up a small portion of rice and gravy, blew on it, and took a bite. *There was nothing quite like a well-cooked supper on an empty stomach.*

"I waited for the better part of an hour with your cat," Val started up again once Madi passed out of earshot. "But you never showed. Horrid shite company that one."

"Alas, Grandpa's entertaining days are long since passed."

"I couldn't believe you had abandoned me." Val pouted innocently as she hooked a hand under his mug's handle and took a long swill.

"And what would you have from me?" he began with a mouth full of food. "I thought you were an angel at the time."

"An angel? Stars save me you're an exceptionally terrible liar."

"Or was it a devil?"

"A devil?" she feigned hurt. "And here I thought you might just simply apologize."

"*Vishura shiroe*," he corrected himself again, pointing his fork at her. "That was it. *Vishura shiroe*."

"Pardon my ignorance."

"Nothing. Just talking to myself. It's probably just best to ignore me."

"You are making that quite impossible right now, I hope you know." She drew the cowl back a bit to reveal the most frighteningly pathetic doe eyes he had ever beheld.

"It was a little joke is all. Something my mum use to say to my pops when he delved too deep in his cups."

"And what, pray tell, does *vishura shiroe* mean exactly?"

"It's Bourystrom folklore. Roughly translated in Midaran, it means 'the changeling.' The myth describes a dream-like fae creature brought about by excess alcohol consumption that seduces her host into wayward and ofttimes violent acts."

"And you believed me such a creature?"

"I must confess. The thought passed through."

Val's lips curled upward. She appeared to be quite enjoying the turn of the conversation. "The young master is just chock-full of random insights, now isn't he?"

"At the detriment of his proper scruples, no doubt. Though please accept my most humble of apologies on his careless behalf."

"And then he says the words all nonchalant. I see your game quite clearly now."

"My game is it?"

"Keep on, giftborn," she said before taking another sip from his mug.

"Was that meant to be a threat then?"

"Take it as you like," she said as Aiden scooped up another steaming bite. "The maidens know it needn't be said, but you are quite possibly the ugliest eater I have ever beheld."

"I'm an ugly eater?" He shoveled another bite past his unkempt beard into his already full mouth. "You mean you don't like this?" he asked between bites.

"Absolutely awful," Val said with a dramatic sigh. "And here I was thinking we might simply name this what it is and get on with it."

"On with it, she says, murderous intent clear in her darkly haunters."

"I was actually thinking of something a mite bit messier than all that." Her smile was far more lethal than any knife end.

"Is that right?" he dared. "And what might that be, I wonder?"

"Well first, I was thinking we drink ourselves proper mad."

"Yeah? Reckon that won't be much of an issue, considering."

"And then I was thinking…we rent a little nook upstairs. And you and me…we fuck each other's brains out."

Aiden nearly choked, the sellsword's words took him by such surprise. They were spoken with an utter dearth of emotion, but those stormy lilac orbs now appeared horribly aglow.

"Tell me you haven't thought about it," she continued matter-of-factly. "You're a man, so I know you have," she answered for him. "You say you wish to make amends, yeah? And actions speak louder than words, now don't they? And from my perspective, you really need to make up for ditching a good time last night, don't you?"

"I…"

"I know, I know." She rolled her eyes. "I'm going light on you, aren't I?

But what's a girl to do? I suppose I'm a bit of a softy for an easy pair of baby blues."

"I daresay, it would appear I am not very good at this after all," he managed. *Rhymona might even be impressed with this one.*

"Good or no, you should well prize, I'm a fantastic lay." She drew the hood up to the edge of her hairline, revealing her whole face to him.

She was nowhere near as beautiful as the angel he remembered from the night before, but she was not unattractive either. Hers was a common sort of beauty, save the ash-colored curls of course, which practically glowed against the contrast of her dark skin. Still, her attractiveness shown a damned sight greater than any other lass in the tavern and comelier than most carousing about the university cobble. It was certainly enough to give pause.

"Listen Val," he began, "you are an unbelievably fetching lass..."

"And here it is." She folded her arms. "I'm no slag, Aiden, if that's your thought." Her expression fixed deadly serious.

"I didn't say you were."

"You know, of all the things you choose to be chivalrous about, this is it? The stars know I hadn't pegged you for the prudish sort."

"It has nothing to do with you. Trust me, I'm doing you the favor here."

"I quite disagree."

"You can disagree until your heart's content, but trust I am a doomed romantic of the utterly hopeless variety."

"Rubbish that. I won't hear another sob story about *Caitie* or your sordid past. I'm not trying to win your hand or your heart here, Captain Manners. In fact, we can skip the courtship rot altogether. I know you fancy me, Aiden. And yes, if you must have the words, I fancy you too. Can't you just let that be what it is? Can't you just allow a little bit of cheer to slip through that enduring pall of gloom? Can't you allow yourself to feel good for one nightfall? With me?"

This woman. Aiden studied his roguish guest. *Come on, buckaroo, she's practically giving it to you on a silver platter.* "The gods know you are well determined, aren't you?" *Caution meet wind.*

"You have no idea." Her doe-eyes returned.

"But I am quite curious," he began.

"Why you?" she finished.

"Well…yeah…"

"And here he goes fishing for flatteries already. Lovely guise, giftborn I must say. What more can a lass do? I've already told you I fancy you. And I've already told you I'm absolute rubbish with folk. So in the rare chance that I do manage to stumble upon a lad I fancy, I rather like to make an impression."

"And you've done that in spades."

"There is also the other matter to discuss," she said, "though I had rather hoped to do that in the after."

His appetite suddenly an afterthought, Aiden leaned back in awe of the creature sitting across from him. "What other matter?"

"You mentioned plans of traveling home soon…to Gallea's Grace."

"I told you that?"

"You did. The great worry of the eve, it was." She took another swig from his mug. "My troupe heads south in a few days, and we will be making a pass outside Gallea's Grace. You are more than welcome to join us if you like. Of course, you will be responsible for your own rations, but otherwise there is always room for another lost soul around the campfire."

Aiden watched Val in silence. Who was this mystery woman that suddenly possessed an answer to all of his bothers? And moreover, what drove her to give the faintest inkling about said bothers? At this point, the intrigue alone was enough to accept her charity. *Ever the foolhard, Aiden Ashborough.* It would seem the drink was not the only bad habit making the rounds these days.

A bygone smile began to take shape at the edge of his rekindled delirium.

What followed was something as though from a dream. Val was tipsy drunk, far more gone than he, but of all folk, who was he to judge?

In the spinning shadows of her starlit bedchambers, she ripped his shirt over his head and her mouth pressed against his. Aiden found her lips soft and full—delicate like a flower—precisely as he'd imagined them, and a heartbeat later, they altered, biting their way down upon his neck then to his chest and his abs before his trousers dropped to the floor.

Fucking hells. Of course, he was already at attention.

He felt the heat of her mouth breathing close against his hardness before her hands pulled away from the back of his legs. He glanced down at her as she began unlacing her boots and found his heart aflutter with feral excitement. He wet his lips as he watched her.

A second later, she stood, licked his cheek, hiccupped, and covered her mouth, giggling as she turned away. She worked her cloak and boots off as she crossed the flat to the other side of the bed. The catch of a match in the chamber's corner illuminated the room as it married to candle, and to his wonder, he found the space considerably larger than expected. There was a decent-sized bed, a bureau, and a bath at the other end. He was honestly surprised at the quality of the chamber, considering the downstairs portion, it appeared as though from a different establishment altogether. But such was a bother for a distant occasion, an occasion in which his cock wasn't out on display at full mast and desperately wanting.

Val leaned her scabbard against the bureau and offered him a mischievous smile as she passed him by, eyeing him from erection to icy blues before settling on a trio of buckets at the bath's stern.

Aiden shook his head incredulously as the sellsword proceeded to fill the bath with water, one bucket after the other. "So you've planned this then?" he ventured. His voice, the gods help him, suddenly taking on a more sensual presence.

"Get in," she slurred a response, pouring in the last of the three buckets.

He obeyed, stepping out of his trousers, removing his socks, and tiptoeing awkwardly across the creaking hardwood to the bath. The water was tepid as he sank in.

Silently, Val knelt down behind him once he settled and placed a cloth that smelled of lavender upon his shoulder, coursing it across and down his chest under the water's plane to his patch of pubic hair, and cupped it gently around his prick and balls. She stroked it up and down his shaft slowly, her grip tightening with each stroke causing his body to tense, and with her other hand, she guided his face sidelong into her warm lips, her tongue luring his into her mouth.

She released her grip of him and traced the cloth, now a sodden bunch, back up his stomach to his neck where she daubed at him attentively as though caring after a wounded patient. He fought the urge to pull her in with him, clutching the sides of the bath, and instead closed his eyes imagining her naked body and all the things he wanted to do to it. And there were far too many things. He wanted to taste her silky skin and the folds of her cunt, he wanted to ride her raw, from every angle imaginable, until bruises painted his—

"Sit up," she instructed, dipping the cloth under water again.

He complied, losing his focus, utterly beguiled. He was now hers to command apparently.

She wrung the water down his backside before placing the cloth against a shoulder blade, scrubbing and massaging deeply.

He became lost within her unexpected tenderness, falling into a place of solace, a place he hadn't found in quite some time, before he heard a splash at the other end of the bath. His eyes opened at the sound of footsteps, and he watched the wash-cloth sink between his legs.

He turned his head after her and gaped breathlessly as she unbuttoned her blouse and let it drop to the floor between them. Afterward, she waited for his eyes to meet hers and she unclasped the pins holding the linen wraps around her breasts.

The air between them thrummed with untamed energy, and her mouth twitched up ever so slightly.

He had thought it before fully shit-panned, and he was thinking it again stone-faced sober. This girl was simply too much.

Val placed a hand seductively against a breast, loosening the outer layer of wrap, and eased it behind her back, capturing it with her other hand, revealing something of her bosom size in the process, unwinding it once more until it came completely loose from her bust and drooped down to her waist.

Aiden's eyes widened in anticipation and she clutched an arm across her breasts just before their exposure. Her lips pouted suggestively and she turned away from him, blowing out the candle on the night table.

You've got to be fucking kidding me, his cock complained. Contrarily, his mind was somewhere the next galaxy over.

She stood in the ashen wash of starlight pouring through the bedchamber's half-curtained window and glanced sidelong over her shoulder at the archivist. Her elfin grin remained. Oh, she was most definitely toying with him now. And it was fucking irresistible.

Her arm lowered from its clutch across her bosom, and next, he could hear the jingle of her belt buckle coming unfastened. Casually, like a falling feather, she drifted down onto the bed beside her and shimmied off her trousers, lying still atop the mattress once she was completely naked. He gawked as she ran a hand through her tangle of curls before the silhouette of her arms stretched skyward.

"You just going to sit there in the bath all night then?" she called, her tone at once both sultry and shy.

At that, Aiden was up in more ways than one.

In a blink, he found her side, and a moment later, she straddled atop him, forcing him against the headboard. *You're a rough one, aren't you?* Without words, she urged him to taste of her breasts and any part of her body he craved for, as she fondled his shaft only inches below her cunt. Acquiescently, he kissed and sucked at her anywhere and everywhere his lips could find untouched skin until she grabbed a fistful of his long, damp hair and pulled his head away from her.

Neither one broke eye contact as she lowered herself slightly so the tip of his swollen cock grazed the lips of her cunt. She rubbed herself slowly, then roughly against the underside of his shaft, and he took a breast in his mouth, sucking at her velvety skin, tracing a tongue back and forth across her nipple.

"Yes, keep doing that," Val breathed heavily, shuddering. "I'm so wet," she whispered, and Aiden took the other breast in his mouth, licking around her areola before biting down. "Mmm," she moaned, wrapping her fingers around his hardness, and he slapped her ass, palming it violently, as she guided him inside her. A long moan followed from both as he pushed deeper into her wetness. She rode him hard, thrusting her hips forward in a gyrating motion, gripping the headboard for leverage. And it didn't take long before he could feel bruises forming around his pelvis from the sticky friction. He fancied every wicked stabbing ache of it.

They had become a tangle of hair, sweat, saliva, and savage pleasure.

He took her up along the small of her back, lifting her and laying her down beneath him, sliding back inside as he lowered himself against her. The transition was smoother than it had been with any other woman before, like their bodies were intended to fit with one another. They locked lips again as he plunged himself deeper and deeper inside of her, closing his eyes in concentration, determined to pleasure her to completion. He wanted nothing more than to see her wholly satisfied, though her moans were fastly becoming a problem, each one more stimulating than the last.

He tried to think of spell wards, listing them in backward order, listing them in any order at all.

Then she clasped him tight, a hand gripping each side of his buttocks, mindful of his game, forcing him in harder as she constricted her legs around his. Her moans came louder and louder still as she manipulated his movements to her delights and her nails dug into his backside, just below his shoulder blades, through layers of flesh, with the anticipation of orgasm, drawing forth lines of trickling blood that crawled lazily down his flank with each subsequent thrust. Between the sounds of her gratification and the sudden rush of pain conjured from her fingernails, he came first, unable to further suppress his body's urges. Its occurrence felt a seemingly inevitable consequence. Slowed by his sudden descent into ecstasy, he struggled mightily with each stroke thereafter.

"Stay with me," Val demanded as she rolled atop him, pinning him down again under knife-like fingers and clenching him inside of her as she gyrated against his shrinking manhood. "I'm so close," she repeated, breathlessly, over and over again, touching herself and grinding almost methodically against him until, at last, her movements began to gradually slow and her body became suddenly quite tense.

CHAPTER TWELVE

After the madness of Westerly's laboratory, Remy tried to find some shut-eye, but sleep would not have his company. His mind simply would not stop, racing from one horrible thought to the next as he stewed over Lieutenant Shore's ominous words.

He wound up haunting the halls of the barracks like some heartbroken cellar banshee until the morning, and eventually made his way outside into the tourney yard where he spent the better part of the afternoon masking his worries behind a gravedigger's glower and the scrape of a whetstone.

Rhymona passed him by sometime after midday whilst he watched his swordbrothers sparring in the distance, and she ordered a rendezvous at a lower city tavern after sup, rushing off before he could muster even the faintest breath of response.

Delight of delights, that, he thought in her ill-bred wake. *More Rhymona Curie high jinks.* How could he possibly decline?

For an establishment named the Angry Dog Alehouse, Remy found its accommodations surprisingly tame, if not dreary, and its few patrons woefully subdued. Not that he had frequented many alehouses in his day (to wit, he could almost unquestionably name all of them on a single hand), but any place with the word alehouse in its title rather painted a certain indelicate expectation, did it not? The gods know the silence was so loud he could hear what little bit remained of the evening's firewood crackling and hissing inside her low-burning hearth. In fact, the dingy, woodland smell was perhaps the only feature of the old haunt that did not wholly betray its name.

Verily, he and Curie looked about the roughest pair amidst the legless lot, a discovery from which he drew scant little satisfaction. Though, he was a damned long sight from the boy who fled Lancastle's stately courtyards last cycle, a damned long sight indeed with his patchwork shadow of a beard and long, greasy curls.

"And what is that face for?" Curie questioned from across the table, her roguish scowl in fine form, the dance of firelight from the candle betwixt them shifting the darkness from one side of her face to the other.

"What face?" he muttered as he set to packing his pipe.

"What face, he says. The face like someone just pinched a turd in your apple pie, mate. Have a bloody drink, why don't you? If not for yourself, then for the rest of us lot that have to take in your ugly, sullen mug." She washed the comment down with a swig of her own.

In spite of his dourness, he nearly split a smile at her brazen humor. It used to be he would scold any cur that came at him with such a vile tongue. Back when he initially joined the Kingswatch. Back when he had spirit and half a spine. Or at least back when he thought he did. And he had been horridly expectant in those early days at The Wall too, and doubly judgmental, thinking the world somehow owed him something, thinking that he was doing the rest a favor. But he quickly learned from his swordbrothers what expectancy earned you beyond the stones of court. In his case, it had been a shite burn name and a long series of japes and pratfalls to rival the savage songs written over the cycles at his family's expense. But now those days, too, were gone, it would seem, gone to the grave with his closest swordbrothers back in Brymshire and Hearth before her, leaving just himself and Curie to carry on the banner of the Black Stags Company.

He took up his cup in remembrance of those now fallen and eased it back, draining it to the half in three heavy quaffs. "Happy now?" he murmured before the brackish after-taste scrunched up his face. It was without a doubt the worst ale he had ever partaken.

Curie's scowl lightened by a shade at that. "There you go, lad," she said like a proper Southlands pub-crawler. "Bit of rot for your gut and hair for your chest." And she turned up another swill at the toast.

Remy wriggled the candle from its holder, turned its flame into his pipe, and pulled a massive drag followed by a series of smaller puffs to stoke the burn. It was his first drag since the innhouse horror in Brymshire, and mercy of Myrenna, was it a fine one.

"So I've given some thought to your grimoire's owner," Curie added afterward.

This ought to be rich. "And?" he offered, not expecting much.

"And, do you recall the knight in crimson? From the privy council?"

Tall, dashing, and mysterious? How could I forget? "Of course," Remy said. "He rather made an impression, I would say."

"Right. Well, I don't know about a woman named Tarboril. But I seem to recall a man hailing by such a name."

Beldroth did make mention of a brother. "And you believe this man to be the crimson knight?"

"Aye."

"And what else do you know of him?"

"Little to nothing really. Though he seems to carry some high favor amidst the council and Palatian guard both. As such, we may have some degree of difficulty finding an audience. Which begs the question, does it not, of the reasoning behind your own abdication."

The sudden turn in topics took him by surprise.

"I mean for fuck's sake, Toff, why in the nine hells would you abandon a bloody kingship to piss about this rotty bollocks?"

A fair curiosity. "I have my reasons," he answered tersely, hoping to table the matter.

"Oh, woe is me, is that it?" she mocked, her attitude as rude and patronizing as ever. "Life amongst the posh folk too tough for you then? Too much food and warmth for the young master, was it? Oh, but Mother didn't love you enough, did she? Tut, it's always the same old song with you lot, isn't it?"

The same old song? And what could you possibly know about royal affairs, Curie? Hands and elbows all over the table, an absolute dearth of manners or refinement. Doubtful they would let a mongrel like you anywhere near the citadel much less within the council chambers. "You don't know half as much as you think you do," he muttered before taking another heavy pull.

"What's that then? You have something to say about it?" She displayed a toothy smile and cupped a hand behind an ear. "By all means, Your Highness, regale away."

Her expression was jarring. He was not accustomed to regarding a woman's smile so openly. The women of court typically concealed their faces during such an act, either with a hand or, in the summer, with their fans of silk. It was considered proper etiquette after all. Something Curie obviously knew fuck all about. The gods know it was a ghastly wicked grin too. "And what would a robling like you know about a kingship anyway?"

"A robling?" Her smile somehow grew wider and more pompous. "If only." And just as quickly as it had spawned, the loathsome smile evaporated and her expression became quite grim and ugly. "I'll grant you I know fuck all about a kingship Remy, if that's what you need to hear. But that's not what this is really about, now is it?"

And here we go. If Remy was proficient at any one thing in all the world, it was sussing out a looming lecture. The gods know they had found him aplenty over the cycles. And he would be damned before he suffered another one from Rhymona bloody Curie of all folk. "I'll manage," he said dismissively before drowning another lengthy swig. It was just as horrid as the first chug and yet somehow a mite easier.

"You'll manage, will you? Because you've done such a brilliant job of managing thus far, haven't you? You were knocking at The Hood's Door by the time I got to you. More than like beyond it already. Nearly bled myself dry bringing your sorry arse back from the grave, I did."

"And you've had my gratitude, haven't you? What else would you have from me?"

"I'm afraid you have me all wrong," Curie said, her voice every measure as grim as her countenance. "I don't want anything from you, Toff. Quite the opposite, in fact. I'm trying to give *you* something." She shifted away from him. "The gods know but you're just as stubborn as he is, aren't you?"

"What?"

"Nothing. Forget it."

"Listen, I don't know who he is or what you're on about, but it's just as well we keep things simple between us, yeah."

Her eyes darted back up to his. "Is that how it is then? Fuck me, yeah? Rhymona fucking Curie, yeah. She thrives on discord, yeah. She's a fucking cunt, yeah? The heavens forbid you dally below your station for even a single fucking moment, Toff. Tut, but you're better than all that, aren't you? That's why you're out here, isn't it? So be better than all that, yeah. You're certainly going to have to be better than all that if you want this partnership to work. You want me by your side, you get all of me, yeah. I can't play fucking handmaid for you or whatever it was you were hoping for. And this is not me trying to get the better of you or learn you up on some old useless bollocks your Nan used to natter on about during beddy-bye. Trust, this is me putting in the effort, yeah, the genuine fucking effort, to help you. Something I'm well aware you're probably not much accustomed to. But here it is anyway. Take it for what it is, yeah. As you say, I know fuck all about a kingship. And I certainly won't argue on that. Truth's witness, I couldn't give a sloppy, wet shit about Lancastle or which fuckwit soils its dirty, decrepit throne, rot, rot, bloody rot, and onward. But you better believe I know plenty about suffering and doubly more about abuse and betrayal. About being made to feel like nothing. Like less than nothing most days. About feeling completely and utterly empty and unloved. About running from my troubles like you have, like anything and anywhere in all the world would be better than my current lot. Prize well, I know a great deal about that bit."

It was not exactly the response he had expected from the woman who supposedly cared about nothing and no one. Remy held her glower, her uneven bangs now concealing an eye, but she did not for even an instant back down.

"Given all that," she kept on, "it makes your mask rather useless on me, wouldn't you say?"

"My mask?"

"Your fucking mask, mate." She clutched a hand over her face. "It's all just woefully evident, isn't it?"

"You're bent."

"Tipsy at best, but I can still read your bollocks like a fucking book. You and me, we're more similar than you realize."

"I doubt that."

"Spoken like a true-blue unlettered fuckwit. You're a fucking shell, Remy. A stock character from a Chandiian tragedy or some such tripe. A one-note fucking cog, mate."

"Fuck off then."

"Well, that's what those buck-ass pretenders told you, right? Over and over again, wasn't it? Relentlessly? Every day? Like it was their fucking job? That you're nothing. That you're less than nothing. Less than shit even. And I'm sure there's worse than all that to go along with it. There's always fucking worse. But, finally, one day they broke you, didn't they? And that's precisely what you decided to become to cope with all the trauma they caused you. Little Remy put on his sad little nothing cog mask so that he wouldn't have to make the hard choice."

"Fuck you," he said, banging a fist on the table. "I did make the hard choice." His heart was hammering against his ribcage, tears welling behind his sneer, his chin raised high as a lord.

"You ran, Remy. Like a useless fucking craven. A shit choice by a shit king."

"I ran because I refused to let them control me any longer. I refused to be their pathetic little puppet. I refused to play their sick games."

Curie shook her head. "You should know better by now having lived in the court of courts for as long as you have. The game is never over. It merely alternates its players. No doubt living in Lancastle you've seen the wheel spin a dozen times over. You remain their puppet still, Remy, whether you accept it or not. They still control you. Even out here with the dogs."

"They have nothing to do with me out here."

"They have everything to do with you out here. Emyria's lament, they are the sole fucking reason you're out here, Remy. Not you. Try as you might to convince yourself otherwise. And they will control you until you confront them."

"Out of sight, out of mind," he snapped crossly. They were words he had told himself a thousand times before. Words he had convinced himself of. Words that felt more and more like a lie with each telling.

"And do you feel rid of them now?" Curie asked. "Truly? Or are they all you still think about? Like a festering wound."

"Rid enough," he spat.

"Rid enough, he says. Fuck *enough*. Any man who claims enough is all he needs is a fucking wanker, yeah."

"Then I'm a fucking wanker. Mercy of Myrenna, what else would you have me say? All that's going on right now and you choose to focus on this?"

"I'd have you say what you really want, Toff. Tell me one bloody thing you care about. Tell me one thing this second and I'll drop it."

"I don't know," he said, almost confused by his own words, grasping at any other explanation. But nothing arose. "I don't know what I really want. All right? I'm concerned with more important matters just now if you must know. What are you on about anyway? What is the purpose of all this?"

"The purpose?" Curie's expression was hell born. "The purpose is you lack purpose, Remy. And those that lack purpose lack drive. And those that lack drive become reckless little fuckups."

"You can keep your bloody platitudes. My business is my own. And I most certainly do not have to explain myself to the likes of you."

"And yet you've made your business my business with this little partnership, haven't you? And you assume I am just ready to take your side in all this. That I am ready to risk my life for you without question. And for the life of me, I can't help but wonder why that is. You think because you believe yourself king that you deserve my loyalty? Because you've some bygone usurper's blood swimming in your veins I am obligated to protect you? Fuck off, Remy. All you've proven thus far is that you're an entitled, over-privileged little shit-stain that deserves what bollocks the world has brought you."

"Then it would seem I have made a most horrible mistake with you, haven't I?"

And Curie's smile returned at that. "You have no idea how horrible. But trust it true, I might be the best mistake you've ever made." *Gods, I hope not.* "I must say, Toff, I would have figured a city boy like you would be hard up for a bit of narcissism. Isn't that what you lot do after all? Talk about yourselves all day?"

Remy felt his lips bending toward a smirk. He didn't much appreciate being lumped in with the lot, as it was so succinctly put, but she wasn't altogether wrong.

"Just answer me this one question. One last question and I will drop it all. Sound fair?"

"Fine," he allowed with a sigh.

"You say you needed to be rid of Lancastle. A place that represents your family, your home, your birthright, everything that most folk hold near and dear. Why is that?"

"Because," he said, and his mind began to wander. He thought of his mother, the Queen, of Marsea and Jules, and then of the beady-eyed wretches of the royal council. And he closed his eyes.

"Because?" Curie echoed.

"Because they were turning me into something I despise."

"And what is that?"

His eyes opened. "You said one question."

"One question provided I get an actual answer. You want me as your partner I need to know what sort of man I'm working with. You understand. Now, what do you despise?"

And with the question returned a violent ringing to his ears coupled with a face he hadn't thought about in nigh on a cycle. It was a face he had gone to great measures to forget. "They wanted me to kill a man," he said, and the words hung in the air between them like prey in a spider's web.

"And did you?"

He remembered Ezra Culver's pale, twisted face in the brilliant cast of starlight. His manic, bloodshot eyes. His bloodstained chin.

"I remember the sister moons were so bright that night." He swallowed hard and looked away from her to the ghoulish figures hunched atop their stools against the bar top. "As though the gods were holding a lantern over me. Watching me. Judging me. Condemning me." A prickling sensation washed over him. "It was my eighteenth birthfall and, of course, they got me good and soused. Honestly, it began as one of the best nights of my life. But the gods know, I was such a fool. I should have seen it coming. I should have realized something was off by the way they were acting. But I didn't want to see it. I wanted their acceptance. It was all I wanted. It was all I cared about back then. And I let them take advantage of me in the hopes that I might gain it."

"They, their, them," Curie echoed, leaning in closer. "Who are they, their, them, Toff?"

"The brothers Harver of course. Vaustian. Ganedys. My stepfather."

"Your stepfather?"

"Raelan Harver. There were others as well," he added sullenly. "After the festivities, Raelan and Gan led me on a stroll, promising a great surprise. And at the time I was too drunk and blind and hopeful to question them. I suspected they were taking me to a prostitute or some such nonsense. Especially considering it was Gan leading the march, a brothel was not by any stretch out of the question. The gods know he teased me mercilessly about my virginity over the cycles. It wasn't until we passed through the eastern gate that I started to become nervous. And it wasn't too much longer in the after that we came upon a small copse where I found a gathering of robed figures concealed under cloak. By then I'd crumbled to bits inside. Instantly, I knew something horrid foul was afoot. And the thought of mine own death came to bare. Especially when I began to recognize some of their voices. They made little effort to mask their voices, honestly. Most I knew to be aristocrats, councilmen, guild associates, and such the like."

Remy took a swill from his mug, and Curie leaned back, never once looking away from him.

"For weeks leading up to my birthfall, Raelan kept telling me there would be a spot opening up on the small council. And being the expectant little twit I was, I thought quite little of it back then. Not once, not one bloody time, did I question how that might come about." He took a long pull from his pipe and held it in, his head wading in his reborn guilt. "They had him stripped bare in the middle of their circle. Bound to timber. His tendons severed. His tongue cut from his throat. And they handed me a blade." He remembered the halting of his heart then, the slowing of his breath in the cold night air, and the weight of the knife inside his closed fist. "I refused it at first. I couldn't believe what they were asking of me. I couldn't accept it. This drew some threats and scathing remarks, of course, and sobered me up quite fastly. And so Raelan came forth and explained to me if I did not comply I would soon after join Sir Ezra in his dreadful fate. He said he could not stop the others if it came to it. That he would not stop them. And so I tried to run away." He recalled how the featureless trees spun crossly about his mad dash and how the forest floor clawed out at him as he neared the eastern gatehouse. "But they sent their quickest after me, trained soldiers, toppers, and cutthroats and the like, and as you might have imagined, they had scant little trouble catching me up."

He remembered the group's laughing and taunting once he had been returned to the circle, bruised and bloodied. He especially remembered Gan's drunken guffaw, like a braying ass, and wanting nothing more than to plunge the knife through his windpipe. Anything to silence the big, dumb oaf's insufferable delight.

"It was Vaustian that offered me the blade this time. The killer of mine brother and the usurper of mine father's throne. The man who took everything from me before I even had a chance to fend for it." He remembered Vaustian's eyes as he offered him the knife's hilt. They were like stone, wholly devoid of emotion, utterly pitiless. "It seemed fair that I might take my chance and run him through right then and there as he did Desmond all those many cycles ago, that I might earn something back for my family, that I might make something new of my sullied name, but no such boldness found me. Such thoughts were merely romantic nonsense. For such an attempt would most assuredly result in mine own death." Remy took another drag and breathed it out quickly. "Besides, I knew nothing of the boy that was my elder brother. Honestly, Desmond seems more a fiction to me than an actual person that once existed. And so the thought crept in, some bit of sanity, I suppose, in hindsight. Why risk my life for a ghost? What good would it prove? What all could it possibly change?

"And so I took the hilt into my hand and examined its features in the starglow. It appeared every measure as unremarkable as any ordinary skinner's knife. And yet I can still imagine it perfectly, as though it were a thing I had constructed with mine own hands. And as I approached Culver, I remember praying, hoping against hope, to unlock a scenario in which I did not have to take his life, but I found only a lonesome sort of silence for my efforts. There was no miraculous answer. No divine revelation. No merciful epiphany. No intervention by the gods. In the end there was only myself, drunk, sore, and exhausted, the infernal blade, and the mute, crippled ruin of Ezra Culver."

"This may come across cold, mate," Curie began, "but it sounds to me like you did what you had to do. Sometimes there is no good outcome, only the lesser of two evils."

"And murder is the lesser of two evils?"

"I reckon it's subjective. But it seems to me he was a dead man long before you came along. You were merely the bladehand. And you more than like did him the favor considering."

Remy had no doubts that a far worse fate would have found Culver had he not seen to the deed himself. The Covenant was not known for their empathy toward traitors. The gods know, his father had been proof of that. But how could death possibly be the best outcome?

"I've found that there are far more killers about than goodly folk these days," Curie added. "That is just the world we live in, yeah. Dog eat dog. Every arsehole for his self."

"It shouldn't be like this," Remy said, feeling every bit a child at the telling, but the words refused to be denied. "The world shouldn't be this way."

"Mayhaps not," Curie agreed, "but to the contrary, no one is completely innocent, now are they?"

"There must be accountability," Remy argued. *Hypocrite*. He thought of the father and daughter in Brymshire.

"Is that what this is then? Is that why you've exiled yourself? You think this is you holding yourself accountable?"

"It's all I can do, isn't it?"

"No. It's not all you can bloody do, Toff." A violent calm roiled in her smoky orbs. "For fuck's sake. The world is not black and white. And not all folk that kill are killers." *Says the obvious killer*. "You need to hear this, mate. You deserve to hear this in the worst way imaginable. Whether you choose to listen or not, that is your choice. But trust there is no denying the truth of it. We're all proper fucked in the end. Every last one of us. Letters on stone, we are. And for the most of us, that's if we're lucky. We've all got a number, yeah. You. Me. Those fat fuckers at the bar over there. No, especially those fat fuckers at the bar over there. And we're all hoping the same thing when it all comes down to it, now aren't we? That the sad fucker sitting there next to us is ultimately more fucked than we are."

He stared daggers into the impossible creature settled across from him. Honestly, it was all he could do.

"That said, it seems to me there must have been a reason for why this Culver fellow found himself in such a nasty predicament in the first place, yeah. What percentage of folk do you think end with their last breaths tied to a torturer's rack? And what percentage of that percentage do you reckon deserved to end up there? It's not fair what they made you do, Remy. It's shit. Horrid shit. Cruelty for the sake of cruelty. And it's senseless. But you of all folk know how cruel this world can be. It's a right fucking bastard to most of us by the end and there will be plenty more to come. There's no sense stewing in it as you are. It's done, yeah. Over. And there's nothing more to be done about it. And no amount of suffering will change that fact.

"Now I don't necessarily agree with your utterly ridiculous standards, mate. Obviously. But you want to do right by Culver? You want to find some measure of forgiveness? Some measure of accountability? Some measure of justice in all this? Then I say you stop living with your old thoughts thinking that your shit don't stink just as bad as the rest of us, yeah? And you pick up your blade there and you hunt down every last fucker that robbed you of your goodness, and when you find him you make him feel it, yeah, you make him feel every last hell-forged inch of it, make him beg screaming for The Hood's Door, and once you've done what needs doing, once you've finally had enough, once you've made what right could be had of it, you finally give the rotten bastard what he wants and you feed his sorry arse through it."

Remy said nothing to her rousing words. He found them quite inspiring, all told. Though he couldn't help but wonder what sorts of horrors she had unbound in life that would spit her back out this way. However, in lieu of another darkly tale, he gripped the handle of his mug and slung back what remained of his rotgut.

And this time he rather thought it tasted just as it should.

CHAPTER THIRTEEN

For the first time in weeks, Aiden awoke in an actual bed. It was a bit unsettling, to have it honest, as unnatural as his sobriety and his freshly washed hair, as though he had somehow stolen away another's life, and likewise swindled the gods. And what's more, he actually felt somewhat well rested, proper fit too, not falsely gained, as though leeched from The Spellbind. Doubly unsettling, that. Almost surreal. He half expected to peek out the window and behold a lush green patch of garden and a perfectly unblemished white picket fence. A smile nearly came to light in spite of his guilty conscience before a breath caressed the back of his neck.

"Caitie?" he said rolling over. But it was not Caitlyn Ellsbury he found beside him as the prior night's events caught up with him.

"The maidens know, I am swiftly growing to hate that bloody name," Val grumbled into her pillow.

"Shit," Aiden said, his face scrunching up nervously, and his heart set to the race. *Well done, fuckwit, peak form.* "Um...yeah...sorry..."

Val tugged the bedsheets back over her head, and an edgy silence descended.

"So about last night..." Aiden began as the evening's events returned to him. And what more could he say, truly? Not only had Val offered him a haven and a warm bed for the night, but she had scrubbed him clean, soused as she was. As clean as he had been in weeks no less.

"We don't have to," Val said with a ghoulish murmur from under the covers.

Submissively, Aiden slunk beneath, tethered to the siren of the cintas grove. "Someone that hates the morning more than I, I daresay I thought such an affair nigh impossible."

He spooned alongside her, pressing his manhood against her bottom, and kissed her shoulder blade on the spot of a tattooed star. He found much of her body was painted in colorful intricately detailed inks. A sleeve raced up her left arm from her knuckles over the arch of her shoulder and across her backside, revealing a mural that comprised everything from beasts and maidens to scripts and symbols captured twixt flowers, waves, clouds, and stars. It was a dream-like assemblage to say the least, almost as though stolen from another world far, far away—as if the sellsword needed anything more to add to her already mystifying allure. Softly, he placed a hand upon her hip and eased it across her stomach toward her inner thigh. He loved the way she felt, smooth as silk, and his hand wandered deeper, his fingers pressing slowly into her.

"You have me wrong, giftborn," she said, rolling back against him, her eyes cracking open, and Aiden held her lilac haunters, fighting the overwhelming urge to immediately steal away at her lips. "I've no quarrel with the morn at all. It's the morn that takes offense to me."

"Is that so?"

"Mmm."

"Well, as it happens, I may know of a place where morning no longer exists." He regretted the words almost instantly, but with Val, he found he couldn't help himself. It was something about her. Something he could not yet explain that compelled him to be completely and irrevocably honest with her.

"You don't say." She smiled sleepily, brushing her wild curls from out of her face.

"You believe me a liar?" he asked, apparently tossing caution to the fire.

"A liar? No. A proper mad lunatic, mayhaps."

Aiden showed a puckish grin. "Well, there is that."

"But I'm a curious lass, aren't I? And in the interest of such a curious affair one of my...shall we say, condition, can't help but indulge. So humor me, giftborn. What would one name such a lovely place? This place with no morn?"

"You're serious? You want to know?"

"Yes, of course. Are you backing out on me?"

A man of sound mind would pass it off as a jape, you know. But you are not a man of sound mind now are you, Aiden? "Hardly." He smirked shrewdly. "It has many names, to wit. The Drag. The Pale. The Tomb of the White Dragon. Yvemathira's Fall. Gloomerton."

"Gloomerton? Surely you've made that one up."

"Did I?"

"It sounds like a place out of The Winterbury Tales."

"Tut, Mervold wishes he was so clever," Aiden derided.

"Stars save me. You're bloody impossible."

"I've heard those amongst the ports, sail-warders and the like, have taken to naming it The Ghost Isle. No doubt you've heard of that one then?"

"Mayhaps." Her smile was kind and infectious.

"Most folk around these haunts name it The Spellbind though. It is a place without time, without consequence, without worry."

"Surely you speak of limbo."

"Limbo? There's a new one. I believe it more akin to paradise, if you must know."

"There's nothing new about limbo, giftborn. It is what the Amendeiya names the plane twixt ours and Hers."

"Hers?"

"Of She who dawns the endless night. Exiled, loathed, cast into plight. You know." Aiden pursed his lips and played the fool. "Surely you've heard the old hearthfire haunter before. The one named amongst The Old Ones as Sin."

Stars save me? Deiya verses? The gods only know how I didn't pick up on it before. "You're a cloth maiden?" To Val, the question must have seemed completely out of the blue.

"Was a cloth maiden," she corrected. "A lifetime ago. When I was but a penniless stray. I needed a place that would take me in without question. A place that was safe. And a nunnery is the last place to turn away a broken, naïve little girl, now isn't it? Another mindless sheep for the flock, yeah."

"So I've bedded a cloth maiden then?" He decided to keep the mood light a bit longer. It would seem his new friend could be quite quick at the turn to despair.

"And here he is. Another dreamer with a bucket list, is it? Am I merely a fresh tally for the young master then?"

"No..." he thought on it a beat longer, "and mayhaps yes? I don't know. I don't think I knew it was there before just now." A devious grin suddenly claimed his countenance. "Can I call you Sister Val next time?"

"Next time? A bit presumptuous, wouldn't you say?"

"Only a bit."

"The maidens know, I liked you better as a bumbling drunkard."

"I've been saying this for cycles now," he preached. "Finally, someone opens an ear."

"And you were saying about The Spellbind?" she asked, bringing the conversation full circle.

"Hold on a tick. That's all I get about Sister Val then?"

"For now," she said cleverly. "And to be more precise I wasn't actually a Sister, I was a Rin."

"A Rin? It sounds like a child's pet."

"Woefully, you're not far off on that. Rin are the handmaids to Ve'Lir. And the Ve'Lir are the Sisters-in-training, so to speak. Something like royalty in the world of organized religion. We Rin were allowed to worship and take in devotions and even attend lectures, but we also had to see to the menial duties about the nunnery. Kitchen chores, dressmaking, supply runs into town, and such the like."

"Well, stars save me," he teased, collecting his hands in prayer.

"Is that you then making fun of me, giftborn?"

"Making fun of a cloth maiden? I would never be so obscene."

"Mmmhmm, you're aiming for a right good smack, you are."

"Oh yeah? And would that be across my left cheek or my right? And furthermore, across my face cheek or my bum?"

Val couldn't stifle a laugh. "Snakes alive, with how much shite you're gushing about, it's tough to tell much of a difference, isn't it?"

"You know I'm fucking adorable and you love it."

"And you know I'm not going to let this bit about The Spellbind go, don't you? No matter how long you try to stall."

She's a clever one, this one. "You should know it's going to hurt like the nine getting there." He rolled over, stretching for his trousers on the floor, and began rummaging through his pockets. "Ice or fire?" he asked, retrieving a pair of binders, one of sapphire, the other of scarlet.

"Surprise me," said the sellsword and apparent former cloth maiden without delay. As if such a creature was even capable of being surprised.

When he shifted back to his lover, he found her sitting up and running a shallow red line across her open palm with a ring razor. "Bloody hell." He couldn't believe his own surprise. "Not your first jaunt, I take it."

"Once before," she admitted, "many quints past."

"And here I thought I was about to take your bind card." He sat up, cross-legged, facing her directly.

"Don't you wish it so?"

He smiled. "Aren't you going to ask me where I got them?"

"I trust you." She smirked. "I mean, I already let you sample the goods, didn't I? Twice, if I recall proper. And I let you stay the night. I can only assume if you wanted me a corpse you'd have already seen to its passing by now."

"Sound logic I reckon."

"Besides, half the swill in The Ports is fermented with sea grime these days and the other half tastes like week-old bath-water. I'd say I am pretty well immune to any shit poison one might use to admix a binder."

"You are sure about this then?"

"Tough to be sure about anything these days, isn't it? Yet here we are anyway."

"Here we are anyway," he echoed, easy-breezy, as he tossed the scarlet candle over his shoulder. "A bit of ice, a bit of stone. A bit of flame, a bit of bone." He took her hand in his, crushing the blood candle between them. "Last chance to back out."

She squeezed tighter. "Not a chance, giftborn. Not for all the coin in the commonwealth."

"It's your funeral, Sister."

"Oh, ye of little faith."

At that he smiled and closed his eyes, concentrating on the candle's form, capturing its essence within his mindscape, and began to channel all of the heat in his body toward it. Almost instantly the wax began to soften. He could practically smell The Spellbind's swaying fields already, free of the city refuse and effluence. They had always reminded him of home, of the farmhouse and her boundless country, of his mother and their many afternoons spent out on the porch reading and debating over anything and everything, of wandering out amidst his father's vineyard in the lagging hours of dusk listening to Tam serenade the stars of nightfall with lilt after lovely lilt. He opened his eyes, clever in his craft, confident in his creation, and focused on the task at hand.

"Once we are inside the ward, we must let go from each other or risk coming out the other side a mongrel."

"A mongrel?"

"It's when two—" he began before halting. He could feel her anxiousness through the candle's meld, try as she might to hide it with japery and nonchalance, and thought the better of it. "You know what, you're probably better off not knowing."

"Such a tease," she said, holding strong to her cool façade.

"As I'm sure you are well aware, you will feel a great swell of agony from the ward's vacuum. It will feel as though your skin is being flayed away bit by bit and your innards are being ripped and torn from your belly. This is normal. It is the extraction process, the body being separated from the soul and consciousness."

"Oh, is that all then?"

"You will come within breaths of The Hood's Door. It will feel like your lungs are being crushed betwixt a closing vise. This, too, is normal. Transporting the mind from the body is an unnatural affair after all, is it not? And there must be some repercussions for defying the gods, yeah? But fear not, it is only your mind fighting the split. Your body will remain in a restorative stasis after extraction, exactly how you left it. And you will return to find that none of your conjured injuries will have come to pass. You might even find that some of your old ones have been cleansed completely, including the entry fee." He could feel the pulse of her heart through the freshly made opening across her palm. "All you need do is trust in the process, Val, and let it guide you."

"Gored, drawn, and quartered before breakfast. Why, it must be my birthfall."

"And she takes to the gallows humor. A woman after mine own heart."

"Easy there, Galloway."

Galloway? The gods know Cal would've pissed himself to hear that one. "Yeah, yeah, yeah," he returned. "Ready?"

"Re—" she began before he tugged her forward, silencing her with a kiss. She hesitated but for a moment at first, pulling away from him only slightly, before pushing back even harder.

The gods know her lips were swiftly becoming his favorite thing in all the world. *Bloody simpleton.* Rhymona would have had a blade against his bollocks at such a dare, and Caitie would have scolded him until the sun fell from the heavens. But Val took it all with a grain of salt. Almost as if she were inviting his chaotic nature, the bloody temptress. Truth be told, at such a turn, he didn't know whether to be smitten or terrified of such an agreeable creature.

"What was that for?" she asked afterward, playing the innocent with consummate talent.

"In case you're torn to bits in the void, of course," he said, as though chivalry were yet still alive. "Also, I was hoping to distract you."

"Distract me?"

"Reckon I was a bit early."

"Stars save me. Must the young master always carry on so awkwardly?"

"That's odd," he said staring at their clasped hands perplexed.

"What?"

"Usually I'm pretty good at timing these kinds of things."

An eyebrow arched. "Everything all right then?"

"Yes, brilliant, of course," he offered an easy smile, "any second now."

"Oh," she uttered and squeezed his hand tight. It was obviously a reactionary squeeze.

"There it is," he said knowingly, their eyes meeting. "You're feeling a prickling sensation, yeah?"

"To say the least," she said studying the area of her arm whence it came. "Oh," she grunted again, squeezing tighter. "Maidens' mercy. What in the? Motherfuck—" she cried out as the melted candle began to glow a feverishly bright blue.

"Don't fight it," the archivist said. "It'll make it worse."

"Fucking hells, Aiden," she managed through clenched teeth. "What is happening to me?" Suddenly she began to tremble like a leaf as her tiny arm hairs raised and goose pimples sprouted across her skin.

"The candle's magical properties are poisoning your bloodstream," he explained. "I thought you said you had done this before."

"Yeah, like a decade ago and I was three sheets to the nine and baked on shufa at the time." She winced, her teeth grinding, her grip crushing. "Oh, maidens mine, make me thine instrument. Where doubt may dwell… oh, son of a—" she groaned. "It feels like bloody death."

Through their blood pact he could feel every excruciating measure of her surging agony. "That would be an accurate summation, actually," he said, enduring.

"Come again?"

"You are presently in the process of dying. Only for a second though, two at most, that's all it takes to transition."

"What?"

"Only the dead can pass through a translocation rift," he expounded. "This is normal," he promised, panting against their shared pain. "You've done it before, remember." He tried to sound reassuring. "Just take a breath and it will all be over in a minute."

"I can't," she gasped for air, her eyes widening, "breathe—"

"I know. I have to let you go now. Just let it take you. I will be right there on the other side." He smiled artlessly, unsure of what else to do to make it easier. "Think happy thoughts."

And at that, her eyes rolled back into her head, his following, and his vision became an endless sapphire film. Concurrently, Val's voice shattered into fragments of sound that echoed from near and far as though trapped within a vast, many-layered labyrinth. He wanted to scream as the melted wax began to expand, both inside and out, racing up his forearm, a creature most ravenous, but it was born of such a bitter cold that it confiscated all prospects of exhalation. The wax tore and pinched at him as it elasticated upon his flesh until such effect that he was fully cocooned within the form-fitting resin. Once swathed inside the hardened chrysalis, an errant drifter kept by the silky allure of some fresh gossamer solace, his sight returned to him and he was promptly hurled rearwards into a conflagrant darkness that hissed and whistled about his rimy armor's exterior. Unfamiliar visions, frayed and ethereal, shocked his mindscape as his petrified body was transported through the flickering maelstrom by a strange opaque serpent-like entity. Despite his paralysis, the turbulence from the rift ravaged his innards to ribbons, twisting his skin taut about his bones. It felt as though he were bound at his waistline and being dragged to the ocean's depths by a galley anchor. Until suddenly the substance began to melt away, extricating itself from his flesh bit by bit, in much the same gruesome manner it had gained attachment, shedding its coat into the whirlwind behind his plight like chunks of falling snow, as gravity began to restore its worth, and the world shown true to his sights yet again in the approaching horizon. At once, the snow became as ash inside the colorless field above, then below as the vortex shifted directions one last time expelling him into the grass a few yards behind Val.

Just as quickly as the transition process had begun, it was settled, the total transport enduring less than a minute's count, and in the after, he found Val on her knees staring off into the far winds at the infamous elder tree. Though it loomed quite some distance away, it was of such a mass that it practically swallowed the entire horizon, lording over all within its dreary haunt. Dozens of branches, thick and twisting, reached far and wide like the tentacles of a great, monstrous sea beast, though some had long since splintered and toppled under their own weight.

"Felt that one in my cunny," Val murmured.

"Yeah, they're like that sometimes," the archivist returned.

The wind was stagnant, nigh to nonexistent, banished evermore from the grace of Thira's scattering tomb. And her sky was a melancholic, deep-set purple, like the cast of a freshly ripened bruise. To sight, there was nary a star or a cloud to be found for fear of their fallen master's wrath. Yet ash, thick and ample, rained down all around them, blanketing the wilting fields and surrounding wood.

Val caught a flake in her hand, and it cracked at the touch, partially crumbling into dust. "Is this...ash?"

"It is the work of Yvemathira's ward," Aiden answered, and he drew in a heavy breath. The air smelled pure. Pure as a distant countryside far away from any city or township.

"Maidens' mercy," Val gasped a moment later as a phantom suddenly appeared, laced in pale sheer dressings, gliding through her, before disappearing and reappearing a short distance away from them.

"Echoes," Aiden explained, walking toward the horizon. "They are the remnants of guests past. Lingering memories, if you will. They cannot harm you."

"It had no face," she said as more began to reappear and disappear all around them.

"Memories fade," he said, enjoying his travel companion's lack of experience. "We are but physical manifestations in this place ourselves. Projections. Apparitions. And though the mind understands this as truth, it still may react to events as though they are actually occurring. Though fear not," he continued, boldly, "you will find no peril in this place, only serenity and healing."

"I could feel it inside me," she breathed, removing herself from the path of another approaching phantom as they traveled. "It was beset by an intense sadness."

"Often memories have emotions attached to them. And sometimes those very emotions are all that are keeping it alive. The feeling will soon pass."

"Are there not others about? Like us?"

"Of course," Aiden said, "they will be the ones with faces." He was beginning to question if she had actually been here before. Drunk or no, high or no, one would think something such as a faceless phantom would be a rather memorable unveiling. But he decided against the turn to skepticism. He was enjoying himself after all. There was no need to spoil such a good thing. "The Spellbind typically projects present visitors far more accurately. Though depending on their knowledge base, we may or may not be able to communicate with them."

"How did The Spellbind come to be this way?"

"All Yvemathira," Aiden said as he dipped below one of the elder tree's enormous branches and rose to trail his hand across it. "It is believed that The Spellbind was created upon her fall and this very tree is its foundation, stretching for many leagues in every direction. And that before her final breath she bound her soul deep within the elder tree's depths, fusing with it the last of her magic, creating a ward that could only be crossed by those with the right bloodline or knowledge base." He pressed his hand firm against a gnarled appendage. "If you place a hand against her, you can feel her moving about inside."

Val followed his instruction, her curiosity gaining the better of her. "Maiden's mercy, it's as cold as steel." She pulled her hand away, and it was stained charcoal as though she had been smearing dried ink about a canvas.

"The tree's original life source has been dead for many centuries now, leaving much of its structure a hollow, empty thing. Yvemathira alone has kept it standing and prospering all this time."

"Surely you're on a fool's charade," Val said.

"Take a gander to the east."

Val followed the archivist's direction and through the ashfall found a series of tall, spiked pillars rising from the ground about a stone's throw away.

"Go on," he continued. "Have a closer look if you don't believe me."

"The stars save me," the sellsword uttered.

Pillars of bones towered high above them to nearly three times their height, curving inward like that of a ribcage, and a trio of faceless phantoms danced amongst them, twisting in and out of the dead dragon's remains. Further down lay the beast's skull, long since rotted and flensed, resting lopsided only a short distance from its high arcing torso.

Aiden watched as Val traced a finger down the length of one of its front fangs. It was nearly the length of a sword. In its day, there was no doubting it. This particular dracari was a most magnificent and terrifying creature.

"So it's true then?" she asked, turning to the archivist, a gaze of awe cast fervently about her countenance.

"I believe it true," he said, "unquestionably."

"So what? She is the tree now? Or how does this work exactly?"

"Something of the like. I can't say for sure. Magic is a most queer creation after all. But I believe she is meant to be the protector of this place. And I believe she is the only thing left severing our world from that of the nether. Though it would seem even the great and powerful Eld are susceptible to The Hood's taking in the end. And I believe Thira's taking will soon come to pass. Her ties to the world of the sentient are diminishing at an ever-increasing pace and have been for some time now."

"But you don't know that for sure," Val said anxiously.

"Ah, but I do," he returned. "I can feel her life force when I am in this place. I can hear her song. Because I, like all who are blessed with the gift, am her progeny. Her blood, her magic, her spirit, flows through my veins, however diluted it may now be."

Val glanced back at the elder tree. "And what do you reckon happens if her connection is broken?"

"Now there's a question I would kill to have an answer for." His lips thinned and his expression became quite grave. "Let us just hope it is not a trial for our lifetimes."

"Wait. What is that?" Val asked, and Aiden followed her gaze back in the direction of the elder tree.

Some distance beyond, slowly approaching, there trudged forth what appeared to be a misshapen figure. And at the very instant he glimpsed its crooked shape, a strange, alien sensation washed over him. It appeared quite different than anything he had ever seen inside The Spellbind before. Its definition was quite vivid, almost angry, screaming through the ashen pallor like that of a stray inkblot on parchment.

"Something is off," Aiden said as he squinted to bring the figure into better focus. And as he pried, he was assaulted by a high-pitched hissing sound that instantly transported him back to his dream from a couple nights prior, right before the cramping in his leg took hold. There was scant similarity in the build of the hooded figure from his dream and the pitiful thing before him, and yet something about the pair struck him as analogous.

"What do you mean?" Val asked.

"I'm not quite sure yet." He took a few steps forward, fighting the residual fear from his freshly conjured nightmare, even though every rational intuition within pleaded with him to stay put. "But whatever it is, it cannot possibly be good."

"Not good as in…?" Val looked worried. "I thought nothing bad could happen here."

Aiden turned back to her, his expression grim. "I thought so too."

"And what is that intended to imply?"

"Stay here," he said apprehensively.

She scowled. "Well, that's just not going to happen, now is it?"

Aiden studied his travel companion then, her words bold and unyielding, her eyes well determined. The gods know he certainly hadn't taken her for the heroic sort. Yet here she was. "This is quite serious, Val."

"And so am I."

"I have never seen anything like this before. Whoever, whatever, that is, they are causing a terrible disturbance in The Spellbind."

"I don't care. I won't be left to the lurch." Her glare was as fierce as he had ever seen before and that included the worst of Rhymona's infamous howlers.

"Then stay behind me," he warned, unwilling to argue the point further.

The sellsword nodded her compliance, and they both watched the figure curiously as they cautiously advanced, side by side. Upon closing the gap, the figure was revealed to be humanoid after all, though horribly hunched, and using what appeared to be a downturned sword as a cane to keep upright. Some short footfalls later, it took notice of their approach and began yelling and flailing its arms about wildly.

Aiden halted, and Val held tensely beside him. "It would appear he is in need of our aid," Val said, turning to the archivist. "He may be wounded."

"This doesn't make any sense. You can't feel pain here."

"Mayhaps it is a ruse then."

"A ruse? To what end? It's not as though he can bloody well rob us."

Val shrugged. "Just a thought...I don't know."

"Physical pain is impossible in The Spellbind," he said to himself, working through the quandary, and scratching his abdomen, unwilling to let it pass, and thusly something of note Rhymona once told him filtered into his recollection. "Unless—" His eyes fixated on the figure once more. *Could it be?*

"Unless what?" Val queried, her worry yet still prevalent.

"Unless he is actually here," he answered. "As in physically here. As in he knows the true location of The Spellbind or somehow lucked upon it."

"Which begs the question, does it not," Val posited, "if he is physically here and we're not, can we actually offer him any aid?"

"The gods know this is supremely fucked," Aiden said, nearing peak exasperation. "I hate to say it, but I haven't the faintest, Val. This is wholly unexplored territory for me."

"It's all right," she said. "We're in this thing together, yeah? Come what may."

He turned to the sellsword with a miserable glower, and her warm expression eased his turmoil, though only slightly.

"We have to try, right?" she asked.

The archivist's voice abandoned him at her question. His instincts told him to cut their connection right then and there, but his curiosity hungered for more. There were just too many lingering questions, questions that would haunt him forever if he robbed himself of the chance to ask them.

"Aiden," Val began again. "We have to try." And without waiting for a response or acknowledgment, she bound off in a full sprint toward the bellowing figure.

"Shit," the archivist grumbled before taking to her trail. "Come on, Aiden," he chided under his breath as he chased after her, "let's just have a nice little morning dip in The Spellbind. It'll be fun. She'll love it. What could possibly go wrong? Fucking knobend." *Anything to get your dick wet, right?*

"Fools!" the hooded figure scolded as they drew near, brandishing the sword out at them. "Stay back. Not one step closer."

"Are you mad?" Val dared. "We were coming to your aid."

The figure was attired to the uppermost button in the blue and gold magian regalia of the highland kingdoms and hobbling about with what appeared to be authentic Kingswatch steel. "I was warding you away. Not bidding you toward me. Damned young'uns never bloody listen." He ripped the cowl back from his head revealing a shock of stark white hair and a pair of otherworldly, clouded, white orbs.

Upon seeing the man's troubled face, Aiden knew immediately that his first inclination was correct. It had been a most horrible mistake to engage him. "Do as he says," Aiden commanded. "Back away."

"What?"

"Now," he rumbled. It was a tone he was quite unaccustomed to taking. It reminded him of his father and their many spats.

"I don't understand," she said.

"We need to be leaving." He took her hand.

"What is happening? What's wrong with him?"

"I don't know. And I don't care to know." Aiden tried to pull her toward him, but she was holding firm to her position, unwilling to relent.

"Aiden, stop," she quibbled, wresting her hand away from his. "You need to explain this right now. Is this some sort of cruel lark?"

"A lark? Don't be daft." He hadn't meant it to sound so harsh.

"Excuse me?" she retorted.

"Apologies, please, just take a step back with me." *The gods know she was a fiery lass.*

"What's happening to him?"

"I don't know, Val. I have never seen anything like this before." He took her by the hand again. "We need to be going. There's nothing more we can do for him."

"You must…warn the kingdoms," the man choked with an eldritch cant, struggling just to form words. It was nothing at all like the wroth voice that had chastised them only moments before.

"Not another step further, sir," Aiden warned as he tugged Val away from the ghastly fiend. "We are leaving, just as you bade us."

:Come famine and sorrow, hunt, wither, and splinter the damned who defy the dead hounds of her winter,: a third, far more sinister persona addressed them.

"What?" Aiden inquired.

"Nightsbridge is a ruin," the man rasped on, his tone changing once again. "Van Wyck is dead, a walking corpse by now no doubt. The King's Wall…fallen. The Kingswatch…compromised. You must…inform… Oathsworn—" The man crumbled to a knee as a series of spasms overtook him accompanied by an uncanny clicking sound, and his head began to twitch and thrash about unnaturally. "My name…Solomon…Darrow," he coughed, "arch-mage…of—"

His head stopped twitching suddenly, his eyes narrowing with malefic intent beneath a furrowed brow, and a wicked smile befell his lips returning the third sinister voice. ***:There you are,:*** it said.

At that, the sword released from his grip, and Darrow collapsed down to his hands and began to gag and retch, a thick, tar-like ichor expelling out of him. When he looked back up at them, his face was stained horrifically in the strange substance, like wildkin war paint, creeping out from his eyes, nose, mouth, and ears.

"Stay away," Darrow growled as the black bile converged below and began to slither outward toward them, a thousand tiny red bubbles emerging in the fel ichor, blinking up at them with the scheming eyes of a watching spiderling's nursery. "It's followed me…here. You must… warn...Oathsworn." He doubled over in pain, retching up another bout of the slimy black ichor, his white orbs now bulbous and pushing away from their sockets. "Now, you fools," he croaked, in the throes of expiry, "sever your bind." And his left eye burst free of its orifice followed by the fracturing of his lower jaw from the upper half of his skull, widening his maw to an unnatural breadth.

His final word trailed off into a low clicking sound, and Darrow collapsed fully into his own pool of sick, asphyxiating on the ichor's seemingly endless gush. But the fel ichor would not be deterred so easily. It stretched out from the body, nearly a thing fully formed, tentacles unfurling out of its core, tiny red eyeballs and all, reaching after them, its progress slow but gaining, dragging the unmoving corpse of Solomon Darrow behind it.

"Let go, Val," Aiden ordered.

"What the fuck is that thing?" she gasped as it rose up high before them, tall as a wngar, nay taller, and rising, Darrow's headless body dangling away from its scaly torso like that of a horridly malformed appendage.

"Let go, dammit!" Aiden pleaded, prying frantically at her fingers.

"Let go?" she uttered.

"I've severed our bind," his voice echoed.

And Val released just as the ward hooked into them once more, the candle's wax swallowing the pair whole yet again, dragging them rearward back into the sightless void, and away from the most grotesque horror he had ever beheld.

CHAPTER FOURTEEN

The morn was significantly warmer than she expected, especially considering the frightful cold front over the past few days, though perhaps it was simply the pleasant company she kept that made her so wonderfully warm.

Marsea couldn't help but dote on gleeful Julia as her younger sister danced and skipped dreamily about the walkways. Her innocence and merriment proved a most welcomed reprieve indeed from the sullen stares, forced condolences, and otherwise gloomy dispositions she received from most everyone else about the kingdom corridors since her apparent assault. And the maidens knew, she was growing evermore weary of playing the damsel card, though to truth's witness, on this day, she found contentment enough that her assortment of aches and pains were beginning to subside. The burning sensation in her face lessened to a dull soreness, no worse than a toothache, and the stabbing pangs that plagued her backside vanished with the night.

"Oh, and I almost forgot," Julia chirped, "I've just learned a new dance from Lady Oona." The younger sister pirouetted into a sun-kissed courtyard from the arcade's dreary shading. "Do you want to see it?"

"Are you kidding?" Marsea said, her expression perfectly rosy. "Of course, I want to see it."

Julia beamed as she kicked off her leathers, yet still devoured by the tenderness of youth, and Marsea readjusted the tie of her sling and took to a cool lean against a wind-scarred column lining one of the many mouths of the square named Cameron's Courtyard after the great conquering Lanier King from centuries past. A rare smile found Marsea's visage as she followed barefooted Julia's dips and swoons and capers about the grass, her raven-black hair and alabaster dress chasing her about like the twinkle of a spriteling's shadow. Oh, and how she moved so elegantly, showing a skill and technique well beyond her cycles. The maidens knew. It would appear Julia Harver possessed a rather keen penchant for the art of dance, much more so than Marsea at the same age. Captivated, Marsea cheered as Jules came into the finale, the younger sister leaping and kicking her legs out wide into a soft landing before bounding up to Marsea all sunny and breathless.

"Maidens' breath, Jules!"

"Yeah? You liked it?"

"Liked it? I loved it! That was brilliant! Leagues better than any dance I've ever performed. And ten times better than Aeralie."

"Really?"

"Yes, really. Has Mother seen it yet?"

"Not yet," Julia said sheepishly. "I think it still needs a little work."

Classic Julia. Ever the perfectionist. "I think you should show her later. I will come with you if you like."

"Maybe," Julia murmured.

"You don't have to," Marsea withdrew. "I'm just proud of you is all. That was truly incredible." This brought a smile back to the younger sister's face. "What was it you said Mister Caruthers got on naming you again?"

"Sprout," Julia answered.

"Sprout," Marsea echoed with a grin of her own. "I like it. It suits you. Young John always had a knack for a good nickname, didn't he? And the maidens know, I had my fair share as a young'un."

"Like what?"

"Let's see there was Smidgen and Shortcake and Lil Bit and Bitsy and Munchkin. Oh, Munchkin, that was the worst of them. And, of course, it had to be Uncle Rho's favorite."

"Munchkin?" Julia's smile arched ear to ear. "So cute."

"Cute unless you're the munchkin," Marsea appended. "Marsea Munch they'd name me, calling it all over the castle and courtyards, as though being short weren't insult enough. 'You better hide, Marsea Munch,' Uncle Rho used to jape when the wind began to swoon so I wouldn't blow far, far away."

"That's funny," said the younger sister.

"You'll be taller than me one day to be sure," Marsea added. *And sooner rather than later by the way of things.* It was Julia's Harver blood that would see to that. Even her half-brother Pion ranged quite tall, despite his hunch and lame leg.

From just outside the courtyard, the sounds of a large group approaching drew their attentions and that of the Queen's Own, a loyal group that stuck to Julia like white on rice. They stepped before the two princesses as the head of the crowd poured through the eastern entrance.

"Come close to me," Marsea implored her younger sister.

"But my leathers."

"We will get them later," Marsea said, taking Julia by the hand and guiding her back into the arcade's shelter.

"Traitorous bastard!" someone bellowed. A man's voice.

"Hang the devil!" cried another. This one a woman's voice, shrill and cross.

"To the gallows with him!" a third voice concurred, followed sharply by a series of foul curses.

Marsea Lanier beheld a scene like this only once before, and that occasion was enough for a lifetime. This spectacle held nowhere near the extravagance of the prior, but it still struck her most abrasively. She remembered the fear in what was left of her father's face as the Midnight Men ripped him away from her mother's arms and thereafter prodded him blindly throughout his kingdom streets to the southernmost gallows where his head was forced down upon the butcher's block and promptly taken from him by some faceless, titleless whoreson.

Absent for three days after the Midnight Men seized control of the throne, her father's body showed a ghastly shell of a man once returned to the upper courts. He ponged of hemlock and no longer possessed a tongue, ears, or eyes. His shirt shown red lash marks throughout, and his arms bore a collection of various-sized cuts and gashes, the sorts of cuts and gashes that would never heal properly. His tormentors wrapped the top half of his head in linens where tufts of graying black hair sprouted out wildly between weakened gaps in the bandaging, and where his ears and eyes once lain, blood and pus had leached through the fabric leaving only yellow and crimson stains.

She wanted like fire to be strong for her father then, but try as she might, his maiming presented such a horror that she could scarce bring herself to look at him, much less hug him. The Midnight Men made of Whit Lanier the most grotesque thing she had ever beheld. At the behest of her mother, she had not witnessed her father's beheading. Instead, she and Remy were taken by the handmaidens to their bedchambers. It would be the last time she ever saw her father. She recalled hearing the crowds and raucousness outside the castle, the revelry persisting long into the nightfall, and thusly her imagination began to fill in the rest.

Whitman Lanier, second of his name, died without dignity, without ceremony, and without family.

Her father, the king of kings, had been found guilty of high treason against the commonwealth by the privy council all those many cycles ago, though from what she had uncovered in the cycles since, there was scant little evidence of any such treachery. Knowing what she knew now of the Midnight Men and their ties with Ravenholme and the Courowne guild lords, she had no doubts he had been set up and made an example of. It was how the Ministry dealt with uncooperative associates, after all. No one was indispensable. No one was above their rule. Not even a king. For in the world made wrong by politics and devils and the mad, as it stood to the present, even the favored found some measure of suffering.

A few bluecoats peppered the throng, surrounding a man in chains with shields held high, but the majority were townsfolk, mostly nobles, many of whom Marsea recognized from courtly festivals and the local shops about the kingdom's upper quarters. Crafters, merchants, performers, and the like. Marsea had never beheld such a diverse gathering in all her days, especially so near to the citadel.

As for the man in chains, he'd taken a merciless flogging. A particularly nasty cut across his right cheek remained open, down to the bone, and severed the lower half of his ear. Yet, somehow, the other side of his face fared worse. Between the burns, blade marks, and patches of swollen flesh, there remained just enough definition for Marsea to determine she didn't recognize the poor fellow.

A half-rotted tomato smashed into the side of his head, followed by a fresh string of curses. Instinctively, Marsea sank back against the wall, pulling Jules in tight as the throng descended upon them. All that now separated them from the teeming mob was a handful of panic-stricken bluecoat soldiers.

"Marsea?" a dark-haired man said, clearing a path through the rabble.

"Raelan?" Marsea answered, recognizing the voice.

"Father?" Jules said simultaneously.

Raelan Harver, the eldest of the Harver brothers and the tallest by far, towered high above most men. Unsurprisingly, his head stuck out above everyone else in the crowd. The rest of him appeared a moment later, parting from the mob, liveried from neck to toe in the navy and gold colors of the Royalguard, his left breast cluttered with medals and the excess of accouterments that named him as a high-ranking official. They were meant to show valor and gallantry, but Marsea rather thought it little more than a prick-measuring contest.

"Mercy of Myrenna, what in vaelnation is the meaning of this, Raelan?" Marsea asked as the chained man was brought before her and lowered to his knees.

The prisoner collapsed onto his side instead, soiling the stones before them with blood and stink. The maidens know, he smelled worse than an open grave.

Marsea tugged Jules back into her chest and covered the younger sister's eyes with her one good hand. The man had not only been beaten and cut open, but he had been branded as well, the sigil of Lanier still bubbling fresh atop his left eye whence the iron had been driven. It matched the eye of hers that Gan had blackened.

"I daresay, I did not expect you would be up and about for a least another day or two," Raelan said.

"As always, you underestimate me," Marsea said with more than a dash of impertinence. With those of the Midnight Men ranks, she found she just couldn't help herself. That and she refused to appear weak in front of him. Not again. Not after what Ganedys had put her through. She had earned this strength. And now was the time to make it useful. Even if she went too far, she knew Raelan would not touch her in front of Julia.

"So it would appear," he admitted, and the man on the ground gurgled something of a response himself. "Get up, filth," Raelan said pitilessly, kicking the man hard in his stomach. The man groaned but made no effort, clearly unable to do so under his own power. "Chuffing hells, will someone put this leaky piss-pot back on his knees," he ordered, and a pair of bluecoat officers forced the man back into a kneeling position, though he wobbled mightily. It was a wonder he'd even made it this far, considering the state of him. Blood and slobber caked the entire lower half of his face.

"The stars save me, Raelan, she's only nine," Marsea argued.

"Come at me with such a righteous tongue, girl," Raelan retorted. "I know you took a few blows, but surely you must recognize this particular heathen."

Marsea stared the poor fellow straight, though he was barely conscious, and his head hung low.

"This was the man that attacked you, Marsea," Raelan clarified, "the man that took your fingers and nearly took your life. Alexander Vardain."

The mention of the man's name riled the mob again, and the bluecoats had to hold fast to keep them at bay. Marsea felt a lump form in her throat, and she couldn't help but wonder if Raelan knew the whole truth. That she had come to be in this condition because of his youngest brother, not this poor sap, and that in arriving here, she took his brother's life to rescue her own. Given the confident glint in his eyes, the pride and the fury, she highly doubted it.

"The state of his face, his own mother might not even recognize him," the princess quibbled.

"Let her look," Raelan countered.

"No."

"She is my blood too, lest you forget. And she is my daughter. I will decide what she can and cannot handle. Not you."

"Spare her this, Raelan," Marsea argued, holding her ground.

"Tell you what. Given your condition and what this wretch did to you, I will meet you halfway," he compromised. "Fair is fair, after all. Half a Harver, half a Waldgrave. We will let her decide which half she favors more then, yeah?"

Marsea pursed her lips, knowing Jules well enough to predict the outcome. She was headstrong, just like her father, ever and always grasping at a maturity far beyond her cycles, ever and always trying to play catch-up with her much older siblings.

"Julie Bug, what say you?" her father asked sweetly. "Do you wish to see what's become of the spineless craven who tried to take your big sister from you?"

"No, Jules, please," Marsea implored. "This sort of thing is not meant for younglings to behold."

"Come off it, Marsea," Raelan scoffed. "It's not as though we are going to flog him in front of her. I mean, I would say he's pretty well done besides," he said gripping a patch of Vardain's hair and forcing the man's ruined face up at her. "What say you wretch? Are you done now? You want to abuse anymore defenseless women?"

Vardain's one remaining eye rolled back into his head, and a fresh spill of blood oozed out over his bottom lip in place of his words.

Raelan nodded before turning back up to the princess. "Mmm, yes, well I suppose it might help if he still had a tongue, yeah?"

"You're a savage," Marsea condemned in a low voice. *Just as horrible as your dead brother.*

"I'm the savage?" Raelan questioned, utterly flummoxed. "Some gratitude. I bring you the man that tried to end your life and you name me a savage?" He said it loud enough for all to hear.

"I want to see," Julia said meekly, interrupting their row. And Marsea could feel her half-sister's fingers begin to pry in-between hers. "I'm old enough, Seasea."

No, Jules, please. Marsea's heart wilted for her little sister as her hand, trembling something awful, lowered to her side at Julia's guidance.

"How about that." Raelan unleashed a deplorable smile. "Harver it is then."

And despite Vardain's ghastly vision, young Julia did not even for a single second back down or turn away.

Is there nothing left to this world that might remain innocent?

CHAPTER FIFTEEN

"Knock, knock, fuckwit," Curie cooed, rapping a knuckle against the chamber door.

Remy sighed. *Fuckwit this, fuckwit that.* Two days in the ornery giftborn's company and he was already nearing the end of his tolerance. The gods know, she'd proven herself every measure as unhinged as his swordbrothers had painted her and doubly as vulgar. Yet still, despite his irritation, he clung to her side like stink on shit, unwilling to bear such a peculiar burden as was the grimoire by his lonesome.

As it stood, they had been on the hunt for hours now, scouring near to every hall of the Palatian Citadel, nigh reduced to badgering and petty beggary, and still they had not found hide nor hair of Tarboril nor her brother. It was a fool's charade to be sure, Remy was convinced of it now, a fool's charade he knew better than to indulge in, and yet somehow, even against his better judgments, here he was, before another unfamiliar doorway cowering in Curie's shadow with his thumb up his ass hoping against hope to find some dullard that maychance know of some other dullard that may know of some cad named Tarboril who may or may not actually exist. Utterly ridiculous, the whole bloody thing, but what else was he to do? The entire city waited in confinement with the blight lurking so near, and his gut simply would not permit him to break the y'deman's promise.

"State your business," a voice grumbled from the other side.

"We're searching for a woman named Tarboril," Curie said. "We were informed we might find her here."

"Yeah, and who wants to know?"

"Your fucking Nan, fuckwit, now open up," Curie said with a scowl.

"My Nan's dead bitch, piss off."

"We seek your High Commander, good knight," Remy explained further. "It is a most delicate affair. You understand."

"And who is this then?"

"This fucker," Curie grumbled to Remy, shaking her head. "He's the bloody Crown Prince of Lancastle, that's who," she called a moment later, "so a fuckwit best mind his betters, yeah."

Remy's face screwed up in agitation. *The gods only know. Must you always act so insolent?* At her response, however, there was a long pause, and he could hear faint voices in discussion on the other side before the door creaked open to reveal a baby-faced bloodcoat guard fresh off a thorough scolding.

Without wait, Curie shoved past the guard, introducing him to both of her middle fingers, and Remy followed in her wake, his hand never leaving the hilt of his blade. This behind-closed-doors sneaking around business was for the dogs, he had decided. Oh, if Marsea and mother could see him now, traipsing about with the dregs of the Vael, they would have had an absolute riot.

"Tarboril?" Remy asked as they came into the room's epicenter and found the crimson-armored knight bare-chested with his chin held high. He certainly cut quite the impressive figure. A young woman ran a straight razor up the knight's neck, over his knobble, and outward away from his jawline.

"Please accept my most humble of apologies for my porter's rather crude manners," the knight greeted.

He spoke with a strange accent that Remy could not quite place. Grounded in peasantry stock, the watchman had no doubts. Though birth station notwithstanding, it was plainly evident the man was well-spoken.

"I suppose we are all a bit edgy what with all the discord happening just outside our fair city," he continued, as the woman wiped the blade clean on a cloth.

"Some more so than others, it would seem," Curie grumbled.

The knight smiled smugly as the courtesan scraped another row of stubble from his neck. "If you've something to say, mage, best to be out with it."

"Yeah? And what'd you have in mind, honey-tits?"

"Honey-tits, is it?" He had a chuckle. "The boys warned me about you. Yes, they did. Mad Mona they name you." The courtesan carefully removed another row of stubble, working around the knight's movements.

"It would seem my reputation precedes me then," Curie offered drolly.

"And so I am quite curious, Mad Mona. Is it true what they say?" His smile was a most deviant one. "That you," he made a clicking sound through his teeth, "took a man's fruits in his sleep at The King's Wall?"

Curie shared his smile. "Why don't you call me Mad Mona one more time, yeah, and mayhaps we'll find out."

"*Dweir ta ka'le du alé rinza*," Remy said, and the knight's eyes fixated on the watchman, his joshing façade from only a moment before all but a forgotten memory. He raised his hand slowly, gripping the woman's arm mid-scrape, and eased the blade away from his neck. A thin line of blood trailed away from the last spot it had touched.

"Say again," the knight bade as he pushed up from the chair. And the gods know he had a perfect physique too, built like a seasoned prize-fighter was this one.

"*Dweir ta ka'le du alé rinza*," Remy repeated as he revealed the archer's tome.

"The blind man's tome," the knight uttered, his eyes wide and glistening with a twinge of madness. "The bastard actually retrieved it." He wrenched the book away from Remy and brushed his hand gently over its uneven jacket before tracing a finger across its leaves. "There are pages missing." He shifted back to Remy, his quizzical expression accentuating his strong, masculine features. "Where are they?"

"I haven't the faintest," Remy answered, though he cared little for the knight's commanding tone. "This is precisely the condition I was given it."

The knight's eyes narrowed. "Did you open it?"

"No," the watchman lied, "of course not." *But she did.*

"Is he dead?" the knight asked, his attentions once again befalling the tome. "Beldroth?"

"I don't know," Remy answered truthfully this time. *So the archer was being sincere after all.*

"And the beast?"

"It was there with him, the ghastly thing," Remy said, "but I haven't the faintest if it's still alive. They left the grimoire with me, and Beldroth bade me bring it to a woman named Tarboril in Palatia. I am assuming you know this woman."

The knight glanced up from the grimoire, eyeing both of his guests warily. "Of course, I know her. I am her liege." The knight turned his back to them and strolled to a table nestled tidily against the chamber's far wall. "But the Lady Tarboril is presently preoccupied."

"We can wait," Curie said, her hand slipping down to Fucker at her waist.

"She may be preoccupied for some time, I'm afraid." The knight rebuffed her as he set the tome down and began to dry his half-shaven face and neck. "However, on her behalf, I thank you for the recovery."

"No," Remy said firmly, matching the knight's patronizing attitude. "I nearly died for that fucking eyesore." His chin rose quite high then. "I demand answers. Beginning with your name, good sir."

The knight bared his teeth, his face suddenly white with fury. Clearly, he was unaccustomed to being spoken to in such a disparaging manner. "I am Lord Davrin of House Tarboril, Your Highness, High Commander of the Palatian Royalguard Regiment."

"Capitol, then it would seem I have found the right man, Lord Davrin of House Tarboril." Somehow courage found his tongue. "And I am Rembrandt Lanier, the rightful King of Lancastle, Lord of the Highlands and the Western Moors, including Palatia and The Morrigan Pass, and more than like whatever disfavored hollow you managed to skive away from, and I will not be brushed aside like some mad stray on a bender, especially not by the likes of a puffed-up lowborn cavalier." He heard his mother's voice slither forth inside his cruel words.

Curie stared sidelong at Remy, a wicked grin sprawled across her face.

"I say, what is the meaning of all this bickering?" a woman proclaimed from behind them, and Curie freed Fucker from its prison.

When Remy turned heel, he was not expecting to find the Queen of Palatia in his sights. The voice, though laced in the same foreign accent as

Davrin's, was as thick and stern as a tourney master's. It did not match her radiant aspect in the slightest. Yet there she stood, a most exquisite vision in the wavering wander of candlelight. Under her cloak of fur, she was clad in shimmering gold and white silks to rival that of the highest nobility, and her long, blond locks lay perfectly still against her high, arching shoulder blades. At Curie's threat, both of the High Lady's guards unsheathed their swords and took a step in advance to sever the magus's path.

"Milady," Remy greeted with a refined air, holding out a hand to ease the tension.

"My king," Lady Dree responded primly behind her guardsmen before her attentions shifted to Davrin, who revealed the grimoire.

"He said the words," the knight answered her silent question.

"Just the one, then?" she queried further.

"So it would seem," he answered as if it were just the pair of them in the chamber.

"You're Tarboril?" Remy said. He hadn't meant for it to sound so mistrustful, but given all that had transpired over the past few days, how could he not?

"Once upon a time," she answered.

Emyria's lament, must everyone act so bloody cryptic in this place? "Beldroth asked that I relay you a message."

"Beldroth spoke? To you?" Confusion washed away some measure of the Queen's prior superiority.

"He did, milady. He said something along the lines of The Eld are risen." Lady Dree's eyes became quite cold and calculating at the telling. "I'm afraid you have me at a disadvantage, in that. Who or what might I ask are The Eld?"

"Chuffing hells," Davrin groaned, setting the grimoire back down upon the table, before retrieving his shirt.

"You bear the blind man's tome and yet you've never heard of The Eld?" the High Lady inquired, her expression mystified.

"It is a Chandiian term," Curie answered, "shorthand for The Eldnumerian."

"Care to expand on that?" Remy asked, his curiosity shifting over to Curie.

"*Eldnu* meaning ancient. *Meria* meaning master," the magus expounded, "though I presume you might better know their import by their hallowed name. The Old Ones."

"Right. And what exactly did Beldroth mean by they are risen?"

"It is prophecy, milord," Lady Dree said, "no doubt you have heard it before by some manner or another. Books, songs, plays, and such the like. In more recent cycles, it has been popularized in sonnet. Mayhaps you have heard of it. 'The Madman's Rime'?"

"Of course," he said. Who hadn't heard of 'The Madman's Rime' after all? It was practically a cradlesong in this day and age. He could remember mother singing it to Jules when she was but still a babe. And he supposed she had sung it to both he and Marsea as well.

"Sadly, its warning has since become reduced to little more than a jape...a nursemaid's lullaby...a silly hearthfire haunter."

Lovers twined tempt Threads of Fate
Torn asunder, unbound Hate
Of She who dawns the Endless Night
Exiled, Loathed, Cast in to Plight
By Six Unnamed, once deemed as Kith
E'er-Curst, the Fey, Reborn of Myth
Towers in Glory of Men thence quake
So too the vain Highborn recanting their wake

"La, lala, lala, and so on. It is a bit overdrawn and pretentious if you ask me, but that doesn't make it any less true, now does it?"

Remy shook his head, counting the lines, trying to recall Gran's version and his uncle's hearthfire stories of the like, but nothing of note came to the surface. Oh, how he wished his Uncle Rho was here with him now. He would have sorted these two charlatans proper in a heartbeat.

"Little else is known about them beyond their legend," she continued, "but it is said they were once a most dreadful collection of creatures beset by great miseries and cruelties who believed themselves horridly wronged by some fashion or another and thereafter set out upon the land to see those very wrongs repaid."

"But what are they?" Remy pressed.

"I am afraid that question is not so easily answered, milord." Her appearance was grave. "Their accounts have become so watered down over the many passing centuries that it is nigh impossible to sort the factual from the false. Some name them revenants, if you can believe it, curst evermore to haunt the shadows. Others name them the gods' chosen, guardians of the devout and goodly. But most magi texts claim they were diseased giftborn who sold their souls to the darkness for greater power and prestige and by doing so became enslaved by their greed. Which brings us back around to the grimoire you so generously brought us." The corners of her mouth curled upward ever so slightly. "For it is believed that somewhere within its many pages lies the truth to such a query. Only..." The word hung but briefly.

"It has a sibling," Davrin finished.

"Yes," the High Lady murmured. "And it is believed both must be acquired to fully unbind the prophecy's riddle."

"And let me guess," Curie scoffed, "you haven't the foggiest idea where the other might be."

"To the contrary," Davrin countered, "we know precisely where it is. Where is not the concern. The concern is the creature whose possession it was last reported to lie within."

"He is known as the bastard born of summer's blood and winter's kiss," Lady Dree elaborated, "ruined before his time he was, stabbed through and through, influence denied, opulence devoured, but The Hood would not harbor such a luckless wretch within his collection. Nor would Nightmare's widow. Thusly he was spat back from the nine some days later, a woeful, unloved thing, returned inside a brand new existence wholly divergent from that of his prior."

"Obviously, we had rather hoped Beldroth would claim both," Davrin said, buttoning his jerkin. "He is amongst the most capable in our employ after all, but if he was only able to gain the one—"

"Yeah, yeah, yeah, rousing tale and all," Curie interjected, "but that still doesn't answer the question of *where* it actually is."

"It was last reported beyond the Southland Bulwark, if you must know," Lady Dree said sharply, flecks of ire beginning to take shape inside her stony orbs.

"The Stranger bloody take me. So half the fucking country away then," Curie grated.

"Though more than like at the university in Kanton, given the nature of the object in question."

"Or it could be in Synner's March, yeah? Or Caejir…or Tavernmast… or up a ruddy wngar's smelly arsehole for all you lot seem to know."

"The gods know, must you always act so unsavory, you filthy bog witch?" Finally, a bit of the bumpkin had come out in the High Lady. Leave it to Rhymona Curie to bring even the most composed and refined down with the riffraff.

"Bog witch, is it?" Curie beamed, her guise clearly deranged. "I've got your filthy bog witch right here." Quick as an alley cat, she bounded for the grimoire, ripping it away from the table's edge before aiming her hatchet at Davrin who swiftly gained the dagger at his belt.

"Put it down, bitch," he threatened. "That belongs to The Covenant."

"The Covenant?" Curie spat. "And of course, they're fucking Ravenholme conspirators. How could it be anything else? I say we ditch these fucking knobends, Toff." She clutched the grimoire against her breasts. "Ravenholme are nothing but bad news. Liars and killers, the ruddy lot."

He was woefully aware.

"You'll want to mind the next words that leave your mouth carefully, gutterwitch," Davrin snapped.

"I'll have you in fucking pieces before you even glance your steel," Curie returned. "I see it in the corner there."

"All right, everybody just keep your heads clear for a second," Lady Dree implored, her eyes wide and alert. "Captain, we are not your enemy, nor are The Covenant. If anything, we are doing all we can to keep you alive."

"Save the lecture for your fuckwit lackeys, Dree. Your poison tongue defiles the eardrums to permit its presence," Curie argued over her shoulder.

"My king, please. You must listen to reason," Lady Dree begged. "The dead already haunt the daylight. You've seen it with your own eyes."

"She's Covenant, Remy," Curie countered. "She will say anything to keep you compliant to their cause."

"What are you not telling us?" Remy asked, never once shifting away from Lady Dree. He could feel his watchman blade begin to call. "What more are you hiding, milady?"

"Best not to meddle in Ministry affairs, boy," Davrin dared. "You of all folk should know better."

"Silence, Davrin," Lady Dree scolded. "We have told you all we know, milord. All the masters will allow for. Anything more and it would put your lives in danger."

As if they weren't already. He was loath to admit it, but he was beginning to side with Curie in all of this.

"Fuck your poxy masters," the magus crackled, ready to explode at any moment.

"Let us handle this, Your Highness," Lady Dree pleaded most desperately. "You did us a great service in bringing us the tome, but we can manage it from here."

I knew I should have buried the ugly wretch, Remy grumbled. *The damned y'deman. What have you gotten me into?* "What does *dweir ta ka'le du alé rinza* mean?" he asked, unmoved by the Tarborils' stories of doom and gloom. When Lady Dree and Davrin locked eyes for a moment as if in silent communication, it became unquestionably clear that he would never gain a straight answer out of these two. Remy gripped tight the hilt of his blade and drew it clean.

"My king," Lady Dree responded, shrinking away from him. "There is no need for violence."

"The lies we tell," Curie mocked, bloodlust wanting in her voice.

"I asked you a question, milady," Remy offered once more. "What does it mean?" *Last chance.*

The High Lady shook her head, her expression altering from innocence to wrath in an instant. "I tried to warn you, my King. Let it be known. I tried to spare you the trouble. But you couldn't leave well enough alone, could you?"

And you couldn't answer a simple fucking question. He clutched the hilt firmly with both hands and crouched low into a guarded stance. "Rhymona, do not let anyone touch that bloody eyesore, no matter what happens."

With only a grunt for acknowledgment, Curie spurred into action, quick as an eye blink, chasing after the High Commander with a series of short hacks and slashes before adjusting to wilder, broader crisscrossing cuts, chopping into table and chair and anything within her warpath, swinging Fucker about like a bloody madwoman. It was all the ill-equipped knight could do to scramble out of the way and find cover.

Concurrently, the High Lady's guards advanced as she disappeared behind them, and Remy reacted by instinct to their threat, parrying left, then right, then left again, before dodging a thrust for his belly, narrowly avoiding the hungry blade's eager bite. Though the strike was a miss, it had enough fury behind it to send him off his balance, and he stumbled away without hope of a proper defense. Given the overwhelming advantage, the second bloodcoat thence drove in at him, twice as hard, and Remy curled away from the brute, taking a gash across the edge of his shoulder, wisps of blood spraying about his plight as he clattered roughly to the floor. *This is it,* he thought as the first bloodcoat stalked after him, *bested by a pair of titleless whoresons.*

But as he raised his sword in desperate cover, Curie appeared, a horror possessed, charging past him to plunge her hatchet into the sliver of flesh twixt the encroaching bloodcoat's sallet and pauldron. It came free with little resistance, and she twirled about in one deft pirouette to bring it around into the hind of the second bloodcoat's helm. He roared as the impact rang his noggin numb, giving Remy enough time to regain his form, and the galvanized watchman kicked the floundering bloodcoat in his chest with all the strength he could muster, sending the wretch sprawling into a violent backward tumble. As he turned around toward the doorway, he watched as Curie sliced her hatchet at the High Commander's petrified porter, nearly cleaving a chunk from the poor bastard's gut, before she cracked him across the face with forward momentum and a nasty elbow.

Afterward, there was naught but stone and torchlight for many minutes as they fled into the citadel's lower corridors. His battered ribs still ached something awful from before, and now his right arm was screaming death from the bloodcoat's blade wound, but he forced himself onward anyway, unwilling to give up, unwilling to give in, concentrating on Curie's backside and the next step forward. Somehow, he was still alive, the fates be damned. And of all the folk in all the world, he had Rhymona Curie to thank for that. Rescued by a bloody madwoman. A madwoman named amongst his swordmates as Mad Mona. If his injuries hadn't screwed his face into a permanent wrinkle of anguish, he might have had a laugh at the absurdity of it all. *Forget Marsea,* he thought, *nine hells forget Mum and the entire round, the whole of the great heavenly pantheon must be having a most raucous laugh at such a barmy turn as this.*

"I know a place we can lay low," she said as they raced down a dark passageway into an empty square, the snowfall coming down in thick patches around them. And Remy was fastly reminded that Palatia's lower quarters were every measure as squalid as was its upper half's splendor. "It's at the end of this street, a few blocks down, the last house on the left. But I will warn you forthwith, the company is as dodgy as they come."

"What are we doing?" Remy huffed as they came to a halt, his expression wild and his eyes erratic.

Curie smiled and offered him the tome with a mocking bow. "I'm following milord's orders, of course."

"What sort of mad Covenant conspiracy have we stumbled upon here?" he asked, stowing the tome back in his satchel. "The Ministry? Ravenholme? The Old Ones? What does it all mean? How does it all connect?"

"Fuck if I know," Curie shrugged, crass as ever.

"Mercy of Myrenna." The burn from his shoulder demanded his attention, and he pressed a hand against it.

"Let us have a look then," Curie offered.

He removed his hand to reveal a bright red palm of blood, and he suddenly felt faint.

"Mmm," she murmured, giving it a quick once over. "Yep, looks like you'll die another day, won't you?"

"I am not in the mood for your insufferable japery, Rhymona," he said with a panicked edge. "How bad is it?"

"The gods know, Toff, relax. It's nothing a few binders couldn't cure."

He took a deep breath and exhaled at the news. "We did the right thing, right? Not giving the tome to the Tarborils."

"Tut, right or no, those two can suck the fucking piss from my cunt. Every last, steaming drop at that. Name me a filthy bog witch, will you?"

"Mayhaps we should turn back," Remy said. "The small council should be apprised—"

"Don't be a bloody fuckwit, Toff. We just killed a bloodcoat. One of the Queen's Own no less."

"As I recall, it was you who killed the bloodcoat."

"Is that how it was, then?" She frowned. "Seems to me I saved your pathetic arse back there. Besides, you think the Tarborils care which one of us is responsible? They will have us both in chains if we turn back. And that's if we're damned lucky."

"Mayhaps the Colonel will listen to reason," he argued, "or Tenbrooks. He seems a competent enough fellow."

"First off, I wouldn't trust Yurien Tenbrooks as far as I could bloody well throw him," Curie said, coldly. "Any bastard who spent twenty cycles milling about the rabble of Six Ports is bound to have a few skeletons, yeah. And as far as the Colonel is concerned, I'd say he's a few bales short of a full load, wouldn't you? A man that's been through as much bollocks as he has? He's a proper mad loon now to be sure. Besides, that wrinkled old bastard couldn't protect us from a pair of Covenant assassins even if he had the entire guard on watch for them. Nasty business, Covenant cronies. And I've no doubts they meant malfeasance with the tome. Nine hells, you could practically taste their addiction. Moreover, who's to say Marlowe isn't in on the whole lot? He suddenly appears just before Brymshire's sacking with an outfit of only seven, promising reinforcements and swinging his cock about the small council like he's bleeding Auzyg the Almighty, forcing the uppers into a kingdom-wide quarantine. You ask me, I would say his arrival here is well fucked to say the least."

Given the turn of the past two days, Remy certainly couldn't argue her logic there. Despite appearances, for all he was aware, Tenbrooks could indeed be a brigand and Marlowe a right proper nutter. Anything was possible anymore, he supposed. Rhymona, however, for all of her faults and frustrations, had proven herself an invaluable ally, bringing him round to health again at her own detriment, and saving him from a most assured death by one of the Queen's Own. It seemed only fair he now grant her a scrap of trust. "So what would you suggest we do then?" he asked, his vitality beginning to wane.

"Fuck me, mate. It's a wonder you've even managed to last this long. First, we rest. Obviously. And then we try to find a way off this blasted shitheap."

"As in off the mountain? Come now, you can't be serious."

"Serious as sin, mate," she affirmed, the decision already made.

"We won't even make it out of the city. The gates are swarming with bloodcoats, not to mention the archers lining her battlements."

"Each one a useless sodding fuckwit to the last. Easy enough."

"All right, let's just say through some act of divine miracle we do actually make it past that lot, have you forgotten about the legion of blighters waiting in the wood just outside?"

"Oh, Toff," she produced that most ghastly smile of hers, "I envy your näivety, truly I do. It'll be better for us out there with the corpses than in here with The Covenant, of that I can promise you. This shit with the Tarborils isn't over. Not by a long shot. Those two fuckers back there, they may look all posh and pretty and speak with a courtly tongue, but they are both dangerous, devious killers, trained killers no less, cogs that answer to even more dangerous and devious folk, folk that hunt malcontents like us for sport, and just now it would seem you possess something they crave most desperately. Let there be no doubt in it, prince or no, right or no, they will hunt us both until they gain the grimoire. And if they fail, there will be a dozen more to take their place. That is how The Covenant works. They are endless and unscrupulous. And they won't be deterred by anyone or anything, nor will they be denied their due."

Remy remembered the y'deman's words at that. *Should you stray from the task, should you break the deal in any way, trust I will know. I know a great many things, mind you. And knowing these great many things as I do, trust it true, I will find you. I will hunt you like a dog hunts the pheasant. And you will not like the consequences that follow.*

The watchman sighed, exhaustion beginning to take its toll, desperation clinging to him like the suffocating stick of wet clothes. "Fine," he grumbled, a man on the cusp of defeat, "we'll play it your way." He hadn't the heart or vigor to argue with her further. Regardless, it was abundantly clear she had already made up her mind on the matter, and like it or not, if he were to endure, he had little choice but to comply. He still needed her after all, as much as it burned him to admit it. And where The Covenant was concerned, substantially more so than she needed him. Besides, in his current condition, he was not long for this world alone. Undoubtedly, his wounds would soon begin to fester without her fel sorcery to mend them. He thought about home then, as he always did when times grew bleak and desperate, about Jules and Marsea and Mother. About the life he might have had had he stayed and simply conformed to Vaustian's demands. Would he be any better off as a pretender? Surely, he would be healthier. But truly, hale or no, would living a lie have found him even the smallest measure of happiness?

No. The watchman quibbled, defiant to the bone, refusing the turn to despair. *That was the old me,* he told himself as he hobbled closely behind his giftborn companion, a long-repressed anger rising within him, *the lesser man's path. You are a bloody Lanier, Remy, last of the pureblood royals. You are their rightful king, usurpers be damned. And you've run from your duties for long enough, haven't you? They are not the problem. You are the problem.*

It would seem Curie's incessant recalcitrance was having a greater effect on him than he could have ever imagined. And at that, he remembered words once had from his uncle not so very long ago after another one of his juvenile tirades. *Act a prisoner and they will treat you like one. Act a fool and they will treat you like one. Act a child and they will treat you like one. Time comes, a man must earn his keep, and sometimes it must be done the hard way.*

The grimoire gained a pound with each step taken, dragging him ever so quietly graveward, but his freshly conjured anger would not be denied. Not this time. Not ever again.

The hard way it is then. He spit to cleanse the taste of blood from his palate. *I'll be seeing you soon, Uncle.*

CHAPTER SIXTEEN

It was a shade past midnight when Marsea arrived, cloaked, outside her lover's private solar. She glanced down both sides of the corridor, staring deep into the darkness beyond the torchlight, awaiting any potential intrusion, before knocking in the cipher she and her love had agreed upon some many quintweeks past.

An eternity elapsed by her reckoning before she heard footsteps approaching from inside followed by the sound of the bolt lock clicking left to right, and the door finally yawned open. She entered silently, rushing past him, head down, and Vaustian bolted the door behind them before chasing after her. She stopped before the hearth, about midway through the dimly lit chamber, the logs within crackling and hissing, the flame bright and hungry, and she removed her hood with her good hand, a mane of fine, honey-gold curls falling free of the cloak, before turning about to face him.

Inside his warmth, she found her heart raced, her skin flushed hot, and she couldn't gather her thoughts clearly. In the days since she had last seen him, she had thought to ask him a thousand, thousand questions upon sight of him, and yet now that she was here, alone in his company, her mind had gone utterly, tragically blank. Just his mere presence had apparently broken her.

You're such an idiot. What did you expect would happen?

Vaustian watched her for a tender moment as she focused on the silver trim upon his gray doublet. The maidens know, she was a lost little thing, hardly even able to take in the sight of him. Vaustian placed the knuckle of his index finger under her chin, forcing her to meet his soothing gaze. Her muscles tightened, ever so slightly, and her breath quickened, and all she could do was blink as he removed her glasses from their rest and placed them upon the hearth's mantle. At his proximity, she tilted her head slightly, grazing her cheek affectionately against his returning hand, longing for his caress, and instantly a wave of tranquility began to wash over her.

"Gran glasses," he said dotingly.

"Shut up," she whispered.

She remembered fondly when she first began to feel this way about him. She remembered the dreams…the urges…the wetness…

Vaustian Harver was nothing at all like his monstrous brothers. Not really. He had an ease about him that neither Raelan nor Ganedys would ever approach. Though he occasionally shared their affinity toward pride and cruelness, he also concealed within another version. A version that belonged to her. A version that was sweet and gentle and just as damaged as she was. And though that version may despise himself for his amorous feelings toward her, he certainly could not deny their existence.

She was nearly in tears as his skin graced hers and a small, involuntary sound escaped her lips. It was truly embarrassing how much she missed him. Their separation felt far longer than only a few days. But what was she to do? This was how she had become. She could no more control her feelings for him than she could the sun and the stars. And the maidens know, she never wanted his touch to end. Then, as though he could hear her very contemplations, Vaustian Harver drew her softly into his chest, careful to avoid her wounded hand, embracing her as close as comfort would allow, and she eagerly snuggled up against him, inhaling his scent, soaking in it, drowning in it, dying in it.

Neither one said a word for many minutes afterward as white-hot tears blistered down the pale plains of her cheeks, one after another, salting the purse of her lips and stinging the rims of her eyes. They too were involuntary. But they were silent, lovely tears all the same. Tears of pure joy. Tears she had rightfully earned. And tears that she wouldn't soon forget. Naturally, her eyes closed as she surrendered in full to his loving care, treasuring the heavy wetness twixt her eyelids, and she listened to his heartbeat, slow and steady, and for the first time since her duel with Ganedys, she actually felt safe. Vaustian's arms were like an impenetrable fortress around her, her fortress, and nothing could take that from her. She was finally protected again. And she nuzzled into his doublet, a smile curling her lips, her breathing falling in pace with his, all of her aches and pains suddenly departed, all of her worries tossed freely to the wind, euphoria nigh, nigh and yielding.

But just as she neared that perfect place of solace, that impossible serenity, her eyes shot open as one of her thousand questions wormed its way into her stream of consciousness and thusly spilled out of her before she could think to bury it away again.

"Who else knows?" she asked. It barely registered as more than a whisper, but it lingered like a roll of thunder for some endless seconds thereafter, afloat somewhere amidst the chamber's infinite abyss, each second of ensuing silence seemingly spanning that of a lifetime.

"Casilvieri, of course," he said, his voice sounding raspier than usual, and she couldn't help but wonder just how deep into his cups he had fallen, "a few resident members of the Ravenholme council as well, but otherwise just you and I, my love."

"Not Raelan?"

"Not Raelan," he confirmed. "My brother can never know the truth of this."

She thought to end the inquiry there with how serious he had become, but something within wouldn't allow for it. "And who is this Vardain fellow that will suffer for my transgressions?"

"He is but a loose end," Vaustian promised.

And by his wintry tone, Marsea suspected she would get little more than that about the man, so she altered course and said with an unsure tongue, "Ganedys…"

"I know," her love said evenly.

"He…" She sagged against him as the memory of her duel and Gan's dastardly actions choked the life from her words.

"I know," Vaustian said once more, and she could feel his embrace tighten ever so slightly as one of his hands coursed delicately down her backside, sending a tingling sensation throughout the entirety of her body. She shuddered. The feeling was somehow both wonderful and terrifying at the same time. "As usual, Cas was exceedingly thorough in his report."

Nestled close against his chest, she felt the vibration of each word escaping from inside him. "It was your hidden blade that saved me," she responded to his vibrations.

"The blade was but a means, love. You were what saved you." And there was more than a hint of bitterness to the statement.

"But I couldn't finish the task," she confessed.

She could never lie to her love. Not anymore. Nor could she conceal the truth from him. Both were pointless endeavors where she and Vaustian were concerned. He would know almost immediately were she to try, besides. And she had tried. For cycles and cycles she had tried. But he read her too well—controlled her too well—trained her too well. The gods know he knew her better than she even knew herself. And eventually he broke her as she had broken him. And she acquiesced. It was the only power left to her. Her devotion for his obsession.

"I tried," she avowed, "but I heard footsteps. And—"

"I know," he said again, softer. "Cas saw to its conclusion. It appears my dear brother in his drunken stupor ran afoul a rather nasty band of wildkin." He released his hold of her. "A fitting end if you ask me."

There was that Harver cruelness, she thought. "He hated you just as well," she said instead.

"With good reason," Vaustian admitted. "I showed my baby brother scarce little love even from a young age. Though, verily, he put in scarce little effort to ever earn it. Still, Gan knew better than to cross me. And he should have known better than to threaten Ravenholme."

"Hearing his words, seeing his bloodlust, I have no doubts that he was planning your expiry just the same," she added.

"Nor do I," Vaustian agreed. "But Gan was always a bit of a wastrel, wasn't he? All bark. And very little bite. Especially involving matters of great import. Truly frustrating, my brother. Mayhaps this might best explain why we were never able to establish a proper bond."

Bite enough, Marsea thought as she remembered how ferociously he had beaten at her. "So you are not angry with me?" she asked artlessly.

"No, Marsea, of course not. I daresay at this point you would have to go to great lengths to draw mine ire."

"And the masters were pleased?"

His answer wasn't immediate as he ambled over to his desk where amongst the clutter of tomes and contrivances there rested a carafe and a single glass of wine, both half-emptied. He offered her the glass and took the carafe for himself, turning it up. Afterward he doted upon her, his demeanor altering into something a little more sensitive as he caressed the flats between his knuckles against the swell of her bruised cheek. "The plan was never for you to become like this, my love."

"I know," she said, almost ashamed.

Vaustian had that effect on folk quite often. And much of the time, she noted, it was not done to be intentionally cruel. He expected greatness from himself and, therefore, expected nothing less from that of his peers. He was a hard man that had lived a hard life and through his many trials had managed to rise from the peasantry stock to the Viceroy of Lancastle Citadel, the lordliest kingdom in all of the Midaran Commonwealth. Thusly he had scant little time for soft things as it were and even less understanding of them. Though somehow, over the cycles, for reasons she still couldn't entirely fathom herself, she had managed to surmount those very feelings. She, the softest thing in all the Vael. Or so ofttimes that was how it felt.

"I fear I have pushed you along too fast," he said.

"No, my love," Marsea began, remembering the warrior from the wood, Casilvieri's words, and all that she had done over the past fortnight to prove herself to the Ravenholme masters, "this was meant to happen. This had to happen." *Something had to change,* she thought. *Anything at all.* And if that meant nearly losing a hand and her very life to see it through, then so be it. "This is how I ascend." She set down her wine glass without touching a drop and leaned in close against him, driving him flush against the desk. "This is how I become useful." Against the push of their combined weight, the desk complained backward, and Vaustian clutched her tightly, reflexively lifting her upon him as he collapsed atop the desk's surface to halt their plight before it even began. And somehow the carafe managed to survive the awkward incident. Though the inkwell at the other end was not near as fortunate.

"Oh, and then there's that," she said, now lying atop him, his hardness pressing against her.

"Are you all right?" he asked, ignoring her blushing embarrassment. "Your hand..."

"I'm fine." One would think she was the sot given what had just transpired.

An unexpected chuckle erupted from her love, and she couldn't help but grin at his sudden amusement. It had been quite some time since she had heard him laugh in such a manner. In fact, it had been some time since last she had heard her love laugh at all.

"Well, someone is mighty pleased with himself," she murmured as she collected herself.

Vaustian sat up, massaging at the small of his back where a pair of tomes had stabbed at him upon impact of their fall. "Marsea, I must confess, you might be the last person left to the Vael that can still make me laugh in such a manner."

This made her smile grow that much more despite the sting of her busted lip, and she licked at the crooked notch, having forgotten it for the thinnest of moments. The edge of her tongue tasted blood from a freshly made fissure in the scab's crust, and her smile quickly faded. She daubed at it with the edge of her sleeve, revealing a smear of red. *The maidens know,* she thought, *how dare you, Marsea. How dare you show even the slightest inkling of merriment.* "I said the words," she murmured in place of her aggravation, holding her sleeve to her lip.

Emotion cowered away from Vaustian Harver as he held her suddenly stormy gaze.

"I will not let my past define me," she recited, making her prior comment clear. The words came easier and easier with every breath.

"Saying and meaning are two very different concepts," he said, turning his cheek to her, staring out the balcony doorway at the star-filled skies beyond.

"I meant them," she said in such a serious manner as to force his attention. "Consult Cas and he will confirm. I meant them wholeheartedly." *I nearly died for them, after all, didn't I?*

Wordlessly, he simply stared back at her, *into* her really, his eyes like the heavens during snowfall, somehow both light and dark, and maddeningly unreadable.

"I agreed to the assignment," she maintained her boldness, "and I knew the risks."

"You were not ready," he countered, the words already in wait. "And I knew you weren't. I knew better and I allowed for it anyway."

"And yet the maidens saw me through." Her eyes were wide with conviction.

He shook his head, his lips thinning to a rigid line, a rumor of frustration befalling his calculating countenance. And Marsea knew she would gain little ground speaking of faith and fortune with Vaustian Harver, for the Viceroy considered neither. "You made a decision in a moment. A decision that preserved your life. Nothing more, nothing less. And I had a moment of weakness, a moment of foolishness, and I nearly lost you for it. I nearly fucking lost you." He shifted away from her. "That will not happen again."

"You cannot control everything, Vaustian," she argued, her escalating emotions conjuring a fresh burn of tears behind her eyes, though she fought mightily against their recurrence.

"I cannot lose you, Marsea," he thundered possessively. "What must I say for you to understand this?"

"You won't lose me." *Must it always come back to this?*

"The fool I am. I sent you to slaughter," he said, his tone dangerous and arcane. "I let you convince me. I let you blind me." He took up the carafe by the neck and turned up another swallow.

"Must you always focus on the imperfections, darling? I am still alive, aren't I? And the assignment was fulfilled."

He said nothing. Though behind his cold visage, it was evident he was suffering some manner of great turmoil.

"You promised," she said as his silence became extended. "Have I not paid my toll for your promise?"

"Marsea—"

"What more must I do to convince you that I am loyal to the cause—that I am worthy?"

He set down the carafe and held her darkened haunters as he reached out to take her wounded hand. He cupped it delicately and lifted it gently as he eased the sling over her head. "May I?"

Of course, my love. She consented with an obedient nod, her eyes speaking in place of her lips.

He removed the pin from the cloth and began unwinding, his calloused hands working slowly together as he unraveled the bandaging, layer by darkening layer, again and again and again in quick, rhythmic circles until a sliver of bruised flesh appeared beneath. He stopped at the sight of it and stared grimly at the discoloration, holding an unmoving hand under hers for support. Her hand, though swollen, was still quite small by comparison to his. "May I?" he asked again.

And she nodded again, her breath halting, as he lifted her hand tenderly to his lips and pressed them against the thin expanse of exposed skin. His stubble was thick and rough, the tiny hairs prickling into her flesh ever so faintly. It was a small pain she had grown quite fond of, a subtle reminder of his manliness.

"I know that I am quite mistrustful," he began. "It is my nature, I am afraid. I have warred with this world since I left the womb. I have warred with foe and family alike as you well know. I have made enemies of many. A volume's worth. More than I ever care to count. War, I understand. And, dare I confess, find some measure of comfort in." The last bit was stated with jarring confidence. "For war is a defined pain. An understandable construct. A construct with absolute confines." He spoke with smooth, stark inflections and stared deep into her shimmering silver orbs, stimulating a tide of goose pimples across the expanse of her skin. "But you. You, Marsea Lanier. You represent what I can only ascertain is the opposite of war for me. That is not to say that you embody peace or compassion or love or that I have not felt such emotions before. I have encountered all three on numerous occasions in the most profound of capacities. It is more to say that to me you are something beyond those mere sentiments. You are something I cannot properly describe, something that is decidedly both healthy and unhealthy for me, something that more than like I will never fully comprehend. I have resigned myself to such a theory. And I have endeavored to warm myself to it. However long it may take. I have a wife, yes, and I have a daughter, both of whom I love in my own conflicted method. I also have an overbearing older brother and a host of leal servants. And through all of it, through blood and oath and law and fealty, it always comes back to you. And do you know why that is?"

Her tongue failed her in spite of her want. Hells, the concept of language itself as a practical preexisting entity failed her.

"You are the only one that I believe when you say I can trust you. You are the only one that has not yet betrayed me by some manner or another." A brief pause inserted itself into his words, and a wistful expression befell him. "It is a truly terrible concept of our humanity to question that of our own bloodkin, that of our own progeny."

Marsea rather thought the same about her own kin. Her mother had betrayed her father all those many cycles ago. And thusly she had betrayed them all. Centuries of Lanier reign cast to ruin in an instant. And Remy...well, he had become something else entirely. Marsea had never truly gotten on well with her younger brother. He was a bad mix to be sure, every bit as arrogant and headstrong as their older brother Des had been, though Remy lacked the confidence and the backbone. In the least, he'd grown clever enough to escape this prison when the time came, yet to what end she hadn't the faintest. All of life was a prison, she had come to believe, and she would just as soon have the prison she knew than the one out there.

"I apologize for the gloomy digression," Vaustian said as he resumed unfurling her bandages. "That was most certainly not my intention. The short of it is this, my love. Your worthiness was never in question. Though trust, by contrast, there have been many nights when I've questioned mine own worthiness of you."

Her inquisitive watch softened, and seconds elapsed—too many seconds—far too many seconds. *Words, Marsea,* she reminded. *Fucking words. Get there.*

"You cannot shelter me forever, you know," she found herself saying. *And there we are then.* "I am awake now," she kept on, apparently unable to stop herself, letting the bloodstained linens fall loose to the stones below. "You have awoken me. You set me to this path. You created this." She held her hideous, misshapen horror of a hand between them so they could share in the fruits of her darkly labors. "I now see the wolves in the halls. Because of you. I hear their secrets through the stone. Because of you. I know their conniving schemes behind closed doors. Because of you. And I cannot simply ignore them any longer. Nor can I cower from them. You are absolutely right to be the way you are, my love. You have every claim to your mistrustfulness. You should know even your closest conspire against you. Your man Cas would sooner have me a killer than a queen, in spite of your wishes. Though, if I am being completely honest, because of you, I cannot say I disagree."

They were words that had been long in the loom, to be sure, though a sense of nervousness swiftly replaced what relief was found by their unfolding as she waited heartbeat after thrumming heartbeat for his next suggestion.

"Once a robling, always a robling," Vaustian muttered. "Cas is a stray dog that managed more cycles than he ought and a far higher station than he rightfully deserves. He should better know his place than to put daft thoughts in the minds of the untried. And you should know better than to entertain the words of the lowly wicked." *And there was that Harver pride, ever near, to rear its ugly head.* "In any event, there are yet still more pressing matters beyond us we need discuss." He shifted away from her at that, toward the balcony's darkness, and retrieved his coat in course, fishing his cob from one of the pockets once he had it on.

The maidens know he could avoid with the best of them. Marsea clutched her wounded hand against her bosom and followed.

The king's balcony overlooked near all of Kingdom Lancastle below, and its view stretched long across the stone buildings and scattered streetlamps of the sprawling city into the hovelled cabins of the farthest hamlets before the Kingswood's obscurity swallowed the remaining horizon like a giant black wave. It was a quaint little hideaway, where she recalled her father had spent many of his days and even more of his nights. It had taken Marsea many cycles after his death to share in his appreciation of the king's balcony. But here she was again. Inside Vaustian's version of it. The high lord's balcony. And every time she passed upon it, she couldn't help but wonder the same exact thing. What would her father think of her now, consorting with the man that had orchestrated his demise? She inhaled slowly, the winds crisp and biting, and breathed out through her mouth, forming a cold cloud before her face. The morning's fleeting warmth was already a long-forgotten memory, almost a dream in its swift passing.

Vaustian, huddling close to the wall with the cob clutched tight in his teeth, scratched a match once the wind died for a moment, and quickly lowered the tiny flame inside the bowl. He took a heavy pull, followed by a second, and a third to stoke the burn before turning back toward her.

"Drag?" he offered.

The wind carried a scent of shufa to her, and she declined with a wave of her good hand. She wanted nothing more than to partake, to unwind, to find the smallest inkling of relief, but something in her gut was telling her to keep her head as clear as possible this nightfall.

Vaustian took another long drag, and this time he held it in, savoring in its bliss until only a thin wisp breathed out through his nose. Afterward he studied Marsea with heavy, stoned eyes, eyes that concealed behind their watch a most deep-rooted melancholy. "By now I am sure you have heard tale of the conflicts in the north."

"Cas made mention," she said bundling up inside her cloak, "as did Pion."

"Pion?" Vaustian scoffed. "And what would my bumbling nephew know of war? He can scarce bring himself out of bed in the morning for a proper piss, much less wield a sword and shield."

Despite his harsh and seemingly dismissive words, Marsea did not believe for a second that her love underestimated his clever bloodkin. Vaustian Harver never underestimated anyone. He might believe himself better than most, but he never took a man at face value. Besides, she had overheard him with the privy council discussing Pion before not so many quints past and Vaustian had not been so dismissive then. In fact, the way they spoke about him that eventide, one would think Pion Harver was one of the greatest strategists to ever live.

"In any case," he started again, "it is still unclear as of yet what all parties are involved. However, rumors of the blight returning to Midara have been confirmed. Latest reports claim the ashaeydir are responsible, alleging it was one of their gravedancers that summoned a lich back from the nether to wreak havoc on the northern hollows."

A lich? Had it come from anyone else's lips, she would have thought the divulgence utterly preposterous. "You are serious?"

"Though I wish that I were not," he said gravely. "Amongst the fallen are Stone's Throw, Avindell, Brymshire, and Hearth, with Palatia presumed to be next." He leaned down against the stone balustrade and turned to her with a grim expression, his black curls flowing slightly in the seeking breeze. "This information was had only a few hours past."

"How bad are we talking?" she asked, joining him at the balustrade. "Another Black Dawn?" She watched just below them as a pair of bluecoats patrolled the parapets on the next tier down. One of them began laughing suddenly, and she felt a swell of rage rise up within her. Cheerfulness of any sort seemed a ridiculous concept given the conversation's turn.

"It is much too early to tell, but another Black Dawn is entirely possible. The ashaeydir are nothing if not practiced opportunists. Opportunists and proven conquerors. And what would make Vaelsyntheria any different than Y'dema or Ashira before her? Conquest will ever and always be in the ashaeydir's blood and bones, and for the most, they have proven quite effective at it. Whether the reports of their current involvement are true or not, I have no doubts they will eventually make their presence known. I tell you this now, Marsea, because there is a very real chance we will come to face these creatures and soon. The threat is imminent. And the coming reports have grown more and more dire by the hour. So dire that on the morrow, a mandatory draft will be conducted about the surrounding hollows calling to service all men and women of suitable age that are fit for combat."

"Are we in danger then?" she asked, knowing well his insinuation. "Is Lancastle in danger?"

"*We* are not in danger, my love," he assured. "Ravenholme already has contingencies in place for its own. I can keep you safe." His expression became deadly serious. "I will keep you safe. Anywhere I go, you will go with me. Is that clear?"

She held his glare and nodded.

"Good."

"Are you afraid?" she couldn't help but inquire.

And he gazed not at her but into her. "Honestly? I'm fucking terrified. You know me as well as any other. I am the worst manner of cynic and a terrible worrier. I fear the worst all the time. And I always expect it. As such, I believe it is no longer a matter of *if* Palatia falls, but rather *when*. And I suspect, given the savagery described in the coming reports, that once she is taken, the ashaeydir and their legion of monstrosities will next turn their attentions southward."

"But we repelled them before—"

"*We* did not," he said sharply. "Our forebears did. And they repelled them because the ashaeydir were greedy and arrogant, fresh off their victory on Y'dema. They thought they were invincible, and they misjudged our legions, badly. And we rallied behind great men in those times, heroic men. Men, that suffice to say, are few and far between in this soft version of society. In those days we also held a fruitful alliance with that of the y'deman and loraai aristocracies and the mountain folk alike, an alliance that has since become dissolved by petty feuds and infighting, an alliance that despite appearances no longer exists. Midara's commonwealth is now and has long been fractured, more than like beyond repair, the many races falling away into their own politics, not to be bothered by those outside their provinces. And you better believe the bloody ashaeydir are well aware of this. Their spies are persistent, and they are countless, the dodgy bastards. And they will not be so foolish this go-round. They will hit us with everything—"

A jarring clatter from outside the solar drew short his words, and they both turned about in consequence. As he took a step forward, a series of knocks rapped against the chamber door, and Vaustian motioned for Marsea to hold position while he tended to the unexpected interruption.

She drifted to the balcony's shadows and listened intently as the bolt lock clicked and the chamber door yawned open once more.

"Aeralie?" Vaustian greeted with just enough surprise. "What in vael-nation was all that racket just now?" There wasn't even the faintest inkling of worry in his tone to betray the severity of their prior conversation.

"A torch hold," she said after a moment of silence. "It just toppled over. The gods only know how."

"Ah, you've awoken the hauntlings then, have you?" he teased.

"Papa, be good. It's far too late an hour to attend your awful humor."

Papa, be good, Marsea mocked. *Good gravy, Aera. Must you always act as a child?*

He chuckled at that. "And what may I inquire, my dear, lovely daughter, has you awake at such an unsightly hour as this?"

"Sleep would not have me this night," she responded guilelessly. "Try as I might to find it." *Like father, like daughter,* Marsea thought sourly. "And so I thought I should like to keep you company as I know you like to keep to the crone's hours."

"Of course, love, of course." His voice was doting, though his sincerity was questionable. "I've missed your company of late."

"And I yours," she retched sweet falsities. "But I know how busy you keep, Papa. I suppose a governor's duties are never truly without end, are they?"

"I expect not," he agreed. "And it would seem your old man has forgotten his sup again as a result. What say you to a wander down to the kitchens?" he asked as the chamber door clicked shut behind them.

Marsea rolled her eyes at her love's little impromptu performance. The gods know he would have been a brilliant actor were the world only slightly skewed. She retrieved her sling, bandages, and glasses as she passed through the chamber and waited a minute's count before peeking out into the corridor. True to the telling, the torch hold down the left side lay unmoving in the middle of the corridor. It was a horridly peculiar occurrence indeed, hauntlings or no. But there was no time to investigate as she heard the clanging approach of a bluecoat patrol from down the corridor. Marsea closed the door softly behind her and stole away once more into the darkness, away from the guards, as though she were a common thief in the night, as though this place were anywhere but home.

"A close one to be sure, I'd say," a voice called from the shadows as Marsea finally made the passage containing her bedchamber.

She recognized the impish inflections immediately and sighed. As if her day had not already progressed with enough dramatics, she now had another Harver to contend with. Truly, how could it be anything else? She groaned vociferously as she advanced, letting him know her frustration with his presence.

Pion hobbled into the torchlight just before her doorway and took to a casual lean against the wall. "What ails you, sister?" he asked.

Marsea said nothing and kept her eyes down as she pressed past him to her doorway.

"And tell us honest, my dear lovely Seasea," he began noxiously, "did you allow my fool uncle to once again ravage and sully your ladyhood for a fresh course of Ministry propaganda? Truly I would have quite enjoyed watching Uncle's face when cousin Aera opened the door wide to pay her papa call and found you there upon the tabletop taking it like a proper harlot."

Ignore him, Marsea.

"And I'm sure she would have found as much too if I hadn't doused a torch hold for warning."

Maintaining her silence, Marsea retrieved the skeleton key from her cleavage and inserted it into the spyhole of her bedchamber door.

"The silent treatment, is it?" Pion goaded further as the door came unlocked and cracked open. "And did mine uncle gobfuck you mute as well then?"

The princess shuffled inside and slammed the door in his wretched face, falling against it afterward and sliding to the floor.

"I love this little game you're at," he said from the other side. "The one where you believe, and adorably so I must confess, that you can win."

Empty threats, she told herself, *useless empty threats.* Tears streamed down her weary, aching face anyway. They would not be denied. And here she thought she might be all cried out for the evening too. *Just don't let him hear you.*

"Marsea," Pion said in a kinder tongue after a spell of silence. "I am sorry."

She removed her glasses and wiped at the tears that would not stop. *Have you truly become so lachrymose?* The princess could still recall a time when she thought the prospect of tears escaping her nigh to impossible.

"You don't deserve such unpleasant words."

Go away, Pion, you sniveling lech.

"And mayhaps my tact could have been better placed in our meeting, but alas you've made of this man something of a jealous tomfool, haven't you?"

Hardly a man, most say.

"All the same, I come to you with a proposal in stow. A proposal I am hopeful you will accept."

The maidens know, lech, take the bloody hint.

"I am leaving Lancastle on the morrow for Courowne. I fear dreadfully dark times will soon come to find this place. And I should like to be as far away as possible when those times arrive."

Marsea sniffled, and her heartbeat began to hasten at the wonderful news.

"You should come with me," he continued. And she almost laughed aloud at the invitation. "I can offer you protection in Courowne. Your Uncle Rhonyn is there. And no doubt your Aunt Magwyn would be delighted to see you as well."

Neither one spoke for a time after that, but she knew he was still there on the other side awaiting her response.

From her woeful rest on the floor, she stared out her window at the heavens beyond. It had grown gray and cloudy in the last hour since her visit upon the high lord's balcony. She expected Lancastle would soon awake to more snowfall.

Their silence pooled, and her eyelids began to heavy. *Go away, you pathetic creep,* she thought, utterly exhausted. *I'm done with you.*

And as though he could feel her drifting, Pion said, "I know you will never care for me as I do you, Marsea, but prize well, I still have a desire to see you happy and hale...to see you safe."

"Go away, Pion," she finally spoke the words that had been circling about her thoughts since she arrived at her bedchamber door.

"He's burrowed too far into your head, hasn't he?" Pion asked, a forlorn sadness thick upon his tongue.

Marsea frowned and groaned as she lifted her aching body back up to its feet.

"Why can't you see what he is?" Pion questioned further.

"I said sod off."

"Are you truly so blind, Seasea? So grateful he's fixed you that you forgot he was the one that caused your misery in the first place. I can offer you what you have wanted all along. I can offer you a path away from this place...away from this suffering. I can offer you some measure of freedom."

"I don't want a path away from this place," she said icily. *This is my home, after all. My kingdom.* "And you should know better than any of us, Pion. Freedom is a lie." *A myth really.* "None of us are truly free. Not you. Not me. Not Vaustian. Not any of us. No matter where we run to."

"He will be the death of you," Pion said gravely.

But Marsea deafened herself to his words. *Go away, Pion,* she thought. *Go to Courowne if you must. Go to the other end of the bloody Vael for all I care. Just promise wherever you go you will never return here.* And the princess trudged to her bed where she collapsed upon it and closed her eyes as she softly began to trace a finger over the jagged rows of sewn together flesh about her ruined left hand.

CHAPTER SEVENTEEN

A songbird's serenade from just outside the bedchamber window struck him like a hard slap to the face, and Remy jolted awake for the umpteenth time. Yet again he found himself inside the freezing darkness amongst the creaks, the muffled voices, and the dancing shadows. He groaned at the vicious recurrence and massaged gingerly at his cheekbones, driving up into the hollows around his eyes. It would seem amidst the spiraling madness, his insomnia had returned once more for the haunt, and so he set himself to the most tedious of tasks, marrying stone to sword. By and by, if the world would have him awake at such an hour, he'd manage something of use from it. A cleanly sharpened blade.

In the least, the dull ache behind his bloodshot delirium had become something of a distraction from his sore ribs and burning shoulder. And by the gods' mercy, he took some small comfort in the fact that he hadn't been stirred this time by the sound of some moaning whore in the next room over or another shit-panned patron staggering about the hallway outside. *There was something, wasn't it,* he mocked his lack of pride. *And there goes my boastful standards and the gods only know what else right along with them.*

He appeared anything but a king now, silenced by filth, plagued by ignominy, existing somewhere betwixt yet wholly separate of both the nobility and the peasantry. He'd become an outcast in the truest form, ostracization incarnate, and accordingly, here he now found himself, cowering in a brothel of all places, a fearful, broken fugitive. Oh, but it was a most wretched whorehouse too. The skunk hole at the edge of town, and even that title rang generous. Leave it to Rhymona bloody Curie to find refuge in such a repulsing haunt.

Who was he kidding? Of course, it was a damned brothel. How could it be anything else, really? So long as it was dank, distasteful, and depraved, she was game for it. Or so it would seem. Though he supposed, all affairs considered, it could have been much worse. Breath still found his lungs, did it not? And without question, he had Curie to thank for that bit too.

Their room was at the end of a long corridor and reeked of body odor, excrement, and spilled alcohol, a collective stench that put even the worst of stables to shame—as if he hadn't lost enough faith in his fellow man already. But given the turn of things, what other choice did he have? It was either imprisonment inside the citadel dungeons or freedom within the confines of an outhouse, and this was indeed an outhouse whether it housed an actual privy or not. Thusly into the shitpot he leapt with an eager want in his weary eyes and bells adorning his bootstrings. Pride was a worthless fancy to the dead, yeah? And given the turn of things, the value of anonymity rated gold to pride's dross.

The room itself was plain, sparsely furnished, and only slightly warmer than the chill lingering just outside. The bed merited no blankets or pillows, the nightstand lacked a candle or candleholder, and the stool, of which he presently occupied, might have once been some fashion of chair. No doubt the space would have served them just as well completely bare. The sister moons provided a scant allowance of light, shining through the spiderwebbed cracks in the room's lone windowpane, and Remy rather thought that bit for the best. All told, the malodorous stench alone would be sight enough of the place.

The watchman turned up what remained of the whiskey and felt the warmth settle inside his chest, only to desert him again seconds later.

He shifted his attentions toward Curie. She had fashioned herself a pillow with her fur cloak, and she lay unmoving atop the otherwise barren mattress. To wit, she hadn't moved from that very spot in hours, since her failed attempts to heal him through The Spellbind. At least she had cleaned his wound for him and closed it with twine as he quaffed his way through the pain of her slapdash surgery. But afterward she had walled herself off from him, clearly disturbed by her sudden inability to commune with what she referred to as the giftwell. And he decided it best to give her what time and space he could, as though he actually had any of either to spare.

"Rhymona," he said, pushing up from the broken chair. He found his entire torso had become stiff and uncooperative. She offered no response, and he waited a little longer in silence just staring at her. She actually appeared quite peaceful, almost innocent, in her slumberous state. *Don't be a fuckwit,* he imagined her response to such a line of thought, and he shook the daft reverie from his mind.

"I won't pretend I know anything about The Spellbind or the giftwell, as you say," he began, "or why it won't respond to you. But we need to conjure a plan regardless. The morrow is nearly upon us now. And a decision must be made."

Curie remained quiet and lifeless. And he remained every measure as restless.

"Rhymona," he called a bit louder as he took a step toward the bed. But there was still no response. "Curie," he said, shaking at the toe of her boot. Nothing. Not even a disgruntled twitch. She lay frozen as stone, though in the least he could still hear her drawing shallow breaths.

"Mad Mona," he dared to a deathly silence before touching a hand against her shoulder, and within an eye blink, she seized his collar in her fist, pulling him down to her face with one hand and pressing a blade between his legs with the other. His body became taut as he felt the razor's edge inch dangerously close to his fruits.

"Curie, it's me," he stammered against the strain from his ribs. "Rhymona!"

"Toff?" she grumbled as if waking from a dream most devouring. Her grip weakened at the realization and the blade lowered.

"Mercy of Myrenna, Curie, what in the nine was that?" he spluttered through a coughing fit as he checked his privates for injury.

She snickered in spite of her grogginess. "Didn't your Nan ever warn you?" she rasped. "Never fuck with a sleeping magus."

"My Gran warned me to stay away from giftborn altogether," he said.

"But my Gran passed on cycles ago, the gods rest her soul, and here we are anyway, aren't we?"

"Mmm, dreadfully depressing, Toff, as always," she said, shifting to the side of the bed and retrieving her cloak.

"I give what I get."

"And more's the pity, yeah?"

"Something of the like," he said.

"Any more whiskey?" she asked.

"What do you think?"

"Gods wounds, Toff, I didn't take *you* for a fucking alky."

"It helped with the pain, is all. And I thank you for it. I'll buy you a bloody tavern's worth if we actually manage to escape this nightmare."

"Mmm, building quite the tab then, aren't we?"

"Evidently."

"The gods know it may take a tavern or three to wash all this bollocks away."

They shared a chuckle at that. It was nearly to that point, wasn't it? Where affairs had become so ridiculous that all there was left was to laugh in its face.

"And how's the bad one?" she asked with what sounded like genuine concern.

"It hurts like the bloody nine, but what else is new?"

"Can you move it?"

Remy tenderly flexed his shoulder to test its mobility. It obeyed for the most, but stung horribly when stretched too far. He would need days of rest to restore it to proper use no doubt. Days he did not have. Hells at this point, he didn't even have hours. "I'll manage," he said, fighting a groan at the wound's fresh throb. "And what of The Spellbind?"

"Still quiet," she said ominously.

"Has this ever happened before?" he asked.

"No," she answered with what seemed like genuine honesty, "at least never to me."

"Do you suppose its absence is somehow related to the blight's resurgence?"

"Fuck if I know," Curie said as she affixed the heavy fur cloak to her dark leather jerkin. "I know it's not good news either way. Without the giftwell, we're proper fucked against the likes of a lichlord. Six ways to Sunfell fucked."

"But there is still the possibility of charonisk, is there not?"

Curie snorted. "A dreamer's fancy, that. There is a world's difference between a clever archer ranging open wood and thousands defending a mountaintop. Tenbrooks might be the greatest alchemist Midara has ever seen and he still wouldn't be able to conjure enough Eldn fire to contain the lichlord's army in time. Once the infection breaks through—"

"But wouldn't it work both ways? If giftborn cannot access The Spellbind, how can the lich?"

"The lich don't pull from the giftwell, Toff," she said in her typically patronizing manner. "Magic is called from the blood. Hemomancy, they name it. And the lich are as bloodless as they come, are they not? Nothing more than rotted meat on bones. As such they can't hope to touch magic's gift. It is utterly useless to their lot. Thusly they draw upon the nether instead. And before you ask, yes, the nether too can be accessed by giftborn, but with horrid, perilous consequences. It's not meant to be harnessed by the living. And one should only delve as deep as they are willing to sacrifice. An old friend once warned me of such, and I had to learn the hard lesson."

"You mean to say you've drawn upon the nether before?"

Curie brushed her snow-white hair from out of her eyes and gazed at him properly. "I mean to say. Though it's debatable whether or not I drew from it or it from me." She touched a hand to her cheek and pulled down. "Do you think mine cheeks have always sagged in such an unnatural manner?"

"I expect not," Remy answered plainly. He knew well the dangers of chatting beauty thoughts with the fairer gender and decided to keep his tongue in check.

"Don't you think these crow's feet a mite long for a lass of such few cycles?" she kept on.

He supposed, but in truth, he had no idea how old she was. He might have guessed mid-thirties, mayhaps forty.

"My hair was once as dark as yours, you should well prize. But the nether stole that from me just as well. The nether stole many things from me. And I only borrowed but once. And only for a few seconds."

"If you knew the potential consequences, why did you persist?" he couldn't help but ask. It was the first time he could recall Curie revealing anything even remotely personal about her life to him, and he found he could not simply table his curiosity.

"No doubt the romantic would have me say it was entirely for love," she said. "And I believe that mostly true. But I would be remiss if I said that love was my sole reason for doing it."

"*You* were in love?" Remy could scarce believe the confession, though a wiser man might have questioned it with far less impertinence.

A smile leaked through Curie's ironclad indifference. It was not a sinister smile as what typically found her lips. It was a smile from the eyes, a smile of fondness, and yet a smile of wistfulness all the same. "Reckon I still am, if I'm being honest," she admitted. "And I suspect in a way I always will be."

Curious Curie, ever full of surprises. "And here I thought you had no heart at all, much less one capable of love. I must know. What was his name? This love of yours."

She shook her head, her smile fading to a sly smirk, and turned for the doorway. It was quite clear she had no intention of divulging further.

Bloody hell, but of course the bitch was lying. Always hiding behind humor's shelter aren't we, Rhymona? "You're truly awful you know that?"

And just as Curie released the door's chain lock, the bell tower tolled to life, its peal stark and condemning, followed in quick succession by the horns of war from near and far, announcing an attack. And just as Brymshire had, the sleeping city came alive all at once. The songbird's lonely chirp was thereafter replaced by cries most desperate, hounds baying, and soldiers barking orders. Remy hurried to the window, the pink of dawn but a hint in the distance, and he watched as a trio of bloodcoats on horseback galloped recklessly through the flooding masses toward the southern gatehouse. Torchlights flickered to life in the snow-covered street below as those in residence spilled forth from the brothel's entrance and entrances up and down the avenue.

"We need to be going," Curie said as she opened the door, Fucker at the ready.

Remy grabbed his satchel from beside the chair, pulling it over his head to rest upon his good shoulder, and collected luckless Gray's restored watchman's blade. Wide-eyed and without protest, he followed Curie down the hallway and stairwell into the taproom below where madness had apparently consumed a group of soused patrons who were smashing bottles in every direction and throwing fists at one another. One of the larger ruffians landed a punch in spectacular fashion across another's cheek, dropping the poor unsuspecting bastard cold.

"This is madness," Remy yelled to Curie as a bottle whizzed just overhead to shatter inside the stairwell behind them. A half-dressed, blood-spattered prostitute stumbled down the last few steps of the stairwell then, bounding over the broken glass, and raced past them barefoot into the burgeoning crowd at the brothel's entrance.

"Gods damned bloody fuckwits," Curie groused. "This way," she said, and Remy followed her back up the stairwell, past a mumbling patron and a staggering second, into the first open doorway facing the backside of the building.

"What are we doing?" Remy asked.

"Making an exit, of course," she said, releasing the window's latch and pushing it open.

"Fuck me, you're serious," he said.

She tossed Fucker out the window and turned back to him. "Would you prefer the fuckwit convention downstairs then?" And then she eased herself onto the narrow windowsill, graceful as a cat, and without the thinnest hint of hesitation, disappeared from sight.

"Fuck me," Remy groaned as he rushed up to the window and found Curie on the cobble below having landed with a perfect push into a shoulder roll to retrieve her beloved hatchet.

"Now or never, Toff," she called up to him.

An explosion sounded in the nearby distance, shaking the building enough to nearly take his footing. Immediately, his fingers clutched hard to the window's edge, his eyes squeezed tightly closed, and his heart jumped fully in his mouth.

"Fucking hells," he heard Curie say below as he regained his bearings.

"What was that?" he asked, his fear beginning to cloud rationality from his mind.

"A cask exploding would be my best guess," she said, peeking around the corner of the building. "Cedarholm's boys must be getting nervous."

A cloud of smoke thickened to the east over Palatia's southernmost wall as soldiers by the dozen climbed and settled the ramparts.

"Toss down your shit," Curie commanded. "Now is our chance."

And Remy turned back inside, pacing a nervous circle. "Fucking hells." He ran a hand through his dark curls, the ringing from his anxieties chiseling its way into his head again. "Fuck me." *It's never-ending.* He pinched the bridge of his nose and closed his eyes to center his thoughts. *You can do this, Remy. You can do this. You must do this. This is it.*

"You've got ten seconds and I leave your sorry ass," she threatened.

Ghouls, assassins, and now heights. I'm compiling quite the list, aren't I? he thought as he took a series of controlled breaths and approached the window. But when he arrived, Curie was nowhere to be found. "Shit." *She's left me.* Heaviness returned to his chest at her absence, and his breathing became erratic once more. *Just go, Remy,* his mind screamed. *Sink or swim time. Find her. Do something. Do anything.* And without thinking on it a second further, he dropped his sword down to the cobble below and placed an unsteady boot atop the windowsill.

"Oopsie," a voice said from behind, startling him, and he turned about empty-handed to face it. "*Ahda kalare,*" the figure greeted from the doorway. "Rembrandt Lanier, is it?" she asked. "The king of kings himself, yeah?"

Something about her voice made his blood run cold. It was the voice of a most pitiless creature, the voice of a seasoned killer. Somehow, The Covenant had already found them.

"I daresay, we simply must stop meeting like this," she said, her movements like footsteps when no one was coming.

It was a most unexpected remark. "Do I know you?" he found himself asking, questioning if she were really, truly there, or if his nerves had finally brought him round to lunacy's embrace.

"No, I don't expect you do," she answered as a glint of silver kissed the shadow at her side, chased by a vaguely familiar face revealed in the dim cast of dawn's earliest light.

"You?" he said aghast as he backed up against the wall next to the window. The ghost of Brymshire past, she was.

"Oye, tosser," he heard Curie's voice again down below him. "Quit being a craven fuckwit. Let's go."

Curie. She hadn't left him after all. There was still a chance. And a bit of fortitude found him at the thought.

"Imagine my surprise when I came to find out who you truly were," Wade's harlot said as she raised the butcher's knife between them. "The king of kings, fallen straight into my lap. I daresay fortune never favored such a wretch so handsomely."

"What do you want?" he asked, shifting the satchel behind him.

"Many things," she answered evenly, "oh, so many things. You haven't the faintest inkling how many. Truly, I could go on for hours. Though presently I would say your compliance will suffice."

"Come again?" He hadn't expected such an odd response, though his eyes remained thoroughly fastened to the knife inching ever the closer.

"Right. I can see how that might come off a bit confusing for you. Mayhaps I should clarify." And with her free hand, she reached under her blond locks and touched somewhere behind her ear.

The transformation was instantaneous, inside the snap of a finger really. And her irises lightened from a dark, muddied ring to that of a bright yellow-gold as her wan skin dimmed into a deep shade of lilac wisteria. Even her hair became a few shades darker. But her facial features remained exactly the same. How he hadn't noticed the similarities back in Brymshire, he could not say, but there was certainly no denying it now. Wade's harlot and the ashaeydir assassin were indeed the same person.

Remy gawked at the woman utterly speechless, wholly unsure of how to comprehend what he had just borne witness to. He had heard the ashaeydir possessed strange contrivances and abilities beyond magic's cast to wage their many wars, but nothing on the par of this fel sorcery. And the ashaeydir's lopsided smile returned once more as if he needed any more proof as to the truth behind her identity.

"This will only take an instant," she promised.

"The hells?" a second voice uttered from the doorway, and quick as a whip, the ashaeydir turned about and loosed the butcher's knife at the intruder.

Remy heard the blade sink into flesh and bone behind him, and without abandon, he rolled out the window, consequences be damned, though it wasn't the ground that came up to meet him as expected, rather, and the irony was not lost on him, a butcher's wagon. A grunt rippled out of him from the impact, his vision spinning and his body unresponsive.

"Emyria's tits, what in fuck's name was that?" Curie asked as she came to his side.

"Ash...ashaeydir," Remy answered weakly, his breath still eluding him.

"The one from Brymshire," he added, gasping for air, fighting for any manner of movement at all. "Where did the cart come from?"

"Pulled it out of my arsehole," she said, helping him to his feet. "I'm sorry, did you just say ashaeydir?"

He winced and nodded, nursing his tender ribs.

"Fucking hells, Toff. You've a real talent for tomfuckery, haven't you? I leave you alone for two bloody minutes, and you've gone and found yourself a fucking ashaeydir?"

A real talent for something, he thought. "Where to now?" he grumbled instead, ignoring her paltry attempt at japery.

"As far away from the vanguard as we can get," she said. "They're blasting the walls to the south and east, so Northgate first. Reckon it's our best chance." She offered him his watchman's blade. "Out of the frying pan and into the fire once again."

Remy clutched the scabbard with a grimace and drew his blade.

CHAPTER EIGHTEEN

Remy ran, dashing through the swarming city streets behind Curie's wild specter like a man possessed, the misshapen stones of the cobble thrumming hard against the bones of his aching feet and rising up into his ankles and knees, the memory of his tear through Brymshire all too near. But he kept on all the same, enduring the waves of unending pain, dodging and weaving about the faceless blur of the doomed masses like a rat in an overcrowded maze. He knew what they were racing toward, besides, and he knew if he stopped or hesitated for even the slimmest of moments, it could spell the end of him. He remembered how Dennings bit it, helping the cloth maiden, and he would not make the same mistake. He was no hero, nor was he a tenderheart, or a straggler. He would not be undone by some nameless weakling determined to rot no matter how vulnerable or innocent they might be. He remembered the father and his little girl from Brymshire at that, their fraught, haunted faces, and their utter disbelief at his cruel spurning. No, he shook the memory from his mind. He couldn't have helped them even if he had wanted to. More than like they would have only turned him a quick grave right along with them. And at that, he remembered something his Uncle Rho had once told him, something that had long stuck with him despite its callousness.

There are two types of folks in this world, Rembrandt, he began between his second glass of wine and the third one's pour, all those many cycles past, *those that make their own luck and those that hope luck finds them. And then there is a king. A king is not a person, though mortal he may be. A king is a bloody king. A king does not have such a luxury as luck or lack thereof to consider. A king must rule without such a concept as luck to define him. A king must be more than his fellow man. Always and evermore. Without complaint. A king must be able to see beyond what lies plainly before him. For a true blood king has more than himself to account for. Always and evermore. A true blood king must account for all things. His kingdom. His riches. His subjects. His legions. His kinfolk. And most importantly, the continuation of his bloodline. Nothing should be more important to a king than extending the royal bloodline.*

It was really quite simple now, Remy thought, his mind made up. He would press on at full tilt until he was free of this fel madness or until his body finally gave out on him. From here on out, it was just him and Curie. He had no room for another. Not until he reached Lancastle's courtyards. Curie had earned her keep. By the nine, she had earned it by tenfold. But he was done feigning hero for the rest. From here on out, he was the survivor. He would survive for the kingship, for the continuation of the Lanier lineage. He would be faster than the next man, smarter than the one that followed, and more determined than the one thereafter. He would see his home again. He would see his family again. And through hells and high water, he would take back the throne he had so thoughtlessly forsaken before he knew the true nature of the world and its host of utterly dreadful denizens.

His shoulder burned with a fresh fever, and he winced. *What was the old saying?* He questioned, his thoughts becoming more frantic in the mounting chaos. *Whatever doesn't kill you makes you stronger?* He swallowed the taste of blood back down and made a bitter face. *So long as you feel pain, you're still alive, old boy,* he reminded himself as Palatia's towering battlements came into full view through the cascading snowfall and the invading mist. Tendrils of smoke rose high above the miasma, shrouding all favor of dawn's institution, and the thunderous horns of war resounded from all directions. He could only unveil the line of archers by the arrows they set to flame before firing them over the other side. Dogs howled further off to the east, and they were soon accompanied by a ranging chorus of shrieks most morbid, from man, woman, and child alike. A stench of smog and burning flesh thence joined the horrific obscurity as a second ground-shaking explosion stole away all prospects of proper hearing and forced him against a building to steady his footing. Against the stone, Remy pressed a hand over a ringing ear, and he searched the haze before him for Curie, but once again she had vanished from sight.

"Curie," he dared, though he could scarcely hear his own voice before him.

"...Mummy, I'm sorry," he heard in response a few seconds later as he found a soot-caked bloodcoat whimpering and holding a shivering hand to the side of her head where blood streamed in-between fingers. "I'm sorry Mummy, I'm sorry," she repeated over and over again as she rocked herself back and forth, clutching herself tight. And when she looked up at Remy, her face was all ash save for the blood-gush and the vacant, faraway whites of her catatonic eyes. Remy's expression soured at the bloodcoat's disturbing guise, but he held out his sword between them all the same until he passed and she had disappeared into the foggy murk whence he'd come.

As he neared the alley's end, he halted once more, turning a shoulder as a patrol of bloodcoats hurried past. He held his breath and waited a beat, hoping he had not been noticed. Surely they had more pressing matters to attend than a lowly figure in the shadows, and he scoffed at his hesitation and cowardice.

Keep moving, fuckwit, he heard Curie's voice in his head, always spurring him forward.

As he took a step toward the avenue, a bloodcoat tumbled backward into the alley before him, and a second blighted soldier followed, clicking, clawing, and thrashing at the first like a wild beast. Remy stood petrified by the unexpected episode of violence. Immediately afterward Curie appeared, her blood-stained hatchet reared high above her, and she brought it down hard into the ghoulish bloodcoat's skull. The bit stuck as a second ghoul chased maniacally behind her, and something urged Remy forward into a lunge that saw him stick the creature in its belly with his blade, saving Curie from a most gruesome mauling.

Remy forced the flailing ghoul backward into the avenue, its blood-caked maw gnashing for his throat, its gloved hands struggling to find purchase to pull him in for the kill. And it was everything the watchman could do to keep the fiend from ripping him to the ground right along with it as they scuffled amidst the warring masses, crashing from body to body inside a suffocating death pit. This one was freshly dead, too. There was no putrefaction at all. So much so that it almost seemed a raving madman rather than an actual ghoul. But it certainly showed all the mannerisms of a ghoul. It was horridly clumsy yet ravenously undaunted. And at their present pace, it was sending Remy toward a most dizzying demise.

The wound across his bad shoulder blistered to life against the bastard's fight, his arms weakening and his ribs screaming bloody murder, as his knees banged together time and time again. And just as his hold began to slip and his footing began to abandon him atop the snow-slick streets, a tangle-haired Kingswatch soldier scarce older than he buried a knife into the side of the ghoul's head, bringing an abrupt end to its writhing madness.

Remy let the ghoul drop limp before him.

"Headshots work best, mate," the soldier said with a deranged grin, and he was gone again in an instant, lost to the reign of chaos and snowfall and the settling mists.

Headshots work best, mate. By the nine. Of course, they bloody do. And the mistake had nearly cost him his life. He had nearly thrown it all away for her. For Rhymona bloody Curie. A kingship for a madwoman. And yet, by some form of miracle, he still stood, saved once more. And by some no-name random no less. He wagered he must have burned through an entire lifetime of favor by now. And he couldn't help but wonder just how much luck was left to him in all of this.

Remy ripped his sword from the blighter's stomach and searched the circling maelstrom for Curie, but she was gone yet again. And, the gods know, it was growing increasingly difficult to see much past a few yards' distance. The mist had become a cluster of noises. The sounds of footsteps and feasting, of flitting arrows and falling bodies, of clanging steel and the alien prattle of the mindless blight. He wouldn't have imagined it possible only moments before, but already Palatia found itself in worse repair than Brymshire. Much worse.

As far as he could tell, he had two choices now. He could run for cover, away from Northgate, and pray for the best, or he could stick to the plan and press forward into the chaos in the hopes that he might stumble across Curie once again. Without further thought to it, for there was simply no time for thought in such disorder, he started toward the northern gatehouse, or at least what he assumed was the northern gatehouse, jostling desperately through the sea of battling masses before he noticed most everyone fleeing in the opposite direction. Foolishly, stubbornly, against every fiber in his being, Remy kept on anyway, another step forward and a second. He shoved past townsfolk and ghouls alike, brandishing his blade about like a madman, expecting death at any moment, fearing with every footfall he had already exhausted his final favor. And then something like Curie's face blurred past his, and he turned about swiftly and called after her.

"Not that way," she yelled back to him as she hurried up the avenue and a blast of bright white light momentarily awakened the mist behind them followed by the sound of crumbling stone, trembling earth, and screeches most foul. It was close, too close. And it was unmistakable what had caused it. Shadowy forms, mixed and many, surrounded them now, hunting and growing larger by the second, their strange language echoing a most pitiless requiem. He took to Curie's tail at once, trailing her inside another back alley where the mist had not yet blinded all from sight.

"Westgate," she rasped between breaths, blood-spatter both red and black strewn about her face and hair. The gods know she looked a proper savage now. "The North is overrun. Obviously."

"Obviously," Remy agreed.

"Cheers," she added.

"We're not out of this yet."

"In case I don't get another chance to say it then." Her gaze was genuine. "Thank you."

Were he not terrified out of his wits, he might have smiled at her unexpected gratitude. Apparently, he had almost died for something after all.

Westgate drew nigh, only a block away. Mercifully, the mists had not yet consumed the western walks, and the bloodcoats held strong to their position in the distance, a great red wall, beating back at the flood of the blight in unison, shields up and swords cutting down with furious determination. It appeared they were letting folk through in varying spaces, though in such bedlam, where it was becoming increasingly more difficult to distinguish the living from the dead, Remy couldn't help but wonder just how much longer they could afford to maintain such a gamble. It would only take one to send the entire lot into all-out frenzy.

Meanwhile, he found Curie an absolute marvel in action, confirming the many tales of her exploits had from his swordbrothers at The King's Wall. The way she could anticipate and adapt to their movements was truly masterful. Though her technique proved every measure as awkward and unorthodox as her personality; a firm resistance to any lesson had from a tourney master or within the training yards. But damned if the bitch's reckless horror wasn't remarkably effective. She fought like a rampaging bull, all wrath and momentum, darting forward from ghoul to ghoul, Fucker lashing out like a poised fang as it rent through skull after skull, dark blood spraying about her ferocious onslaught.

Remy was merely a fly on her back by comparison, swatting his watchman's blade at whatever remained in her wake. He was sore and exhausted, his limbs heavy, and his breathing ragged. Yet, he was still alive. He growled and stabbed and hacked down at Curie's carnage again and again and again, over and over, all adrenaline, leeching what he could of the madwoman's brutal bloodlust, as he prayed to any god that would listen that it would be enough to guide them through.

An arrow thumped down into a crawling corpse beside him, followed by a second that dropped a ghoul off to his left, and he looked up to find archers on the rooftops, casting down at them. He could only hope one did not mistake him for the dead and quickly shoved the thought to the back of his mind as he plunged his sword into a ghoul's throat and ripped it skyward. Blackened blood spotted the cobblestones before him as the blade burst free from the nape of its neck, and Remy kept onward, teeth bared. Surely they could tell the difference between the blight and their own. Surely.

"This way," Curie ordered as they came upon the wall of bloodcoats where the dead were scattered and heaped to the knees between them. They cut through a cobbler's shop, passing looters and a tussling pair, before bursting through a rear exit into a narrow back alley that ran along the westernmost wall. Curiously, they found the back alley completely empty of movement. A discovery Remy thought greatly disturbing.

But the western gate was within a stone's toss now. And just beyond that lay what constituted as freedom in this poxy version of existence. However, between them and that freedom stretched a trail of butchery like nothing Remy had ever seen before. Bodies lay in tatters, so many bodies, countless really given the method of mutilation, their limbs cleaved away in uneven chunks, their torsos blistered with fist-sized holes, as their blood spray streaked down the walls on either side of the alley in thick, syrupy tears.

Something malefic and otherworldly had made its way through and recently. And it left nothing alive within its violent wake.

"Gods," Remy uttered.

"Not quite," Curie said as she knelt beside a corpse with a severed arm and placed her flask underneath the missing half, collecting its blood drip. "Candles, mate," she answered before he could ask the question. "Doubtful this one had much of the gift in him, but it's red, not black so there's a thing, yeah?"

Remy felt a sickness begin to rise up as he glimpsed the next corpse over and he covered a hand over his mouth and nose.

"Fuck me," Curie groaned as she followed the source of his reaction to the outer wall. The poor bastard was missing the entire right half of his face from nose to ear. "That one's a closed casket to be sure." She shifted back to Remy her smoky orbs deadly serious. "Were I to venture a guess, I would say it was your ashaeydir that passed through this luckless lot. A terrible little ruiner at that. And the fucker was in a hurry too."

"How can you be sure?"

"It may look a shit-show now, but the cuts were cleanly made, served with enchanted steel. Ka'rym chii steel to be more precise. And this one here," she pointed down at the one missing half his face, "ate a wand blast pointe blanc."

Remy dared a closer inspection. He had never seen an injury from a wand strike before and found its result to be quite unsettling. It appeared as though the man's face had been put to the flame and seared away, flesh and bone both, until it was simply gone. A small puddle of blood and ash was all that remained of it.

"Straight through, too," Curie kept on as she inspected the corpse further, "though by the looks of it, it was sparked not thrown, meaning the caster pulled it out of reaction not premeditation. Doubtful the fool ever saw it coming. It's unmistakable really, the leavings of an ashaeydir assassin. And what have we here?" She traced a finger over the blood spatter above the corpse and it began to glow faintly at her touch. "No—"

"What was that?" Remy queried.

She stood and pressed her palm firmly against the cold cobble, and a symbol emanated a faint shade of gold around her hand, its fading magic uncoiling like a knot of snakes to form a burning sigil in the shape of a large X within a smaller triangle. A moment later, Curie turned back to him and split a big mad smile. "It would seem we've managed to curry some measure of favor this day after all."

"What is it?" Remy asked again.

"It's our way out," she answered, pulling away from the sigil, her eyes darting every which way about the alley.

"I don't understand."

"The sigil is a ward," she said as she retrieved her flask and stowed it somewhere inside the folds of her jerkin, "an exile's egress to be more precise. And I believe it fresh enough yet to beggar a free ride."

"Capitol that. Now once more in layman's terms if you will."

"The gods know, Toff, must you always act so impossibly dim? It's a fucking portal, mate. You know? Now you see me, now you don't, poof we're gone, piss off Fuckwit Mountain."

"Gone is good, very good," he said, his excitement growing with hers, "wait a tick, do you mean to say all this time we've been running around like hens with our heads cut off you could have brought up a portal away from this place?"

"Not exactly," she answered. "It takes time and precision to create a translocation ward. And there needs to be a tether."

"A tether?"

Curie's face scrunched up. "Point A," she drew her finger away from the portal and into the distance, "Point B. You can't just portal anywhere you want with a snap of the fingers, this isn't bloody Mervold Chronicles. It needs to be mapped out. You create the source ward at Point A, that's your foundation, then you can call back to it if you know the tether's name, forming a Point B, C, D, however many."

"And you know this one?"

"I know the symbol, yes."

"So you can map it?"

"What? No, it's already mapped, dipshit. But therein lies the rub."

Remy closed his eyes and pinched the bridge of his nose. He was beginning to catch on now. "You don't know where it's mapped to. But, of course, you don't. That would be far too easy, wouldn't it?"

"And why would I?" she scowled. "I didn't scrawl the damned thing, did I? It's a way out, Toff, I know that much. Take it or leave it. We're in a fucking potter's field as it stands. Surely anywhere else is better than here, yeah?"

"Fair point," he granted. *And the gods know we're all proper buggered if Rhymona bloody Curie is the guiding voice of positivity left amongst us.*

The mad magus retrieved a silver-colored wrapper from the pouch at her waist. "And wouldn't you know it? Last one." Her grin was absolutely ghastly. "What is it the lads always say in these dreadfully shite situations? May the luck stones prosper or some such rubbish?"

"Something of the like," he said as he glanced down the alley to its end where folk were frantically crossing back and forth, flailing and falling about, where it was impossible to discern the living from the dead, where another bloodbath most assuredly awaited them, and he gripped tight his blade's hilt.

A deafening explosion from some nearby rest sent a mighty ripple through the buildings down the avenue, shattering windows, and shaking the stones below. Both Remy and Curie stayed their plight against the outer wall as screams and a bright white light flooded through from the next street over. A pair of bowmen dropped down into the alley from a rooftop a block closer to the western gate and made a sprint for it. Remy watched after them until they disappeared into the waiting fray beyond.

When he turned back to Curie, he found her running a ring razor over a palm and ripping the binder's wrapper open with her teeth, revealing a violet-colored candle. Once placed in the palm of her gashed hand, it immediately began to melt, disappearing thus inside the wound. She then placed her hand flat against the ward a second time, and its golden glow returned, its radiance burning bright as a high noon sun. Consequently, the wall around the ward began to soften and liquefy, and within seconds, the once solid stonework had become a puddle of rippling black water. A powerful stench reeking of rotten eggs wafted away from its surface, and Remy had to cover his nose again, breathing through his mouth. There was naught to sight within the pool beyond the glyph's fiery glimmer, only a lightless abyss, black as the nether.

"Is this normal?" he asked, gazing long into the endless void.

"Not even a little," Curie said grimly. "Normally one should be able to glimpse something of what lies on the other side. I will tell you quite plainly there is no promise of safety in this. Anything or anyone could be waiting there on the other side." *More good news, then.* "The only promise is that it will take us away from where we presently stand—for better or worse." *Lovely.* "And might I suggest you sort it out in short order, yeah. This candle won't hold for long."

He turned back to Curie with an indecisive glower.

"No pressure or anything," she offered an uneasy half-smile, "but you're up first. The ward will close the moment I step through it."

It was always something, wasn't it? he thought as he measured the rabbit hole once more, glaring deep into its watery oblivion, searching for something, anything, that would betray its fel obscurity. And now here he was, twixt hells and heathens, grasping for even the tiniest scrap of control, knowing good and well that control was an illusion, a romantic's reverie, a lie told to sustain some semblance of comfortability. But damned if the illusion wasn't all he had left.

At that he took a deep breath, trusting that it wasn't his last, praying he had one more favor left to him in all this, and ducked beneath her arm, stepping through the portal into pitch black darkness.

CHAPTER NINETEEN

"Keep up, girl," Casilvieri grumbled as they rounded yet another dark corner of Lancastle's lower depths. "We're nearly there."

And by there, he meant the castle dungeons. Marsea had always hated the dungeons and avoided their walks as much as possible. Dank and grimy, they reeked of sulfur and corpse rot that clung to the nostrils for days. In Ravenholme's version of Lancastle, to find a dungeon cell meant to find death, typically by torture or starvation. And so it was as they approached the winding underbelly's end that the princess began to ponder—which one of the two horrors had her masters chained up down here, awaiting her attendance?

The remaining fingers of her disfigured hand curled inward at the thought, nearly closing into a half-fist, and ironically, it gave her strength. Hells, the fact that she could feel anything at all of the hand gave her strength, and it was fastly improving. As for the dreadful sight of it, there wasn't much in the way of positivity to cling to, though she was getting more and more accustomed to the wretched thing with every passing hour. It was still her, she told herself, still salvageable, still useful, hideous as it was, and to have it from Cas, it gave her a bit of character. *A bit of character,* she thought at that, *and no doubt it will earn me an equally hideous burn name before too long just the same.* Though, she decided, if Cas saw fit to show even the smallest glimmer of care for it, then it must have been given with some measure of good intent. But then, the maidens only knew, the inquisitor always found his humor in the wrong sorts of delights, didn't he?

"This is it," Casilvieri said as they came upon a rusty iron-pitted door, and he peered through its grille. "Oi, nap time's over, old man," he called inside before inserting a skeleton key into the door's spyhole. "Grab the torch, will you?" he ordered as he disappeared inside the cell.

The doorway opened up into a small lightless room, and the smell hit her before she could even pass through. She covered her bad hand over her nose as she entered, holding the torch high with her other, and she found in the room's center a man in a chair with a sack over his head and shackles about his wrists and ankles.

"Gods dammit, the bastard bloody pissed himself," Cas spat as he ripped the sack away from the man's head. "As if this place couldn't smell any worse, you've got to go on and piss yourself, then, you old codger?"

"Sir Wils?" Marsea uttered, studying the man whose hands were bound behind his back with a chain that was threaded beneath the chair through a metal floor latch to the fetters fixed around his ankles. She couldn't believe the face before her. Despite his ghastly appearance, she immediately recognized the prisoner as Wils Gilcrest, one of Lancastle's longest serving councilmen. He had been around since her father's time. In fact, she recalled he was once quite close with her father. They had been longtime friends, since childhood if she remembered proper, and thusly he had become something of an advisor to her father once he took up the throne.

Clearly rattled, Gilcrest locked eyes with the princess, and she found she could not turn away. Wils Gilcrest had always had the misfortune of appearing quite frail and, as a result, much older than his actual age. And it would seem his time spent in the dungeons, however long that had been, hadn't done him much in the way of favor with either. Verily, stripped to his skivvies, he appeared a beggar nigh on the verge of passing. Moreover, his gaunt features were now lined with dirt and dried tears, and his thinning hair had become matted with sweat from the weight of the prisoner's sack. He tried to speak to her then, to plead with her, his desperation practically palpable in his stink, but the gag that had been roped crudely inside his mouth kept his begging to a sad muffle.

"Do you remember what I told you the other night, Marsea?" Casilvieri asked as he unfurled what appeared to be a physician's surgical kit upon the table in the room's far corner. "About Gan's fall?"

How could I forget? "I do," she answered smartly, walking past the prisoner toward her mentor. "You said that he would not be the last," she added as she lit the sconce near the table, casting the entire chamber in a warm, golden glow.

"Indeed, I did, girl. And so you understand why we are here, then?"

"I do," she said, adjusting her glasses. Even the dimmest of fools knew what the dungeons meant. And knowing Cas and Ravenholme and what happened to those that crossed either of them, there could be no doubt in it. Wils Gilcrest was not long for this world.

"And you think you've the stomach for such a scene?"

"Of course," she answered evenly. *Would there have been a point in saying if I hadn't?*

"It could get nasty in a hurry."

"I will manage," she said, tossing the torch to the stones near the doorway and taking to Casilvieri's side at the table, scanning his assortment of miseries. They ranged from surgical tools to knives and hammers to instruments with purposes she could not even begin to partway imagine. She grabbed the smithy hammer, and it felt every measure as awkward as it looked. To wit, she had never held such an unwieldy instrument before. Off first impressions, she had to admit, she rather preferred a blade.

Casilvieri turned to her with a hard glare, and she met his eyes. "All right. Let's get on with it, then."

Marsea nodded, her silence laced with terrible intent. *He's only a man,* she told herself. *They're only men.*

Cas dragged a chair from the corner and placed it before Gilcrest, shifting it so the back faced forward, and he sat down with his arms resting across the top of its spine. Eerily, it reminded Marsea of his approach in her bedchamber only a few days past. Once settled, he took a breath and acknowledged his prisoner with an emotionless guise. After a moment of scrutiny, he removed the gag from Gilcrest's mouth, and it hung loose like a waiting noose around the old man's neck.

"Have you lost your mind, Merillion?" Gilcrest rasped immediately, his voice nearly as withered as his pale, spotted skin. Marsea had forgotten how insipid the councilman could be. "Harver will hear of this at once."

"No, no, no. That is not how this conversation is going to go, Wils. I will be the one asking the questions, and you will be the one providing the answers. Is that clear?"

"Milady?" Gilcrest called out, craning his neck from side to side over his shoulders in an attempt to bring her into view. "Marsea, listen to me. You cannot trust this man. He is a killer—"

Casilvieri had a chuckle at that. "The girl knows what I am, you old fool. And Harver is the one who gave me your bloody name. He is the one that put you here, so you can save your pathetic council chamber lobbying for the worms."

Gilcrest stared crossly at the inquisitor.

"Right. I thought that might get your attention."

"If Harver is the one who put me here, then I will have it from him. Not you, wretch."

Marsea watched Casilvieri's face at the slight. If he felt any hurt by it, it did not show. Though, by now, Marsea supposed, a man of Casilvieri's misspent youth was far beyond the pains of petty name calling. No doubt he'd been named a wretch and far worse for most of his life.

"You'll have it from me or you'll have it from the end of a blade, you mouthy old git."

Gilcrest's scowl deepened at that, but his tongue remained quiet.

"Ledgermaine," the inquisitor began again.

Ledgermaine? It was a name Marsea hadn't heard in weeks. So much had been made of the missing magus when he first disappeared near half a cycle ago, but the name quickly became forgotten thereafter. Or so she thought.

"See, a little birdy told me you may know something of his whereabouts."

"I assure you that I do not," the councilman said sourly.

"I would advise you against being difficult, Wils."

"I know it is not what you wish to hear, but, as I told your cohorts earlier, I have nothing to give you where Xavien Ledgermaine is involved."

"Mmm, not a good look for you, Wils," Cas said, "not a good look for you at all." And the inquisitor's eyes moved beyond Gilcrest to Marsea. "Did you know I was once a skinner before all this?"

Marsea found herself shaking her head, unsure if he was addressing her or if the tale was meant for Sir Wils.

"And I was damned good at it too," he added with a certain measure of fondness. "The butchers would pay double for old Fiveknives' work, and the fur traders paid the like if not more. It was good business, it was, back in those days. Good business indeed. Eye-catching business some might name it, if you catch my meaning. After all, there is not much difference between a skinner and a torturer when it comes down to it, now is there? Matter-of-fact, I'd say about the only difference between the two is that a skinner's game is already dead before he starts tearing at them."

"Your meandering threats are quite unnecessary," Gilcrest retorted. "I don't know where Ledgermaine is. How could I possibly know? He has been gone for some months now, hasn't he? And no amount of violence you bring me will change this."

"Mayhaps there is some truth to that," Cas said, his voice even. "But you knew where he was going initially, didn't you?"

"No," the councilman maintained. "He told me of his plans to leave, yes. But that was all. Nothing more. He didn't trust me with his secrets any more than he did the rest of you."

"Girl," Cas called.

A spell of fresh air filled Marsea's lungs at the summoning.

"Bring over that hammer there, would you?"

And Marsea's good hand tightened about the hammer's handle. She had nearly forgotten she was still holding it, she had become so absorbed in the excitement of the exchange.

"It would seem Sir Wils here has forgotten his place."

"Forgotten *my* place!" Gilcrest howled. "I've answered your questions, haven't I? What more would you have?"

The inquisitor's mouth quirked slightly. "And he has become quite disagreeable."

"Disagreeable? How dare you!"

"How dare I?" Casilvieri returned. "How dare *I*? I warned you against being difficult, did I not?"

"You're mad!"

"Mmm, and there it is, yeah, the first honest thing to leave your mouth yet. Carry on then."

"You're off your head!" Gilcrest struggled against the chair and his chains. "I've answered your bloody questions."

"Girl," Cas began as she arrived at his side, "you up for a bit of work then?"

"Of course," she answered, betraying the knots in her stomach. Though, strangely, she found she quite enjoyed the nervy sensation, just as she had with Ganedys. It gave her a sense of resolve, a sense of meaning, like she might actually be useful for once, like she might actually be getting somewhere.

"Right, of course," he echoed. There was the trace of a true smile amidst his permanent one. "Then I want you to take that hammer there, and I want you to smash it down into old boy's knee here hard as you can. Leave nothing to waste."

"No," the councilman shouted incredulously. "What?"

"No?" Cas mocked, his true smile vanishing. "No? Come now, Wils, I know you've more mettle than all that. Where is all that cunning now, eh? Where is all that council chamber smarm?"

Gilcrest simply stared at them, slack-jawed.

"Is it starting to sink in yet? Are you starting to grasp the severity of the situation you're in here?" The prisoner remained silent. "All right. Now this is my expectation of you, old man. It's quite simple really. I ask you a question, you tell me precisely and concisely what I want to know involving said question, and I spare you the result of excruciating pain. Savvy?"

"And I'm telling you, I don't know anything," Gilcrest said with an arrogant edge to his tone. "There is nothing to tell. Vaustian has this wrong. You have this wrong, Merillion. Your masters have this wrong. You are expecting an answer that does not exist."

"Defiant 'til the end is it?" Cas said calmly as he stood tall next to his apprentice. "Reckon we ought to help our guest along here then, eh girl? We haven't got all night, have we?"

Marsea took a step toward the councilman.

"No." Gilcrest wrested the princess with a desperate gaze bordering on hysteria. "Milady, this is madness. I beseech you. Your father would not condone this sort of behavior from his most beloved daughter. His Little

Dove. This is not you. This is Ravenholme. This is all Ravenholme. They have conditioned you. They have bent you—"

Little Dove? It had been a wolf's age since she heard the telling. "Do not pretend that you know me now, old man."

"Old man?" Gilcrest murmured in utter disbelief of the princess's turn.

Casilvieri snorted. "Tell you what, Wils. Not that you deserve this. You've been awfully argumentative, condescending, and just plain unpleasant, really, in our short time together. But even still I will offer you a choice here." A dagger suddenly appeared in Casilvieri's hand. "Option one. As we've discussed. The girl bashes a leg with the hammer every time you fail to answer a question to mine liking."

"I don't know anything," the councilman swore, spittle flying from his mouth as he began to squirm.

Marsea rather thought he was starting to get it now.

"Or option two," the inquisitor continued, in spite of the councilman's professed ignorance, "I take this blade here and I get to peeling back that massive beak of yours, layer by bloody layer. What say you, girl, an inch or three might have it looking a mite more natural, yeah?"

Marsea's heart began to race, and her palm felt sweaty against the hammer's grip.

"You must be reasonable," Gilcrest cried. "I don't know anything. I can't give you the impossible."

"Me giving you a choice *is* me being reasonable," Cas said. "In fact, you should be thanking me. I am the sole reason you aren't a corpse already. I told the uppers you would be most cooperative. That you would be delighted to share any information you had about Ledgermaine's whereabouts. And yet you give me attitude and this bloody tripe. I must say I am sorely disappointed in you, Wils."

"I don't know anything," Gilcrest bellowed once more.

And Cas drove forward, quick as an eye blink, and sank his fist into the councilman's gut, doubling him over. "You say those words one more fucking time and I will choose for you, yeah."

Gilcrest coughed and spluttered from the blow, his breathing thin and erratic, and he shifted his gaze back to Marsea.

Marsea had never beheld such an utterly pathetic creature before. It was disgraceful, really. This was a man that had once earned the respect of a king, enough so to fill a seat at her father's round and hold it for decades. He was a man of influence, a man admired in the courts, formidable in the council chambers, and had commanded great power within the halls of Lancastle. **And yet still**, her other chimed in, **despite all of that power, this pathetic creature didn't lift a finger to help you or your kin when the Midnight Men came to prey, did he? No, this pathetic creature allowed your suffering to persist, didn't he? This pathetic creature deserves what's coming to him, Marsea. This pathetic creature has earned his misery**.

"Now which will it be, old man?" Casilvieri asked.

Remember their words, girl. Remember how they did you and your kin.

Only the favored shall feast. The words raged within.

Only. The. Favored. Shall. Feast.

"It should be me," Marsea said, and both men turned to the princess.

"Milady, you cannot mean this," Gilcrest said utterly flummoxed.

"I do mean this," Marsea said, her reason giving way to compulsion. *Never let them know your fear,* she remembered Casilvieri's words from before, some many quints ago. "You deserve this pain, Wils."

"Mi...milady..."

"He was your friend," she said coldly. "He trusted you. And you turned your back on him when he needed you most."

"You have it wrong, milady," Gilcrest's lip trembled. "I tried to save your father. I did. I warned him time and time again of Ravenholme's menace, but he would not hear my behests."

No, you have it wrong, Wils. Marsea narrowed her eyes, studying the councilman's woeful face. "You should have done more."

"What more could I have done? He was a king, milady, and I merely a humble advisor."

"You should have found a way," she said, her words dripping with acid. "You owed him at least that much."

"Milady..." His voice was barely a whisper.

"Instead you turned your back on him to save your own skin, didn't you?"

The answer was written plainly across his pitiful countenance.

"And you turned your back on all of us." She lifted the hammer, and Gilcrest shrank away from her approach, his eyes squeezing shut, his teeth clenching. "Father," she cried, slamming the hammer down into the meat of his thigh, feeling the bone give slightly beneath. Oh, how the councilman howled at that. "Des." She drove it down again nearer the kneecap. And he let out an ungodly screech, writhing about the chair and chains like a man on fire. "Remy." She came in with a third blow to the side of his knee and the leg made an unnatural sound of complaint to fill the space between his screams. "And Marsea," she said raising the hammer high above her shoulder once more.

"Stella!" the old man wailed. And the princess halted midway into the hammer's descent. "Stella. Gods! Please! No more. No more."

"Stella?" Cas echoed.

"Yes," Gilcrest managed through a whimper. "Stella. He mentioned something of Stella the day before he disappeared."

"And who is Stella?" the inquisitor asked.

Stella, Marsea mused, easing her glasses back to their proper placement with the back of her bad hand. *Why does that name sound so familiar?* The hammer lowered casually to her side in her contemplation as something of the name came back to her from the depths of her childhood. *It couldn't be.*

"Critchlow," the councilman offered as he examined the gruesome damage to his leg.

"And what is Ledgermaine's connection with this Stella Critchlow?" Cas inquired further.

"They were in love," Marsea said.

"In love?" Cas had a snort. "Good one, girl. The gods know, Wils, even the girl can suss out your pathetic bollocks."

"She was a soldier," Marsea clarified, the image of the woman taking shape, "a magus that saw to the citadel library some cycles back."

Casilvieri turned to Marsea, and his wry smile disappeared. "You're serious?"

"I remember the name," the princess confirmed. "Stella Critchlow. She would read to me sometimes when I wandered down to the archives. She was quite unforgettable really, remarkably clever, and beautiful, more beautiful than most ladies of court, as I recall." The image of a soothing pink smile flashing between ruby-colored curls befell her. "Yet she was always clad in the dull livery of the Royalguard, never a flowing dress, as donned by a proper lady. I remember thinking it awfully peculiar. If any lovely face could out-shine a fancy dress, it was most certainly Stella's.

Though hers was a story straight out of a hearthfire romance, every measure as tragic as it was tender. And one day, some months into our strange friendship, for reasons I could never properly explain, she confessed to me that she was in love." The fragments from her sessions with Stella were beginning to slide together. "She told me this in confidence, I believe. More than like because she had no one else to confide in and a curious youngling would provide aptly minimal risk. Often, I remember thinking she seemed an awfully lonely person, which I also thought unusual because I rather enjoyed her company. She seemed a goodly sort, kind and selfless. And I remember thinking if any one person in all the world deserved to have her love's desire, it was Stella. But she said her love could never be fully consummated because of her duty to the crown and his duties elsewhere." For all the coin in the world, Marsea could not comprehend why this particular memory had stayed with her for all these cycles. "And when I asked her the man's name, she made me promise never to divulge it." *Cross my heart and hope to die.* "Prize well, it was a name I had not in the least expected, for at the time I rather thought him quite ordinary looking, in particular for a woman as fair as Stella. Yet it was his name all the same that she gave me. And that name was Xavien Ledgermaine."

"Hunh," Cas grunted, "and here I always took Ledge for a bender. You're sure about this, girl?"

"Positive." Stella was arguably Marsea's favorite to ever serve as archivist to their family's library, and during the princess's younger cycles, she was one of a very few folk that had treated her like an actual living being rather than some obnoxious, entitled little bother.

Casilvieri tilted his head back to the councilman. "And where is Critchlow now, old man?"

"The Southlands, last I heard."

"The Southlands, eh? And who else knows about this?"

"I don't..." Gilcrest began again before thinking better about the words. "As I said before, Ledgermaine wasn't exactly forthcoming about his personal affairs." He winced as he struggled to move his body back upright. "It is doubtful he confided in anyone within the citadel. That is all I know. I swear it."

"All right, Wils, all right. I believe you," Cas said as he circled around the prisoner, stalling just behind him. "But the masters called your name, didn't they? So, it is done, yeah. Your death warrant is signed and sealed. You know how it is."

"What?"

"There is nothing to be done about all that."

"But—"

"I don't kill you, then they kill me. And then they kill you anyway. So, you see my hands are tied here."

"I gave you all I know. I gave you what you wanted. I can still be useful."

"You did well enough. And I appreciate that." Cas placed a hand on the councilman's shoulder. "But rules are rules, yeah." Gilcrest began to squirm. "You've been in this game long enough. You know how all this works."

Marsea thought about her father then. About the mummified version she beheld upon their last meeting, trotted out before the entire kingdom like the lowliest of stable thieves. About the three days he had been missing after the coup. He had been in a place like this. Mayhaps even this very room. Only the Ravenholme cronies that had seen to his torture had not been quite as kind as Cas was being with Sir Wils. A dreadful, sour feeling stewed in the pit of her stomach at the thought, and she clutched tight the handle of the hammer once more.

"Now I can kill you right now, old man," Cas continued, "I can make it painless, sweet, and easy, soft as the siren's song. End your suffering before it becomes too unbearable." He let the words resonate for a beat. "Or I can leave you here to rot out your final days with the fresh gimper there, confined to this chair in darkness and misery. The choice is yours." He removed his hand from the councilman's shoulder. "Now you have a minute to decide, or the girl decides for you."

CHAPTER TWENTY

He chose to rot. He actually chose to rot—to suffer—to endure. And for what? For an inkling of hope? For a few more agonizing hours? For breaths that would be defiled by shame until there were no more? Are we all so desperate? Are we all so dreadfully woeful?

Stop, Marsea!

What is this?

The princess barely recognized herself as she sat trembling at her vanity table, clutching her bad hand close, the stench of the dungeons clinging to her like a crone's curse, her own ripeness thick upon her clothes. She could hardly believe her actions. She had lost herself again, turned herself over to her rage, just as she had with Ganedys in the Kingswood, and she nearly took another life because of it.

You deserve this pain, Wils.

She removed her glasses and blinked through the building pressure behind her eyes as she stared at the distorted creature in the mirror before her.

Don't you dare fucking cry, Marsea.

A tangle of loose curls hung down low, grazing the tip of her nose like that of a used harlot and she brushed it behind an ear.

What is this feeling? This isn't you.

Her mind had become a maelstrom since the dungeons, spiraling too fast for proper thought, and it wasn't slowing.

What is happening to me?

Out of habit, fresh as it was, she licked at the jagged scar on her upper lip. The scab had finally come away that morning and left beneath it a tiny mark that flushed cotton candy pink whenever she moved her mouth.

Who am I?

What am I becoming?

She had agreed to the Ganedys assignment for personal reasons. True, it was a means to gain Ravenholme's attentions, and that played into it, but Gan had also tormented both she and Remy for most of their days, even beating on her little brother when the boy caught a clever tongue, which was more often than not, especially once he had come of age. Poor Remy, ever the white knight, had even taken a few lumps on her behalf over the cycles. Plainly put, Ganedys was a thug and an awful human being that deserved his comeuppance and probably much worse. She could make sense of her hatred toward Gan. And she felt no remorse for what she had done to him. She only wished Remy had been there to share in the wretch's misery.

Something is broken inside of you.

She focused on the blur of guttering candlelight behind her in the mirror's reflection.

But Sir Wils? Sir Wils was different. The man may have done wrong by her father, but he had always been kind to her. And there had always been a sense of guilt in his eyes. A guilt that he had done his best to make amends for over the cycles. And truthfully, that was more than she could say for most folks. Besides, he wasn't the only one to turn on the king all those many cycles ago. In the end, near all of Lancastle turned on Whitman Lanier. His wife. His brother-in-law. His best friend. The small council. The common folk. Everyone. To her knowledge, not a single soul spoke out against his murder as he was prodded out to the butcher's block at the city's southernmost edge. And she couldn't very well hold an entire kingdom to the same cruel standard she tried to impress upon Gilcrest, now could she?

Marsea pushed away from her mirror with a mannered sigh and strayed over to the window to take in the snowy nightfall.

Past her many wind-beaten parapets, Lancastle Citadel towered high over the seven kingdom hamlets, a great razor-spined leviathan of a thing, and despite the hour and the cold, her cobble mired still in an ungodly breed of chaos and devilry, lit as a holiday festival, folk milling about her rutted avenues like fleas upon a verminous beast.

The kingdom had changed mightily over the past few hours. News of the blight had driven folk inward from the outer hamlets, and the lower city quarters had become overrun and were now governed savagely by bluecoat patrols and patches of monolithic spiked barricades. Marsea supposed the guard had managed to institute some manner of order within the madness, for the upper quarters remained somewhat fixed and no one was yet storming the castle. Banners of navy and gold stitched with the Lanier House crest now hung from many of the major hamlet establishments, establishments now commissioned and occupied by the Royalguard, to accompany those of the citadel battlements. The maidens knew, the princess had never seen so many gold griffins in all her life. And Lancastle's once-fair streets, dappled in snowdrifts and the hazy glow of ocher lamplight, were now littered with Royalguard propaganda, the parchment flowing every which way in the ruffling winds, cascading down walls and windows like a fresh layer of paint. It was a different city to say the least, a city in wartime, something Marsea knew exactly fuck all about, and affairs only promised to worsen on the morrow.

A soft rapping at her bedchamber door drew her from her dreary contemplations, and she stared at it wide-eyed and breathless, unsure if the noise was real or if the hauntlings had come round for an evening scare. She licked at the split in her upper lip once more and waited tensely.

"Lady Marsea," a timorous voice called from the other side a moment later. "It's Effie."

Effie? This was quite unexpected at such an unseemly hour, especially by a cloth maiden with an abbey curfew to contend with.

Promptly, Marsea retrieved her glasses, raked the better hand through her hair, and spritzed herself in perfume (mayhaps a few times too many), hoping it might cut the stink of violence that had followed her up from the lower quarters.

"Just a moment," she responded as she scanned the rest of the chamber, making sure it was suitable for company. One would have thought *her* the bloody handmaiden by the way she dashed about, readying herself, and tidying up.

Once settled, Marsea took a deep breath, brushed down the front of her plain emerald dress, and opened the door with a forced smile that implied her already splendid night couldn't possibly progress any more splendidly.

"Milady," Effie greeted, "I...I missed you at devotions the other day. I asked around and folks told me about the assault. And I just...I—"

"Come in," Marsea said, pulling the stammering girl inside, glancing to and fro down each side of the long torch-lit corridor, before bolting the door behind them.

"I hope you don't think me untoward. I just...I had to see you, milady. I had to be sure you were..."

"Thank you," Marsea replied. *Sweet, innocent Effie. A rare bird indeed.* "Honestly, it's nice to see a kind face." And wasn't that the truth of it?

"I would have come sooner, but my duties in the kitchens called. And Lirae Thirsby...she's been in a terrible foul mood, especially since the draft began this morning."

"I'm quite all right now," Marsea assured, though she really wasn't.

"Your face..." Effie uttered, and her gentle-eyed gaze shifted downward, "your hand."

"They are much better, really." Though they really weren't.

The cloth maiden swung her satchel round in front of her and began rummaging through it. "I know it might be unnecessary at this point, but I brought some ointments and herbs anyway. I have some practice in the healing arts, milady. My mother was an herbalist for many cycles in Kastilla before she became sick. And she—"

"Effie," Marsea said, placing her good hand over the satchel's flap. "Effie, slow down. There will be time for all that." Effie glanced up at the princess with a wounded look. "It's rather late, after all, isn't it? Well past the maiden mother's curfew. How did you even get past the guards?"

Effie's wounded look turned to that of shame. "I may have told them a tiny little lie, milady." Her response was scarcely a murmur.

The trace of a smile pulled upon the edge of Marsea's lips. "Did you now?"

"I showed them my medicine bag and told them you had requested me."

"And they believed you at that? Without a summons?" Marsea didn't know which she was more appalled at. The fact that golden girl Effie had actually spoken a lie or that her alleged guards were keen to just let her up at her word. The maidens know, it could have been anyone masquerading about as a cloth maiden, especially with all the turmoil surrounding the highlands of late. Vaustian would have lost his wits to learn of such negligence.

"I'm sorry, Your Highness, I meant no disrespect." Effie lowered her eyes.

"Trust, I am not upset at you, Effie." Though, without a doubt, she would have the names of the night watchmen outside her wing by morning's dawn.

"I only meant to check on you," the cloth maiden added, all rustic charm. "I wanted to be there for you as best I could. I know it sounds silly coming from a bumpkin like me, but I do see you as a good friend, milady."

The girl's words struck her like a lance to the heart. *I do see you as a good friend.* They were so simple and said with such tenderness and sincerity. Marsea found herself quite lost for a response. No one had ever said such a thing to her before. At least not that she could fastly recall. And she had a damned good memory by her estimation. It was almost as though she were an actual person for once and not just a title or means to an end.

And before she could think to stop them, tears began to stream down her face—and her ears began to pop—and her lips began to quiver—and her nose became snotty as all the pent-up pressure began to leak out of her at once, and she found herself bending against the cloth maiden, an utter mess of emotions. The girl was still cold from her winter waltz through the courtyards, but the princess could not have cared less. A moment later, she felt movement between them, and a long arm arched out from below and across her back, pulling her in closer.

Marsea's head sank against the cloth maiden's shoulder and the scent of the girl, so natural and pure, like a pristine forest, reminded her of the abbey, of devotions, of goodness, of hope. It was a stark contrast to her own dreadful stench, masked but faintly beneath a veil of manufactured fragrances.

"Effie," Marsea sniffled, "you should well prize. I am not a good person." A confession began to take shape upon the tip of her tongue, and she had to fight to swallow it back down. **No. You've come too far to risk it**.

"Of course, you are, milady."

Of course, I am. If you only knew, Effie. Would you still embrace me if I gave you my truth? Would we still be friends then? If you knew I had taken a life? Would you still readily bow your head and bend the knee to a killer? Marsea snuggled up tight against the girl and hugged an arm around her.

Even if it was false, and the princess hoped it wasn't, it still felt good to hold and be held. She could pretend with the best of them most days, partially because she wasn't even sure of her own truth anymore, but she found she couldn't lie to herself when her heart was like this. It was the only method left to her to decipher her own individuality—her own desires—from that of Vaustian's and Ravenholme.

It went without saying really, but she needed this. She couldn't thank the maidens enough for Effie in this moment. The tiny scar crawling away from the edge of her upper lip most certainly showed a screaming pink now, pink as cherry blossoms in the height of springtide.

"Milady, I would really like to tend to your hand, if I may," the cloth maiden said, restoring the princess from her distant reverie. "Not that your physicians haven't done a fine job, I'm sure they have, but I would like to see if I can help minimize the scarring if possible."

Reluctantly, Marsea pulled away from their embrace and began to slowly undress her hand, a process that had become all too familiar to her over the past three days. To have it true, she wasn't in a mood to contend with the ugly thing just then, but for Effie's sake, for the sake of their friendship, she buried her aversion. The girl had come all this way after all, and Marsea believed she meant well.

Another knock rang out from the chamber's entrance, and the two girls stared at each other but briefly before simultaneously turning toward the door. Marsea recognized the knock instantly and her face fell.

"Marsea," a voice called from the other side, its refinement unmistakable, bought from a lifetime spent in the contest of court.

Mother. Speaking on things she didn't care to contend with. "Just a moment," Marsea answered again, wiping the tears from her cheeks with a sleeve and dotting the wetness at the tip of her nose.

"Shall I, milady?" Effie asked in a whisper once the princess had somewhat composed herself.

Marsea eased her head forward in a gracious nod. She had avoided the woman for long enough she supposed. But it had finally come time, hadn't it? Bandage off literally and metaphorically, it would seem.

And the very instant Effie turned the bolt lock, Larissa barged in, radiant in a fur-lined cloak and lavender gown, her long, bouncing blond locks but a shade lighter than Marsea's. She was clearly upset, though this was fairly routine where the Queen was concerned. A pair of leather-clad bluecoats, the Queen's Own, remained in the hallway with their backs turned to the room blocking the entrance and any means of a clean escape.

"Good evening, daughter," the Queen greeted, and by her tone, Marsea knew it to mean quite the opposite. Despite her eloquence and grandeur, her mother could be quite sardonic when driven to it.

"Mother," Marsea offered, hiding her half-exposed bad hand behind her back.

"Mother? Is that all you have to say to me, Marsea?"

"Good evening, Mother?" It was already starting. *Stars save me, can we not even make it past a greeting anymore?*

"It's been a week, Marsea," Larissa said sourly, "a bloody week. And I've invited you to dinner every night, haven't I?" Her chin turned up suddenly. "Hrathgon's horror, I daresay what in the devil is that awful smell?" She covered a hand over her nose. "It reeks like a yokel's pigsty in here." Larissa turned reproachfully toward Effie, and the cloth maiden shrank against the wall apologetically, the color draining from her face.

"It's not Effie," Marsea said. "I was in the cellars earlier. With Cas."

The Queen shifted back to her daughter. Say one thing about Larissa Waldgrave, say she had eyes that could cut even the boldest of challengers to ribbons. It was a talent born from cycles upon cycles of contending with the cruelest of the upper crust. The Queen was a youthful forty-one despite her constant courtly war games. And though Marsea was half her mother's age, there could be no denying by appearance they could have been sisters. The scant bit of age that had managed to find her, a small etching of crow's feet here, a whisper of marionette lines there, had only worked to make her appear that much more daunting. She became a queen at the age of fifteen and a mother at eighteen and had two more by the time she had reached her mid-twenties. The maidens knew, such was a prospect Marsea couldn't even begin to fathom. At the very least, she had to grant her mother some measure of respect for the effort.

"And why, pray tell, were you in the cellars with Cas?"

Marsea's attentions swung to Effie, who appeared thoroughly dismayed, her stare fixed on the stones at her feet, then back to her mother. There would be no point in lying. Her mother was far too intuitive, mayhaps even more so than Vaustian. And she was no novice to the backstabbing theatrics of the small council and their den of thieves and killers. One did not remain atop the throne for a quarter-century without achieving some measure of cunning and survivability, after all.

"Surely your *darling* husband has already apprised you, Mother," she dared.

The Queen seized her daughter with an icy stare. "Honestly, I haven't seen sight nor shade of Raelan since breakfast."

"Mayhaps he's found another flogged corpse to prod about town then," Marsea disparaged.

"Enough," Larissa said shortly. "And you know how I feel about your carrying on with that heathen. The gods know he's scarcely more civilized than a wildkin savage."

"Oh, and how he loves when folk name him that," Marsea said, the image of Casilvieri lording over Gilcrest still fresh in her head, "or mongrel. That's his favorite, I'm told."

"He is dangerous, Marsea. Do you have any idea what they name him outside the courts?"

"Fiveknives," Marsea returned, venom on her tongue. "Rillion bloody Fiveknives."

Larissa sighed. "Why must you insist on behaving this way? I know I've raised you better than this."

You didn't raise me at all, Mother. No, that chore was left to your bitter serving staff, wasn't it? "And what way would that be?"

"Rebelliously," Larissa answered with a candor that chilled Marsea's flesh. The Queen boasted a manner of speaking that was always genteel and that much more threatening. "Secretively," she appended. "All I ask is for a proper conversation with my own daughter—at least once in a maker's moon." Marsea knew exactly what a proper conversation with her mother looked like, and it typically turned into a lecture. "I simply cannot understand why you must persistently defy me your company. Don't you think it pains me to see you like this?" Her mother's ability to shift any topic to how it affected her was indeed masterful.

"You want to have *this* conversation, Mother? You want to have it out right now? In front of my friend and your lapdogs and anyone else within earshot?" The words gushed out of her, boiling with contempt.

"Your friend?" Larissa turned sidelong to Effie. "This scullery maid is not your friend, Marsea, I can assure you that. Whatever she is to you, she is only using you. But so be it. If this is what it takes to get you to talk to me, I will oblige."

"Don't judge Effie by your own failed relations, Mother. You know nothing about her."

"I am only trying to help you, Marsea."

"Help me? From what exactly?" She had a little titter of amusement. "What do you believe ails me, Mother?" Marsea revealed her half-bandaged hand from behind her back, the linens hanging down loose about her arm, and restored her glasses to the bridge of her nose. "Better yet, what do you believe will fix me? You've already pushed Remy away with your incessant badgering, haven't you? So we know that method won't work with us, will it? All because you couldn't approve of his—"

"Mind, daughter," Larissa scolded. "There is no need for ugliness."

Marsea thought about her behavior in the cellars. *Oh Mother, you have no idea how ugly I can be.* "Is that what you're naming it then? Ugliness?"

"Marsea, stop projecting. It's really quite irritating."

"So he likes cock," she kept on. "So do I. So do you. What's the difference?"

"I will not be addressed by such a coarse tongue! Is that clear, Marsea Anne? And that is not at all what this is about. Now I have done my best to be understanding—"

"No, you haven't," the princess snapped.

"I have," Larissa stated firmly, "and I will have your respect, like it or not." *Useless threats.* "Besides, Rembrandt left of his own volition, didn't he? Truly, with all that's going on in the northern hollows, do you think I wish him out there in the middle of all of it? I don't like it any more than you do. I miss him, horribly. And I want him home just as well. Especially now."

"You're Queen, Mother, no doubt you could have him home if you truly wanted. You could have had him home at any time."

"Despite your feelings of me, I try to give you both your space. I try to allow for you both to find some measure of your own desires." *Sure, of course, Mother. As long as it also suits your own.* "Having him dragged back here against his wishes would have only caused a further stir. And he's just as stubborn as his father in the end, isn't he? Not a one of you missed out on that trait, did you?"

"And now he may be dead. Brilliant choice, Mother. Truly."

Larissa let out a sound that might have been lament. "I've had a man in watch of him, if you must know."

"What man?" Marsea questioned, her eyes narrowing.

"Someone I trust, of course."

"You will have to forgive me, but I can't exactly take you at your word anymore, now can I?" The maidens know, she was becoming bold indeed. "What is his name, this *man* of yours?"

"Grimbel. He is the son of a childhood friend, a young man of high repute, and a lieutenant of similar age to your brother. He won the Fairer's Tilt a few summers back and the Midwinter Tourney this past cycle, and if he proves himself even half the soldier his father was, Rembrandt is in worthy company."

Something of the name rang familiar. But wasn't that always the case? "You really think one man will be enough considering what's out there? Vaustian talks of lichlords and ashaeydir gravedancers, you think some dullard from bumfuck knobshire is going to stand up against all that?"

"I say, you simply cannot stop yourself, can you?" her mother accused. "It's never enough, is it? The gods know, Marsea, what more would you have of me then?"

Well and true, right now, I'd have you leave me the fuck alone.

They both just stood there in the question's wake, staring at one another through the knife-cutting tension before the Queen finally cleared her throat. "I am still your mother, Marsea."

"I am painfully aware." She made it a point to gaze away from her mother when she said the words, staring at the stars in the night sky beyond her window.

"And I am your Queen. Now I have done my best to accommodate your wishes and support your decisions." *The lies we tell.* "I've even tolerated your little dalliance with Vaustian, obscene as it is. But enough is enough."

"Obscene?" Marsea hissed.

"Yes, daughter, obscene." The Queen's temper met hers. "And look where it's landed you. You've half a hand and—"

"At least I'm doing something, Mother. I won't be what they expect me to be. What you apparently expect me to be."

"And what is that, pray tell?"

"I don't know...some dull, empty-headed simp with a pretty face and a lack of opinions."

"You truly believe that is what I want of mine own daughter?"

"Honestly?"

"Ravenholme is a death trap, Marsea, a club for thugs and filth, not ladies of nobility, and if you're too fool to see that, then you truly are a lost cause, aren't you? As for Vaustian, he is a taken man, isn't he? Not to mention twice your age. And the gods know, Marsea, he has a daughter near as old as you are. I know you know better. The entire affair is absolutely deplorable."

"It's no more deplorable than was your marriage to his brother."

The Queen bit her lip at that, and a renewed silence stretched between them, pooling like blood-gush from a fatally driven flesh wound. It was the same old song and dance. And the conversation was not going to improve any time soon.

"Are we done *now*?" Marsea asked crossly after a few endless seconds, the pain and resentment inside her too great to push back down. "Was this what you wanted?" She could tell her mother struggled to maintain her near impervious composure at the dig, and given her mood, she was well tempted to push the Queen beyond it.

Larissa simply shook her head and turned away from her daughter, departing without further response. More of the same.

"Lovely chat, Mother," Marsea spat as she trailed her mother to the chamber's entrance, "as always," and she slammed the door shut behind her, resting her head against it in the after.

"Bitch," she grumbled into the woodwork, her body set to a trembling excitement.

She inhaled to calm herself, and with the exhale, her eyelids crashed shut like a dropped portcullis. Suddenly, it was very quiet again, and once more she found herself drifting atop her endless ocean, the tiny waves from her heartbeats ebbing and rolling gently away from her.

Away, away, gently away—

But then a subtle shifting sound came from somewhere behind her, something that shouldn't be there, and the gates were drawn open.

It was only then that she remembered Effie.

The girl didn't need to say anything as Marsea circled slowly round to face her. The truth of it was plainly written in her downcast eyes as they twitched up to meet hers.

Maidens keep me.

And a cracking sound quaked through the princess in that first instant of eye contact, a thunderous sound that only she could hearken, and yet it was the loudest sound in all the world.

Unmistakably, irrevocably, it was the sound of her heart splintering in two.

CHAPTER TWENTY-ONE

Drenched in sweat, Marsea wiped her face against the mantle of her blouse before training her sword on Vaustian once more. He paced around her, as she gasped for breath, spinning his blade effortlessly, baring that ridiculously fetching smile, making a show of it between their break. *Keep your head clear and your form honest.* She kept her bad hand tucked neatly behind her back all the while. *He's only a man.*

"Ready?" he asked.

"Ready," she confirmed.

"It's going to be a little harder this time."

"Bring it."

And Vaustian was on her in a breath's take, slashing about her feverishly, like a human hurricane, his actions unpredictable and wholly devoid of form, completely bought by emotion, but Marsea did not relent from the onslaught, and she would not turn away.

Steel cracking against its brethren echoed like shattering crystals in the Hall of Glass as the long marble-floored chamber fired all measure of sound in a thousand different directions with each joining blow.

This set existed separate from any technique she had ever defended against before. In fact, it lacked any semblance of technique altogether.

Nevertheless, she played their contest prudently, careful not to become too eager or impatient, matching the pace of her mentor, cutting his thrusts sidelong and his swipes downward, all the while searching for a flaw in the feral assault.

Another series of parries more and her opening arrived. She took to the offensive, lunging forward, quick as her weary body would allow, thinking she had finally bested her mentor. But Vaustian was keen to the serving, catching the thrust just in time, sending it wide, and Marsea sprawled past right along with it. Keeping her feet under her stretched her skills beyond her limits as she staggered forward, eventually dropping to a knee and turning her shoulder into a roll, before pushing back up to her feet with what remained of her momentum.

Her knee burned like hellfire from the impact, but rest wasn't an option. Vaustian was back on her in a heartbeat, silky smooth dexterity like a slithering serpent, and their blades locked together, the mentor bearing down upon his apprentice with all the strength he could muster, his steel lusting for her neckline, forcing Marsea's blade back into the padded leathers over her chest, cutting into the fabric of her tunic. And he snarled in her face like a monstrous ogre, his weight crushing against her.

Marsea felt her knees begin to wobble, struggling to keep her upright. **Let me out**, the thing within bade at the threat, **or he will win**. And with one final effort, she caught against the flat of the blade with her bad hand, yowling from the contact, and pushed against Vaustian's might to give herself what bit of breathing room could be had, before releasing into freefall, turning her chin and shifting to her side as much as possible, sending her mentor blundering recklessly forward.

Marsea's body screamed at the impact as the marble surface came up to meet her, punching out what little air was left in her, and Vaustian trampled over top.

Get up.

It took every ounce of strength she could conjure just to move in the after, much less to find her feet, but she was no longer in control, was she? She was merely a passenger now, dog-tired, beyond beaten, bruised and broken, her body complaining at every slight inch of movement. But her other could not be bothered by such limitations. Her other believed she could still take this contest, and she was willfully determined. **Still**

here, her other thought, pushing up for another go, leaning heavily upon her blade for support, favoring her bad hand before balling it into a leaking fist. **Use it**.

Vaustian readied his blade, briefly catching the firelight in its luster, as a deep growl loosed from his throat and he came at Marsea again, lightning quick. The princess caught the first cut mid-blade and felt the vibration course throughout the entirety of her body. She sent it scraping down the steel's end away from her, but her mentor was keen to the maneuver reversing momentum with a low grunt. It missed her gut by the thinnest of margins, and once again Marsea found herself on her heels as Vaustian pursued, swatting his sword about like a madman. He cut hard with a juke to the left then countered, sharp as a slitpurse, with a slice from the right. Marsea parried the effort just wide enough to keep it from flesh, blood from the cuts on her hand loosing on the air, spattering across the nearby mirrored wall. Vaustian had become a well of aggression, vicious, feverish, daring aggression, and he matched her fury, thrusting upward, downward, then to the right, again, again, and again in brutal waves, wearing Marsea's other down just as fast as he'd done her.

Her legs began to falter in their stance, her bloodied grip slipping, her concentration slowing, and with the bad hand, despite her other's spirit, scant opportunity for retaliation existed. It was only a matter of time now before one of the lot betrayed her.

And then, as though suddenly bored by an old, uninteresting plaything, he relented, shouldering his blade, and spinning away from her into a showy strut, suave as you like.

Say one thing for Vaustian Harver, say he had a flair and style unmatched by any.

Her body gave out in response, reducing her to a pile of pain as she eased herself onto the floor. Blood spilled from between her stitches, dripping messily away from her. Briefly, she observed herself in one of the many mirrors lining the vaulted magnificence of the Hall of Glass. And what a fine mess she found awaiting her there.

"Not bad," Vaustian said with an imperial smile as he leaned his sword against the wall and began removing his shirt. *Ever the man's man,* she thought taking in her love. *Charming, strong, commanding.*

"What was that?" she asked through tired breaths.

"*That* was you taking on a wolld warrior," he said as he offered her his shirt. "How's the bad one?"

"I can still feel it." She cringed as she wrapped the shirt gently around her hand. "So there's that."

"You're improving," he said. "I could feel the fire there toward the end, yearning to be let loose. You'll need that. You might have had one in the grave with that fire. Though prize well, wildkin savages are impossible to predict. Not a one of them fight the same way. They do not practice proper training as the courts demand or observe anything nearing swordsmanship honor or duel etiquette."

"You've fought one of these beasts before?"

"I have. A few of them, mind you. During my apprenticeship with Ravenholme. It was part of our trials. Six of us were sent out into the wilds beyond The Scar and were bid to return with the head of a wolld war chief. I was the only one to make it back."

"You killed a wildkin war chief?"

"I killed *a* wildkin," he said, drying his forehead with a linen cloth. "A nasty looking bastard too, big and ugly as you could imagine. Riddled with scars and inks and exposed bones, the whole nine. Looked the part of a war chief, if you ask me. I daresay by comparison he made Cas seem a dashing prince of a fetch."

Marsea found that hard to believe. Though she couldn't help but find the stark irony between this tale and the one Cas had regaled her with involving his experience with the wolld.

"I tell you this because after some long deliberating hours, the masters have decided to grant you trial for acceptance into Ravenholme."

Her breath froze mid-inhalation, her heart paused the like, and her eyes grew wide as her bottom lip pouted outward and the scar upon her upper burned bright. "You're serious?"

"Yes." His opinion of it was maddeningly unreadable. "We will travel to Vinth in two days, once this tax business with the Ministry concludes."

"I...I don't know what to say..." *Vinth?* The thought sent a shiver up her spine and twisted her stomach in knots.

Tell him no, you stupid girl. It will ruin everything.

It was only a few weeks past that she had stepped foot outside the kingdom walls for the first time and even that little leap was a nerve-wracking trial. Vinth would be a bloody nightmare by comparison.

Tell him no, Marsea. Tell him you don't want this. You're not ready. He will understand.

At the thought, her heart hammered back to life, her vision spinning, undulating around her, and she suddenly found she had to focus just to steady her breathing, swallowing in-between each intake of air.

"I must admit I still have my reservations in spite of your marked progress," Vaustian said, "but come week's end, Vinth will more than like be safer than Lancastle."

"Oh?" she uttered. *Then why does it feel like I'm walking the plank?*

"As I am sure you are aware, there have already been sightings of the blight near as The Straights and Elkmark. And their appearances are coming more rapidly now. Doubtful the outer hollows will survive their legions, though I am confident we can keep them from breaching the city."

"What about Aera and Sylvie?" *Dumb question, Marsea. Tell him you wish to stay. You have to stay.*

"They will remain here, of course," he said with an almost inhuman indifference. "Ravenholme is exceptionally strict about its tenants. And I trust Raelan to keep their best interests, my best interests, in mind." He flashed his confident, handsome smile once more. The one that instantly melted her heart every single time. "Besides, I told you I would keep you safe, did I not?"

"You did."

"And I like to think I'm a man of my word."

"You are." *Dammit, Marsea.*

"Then it's settled."

She forced a smile and glanced sidelong at her wet reflection in the blood-speckled mirror. The curved monstrosity inhabiting the lower half of her face was absolutely ghastly.

Useless.

"Milord," a voice called from outside the chamber just before entering. "Apologies, Your Highness," Bromas Aldridge said as he bowed to Marsea.

"As you were, Captain," Vaustian commanded.

"There is an urgent matter that requires your attendance, sir. The small council is convening as we speak."

"And what could possibly be so pressing this early in the day, Aldridge? It's scarcely reached breakfast yet."

"Rightly, sir, you will have to see it to believe it."

"Don't test my patience, Captain," Vaustian said with a hard menace.

"A y'deman drifter, sir, has arrived naming himself an emissary of House Beldroth."

"House Beldroth? And why should I bother myself with a drifter from a long since fallen Fae house, Captain? Send him on his way."

"I understand, sir, but General Harver has already brought him in and offered him immunity. He claims he has a method for combating the blight, sir."

Vaustian's eyes narrowed on the soldier. "Very well," he said with an irritated sigh, "since my brother has taken it upon himself to apparently decide such matters, I suppose I don't have much choice, do I?"

"Permission to comment, sir."

"Granted."

"The y'deman's claim appears legit, sir. There are others, armed watchmen that came in with him that swear to its truth. They speak of Chandii magics, the Eldnumerian, and a wolf the size of a wngar."

Vaustian turned back to Marsea, clearly expecting the conversation to be concluded at that, but Aldridge remained. The Viceroy waited a tense second before shifting back to the bluecoat. "Was there something else, Captain?"

"Sorry, sir, your brother ordered that I personally escort you to the Lord's round."

"My brother ordered, did he?"

What Marsea would have given to behold the expression on Vaustian's face in that moment. Verily, Aldridge quite looked ready to soil himself post haste.

"Fucking Raelan. Always bloody something. Give us a moment then," the Viceroy muttered before turning back to the princess. He waited for Captain Aldridge to remove himself before addressing her. "It would seem this is going to be a thing for today."

"So it is," she answered. *Keep it together, girl.*

"Tonight, after sup, meet in Alistair's Courtyard. There's more we need discuss about Vinth and your trials."

"Of course," she said, detesting her lack of courage.

"And not a word about Ravenholme to anyone else in the meantime," he ordered, collecting his sword and sliding it smoothly into its scabbard.

She nodded.

"I love you," he added with a velvety allure.

"I know," she muttered to his ghost before turning back to her woeful blood-spattered twin in the mirror's expanse.

CHAPTER TWENTY-TWO

Two days had passed since the horror in The Spellbind and somehow through all the change, through all the chaos, through all the scouring of Perciya University's *peerless* stacks for an account or registry describing the Oathsworn, they landed on Tavernmast as their next destination.

Not a single oil escaped their burning, whether midday, midnight, or otherwise as the hours took on a life of their own. It was a tedious chore to say the least, almost as though he was enrolled in uni again and saddled with yet another convoluted assignment he had procrastinated over. But in spite of his reluctance, the fates had seen fit to affix this task to his conscience all the same. Admittedly, Aiden might have just shrugged it off had it just been him in The Spellbind. *The creature would carry on just as well as some other sad sack's bizarre quandary, wouldn't it?* No skin off his back. He could find a way to deal with the horror. He had buried things before. Besides, what was another skeleton for a cupboard such as his anyway?

But, of course, he hadn't been alone, had he?

No, there was Val's involvement too, wasn't there? And as much as the sellsword claimed to avoid folk and confrontation, she had an awfully peculiar penchant for finding herself well deep in the thick of things, didn't she? No doubt her services would have been better served as an officer or a watchman rather than a sellsword. But either way, what was done was done, and it had become abundantly clear with her attachment he would have no other choice but to investigate further. He certainly couldn't in good conscience leave her to this lunacy alone.

So he bought in and they turned Withers on her head once more.

But the gods knew, how he hated participating.

And then, just when the search seemed at its fruitless culmination, something of note found them. Something barely there, something almost missed, some little inkling of a thing in the billionth book he'd turned, some trivial blurb about a sailwarder named Arys Redding.

Evidently, Redding, noted pirate of the era, expropriated some bygone lord's seaside manor in Tavernmast nearly a century past, a haunt named the Heart House, and created something of an archive from its remains, rot, rot, bloody rot, irrelevant. What was relevant, however, was the description of Captain Redding. Not the pirate bit, of course. But the suspected Oathsworn affiliate bit.

Sure, after all that digging, it was a turd of a lead at best, but, in the least, it was something. And only a township over. What could a little holiday excursion hurt?

They reached Tavernmast as twilight shifted to full dark, the arches of his feet barking from the wear of the road. Still unable to locate his boots, he settled for an old pair of leathers he'd worn to tatters ages ago. In terms of comfort, they proved only slightly better than walking around barefooted.

Looted corpses were piled in uneven rows just outside the city gates, awaiting the torch, and dark scowls followed the pair's staggered plod as they entered the sinister hum of the inner cobble. To call the city run-down would have been a most generous compliment. Though only half the city lay on land to begin with, so the expectation going in was decidedly low. The other half was a shambles, supported by thick wooden stilts that rose and creaked above the salted stain of the Aurabus shoreline, but only just. Yet, in the face of commerce's institution over the past century and the inevitable appendage of banditry that came along with it, Tavernmast, at its soul, still remained very much a quaint little fisherman's village.

Despite its coarse, poverty-stricken exterior, Tavernmast was not altogether dissimilar to Kanton. The same narrow, uneven walkways, the same stone building structures steeped in tradition and simplicity, and the same dark, dreary back alleys one knew to avoid, marked its character. However, where Kanton's quarters had been restored under countless coats of veneer over the cycles, Tavernmast's had been ever left to languish and molder, rendering it in a far more ancient and rustic appeal.

The Heart House itself stood a pale horse, appearing quite like a vinteyaman plantation manor, its front extravagantly pillared, tragically sun-washed, and nothing at all like Aiden had imagined. Even by Tavernmast's dated standards, it appeared a creature out of time. It rose four stories tall, the largest building in sight, its many windows shuttered, save a missing few, and much of its siding had become consumed by a dense rash of ivy.

Inside, the archivist's eyes widened at the sheer spectacle of the place. It was a palace, sensory overload, reeking strongly of fighting and fornication and something else Aiden could not quite readily name. And for obvious reasons, he couldn't help but compare the innards to Withers, for indeed the Heart House was an actual library, somehow, housing rows upon rows of tomes on shelves that were, given the patrons in question, surprisingly still full. The downstairs also doubled as a tavern, complete with shufa den, and he imagined, from what little he saw of it, that the upstairs accommodated a series of lodging quarters, most of which, no doubt, charged rent by the hour.

He slung back another swallow of Aberynt Red as a pissed musician began plucking at chords from the smoky dream at the other end of the tavern. The gods know, he was making an absolute sodden mess of the lyrics to "Darmoon, Ever Frail," though in the least his string work was passable.

Good for that guy.

"Rumor amongst the guard is the wolld are running a red tide across the highlands right now," a woman's voice said from the next table over, and Aiden couldn't help but pry.

"Is that right?" responded the man sitting across from her, his long, greasy red curls hiding half his impish smile. "And to think you'd been whoring about the Royalguard ranks all these bloody months for nothing."

"Ye jealous, Malkin?"

Malkin croaked something like a laugh. "Jealous? Trust it true love, I wouldn't fuck you full tilt shit-panned with Cus's cock and that's a damn promise."

"Oye, I heard that," a disembodied voice rose from the shufa den. "You two keep Little Cus out of it, ya hear."

"Oh, that's right," the woman fired back at her table mate, "ye rather fancy the menfolk this week, I heard."

"I rather fancy keeping the rot off me fruits more like," Malkin was quick to the cut. "Nine hells, as it stands, I count my ruddy luck stones every time I have a piss and don't see blood. 'Sides, everyone knows the lands north of the bulwark are a proper fuckshow. Worse than wolld up them ways to be sure."

"It's the ashaeydir, I'm tellin' ye. Back for another go," the dark one with the facial tattoo said, twisting a pinky inside his ear. "It's always the damned ashaeydir."

Ashaeydir? This seized Aiden's attention. It had been some time indeed since last he'd heard tell of anything involving the ashaeydir. Since Rhymona, really. And it was a fair assessment to say she had a terrible little fascination with their lot back when. From study and folktale, he knew the gist of their records. They were a race of beings, similar in form to humans, with alien devices and supernatural abilities far beyond the scope of even the most powerful of giftborn. Often RC would liken them to demons and fae and other sundry mystical creatures. And she would describe such queer magics as shapeshifting and ward-spelling amongst their many talents. How strange to hear of them again from within a band of tramps and drifters of all places.

"Aye," Cus agreed, joining the table from the smoky abyss, "and mayhaps this go they'll finally rid us of that worthless twat Dalivant while they're at it."

Aiden recognized this fellow, Cus. His eyes narrowed on the short, skinny man and it dawned on him. *Rat-face? Fucking hells.* He was one of the anglers from a few mornings back. *Small place, this old moon.* Now his interest was most certainly piqued.

"Him and the rest of the royal court lackwits with any act of the gods' mercies," Malkin added. "Serves them bloody highborn pricks proper, ye ask me. They sit all high and mighty in their perfumed chambers and their posh banquet halls with their honeyed words, fattening their bellies, and hosting a festival for this little Lady and that little Lord just so they can have a poke and a tug at each other. All the while the rest of us are left to the black to freeze and starve and count the fucking corpses, rot, rot, bloody rot and onward. At least have the gods' damned common decency to look me in the eye when you're fucking me like a syphilitic whore, yeah. And if you're going to bend me over and just take it, maybe offer to finger the anus first."

"You've a lovely way with words, Malkin," an old man said as he approached their table, slinging a damp washcloth over his shoulder, "truly." And his gaze shifted up and froze on Aiden. They locked eyes.

There was an instant familiarity about him, a familiarity the archivist couldn't quite place, and yet it burrowed in like a nagging itch at the back of his skull. He found he could not turn away. It wasn't the scholarly sea-green haunters or the long, wispy gray hair, lined ever so thinly with echoes from its blackened past, or the thick salt and pepper beard that came to a messy finish just below his neckline. No, none of that. He seemed about as ordinary as geezers come considering. No, something about his posture, his form, Aiden cogitated. It was obvious the man had once been quite fit, his burly build matching the soldierly type, but that figure had since taken on a bit of weight in his later cycles, more than like from the drink. Though, all told, he still seemed more than capable were it to come to blades or knuckles or general devilry.

"As I live and breathe," he uttered.

"Do I know you?" Aiden asked as the elder advanced.

"Still don't recognize me." The man shook his head, a long veiny crease stabbing down from the arch of his widow's peak. "I'm not surprised, considering." A frown formed. "You knew me once, Aiden." *The fuck?* "In another life." The big man heaved a sigh. "It just goes to show you, you can prepare and prepare and prepare and still never find the right time. So be it. You're here now."

"How do you know my name? Who are you?" And the realization struck the archivist like a cold, hard slap to the face, as a silhouette blurred into retention from the fringes of his jumbled memory. "You were at the beach…the other morning, with the other fellow there."

"I was," the old man confessed. "We've much to discuss, Aiden. Much indeed. But first, there is someone you need speak with."

"How do you know my name again?" Aiden repeated.

"Follow me, lad, and I promise you will have your answers."

From begging and bingeing to folly-hunting and full-on tomfuckery. Indeed, a fine line separated the brave from the foolish, and apparently, he was apt to straddle it all the way to the bloody grave. It would seem he was daring just about anyone these days to put him there. Had he truly become so unconcerned with his wellbeing? Sadly, it had become a necessary question over the past few weeks and perhaps even worse, it was a question for which he held no suitable answer. At least he had Val with him, and that brought him some small measure of comfort. She was a sellsword after all, but even still, when it all came down to it, could she really be trusted any more than the rest?

A rat brushed against his ankles as he descended the final step of the narrow spiraling staircase into the Heart House cellars. Unsurprisingly, the room reeked of death rot and excrement, and it felt as though they were suddenly walking through a cup of boiling soup in the middle of summertide.

And for some reason, he heard his father in his head complaining it was hotter than two rabbits humping in a wool sock. Say one thing about Vincent Ashborough, say he had a barmy phrase for near every occasion. Aiden might have even had a laugh at the memory were the surroundings not so horribly grim.

There were three bodies chained to the surrounding walls. The one nearest the entrance slumped against the wall, unmoving, dead, his guts freed of their confines, his dark, slimy intestines coiling out from the spill of his innards like a loose feed of rope. He had been left there, long to the rot, and the skin of his face had since shriveled to the protrusion of bone, further accentuating the bearing of his pre-existing skeletal features. His upper lip now curled back from his teeth and his jaw sagged unnaturally low as though some creature had crawled forth from the space behind his tongue.

The other two were still moving inside the shadows—the one, but barely.

Aiden studied what could be made of them in the guttering torchlight of the dank circular chamber. They were both stripped bare. One was a man, mayhaps around his own age, but in the poor lighting, it was impossible to tell. He came forward, his chains dragging against the stones, and stopped as the shackles reached their limitations from the wall anchor. His face had been altered into a mask of horror. A mask that featured emptied eye sockets and a severed tongue to accompany the various gashes opened about his emaciated torso.

It hurt the archivist just to take him in, and so he turned his cheek.

The other was a young woman with a partly shaved head and a bevy of bruises. Both alterations were fresh. And Aiden knew the game well enough. She was stripped of her beauty as a form of punishment, though by comparison to her cellmate, she remained practically radiant. Unlike her cellmate, she did not bother to move from the stones she lay upon.

"What the fuck is this?" Val asked, taking the words from Aiden's mouth, a hand collapsing upon her hilt.

"Redding's Room," the old man said.

"My left ass cheek," Aiden groused, issuing a look that fell somewhere between a scowl and bewilderment. "I know a fucking summoning chamber when I see one." (Though, properly, he had never actually seen one before).

"Who are these people?" Val pressed. "Why are they down here?"

"Save your pity and contempt," the old man said. "This one here," he inclined his head toward the man, "is a murderous knobend piece of shit." The old man spat at him, and the wretch moaned back at them in his new incomprehensible half-language. "Butchered one of the girls a few nights back, he did. Decent girl too. One that deserved a mite bit better than this Fuckhead's knife-end at least. And this cunt," he turned to the woman who lay on her side sobbing, "was the one who put him up to it."

You're well in it now, aren't you, fuckwit? Aiden heard Rhymona's voice in his head.

"And shitbag over there was a bloody marsher. Fucking Dalivant's got his pisscoats all over the ports these days, even this far east. It seems he's well determined to expand his empire."

The old man strolled over to an indentation, like a shelf, in the wall and retrieved a jar. Inside the jar was a black substance that put Aiden's heart to the hammer.

It couldn't be.

A pang of apprehension tremored throughout the archivist as the vision of Darrow's jaw unhinging and exploding into the strange black ichor came to haunt.

But it was.

"Now normally I would accommodate a choice for you here," the old man said, his eyes mirroring a multitude of fluctuating colors in the drab filter of firelight, "but seeing as Fuckhead had to go running his mouth earlier, you're stuck with Princess Pillow Talk."

You could be at the Brass Lantern right now, lit as a lord, but no, you had to keep pushing it, didn't you?

The old man placed the jar on a stone dais that rose up from the chamber's epicenter like some fancy courtyard statue and began chanting in a strange language as he revealed a small dagger and ran it across his palm. In sequence with the cut, he unscrewed the jar's lid and dripped blood onto the black ichor inside, once, twice, three times, all the while chanting, and quickly spun the lid tight about its ridges once more.

An eerie silence followed the act, sending a creeping shiver up the archivist's spine. It was like the silence of a cemetery once inside the witching hour.

A choking cough heaved out of the beaten girl on the ground, followed by a deep gasp of breath and a wheezy exhale. A moment later, she rose and came into the torchlight. Thick black tears streaked down her face, from below her glowing emerald orbs, just like it had from Darrow's. And it studied its temporary skin, cupping the girl's breasts and fingering her cunt, the chains rattling with each subtle movement, before it turned up to them, immediately settling its foxfire gaze upon Aiden.

"*And who is this one, Ledge?*" it asked, white clouds forming before its face, defying the chamber's dense swelter. "*I know you, don't I? How do I know you?*" The girl's face became quite inquisitive in the dangling silence. "*You're the one he's after, aren't you?*" She sniffed at him, like a beast hunting the wind. "*Yes. It is you.*"

"What's she…er he…whatever it is on about?" Aiden glowered at the old man.

"He doesn't know?" the girl asked, a slow curling smile taking shape. *"You haven't told him yet, have you, Xavien?"*

The old man's expression bent sour.

The girl cackled. *"What say you, Ledge? Would you like to have the honors? Or shall I?"*

"Who are you?" Aiden asked.

"Who am I? Nothing to no one, most would name me," the creature introduced itself, shifting its gaze to the one it named as Ledge, *"at least not anymore."*

"This is Arys Redding," Ledge said.

"Though my name should be the last of your cares, boy. Tell him, Ledge. Tell him his truth or I will tell him for you."

The archivist glanced sidelong at the old man.

"There was never going to be a good way to tell you this. And you should know. We had planned to tell you together."

"Spare me the rigmarole, old man, and spit it out already." His patience was getting shorter by the second. "I mean we're talking about the nether here and gravedancing whatever the fuck she is. How much stranger can it possibly get?"

"Very well, lad, very well." A certain measure of regret colored his tone. And an even greater shame inhabited his eyes. "Your name is not Aiden Ashborough," he began. "At least not by birth." The words came over him in slow rolling waves. "Stella is not your mother. Vincent is not your father. And Autumn is not your sister. At least not fully."

"How do you know those names?" The scar on his stomach began to itch, and he pressed a fist into it.

"Such a cruel thing to keep away from one so young and utterly without, I must say," Redding chirped. *"But surely it cannot come as much of a surprise at this point. Tell me, boy, all these cycles, did you never think to ask yourself why the memories of your early life were such a blur?"* The creature's smug delight perverted the girl's once delicate features. *"I think somewhere deep down inside you have always known the truth. Or at least you have suspected for some time now."* It wandered back into the shadows, the chains jangling behind its host like an iron tail. *"I think you have denied its possibility to circumvent the heartbreak that would come along were your fears to ever be counted true.*

And trust there isn't a soul alive that can blame you for acting as such. Desmond Lanier."

The name swept over him like a plague as echoes of its former calling burrowed free from the catacombs of his subconscious mind.

"Very few have suffered more than you, Desmond. You lost your family. Your name. Your titles. Your wealth. Your fame. Your friends. Your memory. Fucking hells, you even lost your own bloody life. But all the same, flip the coin, and no one has been given more than you either. You were brought back from death, you were. From the very bowels of the nether. Without regret. Without pain. Without expectation."

"You're off your fucking face." Aiden turned back for the stairwell, wishing he'd taken down a mite more tavern courage before embarking on this bit of madness.

"And there's that Lanier blood, come back to rear its ugly, impetuous head, yeah."

The archivist stopped; leathers sunk heavily atop the first stair, urging him forward, back to some bastion of sanity.

"Walk away, sulk, deny it all you like, boy, but deep down you know I'm telling you true. In order to survive the trauma of the ghastly experience, you fractured yourself. This is why you cannot remember."

Close-fisted, fire bristling feverishly in his icy blues, Aiden rounded on the creature, staring hard at its black shape in the veil of shadows, nails digging deep into the skin of his sweaty palms.

"You created a wall within yourself to sever your mind from the horror of it all. And Stella and Ledge, they are the ones that put it there and helped you nurture it."

"To protect you, Desmond," Ledge added.

"That's not my name, asshole," Aiden growled.

"Aiden," Val chimed in.

"No, Val. This is not why we're here. I'll not hear another word of it."

"This is absolutely why you're here." The girl came forward from the darkness again, her expression hard and menacing. *"It's not just you, Desmond. You're all bound by the shackles of causality. Shackles forged long before calendars were conceived and ages were named. And you've all been living on borrowed time, you have. Midara is cursed, and make no mistake about it, her time is short. Meaning your time is short. She's being torn apart, you see, even*

now as we speak, by an inescapable affliction. One that will not relent until its appetite is seen to. And soon her beautiful, bountiful frontier will begin to alter, and she'll start to darken and fissure and lose all of her lovely, lovely luster, and it won't be long after that until her entirety dons the same wretched appearance as the cold and hopeless badlands lining the Aryndrath Coast.

"No one living remembers the world before the Age of Dragons, before magic poisoned the elements, save the Eld of course, assuming the Old Ones ever existed at all, but there must be repercussions for things stolen, yeah. There is a system to mind after all. And what was once taken must eventually be returned. As such that time has finally come, hasn't it? And there will be a feasting of the world to reset the scale."

"You speak of the blight?" Val asked.

"The blight?" it scoffed. *"The blight is but a prologue, girl. I speak of the massive impenetrable cancer rising from the tides and slowly devouring this landmass from the outside in. The one your fellow denizens seem so thoughtlessly content to ignore.*

"It is the inevitable consequence for cultivating esoteric gifts from the beyond. You see, for as magic scattered, bonding with the elements of this world and fusing amongst her unwitting populace, so too did its scourge. And in the cycles to follow we took too much. All of us. Every heathen, every craven, every butcher, every maiden, every vile greedy bastard walking this moon. And there had to be a balance to all that taking, didn't there, a place to put all that used up energy."

"The nether," Aiden answered.

"There he is. Turns out you're a quick study, kiddo," Redding teased, *"and what do we know of the nether? Aside from the fact that it's a massive fucking knobend? Oh, that's right,"* it began before a response could be made. *"We know it's poison to all housing magic, however small, however untapped, within their bloodstream. And the more you have of it, the worse it will be for you in the end."* The image of Darrow's body splitting apart flashed in his head once more. *"Now I don't know about you lot, but I would name that equilibrium at its finest. One cannot blossom without the other and neither would exist without its proper counterpart, rot, rot, bloody rot. The gods are dead. May the frail inherit her ashes."*

"How long have you known this?" Aiden posited for the room. "I watched Darrow die."

"Darrow?" the girl hissed with a cold grit. *"Solomon Darrow?"*

"That was what he named himself," Aiden confirmed.

"What has the fool done now?"

"We found him in The Spellbind. Or rather he found us."

"And what in vaelnation were you *doing in The Spellbind?"*

"I don't know. Having a piss." *Trying to impress a girl, like a right proper fuckwit. Pretty standard me bullshit really.*

"Seems about right," Redding muttered. *"I suppose no one can ever say prophecy doesn't come without a sense of humor."*

"We saw that same shit there," Aiden nodded toward the jar of nether, "though a lot more of it, blasting out of him before the elder tree."

"Before the elder tree?" it echoed. *"You mean to say he was inside the ward?"*

"I mean to say."

"As in physically there?"

"Physically there."

"You're sure?"

"Positive."

The girl crossed dirty arms over naked breasts. *"If what you say is true, if Darrow brought the nether to the dragon, then you're all well and truly fucked already, aren't you? You may as well pack it in, grab a pint, and wait for the shit-show to unfurl."*

An awkward silence followed.

"All right," Aiden began, "well, since you're being a cracking fine help about all this, where exactly is The Spellbind?" *You may as well get something out of this whole Oathsworn debacle.*

"The Spellbind is not a question of where, but when," Redding said. *"You see, this has all happened before. Only during the previous revolution one of the Last Seed got clever. And Yvemathira used what remained of her magic to bind with the elder tree, using its amber to slow time inside her ward, protecting her from the nether's hunger. This also caused a host of irregularities outside of her tomb, most notably the scattering of magic. But if the nether is already in the past—"*

"He asked where," Val reiterated.

"Far to the north," the creature returned, *"well beyond the King's Wall, on the southern edge of The Scar near a hollow named Nocthun, deep in what is now ashaeydir territory."*

"Nocthun?" Val uttered.

"You know it?" Aiden asked.

She turned to the archivist, the portrait of dread itself plastered upon her face. "I..." Her voice withered in response.

"What is it?" He had never beheld such a fearful aspect upon her before, not even during their nightmare spin through The Spellbind.

Horrorstruck, she stared deep into his icy blues, sorrow washing over her as though the weight of the world just crashed upon her shoulders, and she drew her blade, whirling it about quick so the hilt was offered out to him and the blade rested flat against her side. "Here," she said. "Take it."

"What are you doing?" he asked, reluctantly reaching for the hilt. "You're scaring me."

"I'm preparing you as best I can," she answered as her eyes lowered.

"Preparing me? For what?" he asked as he took up the hilt and recognized the make of the blade to be ka'rym chii steel.

"Just know what happens next, I mean you no injury." She backed away from him and reached a hand behind her ear. "I'm still the same girl, all right?"

"What are you on about, Val? What is this?"

"Say you understand, Aiden. Say you believe me."

"And what am I to believe, exactly? You're not making any fucking sense."

"That I am the same girl. Say it."

"What the hells, Val?" His pulse quickened.

"Please," she begged.

"You're the same, all right. You're the bloody same. Whatever the hells that means."

And as she rested her fingertips against the space just behind her earlobe, he had his answer.

Sound shattered at the sight of her. Air ceased to fill his lungs. And his body quit all manner of proper functionality.

Her skin lightened to a pale lilac shade, her long frizzy curls darkened from ash to obsidian, and her irises, now returned to meet his, had become gilt as the king's coin.

Ledge aimed his ritual dagger out at her as Aiden stood aghast, neither one willing to believe the sight before them.

"Stay your blade," she said, hands held out between them. "There is no need for violence."

"The hells there isn't," Ledge seethed.

"You're a bloody ashaeydir," Aiden uttered, his heart in his throat, a sickness beginning to wash over him.

"I am, but that doesn't change anything. I am still the same girl."

"Are you fucking mad? It changes everything!" Aiden argued, leveling the mae'chii at her, a howling lament burning through the entirety of his being like the windswept wander of newly conjured wildfire.

"Don't you dare put this all on me, Aiden. You knew I was trouble the moment we met. I saw it in your drunken, shufa-shot eyes. I watched you make the decision to let me in."

"Why?" he huffed, fighting mightily to keep his head. "Why do this now? Why do this at all?" He thought it a fair question. Had he the ability of shapeshifting, he might never look his true form ever again.

"It was bound to happen sooner or later," she answered simply, an air of anguish in her rueful voice. "It nearly happened after The Spellbind. I wanted to tell you then. But I had to be sure."

"Had to be sure of what?"

"I was sent to find you," she said, "to bring you back."

Aiden pinched the bridge of his nose in frustration. "So what, it was all a lie then?"

"No. Not all of it."

"We...you...I fucked an ashaeydir?"

"Not to split hairs, delicate matters and all," she said, "but you've actually fucked two."

"What?" The blade lowered.

"Because right now seems an appropriate time for a lover's quarrel," Redding's vessel carped from her haunt in the shadows.

"And you can fuck all the way off, Redding," Aiden snapped, raising the blade at the fiend. He was coming apart at the seams now and apt to do something quite foolish the way things were.

"As I recall, it was you who summoned me, you ungrateful little shit."

"I believe you know her as Rhymona Curie," Val expounded, restoring the archivist's attentions.

Rhymona?

And yet, somehow, he already knew.

He didn't even feel the sword release from his grip. Nor did he hear it as it clattered to the stones below. It was all too much. Too much all at once. And none of it good. It was all the same old rubbish he'd always known. Just different faces attached to the delivery. How was he supposed to be about all of this anyway? How was he supposed to react to all this?

Fuck it.

Same old Aiden it is then.

Fuck all of it.

CHAPTER TWENTY-THREE

"We have to sort this," Val hollered after him as he stormed through the library and out into the streets, shoving through the swarm of harlots and vagabonds into the back alley running alongside the Heart House's right wing. "I will tell you everything. Anything you want to know. Just give me a chance to explain."

"Rhymona!" he said, circling about and meeting her in the lamplight at the alley's mouth. The sellsword had concealed her true form once again for obvious reasons. "Where is she?"

"I don't know." Val could barely bring herself to meet his eyes. "Can we please go somewhere more private?"

"You must be daft to think I would go anywhere alone with you."

"I could make you if I wanted."

"Then fucking make me, Val." The words were childish at best, but this is what he had been given. And he was nearly at his wit's end with all of it.

"I'm sorry, Aiden. I didn't mean it like that. I'm not like that. But you have to believe I am on your side."

You sure do have a funny way of showing it. "What does that even mean? *I* don't even know what side I'm on." *Ten minutes ago, I didn't even know there were sides.* "I don't even know who I really am anymore apparently."

"You are Desmond Lanier," she promised without missing a beat.

"That much I know for truth. How you returned from the grave, that bit is still just as much a mystery to me as it is to you, though you may want to question Ledge about it. Seems he's not all he appears either."

This is what you deserve, Aiden. This is what happens when you lie to yourself. When you ignore your intuitions. You find yourself lost amongst liars and whores and, evidently, ashaeydir. Oh, what he would give to be back at Withers, feet kicked up, high on shufa, and drowning in a keg with Calem. *Yessir, that would be real fucking swell, wouldn't it?* ***:Another lie, though.:*** *Fuck me, right?*

But what he really wanted was to curl up inside a box somewhere in the fetal position and just lay there unworried, unbothered, and unfucked with.

"And who are *you* really, Val?" he pushed back instead, determined to reassert some measure of control over his swiftly deteriorating grasp on reality. Because that's what sane folk do in these dreadfully shite situations, right?

"My name is Valestriel-shan of High House Alyfain."

Pretty words, those. "And Rhymona?"

"Curie was a vassal to mine House named Morgandrel, formerly of House Tully, and she was on assignment by way of mine uncle to bring you back to Lancastle some cycles ago. But something happened, something we are still unsure of, and she quit her objective, suddenly cutting all ties with us, abandoning her station and her fealty entirely. She'd grown reckless and unreliable over the later cycles, to have it from mine lord father, so my family decided to relinquish her services altogether rather than put her to the chase. The Tullys were a dead House anyway. So, they let it be just that. And eventually I was sent in her place to resume the assignment."

"So the *young master* is an assignment then?"

"Don't be like that, Aiden, please."

"Then answer the bloody question."

"That was how it started, yes." She paced away from him, deeper into the alley's darkness, hugging along the ivy-caped siding, passing through bandlight from the library windows. "Though it's something quite more now, isn't it?"

Against his better judgments, he followed after her, clutching tight the strap of the satchel housing his grimoire. It was a wonder indeed that the cloth yet held considering how rough he'd been on it of late.

"And do all ashaeydir typically make it a point to sleep with their assignments, or was that bit saved specially for me?"

"I slept with you because she did," she said sharply, its truth undeniable. "Because I had to know. Because—"

He watched her silhouette shrivel in the absence of words, and they both came to the exact same realization in chorus.

"Because I loved her."

He couldn't see her face inside the nocturnal void, but he knew exactly the placement of her eyes.

"And I missed her. Morgan...Rhymona...was my friend once, you should well prize, like a sister to me. More so than even my own flesh and blood. And she was my mentor just the like. But over the cycles, she became a jagged soul and a hard woman. The toughest woman I had ever known. And yet somehow you...*you* of all folk...a bloody human had affected something about that. The way she spoke about you the last time—"

Val glanced away from him, her silence deafening.

"You were the last thing I knew of her. My only starting point, really. And I believed you the rightful heir, so of course I took up her assignment. At the very least, you were a possible answer to mine family's future designs."

"And what designs might those be?"

"To infiltrate kingdom Lancastle, House Lanier and Ravenholme both —to repair our reputation—to exact revenge."

"Revenge for what?"

They were exactly midway down the empty back alley now, leagues away from anyone else. Unquestionably, he was a dead man if she wished it so. Not that he would find much aid round these parts besides.

"We had a coup of our own after the first few failed attempts of conquering Vaelsyntheria. A coup against High House Tully, Morgandrel's House. My House, High House Vystaris, and House Ur'Dusk. House Tully was viewed as the weak link amongst the upper Houses and thusly suffered the blame for our failed expansion. As a result, our Houses banded together and slaughtered everyone in House Tully, from her father Lord Refyn all the way down the ranks to the serving staff and stable boys. Everyone but little Morgan. It was my father's way of slighting House Tully even after death.

"The story I gave you the night we met about family. Those were Morgan's words. And in the cycles to follow, he would parade her about like a slave for the company, every chance he got, having her serve meals and clean the scullery, amongst an assortment of even more degrading tasks, demeaning her all the while. And that was when he was feeling generous. I hated my father for all that. The maidens know, I still do. But through it all, Morgandrel would not be kept down. She fought on with every angry beat of her heart. Eventually gaining mine uncle's eye and my mother's endorsement, until she somehow earned her way onto our House guard. And not only that, but she exceeded the quality of most within the ranks. Those that had every advantage over her. My elder sisters included. An accomplishment my sisters have despised her for every day since. But not me."

She drew in a heavy breath and exhaled.

"Now my House stands to suffer the same culling as Morgan's did all those many cycles ago. Only we've fashioned a plan. A plan of unity—with your House. House Lanier. And the other true blood Houses of the highlands."

"An Ashaeydir-Midaran alliance? Impossible. The Ministry would never allow it."

"The Ministry is the old way," she said dismissively. "We can forge a new way."

"You speak of mutiny."

"No, Aiden, I speak of revolution."

"A romantic notion."

"Only to those without proper cause."

"And how do you propose this revolution?"

"It's already happening as we speak. Mine uncle and sisters have been circling the Lancastle halls for months now, planting their little seeds. And I have no doubts that they've already dug their claws deep into some of your family's most trusted. Turning folk for or against one another to benefit our own is kind of what my kin do best. Reckon I'm a bit of a black sheep in all that. I blame Morgan for that bit."

Same old girl, right?

A sea breeze drifted past them as they approached the other end of the alley that opened onto the harbor, and it calmed what remained of his crossness. Though his thoughts spun round and round like a great unstoppable tempest.

"She loves you, you know?" Valestriel said as they came to the ocean view, the red, white, and green reflections from the sister moons mottled upon the Aurabus surface like that of a painter's mixing board. "She once told me she loved you so much that she hated you."

Now that I believe. "Rhymona was always an odd piece, wasn't she?" Aiden mused as they sat upon the harbor's edge. He wished he'd had a drink with him. Anything would do. Anything at all. And the gods know he needed something after all this bollocks, something strong as hell.

"She was," Valestriel agreed, gazing long into the crimson-stained heavens, all the way up to its violent collision against a most ominous horizon. "And she's out there somewhere."

"She is," he said, "and I intend to find her."

"And what about what Redding said?"

"Bridges we'll cross if we get there."

"We?" she murmured, listing slightly toward him.

"Don't push it, yeah."

"No pushing. Promise."

"Besides, it would seem you know something about The Spellbind that I do not. Nocthun. You've been there, right?"

"Been there? I was born there."

Of course, you were. "The shackles of causality and all that, yeah?"

"I reckon so. Though not at all what I expected from an Oathsworn, that one."

"You'll find no argument here."

"So…are we…?" she started.

"I don't know yet," he answered before she could finish. And it was the gods' honest truth. It took guts for her to come out as she did, he had to give her that, and he understood why she felt the need to hide her true identity from him, but all the same, cycles upon cycles of her kinfolk's sadistic history now stacked up mightily against her.

Time will tell, he supposed. *One breath at a time, right?* "You said you went into The Spellbind once. Was that true?"

"It was."

"Was it with her?"

"What do you think?"

"Do you reckon she knew something about all this?"

"Knowing Morgan, I have to believe so. The girl has an impossible way with trouble. Always has. And it finds her about as often as she finds it. I swear she's hexed."

I know the feeling.

They sat in silence for a while after that, listening to the waves cascade against the stonework beneath them, and watching the dockworkers across the harbor unload cargo from a galleon named Blackhall's Banshee. It was actually quite pleasant considering all the other horseshit goings-on of the day...week...cycle...decade. At some point, Val moved in closer to him and relaxed her head against his shoulder, and the distant scent of cintas flowers, somehow, impressively considering the city's stink, swept over him once more. He didn't have the heart to fight with her over the gesture. He believed her words genuine besides. The gods know had she truly wanted him dead, he would have likely become a corpse already.

Again.

Apparently.

He thought of the first night they fucked and of the bath she had drawn him prior. Of how delicate and attentive she had been washing him. No one had ever done anything like that for him before. Not Rhymona, not Caitie, not any of the other one-night strumpets he had ever paid call. Just her. The notion of a smirk befell his lips. He quite expected a bit worse from an ashaeydir, all told. But then that would have made sense of things, wouldn't it have? And making sense of things would have rather fucked this whole batty shitshow business he presently had going for him.

"You know I was thinking," the archivist said after some time, "Desmond is a fucking terrible name."

"It's not great," Val agreed.

"King Desmond." He let it breathe for a beat. "Nope, can't see it. Sounds like a fucking knobend to me."

Her smile washed over him.

"Mmm, doesn't suit *you* at all, does it?" the ashaeydir said as she snuggled in closer.

"Was that meant to be sarcasm then?" he asked, his shoulder sinking but slightly as his head eased down gently into her soft web of curls.

"I don't know. Was it?" she teased.

And a response immediately filtered through his stream of consciousness. *Reckon we'll find out soon enough, won't we?*

CHAPTER TWENTY-FOUR

"The gods know, this place looks like Hrathgon fucked it, ate it, and shat it back out. Twice," Curie said as they traversed the teeming cobble of Illery inward toward the great towering citadel of Lancastle.

Remy didn't disagree with his companion's assessment, but honestly, he was simply satisfied the portal hadn't led them into a death trap. For all its purported menace, it casually spat them out inside an abandoned shop on the edge of Market Street and Aft.

Once outside, they found some manner of trouble brewing down the way and turned through a pair of back alleys to an innhouse Rhymona held some familiarity with. After a furtive exchange with the innkeeper, the magus returned with a sinister smile, a key, and a bottle of bottom-shelf whiskey.

"Someone owed me a favor," she said nonchalantly, and Remy decided against any further inquiry.

They holed up for the day at the innhouse, where he slept in fits, an hour here, a few minutes there, chasing down the nightmares with the foulest whiskey he'd ever tossed back.

Meanwhile, the turmoil from that morning only grew worse as the day progressed, unveiling all the signs of a military draft. He watched groggily out the upstairs window as Royalguard soldiers pulled folks from out of their homes, herded them down the street, and ushered them off to the gods only knew where.

That night, in the shallow cast of starlight, they finally ate something resembling a poor man's repast. Cold broth and a suspect loaf of bread that may as well have been made from stone for how tough it was to chew. It was all the innkeeper could spare after the Royalguard raided her cupboard the night before. But at least it was something.

For dessert, they drank and drank and rested and drank some more and it wasn't long into their hearty drinking that his pent-up anger began to transform into hearty scheming.

Hearty, purposeful scheming.

He was back home, after all. Back within Lancastle proper. The capital of hearty, purposeful scheming. He would be doing her a disservice by refusing contribution.

And Curie, as Curie was wont to do whilst deep in her drams, proposed the question. *We've already had the talk, yeah. Now that you're home, the fuck you want to do about it?*

It was a dangerous question, a question that did not have an immediate answer.

Only it did.

What did he want to do? What did he really want to do? He wanted to restore his father's sullied name, is what he bloody wanted. He wanted to restore his family's honor. He wanted to restore his family's throne. No, he needed to restore his family's throne. And to do that he needed to remove every heathen at court bearing the surname Harver. Beginning with the usurper Vaustian.

And so Curie kept him honest once the words came snarling out. And she asked the obvious questions. The questions one must ask themselves before undertaking such a darkly initiative. And he answered them one by one until finally a plotline unfolded and they marked their course of action.

Vaustian was rarely alone in a space where he could be taken off-guard, and even when he was, he would prove a toilsome handful. To wit, Remy could only unveil one such circumstance that might find occurrence on his daily routine and that was the Viceroy's evening rounds of the castle courtyards puffing at his shufa sticks and no doubt mulling over what fresh convoluted scheme found his fancy. It was something the watchman had known him to do before. Something he had done for cycles. Something Remy was counting on to have maintained its precedence. But so much had changed in the last cycle, hadn't it?

Not this thing though. Somehow, he knew it, without a shadow of doubt. The time came for every man to meet his maker. Even a snake as shrewd and guileful as Vaustian Harver.

Everyone had an appointment with The Hood. He only needed his to be further down the line than the Viceroy's.

And so here they were, cloaked within the masses, the song of twilight twisting in the heavens underneath the tumble of another endless snowfall. He scratched at a patch of week-old scruff. It was the same damned spot that always itched like a bloody plague in times of worry, and it was being a real shit this day. All the same, he kept his face hidden, especially when they passed near a Royalguard patrol. The entire plan hinged on secrecy, after all. As such he couldn't risk notice. Everything had to play to perfection.

A few more congested blocks in and they came to a blockade at the quarter's end, marked by a squad of bluecoats. The lot of them seemed distracted, if not shithoused. And one of them was chatting up a streetwalker, damned near had his prick out on display for her, the skeezy bastard. *Some protection.* He thought of Liam Wade in that moment. At least Wade had kept his philandering behind closed doors, for the most part.

"Don't suppose they'll just let us through, do you?" He had to ask the question.

"Tossers like that? Not a chance. More than like they'll welcome the trouble, considering we're carrying. And if one of them recognizes you, the shit's over."

His face scrunched up. Of course, she was right. "All right, I know another way."

They picked their way through the faceless masses, eyes upon the icy cobble, down another block and a half eastward to a back alley Remy knew to be named Darrowyn's Rut. His Uncle Rhonyn had shown it to him. It had been constructed in the cycles after the Second Highland War as a means of escape from the castle in the event it became overrun. For cycles, the Royalguard neglected it, assigning the lowest of the bluecoat scabs to guard its gate.

Curie glanced at him as they stood before the foreboding passage then back into it. "Fucking hells, Toff, you're not planning to murder me tonight as well, are you?"

"It's a way in," he said. "Doubtful any bluecoats would bother patrolling the beggar haunts." He crunched forward, his cloak flapping in the cold air, and held tight the bottom of his hood so it didn't come away from his head.

"What's the over-under we find more corpses than living?"

He ignored her, turning his cheek to the wind. Though it only grew harsher the further inward they traversed. The alleyways narrowed after a time; the spaces so thin in places they had to walk one after the other. But as good fortune fell, there were no distractions. Only toward the end did they come about a body, but they passed it by without a word. Truthfully, Remy didn't want to know if it was alive or dead. He just kept moving forward, one step at a time, until they came to the edge of the last corner.

Remy peeked out. A pair of bluecoats sat at a table just inside the castle entrance playing a game of cards. Remy fell against the wall and turned to Curie.

"Two from what I can tell, playing Sick Boy."

"I'll handle it," Curie said.

"Rhymona, do not kill them."

"I'm not a complete savage, you know," she retorted. "Besides, I have these." She cupped her breasts and turned the corner with her best version of a seductive strut.

Through the silent snowfall, beneath the ridge of his cowl, Rembrandt Lanier stared at his quarry across the courtyard with a baleful glower. How fitting to find the godless bastard in the courtyard of Alistair the Arcane. He drew his blade carefully and inched out into the arcade, pressing his back against the nearest pillar, before daring a glance beyond. Curie waited in the passageway's darkness, Fucker lusting for flesh.

And here it is. Through all the bullshit and tomfuckery, you've made it back.

Vaustian was ambling casually parallel to his position, alone, as expected, nearing the turn toward them. It wouldn't be long now. Remy listened to the Viceroy's footsteps as they approached, and his grip tightened around his hilt. He absorbed every detail of the moment. The raw nip of the static winter, the subtle flicker of torchlight buried deep within their sconces, the distant rumble of the kingdom hamlets far below the castle courtyards, the smell of burning wood on the air, the muted wander of snow within the arcade's vast windows. Suddenly the footsteps stopped.

Remy waited. *Patience.*

The silence stretched—or seemed to.

"Whoever you are, I know you're there," Vaustian said in a flat, disarming tone. "I can hear your breathing."

Remy felt a pair of sinister eyes glaring right at him, but he remained motionless. *Cooler heads, old boy.*

"Reveal yourself at once," Vaustian ordered, "or I will be forced to suspect malfeasance."

The watchman held.

"You dare ignore my authority?"

Fuck it. "Oh, I dare, Harver," Remy hissed. "I dare." And he slowly came away from the pillar's shelter. *So much for cooler heads.* From the crook of an eye, he watched as Curie's shape vanished within the pitch of the passageway's gloom.

"Chuffing hells, Lanier, is that really you?"

Remy removed his hood.

"Looking a bit feral these days, I see. The King's Wall not all it appeared to be then? Come back to beg for your old station, have you?" Vaustian pressed toward him, words in full flurry, as was ever his game, sword resting listlessly at his side.

"I've come to take what's mine," Remy answered.

"What's *yours*?" Vaustian had a wolfish grin. "I daresay, the Kingswatch may have made a man of you yet. Grew some big ol' bollocks out there with the hags and heathens then, didn't you? Good on you, boy. Good on you. But you should well prize, crowns are earned these days, not given."

Remy raised his sword, gripping it firmly in two hands.

Vaustian stopped. "Whoa, ho, ho, you might want to think real hard about what you do next, boy."

"I've thought on it long enough." The gods only knew. "And I'm no boy."

Vaustian's hand collapsed upon his hilt, a glint of silver rising slightly from the scabbard's mouth. "No, I suppose not. You're more a man than your father, at least, I'll grant you that. Then again, so was Desmond. At least he picked up a sword when the time came for it. But not old Whit. No, your father hid within his books, didn't he? Hid behind his prophecies and ridiculous philosophies. I daresay, you've already earned more respect out of me in just these past few minutes than your father ever did."

"Like I give a toss about your fucking respect."

"Oh, all right, hurt my feelings then why don't you? Still lugging about that chip on your shoulder, I see."

Remy ranged back a few steps. The wall was very close to him now as the walkway's corner came near.

"You don't want this, boy. I know you don't. I can see it in your fluttery eyes. Tell me, what fool simp put you up to this folly?"

"It's not about what I want anymore. It's about what has to happen."

Vaustian had a condescending chuckle. "Bold words indeed from a lily-livered deserter. Truly, boy, what has all the vainglorious pageantry gained you anyway? Solitude and shame, I would imagine. By the nine, you look a right paltry ruin to me, scarcely worth a trollop's wet fuck for his many efforts."

"I suppose I should count my ruddy luck stones then that I don't much regard the insignificant opinions of fuckwit scoundrels, shouldn't I?"

"Fuckwit scoundrel?" The Viceroy shook his head, his smile returning. "At least you've mastered their coarse language. Though I have my doubts, the blade work is quite as sharp."

"Come find out then, you miserable old fuck."

"A bad egg 'til the end, is it?" the Viceroy unclasped his fur cloak and let it fall to the stones below.

"Reckon so." Remy's gravestone eyes hardened in disgust of the man.

"You're out of your depths, boy." Vaustian unsheathed his blade fully.

And fury, like bile, rose in Remy at the draw as he dashed at his opponent, the feral side from his days amidst the Kingswatch dogs swallowing up his rationality. He cut hard with a feint to the right before shifting to his left and slicing down with both hands at the hilt. Vaustian repelled the attempt easily and pursued the watchman's swing with a powerful strike, catching the young prince's blade against the wall. Sparks galvanized the night as Vaustian scraped his blade against the stonework toward Remy, forcing the watchman backward.

Remy retreated, turning the arcade's corner before falling into a defensive stance.

It was Vaustian who darted forward this time, demon-faced, quick as a slitpurse, stabbing at the waiting watchman again, and again, and again, before lashing a devastating swipe at him. Remy jerked away, just far enough to spare contact, but he certainly felt the intensity behind the swing, and it was horribly alarming.

Realizing his disadvantage in such close quarters, Remy spun away from his opponent, backing down the arcade walkway and out into the falling snow of Alistair's Courtyard.

Vaustian stalked forward without hurry, his blade now a perfect extension of his arm, held out low and away as he crunched into the yard, fat snowflakes floating and shimmering like fireflies about their contest.

"On second thought, I must say, I rather liked you better as a memory," Vaustian said with a sneer. "You should have stayed away from this place, Remy."

Vaustian flailed his sword up like a whip and charged. Their blades came together with spectacular force. The watchman deflected the first strike and countered with one of his own to keep his opponent honest, but it only bought him a few meager seconds as the Viceroy lunged forward again, his steel wanting. Remy managed to parry this attempt just as well, but Vaustian Harver would not be slowed.

The grass, wet and slick underfoot, caused them both to slip in their ringing dance, but neither held back from the lack of purchase. Remy was quick, a soldier true after his spell away from court, briefly surprising the Viceroy, but Vaustian clearly remained the better, slashing about the young prince with an uncanny speed Remy never knew him capable of, making a full show of it.

Now, this was a swordsman. Vaustian's skills were a far cry indeed from the feckless drunks and ill-practiced farm boys of the Kingswatch training yard. His every movement was fluid, his form precise, his technique methodical, and his strength unflagging. Wherever he had trained and whoever trained him did a bang-up job of it.

But there was no time to mind such things. Verily, all the watchman could do was stay ahead as the Viceroy's blade inched ever nearer to flesh. And eventually, their swords locked and their bodies crashed together, their growling faces only inches apart, both straining to gain the advantage.

"Yield," Vaustian ordered.

"Never," Remy rasped.

Their blades separated and both men fell back into a sparring position, circling about the courtyard.

Gritting his teeth, Remy pounded a fist into his screaming ribs, beating at them with each side-step, inciting their agony, waking their fury, before regripping his hilt in both hands.

Anger and adrenaline centered him, sustained him, soaking up his pain, as breath tore ragged from his throat, and a squeezing discomfort settled in his chest.

"I do not wish you further injury, Remy," the Viceroy said. "Your sister—"

"No!" Remy howled. "No. Marsea's nothing to do with this. This is between you and me."

"I doubt she would see it that way."

"I don't care how she would see it. You have no idea what I've been through just to get back here. Just to get to this moment. One way or another, this ends tonight."

"Don't do this, Remy. You are not yet my better."

The hells I'm not. Remy rushed forward, hilt crushed firm inside his palms, and cut down at his opponent.

Vaustian blocked the strike with one hand, making it look effortless, as he curled around Remy's toppling, dropping down to a knee and then back up into a defensive stance.

A shooting pain like the prick of a needle seized Remy's entire body, and he stumbled forward, his momentum sending him sprawling into the muck. His side was on fire, melting away all semblance of the horrid cold that surrounded them. Quivering, he pushed up to a knee and tried to stand, but his legs refused to go any further. He remained kneeling. And barely at that.

"Are you quite finished with this fool's charade now?" Vaustian mocked.

Remy touched a hand to the fresh pain and pulled back dark red wetness. *Shit.* It was in that moment the watchman noticed a second smaller blade in Vaustian's offhand, dripping vermillion tears into the glistening white powder at his boot. *All that struggling, all that favor, for what?* "I'll be finished when breath no longer fills your vile lungs," he groaned defiantly.

"You can't even lift that blade now can you, boy?"

Remy clutched the blade as tight as he could and raised it at the Viceroy with a grunt.

"Enough, Vaustian!" a commanding voice shouted from behind him.

It sent a chill up the watchman's spine.

"Remy?" the same voice uttered inside the otherwise silent stillness.

His arm gave out. And he knew the rest of his body was not far behind.

"Remy, is that you?"

It sounded as though she were inside a bubble. Slouched, he turned his head sidelong to take her in.

She appeared a frail, eldritch creature in the porcelain gash of starlight, trembling, though not from the cold. Inky streaks of black knit a spider's web through the gray-purple bruises below her haunted silvery spheres and down the pale canvas of her face. Weirdly, she wore one of his old tweed hunting jackets. Remy had never beheld his sister in such rustic attire before. Nor had he ever seen her gripping a dagger like the one clutched tight in her right hand. But honestly, it was the other hand that stole away all of his attention. It was a gnarled, hideous horror of a thing, swathed in discolored rags, barely a hand at all anymore.

"Seasea?" her name was choked. He could not believe what he was beholding. His sister, once gentle and ladylike, had since become...this...

I never should have left you.

And her eyes opened large as the sister moons as her attentions shifted back to Vaustian.

Remy followed her wide-eyed gaze, expecting to find a blade racing for his belly, expecting death—*the fool I am*—but instead, he found Vaustian in the last moment of his proper life, still staring at Marsea, like a lost little puppy, every measure as confused as he was, when Fucker came slamming down atop his head with a sickening crunch, splitting him open to the crest of his brow.

Time itself froze—

And just like that, it was over.

Without ceremony, without spectacle, without honor.

Another end.

The end of Vaustian Harver.

A crown for old king killer.

And yet here he was.

A hole in his gut, hardly able to keep himself upright.

Hardly able to breathe.

But he was home.

At last—

Time resumed.

Vaustian collapsed to his knees from the blow, eye level with Remy, his sword falling away from him, as a shaking hand slowly came up to assess the damage. In the freezing cold air, smoke billowed skyward from his gruesome alteration.

Curie just left it there, a third of the way inside his head, stuck, as though it were a stubborn block of firewood, and she looked briefly at Remy before her searching eyes found Marsea.

But Remy couldn't turn away from Harver. An eye drooped sideways in its socket, the iris nearly disappearing entirely, as blood bubbled out, seeping down his face, and then began to pour from his nose, dripping heavily onto his doublet.

"Ma...Ma...Marsea..." The bastard usurper struggled to form the word and reached out his shaking hand toward the Lanier princess as a spout of blood coughed up through his airway.

"Didn't hear me though, did you?" Curie hissed into his ear, cold as the knife that feeds, before she gripped the haft once more, put her boot between his shoulder blades, and hefted the bit from his skull. "Smug sack of shit."

CHAPTER TWENTY-FIVE

The scars that bind us.

And in the end, seemingly in spite of everything, her countless prayers, her ocean of tears, her litany of schemes, her cycles of forced isolation and silent atonement, a fraction of an instant was all the time it took to punch the ill favor in reverse.

It was like the turning of an hourglass that had been pouring on top of her, drowning her, suffocating her all her life. She hardly knew what to do with the fresh air.

Only a man. A slab of meat. And somehow, impossibly, he was still quite fetching, even with a wonky eye—even in death—even with a hatchet sticking out of his head.

Honestly, she thought such a loss would have hit her much worse. And the maidens knew, she wished it had. At least then she could make the argument that there was some measure of her humanity yet still remaining after all this.

Instead, Marsea stared at her dying lover with a harlequin's smile spread across her face long as the Syndin River. She didn't have to see herself to know it was a mad, hideous affair to behold and it endured as he stammered her name and plunged face first into the muck, blood, brain matter, and bits of skull pouring free from the massive cavity in his crown.

The scene hardly appeared real to her. To wit, she could recall dreams with more authenticity. And yet there he was, dressed smartly in fine leathers and furs far above his rightful station, this great, magnificent man, this man that had taken a kingdom at will, had fought wildkin savages every measure as cleverly as he had seasoned politicians, had risen up from abject destitution to strike fear into the hearts of the privileged, all the talent in the world, with all the confidence to back it, and yet now, full circle, once more he was nothing, a ruined corpse, a feast for crows, face in the mud, ass in the air.

Dark fluids wet the snow from the hatchet's end. And just as quickly as the smile came to her, it dissipated, and she followed the bloody horror all the way up to the face of Vaustian's killer.

"Good gravy, Rhymona," reality struck, "I told you we needed him alive."

"Oh, don't be obtuse, Marsea," the magus replied with matching arrogance. "He was a problem, and you know it. And what did I tell you before all this? Sacrifices must be made in order to progress. Including your tragic little daddy issues. You look like shit by the way."

"Pot meet kettle," Marsea returned, pushing up her glasses.

"No, seriously," Rhymona kept on, "the gutterwitch came 'round, said she wants her tailor back."

"Gutterwitch, is it?" Marsea smirked.

"Gutterwitch, indeed."

"Stand the mirror sometime then. You'll find you're about a dashing eye scar away from buck yourself."

"Wait. What?" Remy chimed in. "You two know each other?"

"Obviously," Rhymona said, wiping the blood from her hatchet with Vaustian's raised bottom.

"It's good to see you, little brother," Marsea said, taking him in. "Took you long enough, by the way." She aimed the words at her mangy friend.

"Little brother was a bit of a handful," Rhymona said. "And there were other complications. Mayhaps you've heard?"

"How bad is it out there?" Marsea asked.

"Bad as I've ever seen. Palatia is fucked. And so is most of the north right along with her."

"Marsea, what happened to you?" Remy asked, his voice rasping and tried.

If only we had the time. "Ravenholme," she answered plainly. "Ganedys."

"The bastard. He's next on the list."

"I appreciate your chivalry, but the deed is already done."

"Already done?" Remy uttered. "You mean to say Gan Harver is dead?"

"Dead as a doornail."

"And *you...?*"

"Don't act so surprised, Remy, I'm not completely useless, you know."

"And Raelan?"

Marsea shrugged. "Two out of three."

"Two..." he listed strangely forward, "out of...three," he mumbled before collapsing backward into the snow hard as a sack of grain.

"Remy!" Marsea bellowed as she hurried to his aid.

"I'm fine," he said faintly, his eyes heavy.

"No, you're not fine," she quibbled, inspecting the wound upon his side, finding a wellspring of blood. "Shit. He's been run through. Remy, why the hells didn't you say anything?"

His response was cut off by a sudden coughing fit.

"Gods dammit, Toff. Get him up on the stones, out of the snow." Rhymona ripped out a flask from inside her leathers and sprinted across the courtyard.

Marsea hooked her arms under Remy's armpits and dragged her brother to the balustrade inside the courtyard's walkway. And the maidens knew, he was heavier than he appeared. She eased him into a sitting position against the balusters, her bad hand going numb from the effort.

"Stay with me, Remy." She held his head straight with her good one. "Look at me. Remy, look at me." She could feel his head lolling, his eyes rolling about.

"Marsea, I'm sorry," he said. A streak of blood trailed down from one side of his mouth.

"No. None of that now."

"I love you..."

"I love you too. Now stay with me."

"I thought I might never get to tell you..."

"Keep your chin up and your eyes open." She glanced over her shoulder. "Rhymona! What the hells are you doing?"

"Sorry...I left," he slurred, the color draining from his face. "Shouldn't have left..."

"Remy." She shook him. "Rhymona, hurry!"

Rhymona dropped a torch beside them as she knelt, setting the flask near its flame, and ran Marsea's dagger across her palm. "Lift his shirt."

Marsea obeyed and blood gushed out.

"For fuck's sake, girl, put a hand over it first. Give me a fucking second."

"You said—"

"I know what I fucking said," Rhymona snapped.

Marsea could feel the heat of her brother's blood as it welled between the fingers of her good hand.

"Fuck. It's deep." Rhymona retrieved the flask, pouring its contents over her opened wound. "This isn't going to be enough. Toff, you still hearing me?"

"Unh," he managed.

"Talk to me, Toff," she said as the flask's contents disappeared inside her cut.

"Fucking heard you," he grumbled.

"That's the spirit." Rhymona pressed her hand atop Marsea's. "We're going to need more blood. A lot more. And fast."

Marsea looked the magus straight before her eyes fell upon Vaustian's corpse. *This might as well happen.* "Fine," she said, and she pulled her hand loose and rushed out into the courtyard to Vaustian.

From the battlements, in the distance before her, long into the endless snowfall, a fiery arrow screamed to the clouded heavens like a tiny fever-mad comet followed in sequence by a chorus of war horns. Marsea stammered to a stop and watched its descent before a full volley lit up the sky like a round of holiday bangers. She had never seen anything like it before. Though it could only mean one thing. Dread filled her at the realization. The blight had arrived. And it would have to be a large number to prompt such a massive reaction.

"Marsea!" Rhymona shouted against the war horns' blare. "Any time now!"

The maidens keep us.

She could literally see inside Vaustian's head as she approached, and her stomach lurched. *Only a man. A slab of meat.* She kicked him over on his side, took his cold, dead hand in her good one, and began dragging him back through the snowdrifts toward Remy and…

She halted, her guts in her throat, glasses teetering at the edge of her nose, as her gaze unbound the most terrifying creature she had ever beheld.

It twitched its feverish yellow eyes at her, stealing her breath away. "I'm losing him," it growled.

The elements began to spin violently around them like a snow globe turned on its head.

Funny thing, friendship. All their bar-crawling and drunken rants and late-night bonding, and not once did the topic come up that Rhymona Curie was a bloody ashaeydir.

And with a wail of desperation, Marsea wrenched her dead lover's corpse forward as hard as her tiny, broken frame would allow…

THE END

GLOSSARY

GENERAL TERMS

Charonisk – A man-made concoction with similar effects to Eldn fire.

Dracari, The – The race of dragons. Dracthonir is the name of the dracari language.

Dragonsfall, The – The event comprising both the fall of dragons by man and the spreading of the gift into the elements that would result in The Giftborn Age.

Eldnumerian, The – A Chandiian term. "eldnu" meaning ancient, "meria" meaning master. They are also known as the old ones.

Oathsworn, The – The knights of the round. They are a clandestine order formed to serve the realm of men. There is no head or foot. All are equal. The Oathsworn was founded decades ago by King Cameron Lanier. They protect the realm against darkly creatures and the supernatural.

Quintweek (quint) – A fluid term indicating a general passage of time. There are five days in a week. Six weeks in a month. Nine months in a cycle. Ten cycles in a decade. Ten decades in a century.

Ravenholme – Now synonymous with The Covenant, Ravenholme is a rogue guild created by Malthus Tetherow that split from The Covenant (original). Originally The Covenant was created in opposition to The

Oathsworn. Members of Ravenholme believe that the darkly and supernatural should be revealed to the public, not kept hidden.

Shufa – A powerful drug that can be smoked or consumed with food.

Star maidens, The – The angelic beings followed within the Omedran faith. They are also known as the Amendeiya. Within the order of the cloth maidens are Lirae (a house mother), Rin (a handmaid to a Ve'Lir), and Ve'Lir (a cloth maiden in study).

THE KNOWN UNIVERSE (the sister moons)

Ashira – The crimson moon. It is now wasting away and nearly uninhabitable.

Dalynisa – The big blue planet thought to be completely ocean.

Lumos – The smallest of the sister moons. She is known for her pale white appearance.

Vaelsyntheria – The golden moon.

Y'dema – The giant green moon. It was said to be razed by the ashaeydir after the fall of Ashira.

MAGIC TERMS

Blood candles – They are the stored mold of a giftborn's blood. It allows the user to enhance their inherited abilities, sometimes by considerable margins. They are known to be heavily addictive and can be deadly. The use of varying types of blood can alter and sometimes poison the blood system. Though not entirely banned by The Ministry, the use of blood candles is generally frowned upon through The Midaran Commonwealth especially at the universities of magic.

Blood merchants (warlocks) – Those who hunt fellow giftborn to drain them of their blood for wholesale.

Codices and Grimoires – Tomes and grimoires contain spoken word magic, including spells, recipes, sigils, wards, and bestiaries. This type of magic existed in previous ages, but has become more archaic in the Age of The Giftborn. It is largely considered an inferior form of magic by comparison to gift conjuring.

Giftborn – A person with magical abilities. They can inherently perform great magical feats. The quality varies and is typically bloodline-based. To conjure magic the person must sacrifice something in return. They are less commonly referred to as warders and spellslingers.

Gravedancer – A giftborn with the ability to resurrect the dead.

Kindleblade – An iron-forged weapon, typically a ritual dagger or a sword, that is enchanted and soulmelded to a master.

Night writing – Raised code substituting for words. It is often times used with codices.

Soul magic (black magic) – Magic that feeds off of the soul rather than the physical body. This form of magic is very powerful, but also that much more risky and dangerous. Too much use can twist and deform the conjurer's appearance. It can whiten the hair, pale the skin, and rapidly age the conjurer.

Spellbind, The – A sliver of The Pale that was long ago cut away. It is a pocket dimension. A place out of time and space. One must be greatly gifted or use a blood candle, sacrificing something of their own health to enter. A studied giftborn can transfer their consciousness to The Spellbind. It can be a place of great healing or great destruction.

Totems – Enchanted trinkets, typically made of whittled wood or carved stone.

Wands – Enchanted weapons created by giftborn to channel magic. They form a bond with a master through a soulmeld and will only react to that user's gift.

Wards – There are two primary forms of magic. Elemental-based magic and Soul and body-based magic. Elemental magic consists of Fire (Pyromancy), Water (Hydromancy), Earth (Terramancy), and Wind (Aeromancy). These forms of magic were common during the Age of Dragons. Soul and body-based magic consists of Shadows (Necromancy), Spirit (Psychomancy), Blood (Hemomancy), and Flesh and bone (Carnomancy). These forms of magic are common in the Age of The Giftborn. Powerful giftborn can merge two and three mantia at once.

MILITARY TERMS

Crownswatch, The – Liveried in crimson, they are also known as bloodcoats and redcoats. These soldiers man the northern highlands from The Straights to The Scar.

Emperorswatch, The – Liveried in gold, they are also known as goldcoats (and derogatorily as pisscoats). These soldiers man the Vinteyama swamplands and the flatlands between the highlands and southlands. They are noted for not allowing women to enlist in their guard.

Kingswatch, The – Liveried in blue, they are also known as bluecoats. These soldiers man Lancastle and her surrounding hamlets. They also man The King's Wall, a massive construct that separates the highlands from the lands now occupied by the ashaeydir.

Lordswatch, The – Liveried in gray, they are also known as graycoats. These soldiers man the lands east of the Morrigar Mountains, from the north to the southland provinces just outside Six Ports.

Royalguard, The – The overarching term referencing any coat of arms inside the Midaran military.

WEAPONRY

Helanderan sword – A one-handed sword of varying lengths, edged on both sides, and generally paired with the use of a shield.

Ka'rym chii – A set of ashaeydir weapons primarily indicating a mae'chii and sy'chii.

Mae'chii – A long, slender, single-edged blade.

Sy'chii – A shorter single-edged blade.

Trezsu implant – An implant surgically embedded in ashaeydir soldiers that allows them to alter aspects of their appearance.

ACKNOWLEDGMENTS

The Giftborn novel series has been a decade in the making, melding my undying love of horror, fantasy, and southern gothic literature. I could write a volume alone on how many creators influenced me during that span, artists from a multitude of eras and mediums, from authors and musicians to directors and screenwriters to painters and photographers, and the list goes on and on. But if you're a fan of any of the aforementioned genres, you likely know a good portion of them already. With that being said there are some amazing human beings near and dear to me that I would like to wrap in a word hug for giving my head movie regurgitations even the smallest time of day over the years:

First off, heartfelt gratitude and a thousand cheers to my patient and loving family, for all the support and encouragement along the way. Thank you for affording me the opportunity to dream. Fortune never favored a man so handsomely.

Linda Oshinsky, for teaching me that English is an art and opening the door that would eventually spark my love for writing. Back then I didn't understand what it was within me, but I like to think you did. May your rest remain ever peaceful.

Atia Liaghat Nunnally, for reading The Giftborn Chronicles in its founding stages all those many moons ago, before it even had a proper name. Truly, your honest opinions pushed me to flesh out certain characters far beyond their vapid origins.

Mike Iseman, for the brotherhood and all the adventures, and then that much more for all the endless nights listening to me prattle on about this old tale and that one for hours on end.

Gerard Luat, for taking the time to turn some pages on a whim, and all the positivity and brilliant advice that followed.

Brooks Bevins, for the kind words and indulging a fellow writer. You picked the correct favorite character by the way.

Dan Stemke and Derek Lane, for all the random debates and conversations regarding film and literature. Good times. Great food for thought.

Ashton Dundas, for the trust and opportunity to collaborate and write a different manner of story from my own. Timing is everything and *Olivia* came about when I needed to step away from the world of The Royal Nothings and concentrate on another. To merely call the experience valuable would be a most egregious understatement. The reward upon my return to The Vael was tenfold. And I'd do it again in a heartbeat. Keep after the dream.

Jason Gilbert, for doing your damnedest to include me when I was mostly a ghost, and pushing me to run the con circuit. I can't tell you how much attending writer's panels both influenced and motivated me.

Deepest thanks to Melissa McArthur, John Hartness, Erin Penn, Tuppence Van de Vaarst, and Falstaff Books for the chance to let this misfit make his mark.

And lastly, but certainly not least, thanks to you, for taking a chance on a book about family in a broken world and giving it a read. May you count some measure of hope and inspiration from some place within.

ABOUT THE AUTHOR

Drew Bailey is an emerging author of horror and fantasy. Though he attended college to expand his knowledge of Literature and History, it still took him the better part of a decade to actually mold it into something worth chasing after. Better late than never, as they say. The Royal Nothings is his first novel. In his spare time, Drew is a chronic coffee drinker, avid movie watcher, and follows Liverpool F.C. and the Green Bay Packers. He currently resides in Charleston, South Carolina.

STAY IN TOUCH!

If you enjoyed this book, please leave a review on Amazon, Goodreads, or wherever you like.

If you'd like to hear more about or from the author, please join our mailing list at https://www.subscribepage.com/g8d0a9.

You can get some free short stories just for signing up, and whenever a book gets 50 reviews, the author gets a unicorn. I need another unicorn. The ones I have are getting lonely. So please leave a review and get me another unicorn!

FRIENDS OF FALSTAFF

Thank You to All our Falstaff Books Patrons, who get extra digital content each month! To be featured here and see what other great rewards we offer, go to www.patreon.com/falstaffbooks.

PATRONS

Dino Hicks
John Hooks
John Kilgallon
Larissa Lichty
Travis & Casey Schilling
Staci-Leigh Santore
Sheryl R. Hayes
Scott Norris
Samuel Montgomery-Blinn
Junkle

Made in the USA
Middletown, DE
17 February 2023